The Wounded Kingdom

When their turn came to pass under the archway and be counted, Galaeron glanced into the arrow loop behind the guards and found a familiar cascade of golden hair shining in the depths of the gatehouse. He dipped his head in acknowledgement. The hair moved closer, and Princess Alusair's familiar face appeared on the other side of the loop. Her eyes were red and glassy, though it was impossible to say whether from weeping or exhaustion.

The Elven Enclave

The once-lush grass was gone, burned off or blasted away by battle magic, or withering beneath the rotting corpse of one of the thousands of elf warriors scattered across the field. In the center of the meadow, the marble cliffs of the Three Sisters were speckled around the base with stars of soot and sprays of crusted blood. Atop the hills themselves, curtains of black fume were rising out of the great bluetop forest, coalescing into a single dark cloud that left visible only the lowest reaches of Evereska's majestic towers.

The Dark Empire

Once inside the cloud, the enclave itself grew visible, a huge capsized mountaintop honeycombed with utility passages and ventilation shafts. Malygris began to circle the crags of the overturned peak in a widening spiral, his fear aura keeping the ever-growing colonies of bats and birds at a cautious distance. Even the jewel-eyed sentries who stood constant watch from their _____ out of sight as the drago

FORGOTTEN REALMS®

RETURN OF THE ARCHWIZARDS

Book I

The Summoning
TROY DENNING

Book II

The Siege
TROY DENNING

Realms of Shadow
EDITED BY LIZZ BALDWIN

Book III

The Sorcerer
TROY DENNING

THE
SORCERER

Return of the Archwizards

BOOK
III

TROY
DENNING

THE SORCERER
Return of the Archwizards, Book III

©2002 Wizards of the Coast, Inc.

Distributed in the United States by Holtzbrinck Publishing. Distributed in Canada by Fenn Ltd.

Distributed to the hobby, toy, and comic trade in the United States and Canada by regional distributors.

Distributed worldwide by Wizards of the Coast, Inc. and regional distributors.

Cover art by Jon Sullivan. Map by Dennis Kauth.
First Printing: November 2002
Library of Congress Catalog Card Number: 2001097182

9 8 7 6 5 4 3 2 1

US ISBN: 0-7869-2795-X
UK ISBN: 0-7869-2796-8
620-88616-001-EN

U.S., CANADA,   EUROPEAN HEADQUARTERS
ASIA, PACIFIC, & LATIN AMERICA   Wizards of the Coast, Belgium
Wizards of the Coast, Inc.   P.B. 2031
P.O. Box 707   2600 Berchem
Renton, WA 98057-0707   Belgium
+1-800-324-6496

Visit our web site at **www.wizards.com**

To Ed Greenwood
For sharing his world with so many

Acknowledgments

I would like to thank my editor, Phil Athans, for his patience, good humor, and valuable insight; Eric Boyd for his many contributions to the series; and Andria Hayday for her usual extraordinary patience and support.

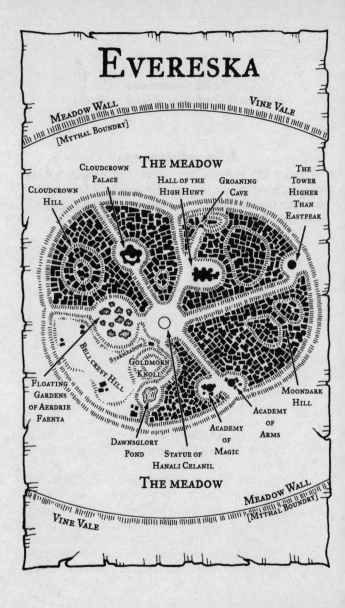

Evereska

MEADOW WALL

VINE VALE

[MYTHAL BOUNDRY]

THE MEADOW

CLOUDCROWN
PALACE

CLOUDCROWN
HILL

HALL OF THE
HIGH HUNT

GROANING
CAVE

THE
TOWER
HIGHER
THAN
EASTPEAK

STARMEADOWS

BELLCREST HILL

GOLDMORN
KNOLL

FLOATING
GARDENS
OF AERDRIE
FAENYA

MOONDARK
HILL

ACADEMY
OF
ARMS

DAWNSGLORY
POND

ACADEMY
OF
MAGIC

STATUE OF
HANALI CELANIL

THE MEADOW

MEADOW WALL

[MYTHAL BOUNDRY]

VINE VALE

CHAPTER ONE

7 Flamerule,
The Year of Wild Magic (1372 DR)

It was the sound of despair, this strained silence that greeted the end of every report. With each account of yet another pact struck by the enemy, with every confession that a realm could raise no more troops, the envoys would drop their gazes to the polished surface of the conference table and study their reflections, and there would be no sound in the room but the sputtering of the oil lamps.

Only Princess Alusair Obarskyr, the Steel Regent of Cormyr, received the news with a raised chin, but it seemed to Galaeron Nihmedu that with each account of another cyclone spawned by the melting of the High Ice, with each description of a new city in flood or a nation's barley fields withering under a blazing sun, the furrows in the princess's brow deepened, the circles beneath her eyes grew larger, darker, and more menacing.

Alusair turned her attention to Galaeron and said, "And what news from Evereska, Sir Nihmedu? How go matters for the elves?"

The question was for the benefit of the others present. Alusair was the one who had told Galaeron much of what he would pass along, and she was doing him an honor by asking him to repeat it on behalf of his city. Galaeron stood.

"Evereska will stand, Your Highness." This good news caused several envoys to raise their heads, and Galaeron continued, "The elven armies are camped outside the Shaeradim, ready to meet the phaerimm the instant the shadowshell falls."

"You're certain it will fall?" asked Korian Hovanay, the ambassador from Sembia. A foppish man with fleshy jowls and an outlandish feathered hat resting on the table before him, Hovanay glared at Galaeron as he spoke. "I see no reason the Shadovar should let it fade. The phaerimm are Shade's archenemies—and the Shadovar have succeeded in all of their other undertakings."

"All of their *diplomatic* undertakings," Alusair corrected. She had aged a decade in the forty days since Tilverton's loss, and her once striking face had become sallow and haggard with worry. "Their army—what remains of it—has been quiet since the Battle of Tilverton."

"My point exactly," Hovanay said. "How do we know they have not been marshaling their strength to renew their attack on the phaerimm?"

"That is wishful thinking, Ambassador," said Piergeiron Paladinson, who had come by magic all the way from Waterdeep. "Sadly, the Shadovar are too cunning to turn their attention elsewhere so our alliance can mobilize against the Melting."

"And the elven armies are as ready to meet the Shadovar as the phaerimm," Galaeron said. "The shadowshell damages

Evereska as much as it does the phaerimm, and our people will prevent the Shadovar from renewing it."

What Galaeron left unsaid was that with two of Mystra's Chosen—Laeral Silverhand and her consort Khelben Arunsun—still trapped in the Shaeradim, Storm Silverhand was just as determined as the elves to bring down the shadowshell. At the first hint of trouble, she would teleport straight to the mystical Splicing that held the dark sphere together and join six of Evermeet's last high mages in preventing the Shadovar from renewing it.

Galaeron felt certain of little else in this strange three-sided war, but he was sure that the shadowshell would fall, and soon. What happened afterward was anyone's guess. With the phaerimm loose in the world, the Shadovar thawing the High Ice, and the weather wreaking flood and famine across all Faerûn, the only thing anyone could predict for sure was calamity.

Hovanay studied Galaeron with a sneer, then finally said, "How wonderful for the elves. I'm sure you'll forgive the rest of us if we don't share your enthusiasm."

"You have reason to wish Evereska ill, Ambassador?" Galaeron asked. "Perhaps Sembia hopes to strike a bargain for our treasure?"

Hovanay's eyes flashed. "I trust you are not suggesting that Sembia would traffic with thieves, Sir Nihmedu."

Galaeron braced his hands on the table and started to rise, but the Harper witch Ruha, seated next to him in her customary veil and head scarf, laid a hand on his forearm.

"Remember your shadow," she said quietly. "You assume too much."

Galaeron felt a sudden surge of anger toward her and knew instantly that something dark and sinister had risen inside him. His shadow self was asserting itself again, trying to make him see dark motives and evil betrayals in those around him. He lowered himself into his seat and folded his hands, then looked across the table to Hovanay.

"My question was unwarranted, Ambassador," he said. It irked Galaeron to apologize, but it was wiser to trust Ruha in such matters than himself. "I hope you will forgive the implication."

Hovanay smirked back at him. "Of course. We are all aware of your affliction."

"Which is not to say that we understand your point, Ambassador," Alusair said. She did not bother to disguise her own suspicion of the man, for there had been no love lost between their two realms since Sembia's not-so-veiled attempt to carve off a piece of Cormyr during the Ghazneth Scourge. "Why shouldn't we want Evereska to survive?"

"It is not Evereska's survival that troubles us," Hovanay answered. "It is the fall of the shadowshell. Commerce has suffered enough as it is. The last thing we need now is a legion of phaerimm making slaves and egg-bags of the few caravanners still bold enough to meet their obligations."

Galaeron restrained the urge to berate the man for worrying about his purse while brave elves were dying—but Alusair did not. She studied Hovanay with a sneer usually reserved for something she scraped off her boot, then shook her head.

"There is more at stake here than gold," she said. "Our subjects cannot eat gold—though I'll be happy to feed you some if you'd like to experiment."

Ruha snickered beneath her veil, and several other envoys had to bite their lips and turn away.

Accepting Alusair's affront with the casual poise of one accustomed to such treatment, Hovanay merely smiled.

"Perhaps we cannot eat gold, but we *do* need it to feed our armies. Is there a realm among us whose treasuries are not barren already?"

When the table remained silent, the ambassador continued, "If our losses grow any worse, I dare say the alliance will lack the means to muster any army at all, much less one powerful enough to defeat the Shadovar and stop the Melting."

Again, a tense silence fell over the council room, and Alusair's face turned stormy with frustration. Already exhausted of both gold and men, the realms of the alliance were stretched to the breaking point, and—just as Hovanay said—any pressure brought by the phaerimm would be enough to crush them. Even to Galaeron, the implications were clear. If Evereska were to survive, it would be at the cost of every other civilized land in Faerûn.

Galaeron began to feel that all eyes were turned on him. When he glanced around the table, it was to see the gazes of the other envoys quickly slipping away.

Lord Nasher Alagondar of Neverwinter, who had come by the same magic as Piergeiron Paladinson, coughed softly into his hand. The quiet thus broken, Alduvar Snowbrand—a Sword of Archendale and one of the three envoys shared by the Dalelands—wrapped his fingers around his chair arms and leaned forward as though he were about to pounce from his seat.

"We are looking at this wrong, I say." A tall, strong man with silky black hair, Alduvar had a spectral face and deep green eyes that seemed strangely distant and dull. "Our enemies are the Shadovar, not the phaerimm."

"That is an easy thing to say when it is someone else's home they have besieged," Galaeron said. "The phaerimm are enemies to the elves, I assure you."

"And who's fault is that?" Alduvar turned to glower at him, but there was no anger in his eyes, no ire or malice—no emotion at all. "Was it not you who freed them in the first place?"

"And who cursed us with the Shadovar?" added Irreph Mulmar, the ruddy-faced Constable of the High Dale. Like Alduvar, he was one of the three envoys from the Dales, and like Alduvar's, his eyes seemed oddly empty. "Were you not the one who brought them back from the Plane of Shadow?"

Somewhere inside, Galaeron realized that the vitriol of the Dalesmen was strangely at odds with their vacant eyes, but his shadow was already rising to the bait, bristling at the accusations and urging him to answer with blade or spell. He started to stand and found Ruha's hand clamped to his arm, her nails digging in hard to remind him that he had to be strong, that to indulge his anger was to yield to the darkness devouring him from the inside.

"What is done is done," she said, continuing to hold Galaeron down. "Is there anyone here who can say he would not have made the same mistake?"

"Mistakes have consequences," said Mourngrym Amcatha, the third and last of the Dalelands envoys. A huge, powerfully built man with a brown mustache and neatly trimmed hair, his eyes were as vacant as those of his fellow Dalesmen. "The elf is the one who made the mistake. It's his people who should suffer for it—not ours."

Mourngrym's comment drew a chorus of astonished murmurs, for he was as respected across much of Faerûn as he was in his own dale. For him to speak so openly against Evereska's interests was to condone the resentment harbored in secret by many of the alliance's lesser leaders, who gathered at night in quiet little groups to complain of the hardships visited upon them by the mistake of one elf.

Galaeron was filled with such a black fury that he forgot about the vacant eyes and no longer felt Ruha's hand on his arm. He was up and leaning across the table toward Mourngrym, his weight braced on his hands and his words tumbling from his mouth of their own accord.

"And who would you blame had the Shadovar unleashed the phaerimm on the Dalelands instead of Evereska?" Galaeron demanded. "Some saurial from Tarkhaldale?"

Mourngrym's lip rose in a sneer, but his eyes remained as blank as before.

"A saurial did not release the phaerimm," he said. "An elf did. You, to be exact."

Suddenly finding himself off balance, Galaeron looked down to find his hand a foot above the table, his fingers curled as though to call a shadow bolt. Ruha was using both hands to hold his arm so he could not cast the spell. Behind her, Piergeiron Paladinson was rising to help, watching the struggle with an expression that was half alarmed and half forbearing.

The sight was enough to shock Galaeron back to his senses. He let his arm go limp.

"Humans!"

Knowing he was still not fully in control of himself, Galaeron freed his arm and turned toward Alusair.

"If the princess will excuse me—"

"She will not, Sir Nihmedu." Motioning him into his seat, she nodded at a pair of Purple Dragons posted along the wall. As they stepped forward to stand guard behind Galaeron's chair, she said, "Actually, I have a keen interest in hearing Lord Mourngrym's answer."

Galaeron sat, and Mourngrym turned to face Alusair.

"What answer would that be, Your Highness?"

"To Galaeron's question, Lord Mourngrym." Alusair replied, her expression growing suspicious. "Who would you blame if the Shadovar had unleashed the phaerimm in the Dalelands instead of Evereska?"

"But they didn't, Princess."

"Lord Mourngrym," Alusair said, "I am asking what if they *had*."

"The question is meaningless, Your Highness. It was the elf who unleashed the phaerimm."

An astonished murmur filled the chamber. Paying no attention, Mourngrym turned to gesture at Galaeron, and at last Galaeron understood what he had been seeing—or rather, not seeing—in the eyes of the Dalesman.

Anger clouded Alusair's face.

"Lord Mourngrym," she said, "as a guest in my realm, you owe me the courtesy of an answer."

Mourngrym responded with an counterfeit smile.

"Of course, Your Highness. What I fail to understand . . ."

Galaeron did not hear the rest of the answer, for his own thoughts were whirling like one of the cyclones that had of late been laying waste to so many of Faerûn's farms and villages. The Dalesmen's attack on him had been carefully coordinated, with the envoys of lesser stature laying the groundwork for a final indictment by their most respected member. Given that the three came from the same area, it seemed entirely plausible they had come together before the council and settled on the strategy, but Galaeron suspected another explanation—a far more menacing one.

He leaned toward Ruha and felt a Purple Dragon's armored hand grasping his shoulder.

"Milord," the soldier whispered. "I think the princess meant for you to stay in your own chair."

"As I will." Though Galaeron answered in an amiable tone, it was all he could do to keep from cursing the man aloud. If he was right—and he was—the last thing he needed was the lout drawing attention to him. "I only wanted to thank Harper Ruha for her support."

Ruha raised her kohl-rimmed eyes to the guard and said, "Galaeron will do me no harm."

The soldier regarded her suspiciously for a moment, then nodded gruffly and released Galaeron's shoulder. Ruha looked to Galaeron, and as Alusair and Mourngrym continued their argument in more heated tones, waited.

"Uh, thank you," Galaeron said. It was all he dared say, at least with one of *them* lurking somewhere in the room, eavesdropping on the council and manipulating its mind-slaves. "I'm afraid I lost control of myself."

Ruha knitted her black eyebrows and replied, "Considering what was said, I thought you did well to keep your shadow in check."

Galaeron continued to look at her, trying to think of some other way to convey his suspicions without alerting the one spying upon them.

Irreph and Alduvar were lending their voices to

Mourngrym's, protesting that Alusair was wasting the council's valuable time with a meaningless exercise of imagination.

"Galaeron," Ruha asked, "is there something else?"

"No," he said. If only she understood fingertalk; as it was, he was beginning to fear he would have to use his own magic to save the council. "That's all."

Ruha nodded—a bit uncertainly—and turned back to the council.

Galaeron sat fidgeting, lost in his own thoughts, trying to think of some other way to do what was needed. It was easily two months since he had last cast a spell. Surely, he could cast this one, not even a very difficult spell. It was just a simple abjuration to reveal the spy he knew to be lurking somewhere in the council chamber putting words in the mouths of the Dalesmen. Of course, he would need to use shadow magic; he was no longer sure that he even *could* use normal magic, but shadow magic was better against the phaerimm anyway. Normal spells had a tendency to ricochet off their magic-resistant scales, but shadow magic always worked.

The thought of touching the Shadow Weave again sent a shiver of anticipation up through Galaeron's body. He could almost feel the cold power rising through him, quenching a thirst that had been building for two months. One simple spell was not going to do any harm. It would hardly give his shadow self the strength to overpower him completely—not for long anyway—and he had to expose the spy, didn't he? He had to make the council see that the Dalesmen's words were those of the enemy, that the phaerimm were trying to split the alliance—

A day never passed when Galaeron did not find some reason just as compelling to break his vow and reach out to the Shadow Weave. The temptation was always there, always awaiting the weak moment, always inviting him down the dark path, but he had only to remember Vala to resist, to think of her enslaved in Escanor's palace in Shade and imagine the abuse being visited on her nightly in the prince's bed.

It had been Galaeron's shadow self that had persuaded him to abandon her there, that had filled his thoughts with so many bitter suspicions that he had finally surrendered to the darkness and vowed to have vengeance on a woman who had never shown him anything but love. It was a mistake he intended never to repeat, even if it meant his life.

And, with Ruha pledged to prevent him from slipping again, it very well might. She was watching him out of the corner of her eye, her thoughts hidden behind her Bedine veil, but her hand not far from the curved dagger stuck behind her sash.

For the second time in as many minutes, Galaeron wished that the witch understood fingertalk—then realized she didn't need to. He caught her eye then dropped his gaze to his lap, where he was running his fingers through the gestures of the magic he wanted her to cast. Though he was not trying to cast anything, the very act of going through motions filled him with a powerful yearning to open himself to the Shadow Weave.

Ruha's eyes widened, and she looked as though she might reach over to interfere. Galaeron stopped in what would have been mid-casting, then started over again. Ruha seemed to relax. He continued the gesture, being careful to make each element slow and precise so that she would have no trouble deciphering what he was doing. When the glimmer of recognition came to her eye, he stopped and looked down the table in the direction of the Dalesmen, who were now pretending that they did not understand the true nature of Alusair's question.

". . . suppose that *had* the Shadovar tried to free the phaerimm beneath Tarkhaldale, there would have been no problem at all," Mourngrym was saying. "The saurials are far too intelligent to breach the Sharn Wall."

Without using his own magic, Galaeron had no way to be certain the phaerimm spy was anywhere near his mind-slaves, but it seemed like a good place to start. He glanced back and found Ruha studying Mourngrym almost too intently, hands lying in her lap and her veil billowing ever-so-slightly as she whispered her incantation.

"Very well, Lord Mourngrym, you win," Alusair said from her end of the table. "You have made it abundantly clear that the Dalelands have no interest in placing the blame for our troubles anywhere but Evereska. Now, would you care to explain why? I fail to see what you hope to accomplish."

Mourngrym's smile was so wooden it was almost a grimace. "Your Highness, the Dalelands have no interest in blaming anyone. We merely wish to point out—"

He was interrupted by the last syllables of a Bedine incantation as Ruha stood. Using the elemental magic of her native Anauroch, she sprinkled a few drops of water in his direction. A sharp crackle blasted through the chamber, and there was a bright flash near the ceiling above and behind the Dalesmen. Galaeron glimpsed the familiar, thorn-covered shape of a phaerimm's conical body, and the thing was gone, vanished in almost the same instant it appeared.

The chamber broke into a wild tumult of shouting and clanging as guards rushed forward. Several of the envoys—most notably Sembia's Korian Hovanay—dived for cover under the table. Others followed the lead of Piergeiron Paladinson. Grabbing polearms from the guards, they leaped onto the table and began to chink the ceiling in an attempt to find the intruder.

The three Dalesmen remained standing in front of their seats. Their vacant gazes were fixed on the envoys and soldiers closest to them, and they held themselves ready to spring into action.

"Order!" Alusair called. She had produced a sword from somewhere beneath her robe of office and was banging the pommel down on the table's polished surface. "It's gone."

Though the princess's assumption was a natural one—phaerimm usually teleported to safety at the first sign of danger—Galaeron rose.

"Actually, Your Highness, I believe it isn't." He pointed over Mourngrym's shoulder. "I think it's probably somewhere there."

A dozen Purple Dragons immediately rushed to investigate. The three Dalesmen stepped away from the table and closed ranks around a spot not too far from where Galaeron had pointed. Caladnei—the slender, red-haired sorcerer who had replaced addled Vangerdahast as Cormyr's royal magician—stepped into view behind Alusair's chair and leveled her staff at the trio.

Before she could speak the word of command, the phaerimm appeared in the midst of the Dalesmen.

Hold! You have nothing to fear from me—unless you earn it.

Galaeron heard the words inside his mind, and he could tell by the startled reactions of those around him that they had as well. Caladnei held her attack, and the guards settled for surrounding the Dalesmen and leveling their poleaxes in the general direction of the phaerimm. Their restraint, Galaeron knew, probably saved their lives.

Better.

Galaeron saw a familiar blankness come to Ambassador Hovanay's eyes and knew the phaerimm was not repaying its enemies' restraint in kind.

Alusair laid her sword on the table and stared across its length at the intruder.

"This is a private council, worm, and you are our enemy." She glanced over her shoulder and motioned Caladnei toward the creature. "Give me a reason I should not have my guards peel the thorny hide from your viper's flesh."

Because they would fail, the phaerimm replied. *And because even enemies need to confer, if they are ever to be anything else.*

Nasher Alagondar's eyes went vacant.

Galaeron leveled a hand in the phaerimm's direction. "Speak through Mourngrym, or not at all." Then, without looking away, he said to Alusair, "Your Highness, this is how the phaerimm make their mind-slaves. Through their thoughtspeech."

Very perceptive. But you have nothing to fear from us, Galaeron. From what I understand, my people are indebted—

"If you know who I am," Galaeron interrupted, "you know that my magic will kill you as fast as a Shadovar's."

I also know you fear to use it.

"Not as much as I fear becoming your slave," Galaeron said. "Another word within my head, and I will use it."

"Another word in anyone's head, and I will command him to," Alusair added. "If you wish to treat with us, you will release your slaves and speak aloud."

"I cannot do both." This time, the phaerimm's words came from Mourngrym's mouth. "Though once we are finished, I am willing to grant your request."

Alusair's eyes flashed at the word "request," but she held her tongue and looked to Galaeron.

He was tempted to lie and claim that the phaerimm was deceiving her, for he already knew by the tenor of the Dalesmen's earlier arguments what the creature intended. But Alusair had treated him with nothing but courtesy and fairness since the day of his arrival, and—even for the sake of Evereska—he would not repay her with treachery.

"Phaerimm speak to each other through magic winds," Galaeron explained. "With other races, they must use thoughtspeech or an intermediary."

Alusair considered this, then nodded to the phaerimm.

"Very well," she said. "What is it you want?"

"Evereska."

Though the answer was exactly what Galaeron had expected, the impact of hearing it actually spoken aloud was more than he could handle. He started to twist his fingers into a spellcasting—then his arm was forced to his side by the mailed hand of one of the Purple Dragons at his back.

Alusair cast a warning scowl in his direction, then said, "When I give the order, Sir Nihmedu—not before."

"Thank you, Princess," the phaerimm said. Its four arms appeared over the heads of the Dalesmen, spreading outward in what seemed to be a gesture of appreciation. "As I was saying, we and our allies from Anauroch will be content with Evereska and its lands."

This elicited a collective gasp from the envoys—at least those who were not still under the phaerimm's mental control—and even Alusair cocked a brow.

"Evereska is not ours to give," she said.

The noncommittal answer caused a dark anger to rise in Galaeron, and he had to fight it down by closing his eyes and reminding himself of all that Alusair had done on his behalf.

"Nor is it yours to defend," the phaerimm answered through Mourngrym. "All we are suggesting is that you concern yourselves with the Shadovar and leave Evereska to our brothers."

"Then you are not from Anauroch?" Alusair asked. She was stalling, trying to buy time to consider all the ramifications of the phaerimm's proposal. "You are here on behalf of the Myth Drannor phaerimm?"

"The Shadovar have made this the fight of all phaerimm," Mourngrym's voice replied. "Much as they have made it the fight of all the human realms."

"And what do we receive in return?" asked Ambassador Hovanay. The selfish light in his eye made clear that he was free of the phaerimm's influence. That was not, at least for Evereska, necessarily a good thing. "How will you repay us for our help?"

The phaerimm pushed its many-fanged mouth over the shoulders of the Dalesmen and said, "A better question would be what will *you* receive for *our* help."

Hovanay waited expectantly, and the phaerimm swung its mouth in Alusair's direction.

"Your enemy is our enemy," the phaerimm said. "Should your alliance strike a bargain with us, it would be in our interest to stop the melting of the High Ice. Your realms would be able to rebuild their armies and feed their people. They would be strong again."

Though every sinew in Galaeron was screaming for him to leap to his feet and denounce the phaerimm as a fraud and a liar, he knew he would win nothing by such a display. The humans would believe—rightly enough—that he was only trying to protect Evereska's interests, that he would claim such a thing whether the phaerimm could be trusted or not. Instead, he had to speak reasonably and make the humans see the pitfalls for themselves, make them realize that by selling out the elves, they would be selling themselves out as well.

"You are promising a lot," Galaeron said, not quite able to keep the quaver out of his voice, "but I've seen the Shadovar magic, and it is not defeated easily. If you can do what you promise, why do you need the humans at all? Why are your cousins still trapped inside the shadowshell?"

Instead of answering Galaeron, the phaerimm had Mourngrym turn to address Korian Hovanay again.

"We would pledge to leave your caravans in peace, even to protect them when it is in our power."

This brought a grin to the Sembian's lips, if to no one else's.

Piergeiron Paladinson said, "You have not spoken to Galaeron's point. If the phaerimm can do what you claim, why does the shadowshell still stand?"

"Because, as you yourselves learned at Tilverton, the Shadovar are formidable enemies," the phaerimm said. "We who are free are too few to prevail, and those who are trapped in the Shaeradim are weak and starving. When the shadowshell falls, that will change."

"So you say," Piergeiron said.

"So we will prove," the phaerimm replied. "You are familiar with the peak Untrivvin, in the east of the High Ice?"

"Where the tomb tappers rise," said Borg Ohlmak, the woolly-headed chieftain sent by the barbarians of the Ride. "We know the place well."

Mourngrym's head nodded to Borg. "There are three shadow blankets at the base of the mount. When the shell falls, we will destroy all three as proof of our capabilities."

"And still we will not be able to come to terms," Alusair said. "Evereska is not ours to bargain away. Wouldn't some other place serve you as well? The Goblin Marches, for instance, are—"

"Worthless wastelands," the phaerimm said. "It must be Evereska. We have no interest in your castoff barrens."

"Then perhaps the Tun Valley," Alusair suggested. "The lands there are as fertile as any in Cormyr, and I'm certain the alliance would be willing to provide any assistance required to take Darkhold."

"Evereska."

Alusair frowned, clearly trying to think of some other place the phaerimm might desire. She was, Galaeron knew, trying to reach an unreachable compromise. The phaerimm wanted Evereska for the same reason they lived in Myth Drannor: its mythal. They needed magic the way other races needed air, and the mythals that surrounded both cities were living mantles of woven magic. Asking a phaerimm to choose another place to live was like asking a fish to make his home someplace other than in the water.

"Evereska is not ours to grant," Alusair continued, still trying. "Name another place."

"He's not going to name another place," Galaeron interjected, though he did not say why. The existence of the mythal was an elven secret, and he no longer felt any trust for the humans gathered there, not even Alusair. "When will you learn? You can't treat with phaerimm—only surrender to them like cowards, or stand and fight them like warriors."

Alusair's head snapped around to glare at him, her eyes furious and black.

"And when will you learn, elf, that it is not wise to call someone a coward when it is her people's blood that must be shed to save that of yours?"

Allowing no opportunity for a reply, Alusair glanced at the guards behind Galaeron's chair and said, "I have heard enough from him."

One Purple Dragon pinned Galaeron's arms to his chair, and the other covered his mouth with a waist sash. A sinister voice whispered to Galaeron that Alusair had betrayed him and would seal the bargain by turning him over to the phaerimm, but he was wise enough not to struggle. The Steel Regent was famous for her fiery temper, and though some part of him knew she would never do as his shadow's voice suggested, he did not think she would hesitate to have him thrown in a very deep, dark dungeon.

Alusair nodded her approval, then turned back to the phaerimm and said, "You were about to name a place it is in the alliance's power to grant."

"Evereska," Mourngrym's mouth said again. "There is no other place. The elf is right about that much."

Alusair sank back in exasperation.

Through its mind-slave, the phaerimm said, "You have until the third blanket vanishes."

The creature drifted out from behind its shield of Dalesmen, and ignoring the ring of guards around it, panicked Borg Ohlmak and Nasher Alagondar by floating to their end of the table.

"We expect your assent by then."

Alusair's eyes hardened. "And if we do not give it?"

The phaerimm braced two of its arms on the table.

You will.

Alusair sat bolt upright and started to order the guards forward, but the phaerimm had already vanished.

Mourngrym and his fellow Dalesmen cried out in bewildered voices, then stumbled toward the nearest chairs, their hands trembling and their mouths hanging agape. The

Purple Dragons looked to Caladnei for orders while the royal magician busied herself casting detection magic. The envoys sat in their chairs looking alternately relieved and uncertain as they considered the wisdom of betraying Evereska.

After a moment, Alusair brought order back to the chamber by turning to her royal magician.

"Can you tell me how that spy came to be in here?" It was a deft maneuver, turning the envoys' thoughts from the phaerimm's proposal to the threat it had displayed in its arrogant use of its power. "It could have killed us all!"

Caladnei paled and shook her head.

"The chamber is warded against invisibility, teleportation, scrying—"

"Obviously, it was not," Alusair interrupted. Still determined to keep the envoys' thoughts on the how of the phaerimm's presence rather than the why—no doubt buying time to gather her own thoughts on the matter—she looked to Galaeron. "Perhaps Sir Nihmedu can explain how it was done?"

When the guard lowered the sash covering Galaeron's mouth, he glanced around the council table and saw—or at least his shadow saw—guilty expressions on every face.

"Galaeron?" Alusair prodded.

No longer able to ignore the outrage rising in his breast, Galaeron glowered at the princess.

"You truly expect an answer?" he asked.

"Why shouldn't I?"

"Because I am no traitor to my people," Galaeron said. "I would never aid allies to the phaerimm."

An indignant drone filled the chamber, but the expression that came to Alusair's face was less anger than surrender.

"Leave us," she said.

The envoys fell silent and began to look to one another, waiting for someone else to take the lead and either object or start the withdrawal.

"Now!" Alusair said. "We will discuss the phaerimm

CHAPTER TWO

10 Flamerule, the Year of Wild Magic

Beyond the shadowshell, Takari Moonsnow saw only dark forms—nebulous disks and hazy pillars that could be monster or mineral, that could be beholders and bugbears or boulders and broken blocks of stone.

They never appeared to move, which favored the inanimate, but whenever she glanced away for a moment and looked back the shapes were in different places. That favored the animate—the sinister, even, and the dangerous. Providing, of course, that the change was not just her imagination playing tricks on her. Reconnoitering through the shadowshell was like peering through an obsidian window. She could tell that something lay on the other side, but what it might be was anyone's guess.

Takari cursed and started back toward camp,

her flesh warming in the hot Anauroch sun as she moved away from the shell's icy darkness behind. According to the latest news from within the Shaeradim, a trio of phaerimm had been seen several days before herding an army of mind-slaves in Takari's direction. Unfortunately, that was all anyone knew. Spying on the phaerimm was invariably lethal, so every report from inside came at a steep price.

Nor could the high mages sent by Evermeet scry the information. While the phaerimm's deadwall had long since fallen victim to the Shadovar shadowshell, the shadowshell itself remained strong enough to turn any spell on itself. Fortunately, the Chosen's ability to hear their names spoken anywhere on Faerûn had returned with the fall of the dead-wall—apparently because the Shadovar had not thought to weave their shell against the god-gifted abilities of the Chosen. Khelben Arunsun and Laeral Silverhand, who remained trapped with Evereska's besieged defenders, were able to relay messages out through Storm Silverhand or another of the Chosen.

Takari reached the field where her reconnaissance company was camped and found it in a bustle, with wood elves strapping on armor, stringing bows, and rushing to assemble at the gathering circle. Her second-in-command, a sloe-eyed male with a sinewy build and a shad-mouthed grin, rushed up to her with their helms and battle cloaks in hand.

"What is it, Wagg?" Takari asked, taking her cloak from him and swinging it around her shoulders. "Shadovar?"

Wagg—actually Wizzle Bendriver, but everyone called him Wagg because he shook his head whenever he smiled, frowned, or spoke—shook his head.

"Lord Ramealaerub has issued the call." He waved a helm over her shoulder, toward the shadowshell, and said, "He thinks it's coming down."

Takari closed the throat clasp of her cloak and turned to find that the black shadowshell had faded to gray-blue. Even from a hundred paces away, the barrier was unbelievably immense, a dark wall stretching beyond the horizon in both directions, the curve of its dome imperceptible as it climbed higher into the air than she could see. Before her eyes, the gray-blue shell faded to just gray. She began to see the terraced crests of the hills of the Desert Border South and looming beyond, the unmistakable crags of the High Shaeradim.

Just inside the fading shell, a broad ridge rose gently away from the desert, snaking its way deep into the foothills before ascending to a high mesa that would serve as the elven army's first staging ground inside the Shaeradim. Takari was relieved to see that the foot of the ridge lay directly in front of her company's campsite. When suggesting campsites to Lord Ramealaerub, she had been forced to recall the terrain inside the shadowshell from memory and guess at good staging points for each arm of the elven advance. That her own company was in proper position meant the others would be, too.

Takari took her war helm from Wagg and with a sigh put the thing on her head. It was one of those gaudy—some would say ornate—pieces of armor made by Gold elves. Gilded in silver and trimmed in gold, it was as heavy as a rock and about as comfortable. A circle of Evermeet's high mages had bestowed on it several useful enchantments, including their most powerful mind-guarding magic and the ability to stay in constant contact with her commander.

Wagg snickered. "You look like a bandit bird—only louder and uglier."

"That's not all bad. Maybe now you'll stop begging me to play night games."

"You're going to wear that awful thing at night?"

"And so are you." Takari pointed at Wagg's helm, then at his head. "The phaerimm don't care when they take their mind-slaves."

Wagg frowned. Shaking his head, he sneered at the adornments hammered into the metal.

"Ships," he grumbled. "It's always ships and sails with that bunch. What's wrong with a few trees?"

"Who knows?" Takari was as genuinely puzzled as her deputy. "Maybe they don't *have* trees on Evermeet."

"You think?"

Wagg's eyes widened at this frightening thought, and Takari shrugged.

The shadowshell had faded from gray to a transparent damson, and it had become more of a struggle to see the flickering barrier than the terrain behind it. Takari saw nothing but boulders, and scattered across the hillside, leafless smokethorn trees and the withered silhouettes of a few spiny soapleafs. The soapleafs she would have to watch. In the two decades she had spent patrolling the Desert Border South with Galaeron Nihmedu and his Tomb Guards, she had never seen one this close to Anauroch.

When Takari didn't see anything else of interest, she turned her thoughts inward and activated her helm's sending magic by picturing Lord Ramealaerub's stern face.

"Lord High Commander," she said.

The image in her mind grew more substantial, assuming the scowling visage of a sharp-featured Gold elf with a dagger-thin nose and eyebrows arched as sharply as ship keels.

Moonsnow, the Gold elf said, his words echoing in her mind. *I was beginning to think something had happened to you.*

"I was at the shadowshell, milord." Takari glanced at Wagg and rolled her eyes. Ramealaerub was a typical Gold, full of himself and the way things ought to be. "Looking for those mind-slaves Khelben warned us about."

Ramealaerub's expression grew impatient.

And?

"I couldn't see a thing, Milord." Annoyed by his attitude, Takari was not going to make anything easy on him. "That was before the shadowshell fell. Everything was too dark."

The shell is not dark now, Ramealaerub said.

"But now I'm back with my company." Takari's tone was innocent. "Didn't you call us to arms?"

A storm cloud came over Ramealaerub's face. Irritated, he said something to someone beside him then composed himself and turned back to Takari.

Moonsnow, the Lady of the Wood and I agreed that the wood elves would serve as the army's reconnaissance company. Though Ramealaerub's eyes looked as though they were about to pop free of their sockets, he spoke in a deliberately patient tone that suggested he did not realize how Takari was playing with him. *Would you be kind enough to take your elves and see if there is any sign of the enemy?*

"Of course—all you had to do was ask." Takari was beginning to worry that Ramealaerub truly did not understand that she was playing a game with him. If so, that did not bode well for the elven army. "But I can tell you already they know we're here."

You can see them?

He was worried.

"Not exactly," Takari said. "It's the trees."

The trees?

"A few shouldn't be here, this close to the sand," Takari explained.

At least Ramealaerub was enough of an elf to understand what that meant.

He grew thoughtful, then asked, *Which ones?*

"The soapleafs," Takari said. "They're the—"

I know what a soapleaf is, Moonsnow.

He looked away and spoke to someone else, then returned to her.

We have a few here, but not enough to slow us down. They're probably just sentries.

"Probably," Takari said, "but with the phaerimm, you can never—"

That's why you need to secure our flank, he said. *We'll be going in fast and hard, but once the shadowshell comes down there's no telling how long it will take the phaerimm to regain their strength. You must stay ahead of us—and let me know when you run into problems.*

"Oh, is *that* what a reconnaissance company does?"

I mean it, Moonsnow, Ramealaerub said. *Toy with me if you like, but not with your mission. You know better than any of us how quickly this can turn into a disaster.*

Maybe this Lord High Commander did have more sense than Evermeet's previous generals.

Takari gave him a coquettish smile and said, "Lord Ramealaerub, I can't imagine why you think I've been toying with you."

She glanced toward the shadowshell and, seeing that it had faded to transparent shimmer, she said, "We'll cross over as soon as we can. If you don't hear from me every quarter hour . . . consider *that* an alarm."

Very sensible, Ramealaerub answered. *And Moonsnow, do try to avoid getting yourself killed. You're the only scout who really knows this part of the Shaeradim.*

Ramealaerub's image vanished from her mind, and Takari turned to find her company waiting at the gathering circle. Though all of the rangers had fastened their battle cloaks and strung their bows, not one had donned the gaudy war helms sent by Evermeet. Most of the helms lay tossed on the ground, and some were being used as footrests or stools.

Takari tapped her own helm and said, "Put 'em on."

"But they're ugly," complained Jysela Whitebark.

"And heavy," added Grimble Oakorn.

Takari shrugged and said, "Suit yourselves, but tell me now what you want done when the phaerimm make mind-slaves of you. Would you rather be killed or let them stick you with an egg?"

There was a scramble for the helms. Takari waited for them to go on, then explained their mission and led the way along a well-beaten trail to what had been the shadowshell. No sign of the barrier remained. The path just ended, and few paces later the rocky slope of their ridge emerged from the sand and began to rise in a jumble of boulders and barren ground toward the distant peaks of the High Shaeradim.

Takari dug into the sand until she found a pebble. Half-expecting it to vanish in a flare of darkness as had the hundreds of others she had tossed through the shadowshell, she threw it as hard as she could.

The stone clattered to the ground thirty paces up the ridge.

She studied the pebble for a moment, not quite able to believe that it had actually landed in the Shaeradim, then turned to her company. They were standing together looking nervous and a little frightened.

"After all this waiting, I guess expected something more somehow."

"I'm just happy it didn't melt or something," Wagg said.

As Wagg spoke, Takari began to speak in fingertalk, her hands issuing silent instructions that were being studied much more attentively than her deputy's ramblings.

"From what you've said about these Shadovar," Wagg continued, "I didn't think it would just disappear. I was sure it was going to explode or something and kill us all."

"Then I thank Rillifane Rallathil you were wrong," Takari said. Her fingers continued to weave commands, warning her warriors to be wary of other things aside from soapleafs. "This job is harder than I bargained for as it is."

Now! she signaled.

Nocking arrows as they moved, the company scattered and loosed. The shafts flew over Takari's head with a low droning whistle, and the slope behind her erupted into pained squeals and strange gurgling howls. She turned.

Where the soapleafs had been a moment earlier, she found half a dozen illithids collapsing to the ground, their bodies peppered with arrows and their mouth tentacles writhing in anguish.

The rest of the slope remained as still as before.

Nocking an arrow in her own bow, Takari dropped into a crouch and rushed forward. Taking cover behind the first boulder she came to, she scratched the surface with the tip of her arrow to make certain it really was a boulder, then looked left and right down the foot of the ridge. Camouflaged as they were by the magic of their battle cloaks, it took a few moments to find the nearest members of her company hiding behind boulders similar to hers. She did not attempt a head count. With the company spread across the width of the entire ridge, she would have been hard-pressed to find them all even had they been standing on tiptoe and waving their arms.

She envisioned her company waiting in the gathering circle a few moments earlier, then whispered, "Reconnaissance company, anything to report?"

When no reply came, she breathed a sigh of relief, then reported their progress to Lord Ramealaerub. He congratulated her on her success, informing her that the moon elves protecting the other flank were advancing as well, then reminded her that the main body of the army would start its advance in five minutes and urged her to keep moving. Takari bit back a sour reply and gave the order to ascend the ridge in two waves, each covering the other as it advanced.

Grimble Oakorn—her partner in this tactic—emerged from behind a boulder thirty paces to her right and raced another thirty paces ahead before ducking back into cover. Takari quickly left her own hiding pace, and weaving erratically to make herself a difficult target, ran sixty paces before finally kneeling behind the big trunk of a dead smokethorn. It was hard work, especially with the hot Anauroch sun beating down on the heavy helm she wore. Sweat began to trickle over her brow.

There was a three-second pause before Grimble and the others in the first wave emerged from new hiding places. Only fools left cover in the same place they entered it, and wood elf scouts were not fools. They raced sixty paces uphill and dropped back into cover. Takari and the second wave crawled to new starting points and rushed up the slope.

The depredations of the strange war had reduced this desert wonderland to a dismal ghost of its former self, leaving hundreds of smokethorns strewn across the hillside, their trunks snapped off at the base or their root-fan ripped whole from the rocky ground. The trees that remained standing were naked and bare, their dagger-shaped leaves scattered around their bases like withered gray skirts. Even the tough thorn-brambles, which seemed to flourish best in ground that was more rock than dirt and blossomed only in the worst of droughts, were withered and drooping, their tiny leaves brittle and brown.

The sight filled Takari with a cold anger, and not only because it pained her to see the Shaeradim defiled by war. The two decades she had spent patrolling the area with Galaeron Nihmedu had been the happiest of her life—even if he had spent the entire time refusing to acknowledge their spirit-bond—and the sight of the land withering away reminded her that her memories were also fading, that eventually she would be left only with the dry fact of the matter: that she had been a Tomb Guard on the Desert Border South and she had been in love with her princep. But the love itself—the simple joy of being always near him, the flutter that had stirred in her heart with his every smile—that would be gone, carried off by war and as lost to her as Galaeron himself.

Takari lost count of the times she and Grimble took turns rushing up the slope, but her breath began to come in ragged gasps, and her hair grew so sweaty it made squishing sounds under the helm. She kneeled behind a broken boulder and wiped her eyes on the shoulder of her cloak, then watched the slope above as Grimble raced ahead and kneeled behind a fallen smokethorn. His battle cloak turned the same pearly gray as the bark, a pair of streaks across his shoulders matching a band of furrows in the trunk. Half wishing she had picked a slower partner, Takari scrambled across the broken ground on all fours, emerged from behind a square boulder, and began her dash.

Takari had taken no more than three steps before her eye was drawn back to Grimble's hiding place. His cloak had turned dark and dappled, and so had his hair, ears, and boot soles—all she could see from behind. As she drew nearer, she could see that both he and his cloak seemed oddly rigid and were covered with tiny flecks of black and red.

Takari dropped behind a knee-high outcropping ten paces below Grimble, then used her helm to call the company to a halt. Without looking out from behind her cover, she pictured Grimble's handsome face.

"Grimble?" she whispered.

There was no reply.

Takari's pulse began to pound in her ears—just when she really needed to hear. She closed her eyes, set her weapons aside, and took a few calming breaths. When the noise finally died away, she picked up a good-sized rock, and rising from behind her outcropping, threw it at Grimble's back.

It struck with a stony clink.

Takari dropped back into her hiding place and activated her helm's sending magic.

"Reconnaissance company, watch yourselves. We're under attack—something turned Grimble into a statue."

Wyeka, too, Wagg whispered. *Didn't see what happened.*

"Me either," Takari answered. "Anybody?"

No one reported anything. Takari was not all that surprised. The phaerimm cast their spells entirely with their thoughts— no gestures or words required—and the eye-magic of their beholder servants was just as silent.

"We need to figure out where this is coming from," Takari said. She lifted her head just high enough to peer over the outcropping. "I'm just below Grimble, and I can see half a dozen good places to hide, starting with a clump of daggerhedge off to the left and ending with a three-boulder pile on the right."

I'm even with Wyeka, Wagg said through her helm. *I can't see the daggerhedge on the left, only the roots of the overturned smokethorn.*

"Then it's somewhere between the roots and the boulder pile," Takari said. "Everyone who can't see that keep advancing and circle a—"

Wait. An image of Alaya Thistledew's rosy-nosed face came to Takari's mind along with her voice. *Something's hissing. Maybe it's nothing, but I'll take—*

Her image vanished from Takari's mind.

"Alaya?"

Turned to rock, said Alaya's partner, Rosl Harp.

Though the two were lovers, Rosl didn't sound overly frantic. With a hundred battle wizards and three circles of high mages in the elven army, there were worse things that could happen to a warrior than being turned to stone.

It got her when she looked around the boulder, he continued. *She couldn't have seen any of the cover you were talking about.*

It's moving around, then, Wagg said.

You mean walking *around,* Rosl said, his voice coming to Takari's mind as a barely audible whisper.

"You're sure?" Takari asked. "Phaerimm float. Beholders, too."

I hear it, Rosl said. *Moving away.*

"A lot of feet?" Takari asked. She was beginning to think she knew what they were facing. "Maybe a tail dragging?"

Sounds like it, Rosl said. *I can't see anything, though.*

Takari rolled her eyes and replied, "You might have to risk a look, Rosl."

I am looking, Rosl spat. *I can't see anything but rocks and . . .*

"It's invisible!" Takari and Rosl reached this conclusion at the same time, then Takari asked, "You're sure you're behind it?"

I'm sure, Rosl said. *What do you think I am, a human? Be ready to cover, everyone. I'll do a cast-and-run.*

Rosl's voice vanished as he prepared his spell. Takari looked to her right. Fifty paces away, Wagg was turning in Rosl's direction, his bow slung across his back so his hands would be free to use his own magic. Though Takari could see none of the other scouts, she knew that everyone within two hundred paces of Rosl's position would be doing the same.

She was just beginning to wonder what was taking so long when a spark of silver cracked down the slope from somewhere above and flashed out of existence. An instant later, a low boom rumbled across the ridge.

"Rosl?" Takari asked.

He's down, Jysela Whitebark, appearing in Takari's mind, said. Her copper-colored eyes were opened wide in shock and horror. *Lightning bolt, I think. It wasn't that powerful. He's still smoking, and alive enough to be thrashing around.*

"Did you see where it came from?" Takari asked.

Jysela shook her head. Though she was undoubtedly the closest elf to Rosl, she did not volunteer—and Takari did not suggest—going to his aid. Their unseen attacker was waiting for just that, and Jysela would only have ended up lying on the ground beside him.

Moonsnow? Lord Ramealaerub's sharp features appeared in Takari's mind. *We heard a bang.*

"We've run into trouble," Takari reported. "An invisible basilisk, I think, and something protecting it."

Just one protector?

"Possibly."

Probably. Gwynanael Tahtrel and her rangers are having trouble with a phaerimm on the other flank. It keeps falling back, fighting to delay the advance. We think they're trying to buy time to recover their magic. You can't let that happen.

"Easily said, milord," Takari replied. "Not so easily done. We don't even know where it's at."

Find out, Ramealaerub ordered. *We're moving into the valley now, and we need you to stay ahead of us.*

"We're taking casualties. . . ."

And you'll continue to take them until you eliminate the problem! Ramealaerub's voice softened when he added, *You're a reconnaissance company, Moonsnow. You're supposed to take casualties. Move up.*

The Lord High Commander's face vanished, leaving Takari's curses to fall on no ears but her own. She peered over her outcropping and studied the slope above but could find no hint of where their attacker might be lurking. Were she the one up there, she would be hiding in the dark cavities within the boulder pile, but she was not. She was not even of the same race. She was an elf, and they were . . . she had no idea what they were facing. It was rare that beholders used lightning bolts, but the attacker could easily be a mind-slave from Evereska or Laeral Silverhand's relief army. Or it might be a phaerimm, as Gwynanael and her moon elves were facing.

Takari found no hints on the slope above.

She pictured Jysela in her mind and said, "Jysela, can you . . . ?"

When her memory of the face did not coalesce into a solid image, Takari realized there was no one there and let the sentence drop. She felt bile burning her throat and tried to swallow it back down. It returned two breaths later.

Hoping her voice did not sound too shaky, she had the entire company report by name. Only Jysela was missing, but as she took the roll call, the basilisk—or whatever it was—turned another scout to stone. Ramealaerub was right about one thing, at least. Hiding in the rocks was not going to spare them any casualties.

"I'm afraid we have to do this like the Golds would," Takari announced.

You mean a charge? Wagg asked.

More accustomed to hunting than fighting, wood elves preferred stealth and ambush to speed and ferocity— especially when speed and ferocity meant charging into the teeth of the enemy's defense.

"Advance in two waves," Takari clarified, "and keep a careful watch up that slope. There isn't much point in this if we don't see where the enemy's hiding. First line, go!"

The first wave had barely left their hiding places before another bolt of lightning crackled down the slope. This one was a little stronger than the first, loud enough that Takari actually felt the crack in the pit of her stomach. It struck about a hundred paces away, just close enough that she saw it blast one of her scouts off his feet. The injured elf's partner left her hiding place to help and was instantly struck by a flight of golden bolts of magic.

Both attacks came from somewhere far to the right of the ridge. Takari focused her attention in that direction but did not bother bringing her arrow to her cheek. Even if the angle were good—and it was not—she still had only a vague idea of where to aim.

The rest of the wave advanced only ten paces before the enemy struck again, this time with a lightning bolt powerful enough that the tip blasted through the victim's body and came out the other side. To Takari, it seemed that the flash had danced down the jagged ridge crest on the far right side, but she still failed to catch exactly where it had come from.

The elves managed another dozen paces before Takari finally saw a ball of red flame appear in the middle of a small cliff's jagged silhouette and streak over the ridge crest to strike a target somewhere beyond. She started to call the location out over her helm, but then a steady stream of dark shafts started to fly back toward the cliff, and she knew the target had been found.

Not that it did them a lot of good. By the time the first wave finished its leg of the advance and began dropping behind cover, an elf in the second wave had been turned to stone by the basilisk, and the hidden attacker had slain yet another in the first.

Each attack seemed just a little more powerful than the last, and Takari didn't think it was only because the victims kept moving closer. The lightning cracked more loudly, the magic bolts grew more numerous, the balls of fire grew larger and burned more brightly. The Weave was repairing itself in the Shaeradim, and as it did so, the enemy was growing stronger.

Their attacker had to be a phaerimm.

Takari's turn to advance came. She crawled a few paces on her hands and knees, then started up the slope at a run. As with the first wave, a lightning bolt lashed down the slope the instant they rose and blasted Yaveen Greeneedle—Takari's closest friend from Rheitheillaethor—into scorched pieces. Takari screamed, not only for Yaveen, but for all of the company's lost elves. These were more than the scouts she had trained to fight phaerimm. These were her childhood friends, her dancing partners and would-be lovers, the sons and daughters of parents who had begged her to bring their children home safe. Each time one died, a little of her died with them, but there was nothing to be done about it except kill the phaerimm and lose more friends doing it.

By the time Takari's wave was ready to find cover, she had lost three more friends. She was also close enough to their attacker to see that it had hidden itself in a rift in the cliff face. Her company's arrows were ricocheting off the opening one after the other, no doubt because the occupant had sealed the crevice with a missile guard and spell shield so it could watch over its invisible pet from safety. A crooked line of elven statues was angling up the slope toward the left side of the ridge, where the attacker's view would soon be blocked by the lip of its own hiding place.

The phaerimm was sending the basilisk to guard its flank. Like Ramealaerub, it was worried about what it could not see.

Again, the first wave of elves rose to renew their charge, and again the phaerimm took one of their number the instant he left cover, sending a ball of fire smoking and hissing into a big smokethorn tree. Young Harla Elmworm came staggering out of the conflagration, engulfed in flames and screaming in agony.

The spells were coming faster, a sure sign that the enemy was recovering all too quickly.

The attack on Harla was also a sign, Takari realized, that her company's camouflage was of little use against this foe. Phaerimm could literally see magic, and given all the magic her scouts were wearing they had to be about as obvious to the enemy as a lantern in the Underdark.

Takari activated her helm's sending magic and said, "Company halt! Find good cover and take it. Here's what I want you to do . . ."

As she explained her plan, Takari was unclasping her cloak and removing her boots, slipping off her rings and bracers, and shedding everything else that carried the faintest dweomer of magic. By the time she was finished, she was stripped down to her leather armor and not much more.

"I'll try to be fast," she finished. "Just keep the enemy's attention focused on you until you see me on top of the cliff, and in the name of the Leaflord, if you hear that basilisk creeping up behind you, don't look! Just fling a magic bolt at the sound and run the other way. I'm sure our good Lord High Commander thinks he has better uses for his battle wizards than turning us all back into people."

The last thing Takari removed was her helm. She bundled it with her cloak and other magic. Wagg and a dozen others began to pelt the phaerimm's hiding place with blasting spells, and the rest of the company began to crawl—very slowly and very cautiously—toward the rift.

The phaerimm countered by targeting its own spells at those advancing on its hiding place. Though scouts took care to stay behind solid cover as much as possible, their enemy was a deadly one, and all too many of its spells struck home.

When Takari judged the assault to be blinding enough, she stood and raced up the hill in her bare feet, carrying no magic at all and little else aside from her weapons. Twenty steps later, a solemn-faced wood elf startled Takari by suddenly falling in at her side. He was a century or two older than Takari, and like her he was stripped down to armor and weapons.

Takari cocked a brow and said, "This is a job for one, Yurne. Two only doubles the risk of being noticed."

"You hear me coming?"

"No," Takari admitted.

"Well, then."

Yurne took the lead, and that was the end of the matter. One of the hermit elves who lived alone in the depths of High Forest, Yurne had wandered into Rheitheillaethor after the reconnaissance company had completed its training and announced he would be coming along. Lord Ramealaerub's officer had made the mistake of suggesting it was too late then promptly found his sleeve pinned to a tree by one of Yurne's throwing daggers. The hermit had stepped over very close and began to quote the officer's lessons word by word, then asked the sputtering Gold what business he had leading a company of wood elf scouts when he could not even tell when he was training one.

After that, no one ever dared tell Yurne what he could or could not do, and a steady chorus of Green elf snickers had driven the affronted Gold elf back to the main army where he belonged. Lord Ramealaerub had transferred command of the company to Takari—who, as a ranger in Galaeron Nihmedu's Tomb Guard patrol, was the only one in the group with any experience that could be considered remotely military.

The conflagration outside the phaerimm's hiding place continued at no small cost in elf lives as Takari and Yurne ascended the slope. As soon as they were higher than the phaerimm's hiding place, Takari dropped to her haunches and, determined to put an end to the costly spell battle as quickly as possible, began to creep toward the little cliff.

Yurne continued up the hill, and Takari flashed an order for him to follow, but he did not see her fingertalk—or chose to ignore it—and proceeded as before. She cursed the hermit's stubbornness and resumed her advance, until she recalled the ease with which he had spied on the reconnaissance company during their training.

Takari cursed the hermit again, this time for his reticence, and followed him up the slope.

Several minutes later, they dropped to all fours and crept across the slope to a fallen smokethorn about twenty paces above the little cliff. They spent a few moments studying the rift from above, though Takari could see nothing in its depths except the constant flash of battle magic.

Yurne closed his eyes and began to sniff the air, and she finally understood why the hermit had insisted on approaching from above. There was not much of a breeze, but what there was came up the slope from Anauroch's hot sands.

Takari could smell nothing but the stench of brimstone and charred flesh, but Yurne's nose was more discerning. Eyes widening, he dropped behind the smokethorn and began to fingertalk in the clumsy gestures of one who seldom practiced the art.

Mime flamer guard!

Mind flayer? Takari asked. *An illithid?*

Yes! The gesture was sharp. *That's wham I seed!*

Where?

How should I nose? I smelled it, not seam it.

Takari peered over the log and saw only rock and dead scrub brush, though that meant nothing. The illithid could be in hiding or simply invisible, and using a spell to find it would be like shouting their presence to the phaerimm. On the other hand, the spell battle was continuing unabated and had diverted the attention of the sentry as well as that of the master. Takari dropped back behind the log.

Anything else down there we can't see? she signed.

A hare, paralyzed by fear, Yurne answered. *Nodding else.*

Really? Takari raised her brow. *That's some nose you have. Why do you thing I lib alone?*

Recalling what a hundred wood elves could smell like after three days of drinking and dancing, Takari made a face and nodded her understanding, then turned to the matter at hand.

I don't think the illithid has noticed us. We need to keep it that way, or the phaerimm will just teleport up the hill and keep attacking.

You have a plant?

Takari nodded and explained her idea.

I lick it, Yurne said. *Except the captain shouldn't go first.*

With that, he slipped over the smokethorn's trunk and crawled down the slope, moving so quickly and gracefully that Takari barely had time to ready her bow before he was at the rift. He dropped to his belly and peered over the edge, doing a convincing job of pretending not to know there was an illithid lurking somewhere nearby. When nothing happened, he rose to a knee and took his bow from his shoulder.

Still lying behind the smokethorn, Takari nocked two arrows on her bow and began to regret she had not tried a more direct plan. Had they just rushed the rift, they would have been attacking by then. The phaerimm might even be dead. Apparently, the illithid's attention remained focused on the battle, and it was unaware—

Yurne gurgled in pain, then let the bow slip from his hands and reached for his head. Takari remained utterly motionless, quietly searching for the source of the attack. She found no hint. The illithid remained as invisible as before, with no telltale footsteps or shuddering bramble twigs to give away his location. Yurne's eyes went blank, and he began to crawl around on his knees, holding his temples and groaning incoherently.

There was a one-sided lull as the phaerimm ceased spellcasting long enough to consult with its minion telepathically, then the conflagration resumed even more fiercely than before. Takari bit her lip and tried to avoid thinking about how many of her friends were dying while she lay there hiding. If the phaerimm was worried enough about its own safety to use invisibility magic so powerful it would keep an attacker hidden, it was worried enough to pick a guard who would not make foolish mistakes.

A seeming eternity later, Yurne lowered his hands and began to shake his head clear. The illithid remained hidden, at least until the hermit stumbled upon his discarded bow. Apparently forgetting he still had a full quiver hanging from his shoulder, he began to search the ground for an arrow he had never drawn. A bramble twig fluttered ten paces behind him, and Yurne's head snapped back as an invisible hand grabbed his hair and jerked him over backward.

That was all the target Takari needed. Rolling to her knees in one swift motion, she set her aim just behind Yurne's head and let fly.

The arrows were still in the air as she leaped over the smokethorn and charged down the hill. The shafts thumped to a stop behind Yurne, in what appeared to be empty air. A cascade of dark blood erupted around the heads of the arrows and poured down on the scout's head. He screamed and rolled away as Takari jumped over him, her bow discarded ten steps up the hill and her sword and dagger already in hand.

A huge mouth filled with fangs and ringed by four thin arms was just rising out of the rift and turning toward the fallen illithid.

Takari knew better than to hesitate. She simply lowered her head and dived past the fangs, slashing and hacking as the thing's dark mouth rose around her. Her sword slashed through something sinuous and tough, then her dagger sank into a mound of ooze as large as her head. The jaws started to close, and she brought her legs to her chest just in time to avoid having them bitten off.

A sour-smelling liquid burbled up from the depths ahead and coated her face in hot, caustic slime. Gagging, Takari pushed off against the back of its teeth, driving herself and her sword deeper into the thing's gullet and dragging her dagger beside her, stabbing and chopping at anything that seemed like it could be cut.

The fleshy passage, now slick and warm with blood and other precious fluids, clamped down and began to push her back toward the mouth. Realizing she was about to be regurgitated, Takari spread her knees to wedge herself in place, then planted her dagger to the hilt and held on.

The muscles began to convulse, squeezing her so tightly she thought she would be crushed. Takari pushed her sword as far as she could reach, twisting the blade to and fro, circling the tip in awkward crescents that sometimes found nothing and sometimes cut through fleshy masses that could only be organs.

When her sword sliced through something soft and gauzy, the phaerimm stopped trying to expel her. A flood of warm blood rose up to fill the dark passage. Everything went limp, and Takari's stomach rose into her chest. She thought they were falling, but the feeling seemed to last forever—a timeless eternity—and a strange chill burned her flesh. She grew queasy and weak, her pulse hammered in her ears, and her mind began to reel.

Then she was simply somewhere else, someplace dark and foul, someplace filled with hot caustic slime. Her flesh was stinging, her eyes were burning. The stuff was in her nose and throat and lungs, suffocating her, choking her, drowning her. She coughed and felt hot flesh all around—not squeezing, merely touching and holding—and she recalled where she was.

Or rather, where she had been when the phaerimm teleported to safety.

Heart hammering, Takari pushed back up the dark passage. The flesh remained limp and motionless around her, but heavy and suffocating. She found herself fighting not to breathe and succeeding—fighting not to cough and failing. More of the phaerimm's foul bile gushed down her throat and made her want to vomit, but she managed to fight back the impulse by reminding herself that she would only end up swallowing more of the awful stuff. She came to the thing's teeth and, finding them clamped shut behind her, pressed her back against the roof of its mouth.

The teeth came apart. A shaft of brilliant sunlight came pouring in from outside, bringing with it a much needed draft of cool mountain air. Inhaling through her fingers to avoid swallowing any more blood or bile, Takari sucked it in, coughed out a flagon full of red mucous that might have been hers or the phaerimm's, then filled her lungs again. Only then, after she had gained control of her reflexes, did she turn and peer out from between the creature's pebbly lips.

Below her lay a vast staircase of dead and barren vineyards, descending toward Evereska's embattled walls in a series of smoke-shrouded terraces, with no living thing in sight except the cone-shaped forms of fifty floating phaerimm.

CHAPTER THREE

12 Flamerule, the Year of Wild Magic

Mount Untrivvin's east wall stood a mile away, a looming face of rock and ice hidden behind a curtain of milk-white steam, its form discernible only as a dim gray wedge against a bright gray sky. A blurry fleck of darkness could be seen in front of the mountain, flying a lazy oval about a third of the way up. When the speck reached the end of its loop and banked around to go in the other direction, it assumed a vaguely crosslike shape with a long, thin body and swept-back wings. Even without the clear-seeing spell she had cast, Arr would have recognized the figure as one of the Shadovar's worm-bat mounts, a veserab.

So we are seen, Tuuh whistled beside her. They were standing on the High Ice, staring at the sentry across the sunken vastness of a Shadovar shadow blanket. *We will not have long to wait.*

Arr turned to Tuuh. With a receding hairline, black beard, and dark eyes, he was an exact double of the famous—and very troublesome—Khelben Arunsun.

"Use your mouth and speak Common," Arr instructed. "The scout may have ears as well as eyes."

If that is so, you are more likely to betray us with your words, Tuuh replied, continuing to speak in Winds, using magic to stir the icy air into the whistling language of the phaerimm. *Even if he is listening, humans have trouble recognizing our voices.*

"The Shadovar are not human."

They are close enough.

"Perhaps, but this is my plan—one endorsed by the entire WarGather. If it fails, do you really wish to give them an excuse to blame you?"

The WarGather does not frighten me. Despite the boast, Tuuh said in Common, "And, if something does go wrong, you are the only one they will blame. I'll see to that."

Tuuh turned, and remembering to use his legs as would a human, he stormed off across the ice. Though she was burning inside to demand a gift of contrition—or at least remind him that the WarGather had placed her in charge—Arr had no choice but to let him go. This was the great shortcoming of the phaerimm, their inability to work toward a common cause.

They all knew it, of course—were they not all geniuses, the wisest race ever to inhabit Toril?—but that did not mean they could overcome their one weakness. Beings of such intelligence were too impatient with the folly of others and too easily bored by any company but their own. Sooner or later, every phaerimm compact was doomed to disintegrate in a tempest of clashing winds and bitter magic. That was the nature of her people, and it was only their fear and hatred of the Shadovar that had kept them working together at all through the dark months of their imprisonment in the Shaeradim.

But if Arr's plan worked, if she could trick the Shadovar and the other two-leg realms into making war on each other, then maybe—just maybe—she could keep her people united long enough to capture Evereska. Once they had claimed its magic-nourishing mythal for their own and the phaerimm saw what they could accomplish together, who knew how long their patience might be extended? Perhaps Arr could find even greater goals to unite them. If she planned carefully and always kept the meat dangled before the teeth of her fellows, it would not surprise her to see them take their natural place as the masters of the world—and she would be the master of masters. Why not? Was she not the wisest and most cunning of the phaerimm?

"Arr!" This from Beze, who had assumed the silver-haired form of Khelben Arunsun's paramour, Laeral Silverhand—right down to the tiny limb sprouting from the stump of the arm Laeral had lost in the Shaeradim. "Your feet!"

Arr looked down to find her feet dangling beneath her, the toes not quite touching the glacier. She felt something warm rush to the cheeks of her human face, then lowered herself through a conscious act of will and started to walk to her place in line.

"Watch your tone, sister," Arr said. Save that she stood a little taller than Beze and wore her silver hair somewhat longer, her appearance was much the same. She and Beze had assumed the shape of the Silverhand sisters, Storm and Laeral. "Remember who is leading this mission."

"How could I forget?" Beze nodded in both directions along the steep bank that led down to the shadow blanket and said, "Your humble followers await."

Arr glared just long enough to make it clear that the sarcasm would not be forgotten, then glanced in both directions Beze had indicated. The shadow blanket had melted a deep basin into the ice, and the rest of their number were carefully spacing themselves along its rim, each about a thousand feet apart.

Like Tuuh, Beze, and Arr herself, the last two phaerimm had assumed the likenesses of Mystra's Chosen: Alustriel Silverhand and Dove Falconhand. Arr would have liked to have a larger force, but given that Syluné was a ghost who never left Shadowdale, Qilué Veladorn seldom involved herself in the affairs of humans, and Elminster was still missing with the Simbul, five was largest number of Chosen they could reasonably impersonate.

Arr waited until Beze and Ryry signaled that everyone was in position—the fog was too thick for her to see Tuuh and Xayn at the far ends—then raised her arms and began to chant. The others joined in at once, gesturing and intoning odd-sounding syllables in a carefully choreographed imitation of a human casting. The process was, of course, absurdly slow and primitive—at least compared to how the phaerimm cast magic—but it seemed a necessary step for humans. Arr and her fellows wasted most of the next minute on this nonsense, then lowered their arms and simply thought the spell.

A long, crescent-shaped blade of magic light appeared before them, the lower lip teetering on the rim of the steep slope at their feet. Arr glanced through the steam bank and saw the dark fleck of the sentry still holding his position in front of Mount Untrivvin. She raised her arm and pointed forward, and as one the five "Chosen" pushed their creation over the bank.

The blanket peeler slid fifty feet to the bottom of the basin, where its lower lip slipped under the shadow blanket's edge and quietly rolled it one yard back.

That was all the sentry needed to see. When Arr next looked, the veserab was vanishing southward through the steam. She allowed herself a moment to savor the genius of her plan, then waved to the others and slid down the icy bank to the shadow blanket.

At the bottom of the pit, they found themselves standing in six inches of icy water. The discomfort was not something phaerimm were accustomed to, but it was a simple matter to fix with a little resistance magic. They soon started to push, and the magic peeler worked just as Arr had planned, cutting the blanket free of the ice and rolling it back on itself. The more material there was, the tighter the tool rolled it.

The only problem came when they encountered stones hidden beneath the ice, a surprisingly frequent occurrence since rocks often fell from the mountain, then were carried forward by the glacier and slowly buried by more snow. Still, the phaerimm quickly learned to push these obstacles out of the way with simple telekinesis magic. Two hours later, they had made so much progress that Mount Untrivvin blocked their entire view of the western horizon, and they could hear the faint ringing that gave the peak its name—in the native tongue, *untrivvin* meant "singing rock."

Arr was beginning to fear that her plan had failed when a jagged line of shadows began to appear in the steam ahead. She continued forward until the line resolved itself into a rank of Shadovar warriors, all fully armored and carrying their deadly black swords. Arr's companions were instantly at her back, arriving by teleport magic even as the enemy began to advance.

Instead of breaking into a charge as Arr had anticipated, the Shadovar line stopped thirty paces from the rolled shadow blanket. A huge warrior with braided hair tails and bright coppery eyes stepped forward and raised his dark blade in salute. He was the one they called Escanor.

"With the phaerimm loose in the world again, I should think the Chosen of Mystra would have better things to do than rob Shade Enclave of its water."

"If Shade kept its water to itself, we would," Arr replied.

She had not expected the Shadovar to be more interested in talking than fighting, but she had to respond in kind. While phaerimm never hesitated to use force, she and her fellows had to behave as the Chosen would, and the Chosen were reluctant to start a fight until they knew they had no other choice.

"Your shadow blankets are flooding half of Faerûn," she continued, "and robbing the rest of rain. Since you refuse to remove them, we will do it for you."

Escanor took one step forward and said, "Faerûn's suffering is the price for restoring Shade to its birthright."

"Then let *Shade* pay the price," Arr said, trying to put herself in Storm's place. "Your birthright is no concern of Faerûn's."

"It is. You abandoned us to the Plane of Shadow for seventeen centuries. You cannot imagine how we suffered."

"We abandoned no one." Arr wondered if she had conversed enough to seem like one of the Chosen, then decided probably not. They talked a lot. "Leaving was your city's choice."

"Choice?" Escanor scoffed. "It was leave or die."

"Then it is a pity Shade did not choose the latter," she said. The Shadovar's talkativeness puzzled Arr. Surely, he knew as well as Arr did that there was going to be a fight—so why was he stalling? "It would have saved everyone a lot of trouble."

"Rude, as well as ungrateful." Escanor looked from Arr to Ryry and said, "You are known to be the reasonable sister, Lady Alustriel. Surely, you can see that opposing us will only lead to more Tilvertons. Wouldn't your energies be better spent helping Faerûn's people adjust to the new climate than adding to their troubles by starting a war you cannot hope to win?"

"No one ever *wins* a war, Prince Escanor," Ryry said, sounding like Alustriel in voice as well as meaning. "They only lose less than the enemy. Given what Shade lost at Tilverton, I should think you would understand that."

"Our city is still here."

"And so are a hundred of ours," Arr countered. "Who do you think can stand to lose more?"

Escanor's eyes flashed orange.

"The question is not how many cities you can lose, Lady Storm." His voice was sharp and seething, yet he seemed as content as before to stand there talking instead of fighting. "The question is how many you can destroy. We have already proven what we can do."

"And if you lose an army with each city, we will not have to destroy your city at all," Arr said. As she spoke, Arr was running her gaze down the Shadovar line, searching for the other princes. "By the third or fourth city, it will be ours for the claiming."

"We have learned from our mistake." Escanor glanced at the shadow blanket rolled up between them and said, "You, apparently, have not. You will remove your tool and allow us to replace the shadow blanket. I will ask this only once."

Arr completed her search of the Shadovar line and finding no more princes placed a hand on her hip in the stubborn way Storm often did.

"And if we refuse?"

"The battle will not be fought here," Escanor said. "It will be Faerûn's cities that pay—"

"Liar."

Nothing would have made Arr happier than to think the prince was telling the truth, but the Shadovar were too cunning to announce their plan in advance. She raised her arm and with a thought unleashed the spell she had spent most of her imprisonment in the Shaeradim developing. A steady stream of silver-white flame boiled out of her fingertips toward the prince. His spell-guard flashed black as the fire struck. The shadow magic in this defense triggered a secondary spell, sending an antimagic beam shooting from the head of the flame stream.

A gapping hole appeared in Escanor's spell-guard, allowing the white stream behind to pour through. The effect was a reasonable imitation of the silver fire of the Chosen, and Escanor fell, screaming and engulfed in flames.

Arr started to whistle a command to her fellows, then caught herself and yelled, "Watch our backs! The other princes—"

She was interrupted by the hissing crash of a dark bolt striking home behind her. Beze went tumbling over the rolled shadow blanket and landed a dozen yards away, wisps of shadow rising from a gaping hole in her chest. She began to thrash about and whistle in pain, then rose into the air, too weak and dazed to hold herself on the ground.

"Laeral, no!" Arr yelled. "Get down and be—"

The word "quiet" was lost to a horrific roar as battle magic—both phaerimm and Shadovar—started to crack and sizzle behind her. Escanor's company answered with a thunderous war cry, then lifted their arms and began to gesture. Arr countered by raising a wall of scintillating color in front of them—Shadovar hated prismatic magic—then she realized she had forgotten herself and neglected to gesture and incant. She covered by waving her arm and booming out a dozen syllables of mystic nonsense, then toppled the wall over on the enemy.

A cacophony of crackling magic and anguished screaming filled the basin for a single instant then came echoing back off Untrivvin's stony face and faded to an low murmur. It was a sound Arr loved well, the sound of astonished survivors struggling to gather their wits and reorganize.

She glanced back to find her companions standing behind their spell-guards hurling magic at half a dozen retreating princes. The bars of a half-completed shadow cage lay at their feet, slowly melting into the slushy water as its unbound energies dispersed.

The sound of sharp commands drew Arr's attention forward again, where the Shadovar survivors had already regrouped. Half a dozen were gathered around their burning prince, attempting to smother Arr's silver flames with their own bodies. The rest, perhaps two dozen in all, were following a tall warrior forward, their swords drawn and their gem-colored eyes glowing with rage.

This time remembering to cast the spell as a human would, Arr called up a wall of flame.

By the time she finished the necessary gesturing and chanting, the Shadovar were almost even with Beze's writhing form. Arr would not normally have hesitated to engulf one of her own in the conflagration, but Beze's defenses had obviously been overpowered by the enemy attack. If the flames killed her, she would revert to true form and reveal the truth about who the Shadovar were fighting.

Arr raised the wall behind the charging warriors, then reached behind her and grabbed Tuuh by the collar.

"Come along, Khelben," she said.

She clambered across the rolled shadow blanket, Tuuh half-stumbling and half-floating over it as she pulled him along. When he turned and saw two dozen angry Shadovar only ten paces away, he forget himself and raised a barrier of thrashing blades without remembering to gesture.

"*Allak thur doog!*" Arr called, improvising.

The incantation was lost to the wet thud of the barrier's blades chopping through Shadovar armor.

Pulling Tuuh after her, Arr started around the far end, shouting, "Remember yourself, Khelben."

"A split second of warning might help next time," Tuuh answered. "Where are we going."

"To help Bez—er, Laeral."

"To *help* her?" Tuuh stopped. "What for?"

"Because she's supposed to be your mate!" Arr hissed. "And because my plan will be ruined if she dies and they see her revert."

They reached the end of the barrier. Arr peered around the corner to find that Beze had fallen unconscious and now lay floating in the air, her arms stretched over her head and her legs twined together in a distinctly tail-like braid. The eight Shadovar—all that had escaped Tuuh's spell—remained trapped between the blade barrier and Arr's wall of fire.

The tall Shadovar saw her looking and raised his hand to cast a spell. Arr pulled back in time to avoid the dark bolt that came streaking past the end of the barrier, then dropped to a knee and sent a fork of lightning crackling back in her attacker's direction. It caught him in the chest and knocked him off his feet, then dissipated harmlessly against his spell-guard. The warrior pointed at Beze and sent his followers rushing in her direction.

A stream of silver-white flame streaked over Arr's head, blasting through the Shadovar's spell-guard and engulfing him in flame. The sight made Arr wince inside. The spell was one of her finest, and though she had willingly shared it for the sake of her plan, it still pained her to see another phaerimm using it.

Arr glanced up and behind her at Tuuh's bearded face and said, "I hope that's the first time you've used my spell here." Because the Chosen could unleash the real silver fire just once every hour, she had instructed her companions to use her spell only one time. "My plan won't work if they realize—"

"It is the first time these Shadovar have seen me use it," Tuuh said. "That is all that counts."

He raised a hand and uttering a single syllable, wagged his fingers. Beze rose above the heads of the Shadovar and started to float in their direction. Several warriors cocked their arms to hurl their swords. Throwing up her hands and crying out something that might have sounded vaguely spell-like, Arr brought a swarm of fiery stars crashing into existence and sent it sweeping across the shadow blanket.

It roared into the Shadovar before they could turn their heads to see what was making the sound. Those who had no spell-guards simply vanished in an eruption of smoke and flame. The others were hurled across the shadow blanket, back through the wall of fire Arr had raised earlier. Judging by the screams and the greasy smoke rising from the other side, it seemed unlikely their protection magic had withstood the trip.

"A little quick for a human, don't you think?" Tuuh brought Beze to their side. "But you saved Beze."

"Well, send her somewhere," Arr ordered, "before she dies and ruins my plan."

Behind them Ryry, speaking in Winds, said, *The fate of your plan has already been decided. The Shadovar are gone.*

Arr turned to find Ryry and Yao standing behind the rolled blanket, staring out across the empty melt basin. In the frigid cold of the High Ice, the cloud of rising steam had already turned to ice and dropped back to the ground, and the slushy water through which they had been wading just a few minutes earlier had frozen into a jagged blue plain. The only sign of the Shadovar princes who had attempted to surprise them from the rear where the soot-smeared craters where they had been hurled into the basin walls by phaerimm spells.

"I am a genius," Arr said. "When we work together, none can challenge us!"

"That will be a great comfort to Beze's ghost," Tuuh said.

Arr looked back and found Beze reverted to true form. She was sinking to the ground, her tail and four arms hanging limp, her mouth open and pouring blood.

"Tuuh, did I not tell you to send her somewhere?" Arr asked. "There still may be spies."

Tuuh touched Beze, and a small tear opened in the air and sucked the corpse out of sight. Judging by the drone of insects and the stench of offal that lingered behind, Arr guessed that he had sent the body to the second or third of the Nine Hells.

Once the portal closed, Arr dismissed the magic walls she had created and was pleased to see the shadow blanket littered with dead Shadovar. There was no sign of Escanor, or of those who had used their own bodies to put out the flames engulfing him.

"I see no wounded," Ryry sounded disappointed. "Where are the wounded?"

"In Shade, by now," Arr said. "The Shadovar took them, I'm sure."

"Truly?" Ryry looked at Arr as though she had hidden the wounded and was keeping them all for herself. "Why?"

Tuuh shrugged and said, "What does it matter? Many two-legs do it, when they can."

Ryry studied him doubtfully, then finally seemed to accept what she was seeing.

"If you say so." She turned back to Arr and asked, "What now?"

"Finish the job," Arr said as she returned to the blanket roll and clambered over it. "That is what the Chosen would do."

CHAPTER FOUR

15 Flamerule, the Year of Wild Magic

Galaeron and the others had been waiting all morning when the muted crackle of a translocational spell finally sounded out in the heart of the courtyard, and their guest appeared in swirl of silver hair, a faint stench of gore and brimstone trailing after her. She was tall even for a human—and especially for a human woman—with a slender build and striking figure. Though her face was a bit rough-featured by elven standards, she was nevertheless a stunning beauty, with twinkling eyes, high cheeks, and a full-lipped mouth.

Ruha poured a goblet of Cormyrean wine—the finest available, though that was not saying much after the ravages of the Goblin War—and went out to meet her. Unsure of the greeting he would receive, Galaeron trailed a pace behind. Aris remained hidden in his sleeping arcade, lest he startle her before she recovered from her teleport afterdaze.

Ruha stopped at the woman's side and said, "Welcome to Arabel, Storm." She pressed the goblet into the woman's hands. "Thank you for coming."

The sound of a familiar voice seemed to bring Storm out of her daze. She quaffed the wine in one long gulp, then made a sour face.

"That's the sourest swill I've had in years." She pressed the goblet back into Ruha's hands. "But I'll have another. I've been trading spells with thornbacks and eyeheads all morning, and the thirst I have could drain the Moonsea."

"Perhaps you'd care to sit?" Galaeron suggested, waving at the table they'd set in the shade of the house—a house they'd bought with the proceeds of the sale of one of Aris's statues. "We can bring out some food, if you're hungry."

Storm eyed him warily, but followed him toward the table. "Sitting is good, but I won't have any food. The battle's not done, and fighting on a full stomach doesn't agree with me."

As they took their seats, Aris emerged from beneath his arcade and came to join them. His grim face looked even more somber than usual. When he sat down beside them, he let his body drop so heavily that the mugs rattled on the table.

Storm craned her neck and looked up into the giant's plate-sized eyes.

"It's good to see you, Aris. You're looking better than the last time we met."

Aris forced a smile and said, "I've been waiting for a chance to thank you properly for saving my life, lady."

The giant reached inside his tabard and brought out a three-foot sculpture of Storm kneeling on the ground. The likeness was perfect, of course, with an expression that was at once angelic and fiercely protective. It struck Galaeron that she looked very much like a human version of Angharradh, the elf goddess of birth, protection, and wisdom.

"Please accept this as a small sign of my gratitude."

Storm took the piece with a gasp.

"It's . . . it's . . . Aris, it's beautiful!" She set it on the table, then rose and studied it from all angles. "Too beautiful to be me . . . or any mortal woman."

"Not at all. That is the face seen by those you help." Aris glanced in Ruha's direction, then added, "Ruha helped me track down some of them, so I know."

Storm tore her eyes—glistening with unshed tears—from the statue and went over to him. Even sitting on the ground, the giant towered over her, and she ended up embracing the side of his arm.

"I'll treasure it always, Aris." She tipped her head back and blew him a kiss, which floated visibly up to his face and planted itself on his cheek like a silver tattoo. "Thank you."

Galaeron was glad to see that Storm treasured Aris's gift so highly—he had expected nothing else, really, for the giant's art never failed to move those who viewed it—but her reaction also dampened his own spirits. The giant did not approve of what Galaeron was about to suggest, and—given that Storm held him responsible for much of Faerûn's trouble—his idea was going to be hard enough to sell without adding any extra weight to Aris's opposition.

Leaving Aris with a foolish smile, Storm returned to her seat and turned to Ruha.

"Suppose we come to the point." Though her manner was brisk, her mood had been much improved by Aris's gift, and the concern behind her words seemed more a matter of time than displeasure. "I doubt you summoned me from the war in the Shaeradim so Aris could present his gift."

Galaeron winced. One did not "summon" a Chosen of Mystra anywhere, and the fact that she had used that word to describe their request for an audience was not a good sign.

If Ruha noticed the word choice, her eyes did not show it.

"Galaeron has an idea. I think it could work." Ruha's gaze rose toward Aris's gray face and she added, "Aris does not."

"And you asked me here to break the tie?"

Noting the sarcasm in Storm's voice, Galaeron said, "I want to bring down Shade."

Storm cocked a brow. "Bring it down?"

"Like the old cities of Netheril," Galaeron explained. "Crash it into the desert."

"If you're asking permission, feel free."

"Actually, I can't do it alone." So far, so good—at least she liked the idea. "To tell the truth, I need you and the other Chosen to do it for me."

Storm rolled her eyes as though she had been expecting something of this sort.

"At the moment, we're rather busy trying to save the Shaeradim. I thought you might have heard."

"And I am telling you how!" Galaeron snapped.

He caught the flash of concern in Aris's eyes, then paused a moment to calm his rising ire.

Finally, he asked, "Are you winning?"

Storm's eyes slid away. "No. Lord Ramealaerub's advance has stalled at the Vyshaen Barrows."

"The Vyshaen Barrows?" Galaeron gasped. "What's he doing there?"

"It's not a good base?"

Galaeron shook his head. "It looks like it from below, but he can't reach Evereska from there," he said. "If the phaerimm come up the Copper Canyon, he'll be trapped against the High Shaeradim."

Storm raised her brow and said, "I'll pass that along. Unfortunately, he's advancing blind."

She let the statement hang, leaving it to Galaeron to ask if he wanted to hear the details. He didn't, but he had to know.

"Blind?" he echoed. "I thought Takari Moonsnow was with him."

"Lost the day the shadowshell fell." Storm's manner grew soft, and for the first time since Galaeron had known her he saw some of the softness portrayed in Aris's sculpture. "She eliminated a phaerimm that was delaying Lord Ramealaerub's advance."

Galaeron fell back in his chair, his heart aching as though someone had punched him in it. He had not seen Takari since shortly after their journey into Karse, when he had returned her, battered and bloody, to Rheitheillaethor and left her there to recover. They had never been lovers, but he had finally come to accept—too late, after leaving her behind—that they were spirit-deep mates, linked on a level more profound than love. The choice to leave with Vala—another woman whom circumstances had forced him to abandon to a cruel fate—had been his own, but one made infinitely less complicated by Takari's harshness as she told him she hoped never to see him again. The thought that those words should be the last he ever heard from her filled him with a raw anguish—and with a bitter fury he knew to be not entirely his own that whispered to him that Storm was lying and demanded that he strike out at her.

Instead, Galaeron lowered his chin and whispered a prayer, asking Takari to forgive his folly and begging the Leaflord to watch over her spirit.

Storm laid a hand on Galaeron's arm—then took it away when his shadow recoiled from her touch and made him flinch.

"You know, Galaeron, you could be very useful to Lord Ramealaerub," she said. "I doubt anyone in the elven army would be foolish enough to turn away your help."

But there was always the question, Galaeron—or perhaps it was his shadow—thought. He was the one who had breached the Sharn Wall in the first place, then invited the Shadovar into the world to undo the damage. He was the cause of all this trouble, and even if they were wise enough not to say it to his face, he knew what his fellow elves would be whispering every time he turned his back.

"Now *that* is a plan that makes sense," Aris said. "Why not return to the Shaeradim, where we can do some good fighting phaerimm?"

Galaeron raised his chin and said, "Because we can't win the war by fighting phaerimm. Nor can we save Evereska that way."

"This is the part that makes no sense," Aris said. "The phaerimm *want* the Shadovar killed, and the Shadovar want the phaerimm killed. Destroying Shade—even if you could— does not help Evereska."

"But it *does*, Aris," Storm said. "The elves have little hope—I would say none—of defeating the phaerimm alone. The rest of Faerûn has been too weakened by the Melting to send help, and the few troops they do have must stay home to defend against the Shadovar. The Shadovar are in the same situation—they dare not engage the phaerimm for fear that the rest of the world will attack them and stop the Melting."

It was a great relief to Galaeron that Storm was the one explaining this. Perhaps one of the Chosen could change the stubborn giant's mind.

Aris burst that dream with a firm shake of his head.

"It won't work."

"Perhaps not at once," Ruha said, "but as the realms recover, they will be able to send troops to join the elves. Not even the phaerimm can stand against the combined might of all Faerûn."

Aris crossed his arms in front of his chest.

To Galaeron's surprise, Storm ignored the giant and turned to face him and Ruha.

"Your plan works only if Shade's destruction is a swift one," she said.

"Without its mythallar, the city will fall," Galaeron said. "The destruction will be instantaneous."

Storm nodded.

"That's what I thought you had planned for us. But how are we to enter the city? Shade's magic is proof against even us."

Galaeron smiled and told her his plan.

When he finished, Storm poured herself more wine, sat back, and thought it over. It took only a few moments before she drank the contents of the goblet and nodded.

"It could work."

"Wonderful!" Galaeron filled goblets for himself and Ruha. "We can be ready—"

"I said *could*." Storm raised her hand to stop him, then looked to Aris and said, "Before deciding, I want to hear Aris's argument."

The giant cast a guilty look in Galaeron's direction, then said, "Because Galaeron can't do it."

Storm furrowed her brow.

"What is there to do? All he need do is appear headstrong and careless." She glanced over at him, then added, "That is not out of character for him."

"Afterward," the giant clarified. "Once he's in the city, his shadow will grow too strong. We'll lose him . . . and this time, I fear it will be for good."

"That is a risk," Ruha agreed. "He's not strong enough to fight Telamont."

Galaeron shrugged and said, "There is cost to every plan. I can resist long enough to make this one work. After that . . . well, I doubt the Chosen will find it difficult to eliminate the problem before it can grow out of hand."

Storm studied him for a long time then said, "You would make that sacrifice?"

Galaeron answered without hesitation, "I have lost more already."

"And that is another wrong thing." Aris planted a big finger in the center of the table and nearly collapsed it. "When he is not talking of Evereska and what it is suffering, he is talking of Vala and what she is enduring. I say he is doing this to save her."

Storm raised a cool gaze to the giant's face and asked, "Why would that be wrong?"

Aris scowled and spent a moment trying to think of an

argument, then gave up and looked away without answering.

Storm looked back to Galaeron and remained just as silent.

Finally, he could bear her scrutiny no longer.

"So you'll do it?" he asked.

Instead of answering his question, Storm asked one of her own, "I want to be clear on this. If your shadow takes you, you're asking me to kill you?"

Galaeron nodded.

Storm shook her head. "No, Galaeron. If you want this, you must say it."

"When . . ." Galaeron's throat went dry, and he had to stop and start again. "When, not if—because I am losing the battle even here—but *when* my shadow takes me, I want you to kill me. More than that, I want you to promise me now that you will. I've brought enough evil into this world through folly and accident. I have no wish to cause it directly."

"If that is what you want, I promise," Storm replied. She stood and turned to Aris. "What about you, my large friend? Will you go with Galaeron?"

"Him?" Galaeron asked, also standing. "This doesn't involve Aris. There's no need for him to return to Shade."

Storm did not look away from the giant.

"Aris goes everywhere with you, Galaeron," she said, "and he has vowed to avenge Thousand Faces. If he suddenly remains behind when you set off to fight the phaerimm, what will the Shadovar think?"

"She's right," Ruha said. "They would grow suspicious, and that suspicion would spoil your plan. This must be done right . . . or not at all."

Galaeron dropped his head. He had nearly killed Aris once already, during their escape from Shade when he had succumbed to his shadow self and used the giant to lure a blue dragon into an ambush. Had Storm not answered Ruha's call for help, Aris would have died, and this time there would be no one to call for help. If matters went wrong—

even if they went right—it might well be the death of them both.

Galaeron shook his head.

"Then we won't do it." He raised his gaze, met Aris's eyes, and said, "This is not something I would ask of you. You have already done more than I could expect even of an elf friend, and I will not see you killed."

"You think that is why I don't like your plan? Because I fear for my life? That is an insult worse than any your shadow has ever spit out."

Aris's big fist crashed down on the table, smashing it to pieces and sending splinters and shards of goblet flying in every direction.

"You saved my life at Thousand Faces," the giant continued. "It is yours to spend."

A tense silence settled over the courtyard. Galaeron was so shocked by the giant's uncharacteristic show of anger that he did not dare look up to apologize.

Finally, Storm rose.

"I guess that settles it, then," she said. She used her hands to brush the wine off her leather armor. "We'll look for you tomorrow, after dawn."

CHAPTER FIVE

15 Flamerule, the Year of Wild Magic

To Malik's astonishment, Escanor was still glowing when he dared enter the presence of the Most High. The prince could be seen from fifty paces away, first as a dim, pearly ball floating beneath the copper flicker of his distinctive eyes, then as a luminous cage of ribs encasing a kernel of pulsing light. A wave of stunned whispers followed him across the throne room, and as he drew closer Malik could see that Escanor was actually staggering. The mantle of shadow that usually served him as a body was bleeding away in wisps, bestowing on him a rather gauzy and serpentine appearance.

Escanor stopped at the foot of the dais, his glow illuminating half a dozen younger princes who were coming up behind him. Though none were in as sorry a condition as Escanor, they had gone with him to attack the Chosen on the High Ice, and three were bleeding shadow from lesser wounds.

Escanor bowed and would have fallen over, had one of his brothers not braved the ghostly light to lend him a hand.

"I apologize for appearing before the Most High in this condition," he said.

"As well you should," Hadrhune said. "It is an insult."

"Indeed," Malik agreed, standing in his customary place just above Hadrhune. Having grown tired of the seneschal's jealousy over his position as Telamont's most trusted advisor—and weary of the constant assassination attempts—Malik had decided to try a strategy of alliance to placate the man. "If the Most High wanted us to see his face, he would show it to us himself . . . though I must admit I am curious to see it myself."

He did not even cringe at this last part of his statement. Much of the reason the Most High valued Malik's advice so highly was the curse placed on him by the harlot Mystra, which always compelled him to tell the truth when he spoke. Telamont Tanthul rarely chastised him for the embarrassing slips that this caused him—and sometimes even seemed to find them amusing.

But not today. A set of icy talons sank into his shoulder, and a cold voice whispered into his ear.

"Your curiosity on that count would kill you, my behorned friend, and slight a prince of mine again and you shall have it satisfied."

Malik's mouth grew as dry as dust. "I meant no offense, Most High . . ." He struggled to end there, but the truth welled up inside him and spilled from his mouth of its own accord. "At least to you, for I have always felt secure in your protection and completely free to insult whomever else I desired."

The Most High removed his icy talons, patted Malik's shoulder, and said, "And now you don't."

Telamont slipped past and descended the stairs toward his

son. Knowing it would be suicide to stand higher than the Most High, Malik followed him down the stairs. The Most High stopped on the bottom step, leaving Malik, Hadrhune, and the rest of the throne room attendants to scramble for places on the floor. In the glow of Escanor's wounds, the sycophants looked ghoulish and wrinkled, with hollow cheeks and sunken red eyes. Only Telamont himself seemed immune to the light and remained hidden in the shadows beneath his cowl.

Taking advantage of the light—he always tried to make the best of every situation—Malik risked a surreptitious glance at his wounds. Though cold spears of anguish still pierced his shoulder where the Most High had grasped him, there were no holes in his flesh, nor any blood on his robe.

Telamont asked, "You engaged the Chosen, my son? They did this to you?"

Keeping his head bowed, Escanor nodded and said, "That is so, Most High."

Telamont's platinum eyes shone brighter in the darkness that was his face.

"Good." He lifted a murky sleeve, motioning Escanor to his feet, and continued, "Rise and tell me how many you killed."

Escanor's shadows seemed to grow even thinner as he stood.

"I fear the answer is none, Most High," he said, his coppery gaze remaining fixed on the floor. "We were defeated."

"Defeated?" It was Hadrhune who asked this. "*Seven* princes of Shade?"

Escanor's eyes swung toward the seneschal. "The Chosen are formidable enemies."

"Which is why I advised the Most High to send seven of you," Hadrhune countered, "and an entire company of the Gate Guard."

Though the effort of defending himself drained Escanor, none of his brothers seemed eager to leap to his defense.

"Your plan did not take into account . . . the quickness of the Chosen. They fling magic as easily as you do aspersions."

Hadrhune responded with a smile—the predatory smile of a hunter in pursuit of crippled prey.

"They are only human," he said. "How could their spell-craft be quicker than that of a shadow lord?"

"That is a mystery to me," Escanor replied, sounding more sincere than sarcastic. "Next time, perhaps you should lead the assault and tell us."

"There will not be a next time," Telamont said in that low even tone that Malik had learned to associate with cold rage. "We cannot afford one."

"Unfortunately, I doubt the choice is yours," Malik said. He had long ago discovered that times like these were when he stood to gain the most with the Most High, since everyone else was too busy cowering in fear to curry favor. "Now that the Chosen have seen how powerless you are to stop them, they will certainly return to roll up the shadow blankets faster than you can lay them."

Telamont whirled on Malik, his platinum eyes shining brightly enough to see by.

"We are not powerless!"

"N-n-no, of course n-not," Malik stammered. "Only, after the losses Shade suffered in Tilverton, you will be if you lose a company of warriors each time you try to stop the Chosen from stealing one of your shadow blankets."

One of Telamont's murk-filled sleeves reached out, and a tendril of shadow knotted itself into Malik's robe and picked him up by the lapels.

"Why must you always be right, little man?"

Malik shrugged and thought it might be wiser to say nothing, but that was never an option when Telamont Tanthul wished an answer. He lasted only a breath before the Most High's will forced him to speak.

"It is my curse, Most High," he said—but of course there was no stopping there. "It is my design always to tell you what you wish to hear—but since that is rarely what is true, before I know it I am foolishly blurting out the things your other advisors are too wise to say."

"Too wise," Escanor asked, glaring pointedly at Hadrhune, "or too cowardly?"

Telamont's glance darted in the prince's direction.

"Careful, my son. You are one of those Malik is talking about."

He lowered Malik back to the floor, then slipped a murky hand through Escanor's ribs and grabbed the prince's still glowing heart.

"Interesting. Tell me about the spell that did this."

Escanor's gaze shifted to the hand in his chest.

"It was the silver fire." His voice was shaky. "It burned through my spell-guard—"

"No." Telamont pulled his arm away, and a glowing palm appeared at the end of his sleeve. "Silver fire is raw Weave magic. If that's what this was, we would be spinning into a dimensional vortex right now."

"Really?" Malik gasped.

He had witnessed enough combat to know that when raw Weave magic contacted raw Shadow Weave magic, the result was a rip in the fabric of reality. It was just such an accident—when the magic bolts of Galaeron Nihmedu's Tomb Guard patrol met one of Melegaunt Tanthul's shadow bolts—that had ripped the Sharn Wall and released the phaerimm in the first place.

"Then you must be . . ." Too late, Malik realized the risk he was taking by revealing that he realized Telamont's true nature. He tried to hold his tongue, but the curse compelled him to finish what he had started. ". . . living shadow magic!"

The Most High's murk-filled cowl turned in Malik's direction.

"Not living, exactly." A faint crescent of purple appeared where a human's smile would have been, and Telamont finished, "No need to feel bad about blurting it out. You were never going to leave here anyway."

"Most High?" Malik looked around as though searching for a door, but of course there was no escape into anything but the shadows. "That is hardly needed! I can keep a secret as—"

"The *enclave*, worm," Hadrhune said. "He means you will never leave Shade Enclave."

"Just so," Telamont said. "I find your advice too . . . *necessary* . . . to let you go."

"Is that all?" Malik sighed in relief. "Then we are in agreement. Why would I wish to leave Shade? I have everything I desire here—Villa Dusari, the ear of the Most High, a stable for my beloved horse and plenty to feed her. I would be a fool to leave all this!"

For once, there was nothing more for his curse to compel him to say.

"How very pleased we are," Hadrhune said, running his thumbnail across his palm. "I am sure the princes are as delighted as I am."

"The only delight that matters is mine," Telamont said. "I will be delighted when someone tells me what to make of this."

He held up his glowing hand.

"Obviously a form of false magic aura," Hadrhune said. "Commonly used in bazaars and such places to make plain weapons appear enchanted."

Telamont remained silent, and when Hadrhune did not add anything more, he turned to Malik. Resolved to jeopardize his position no further that day by being the bearer of bad news, Malik tried to remain silent as well.

Then he found himself saying, "We have a saying in Narjon, where I was once an esteemed merchant: if someone fills your oil jar with sand, it is not because he wishes to give you sand."

Telamont and the princes remained silent and continued to look at him.

"Have you no scale cheats in Shade?" Malik asked, exasperated. "It means someone is trying to deceive you. Whoever created this false aura wishes you to believe his spell is silver fire—"

"Phaerimm!" Telamont and Escanor growled the word together.

"That would explain the swiftness of their spellcasting," Hadrhune said, turning to Escanor. "It surprises me that you failed to see it in the field."

"Had you ever *been* in the field, perhaps you would—"

"Enough," Telamont said in that cold, dangerous tone again. "You are both to blame."

He raised an arm, and with a flick of his sleeve sent Hadrhune crashing into Escanor. They went tumbling across the throne room floor locked in an embrace of pain. Telamont waited until they had vanished into the shadows before turning to the rest of his princes.

"Let that be a lesson to you," he said. "In all things, you succeed or fail together. If one fails me, all fail me."

The princes' eyes dimmed with fear, then somehow speaking in flawless unison they said, "We understand, Most High."

Telamont glared at them for a moment, then finally waved a sleeve in the direction Escanor and Hadrhune had tumbled.

"See to your brother's wounds and your own. This war is too close to lose another prince."

The princes bowed and retreated into the shadows, leaving Malik and the other attendants alone with Telamont. The Most High placed a sleeve around Malik's shoulders, turned him toward the dais, and started to ascend back to his throne.

"It pleases me that you are happy here, Malik."

"Very happy," Malik said. "Except for the frequent attempts on my life, perhaps."

"Ah, yes," Telamont sighed. "Hadrhune."

Malik waited for the Most High to say he would no longer have need to worry or that something would be done about that, but they continued to climb in silence until they came to the step where Malik normally stopped.

Telamont kept his arm around Malik's shoulders, guiding him onto the throne platform itself. This drew an astonished murmur from the attendants below, but the sound faded to silence as the Most High took his seat and stared into Malik's eyes.

"Hadrhune was not so different from you once—if you will forgive being compared to an elf."

Malik's jaw fell at this revelation, for he had never seen enough of Hadrhune's shadow-swathed face to note either arched eyebrows or pointed ears.

"There was a time when he served me as well as your counsel does now," Telamont continued. "I tell you this so you will know that I reward those who aid me with eternal loyalty, even after they have lost their usefulness and become a burden."

Malik inclined his head. "I am honored that you would treat me so."

"I *could*," Telamont said, his voice again assuming that dangerous coldness, "were this debacle not your fault."

"*My* fault?" Malik broke into a cold sweat. "How have I caused this, Most High?"

"This happened because we did not anticipate the phaerimm's plan. We did not anticipate their plan because we do not have the knowledge my son Melegaunt passed on to Galaeron. We do not have Galaeron because he is still in Arabel."

Telamont sank back into his throne and continued, "Did you not tell me that if we sent Vala to be Escanor's bed slave, Galaeron would return to Shade and try to rescue her?"

"I may have said, er, uh—" Compelled by Mystra's curse to tell the exact truth, Malik stammered to a stop then was forced to continue, "I *did* say that was the surest way to draw him back in a rush. I have no dou—er, a reasonable belief—that my plan will still work . . . eventually."

Telamont's eyes grew white and icy. "*Eventually*, my patience will come to an end. One might even say that it is waning now."

A lump the size of a fist appeared in Malik's throat, but he still managed to say, "Indeed?"

Telamont remained silent.

Malik found that he had another question, a question he desperately did not want answered but which was rising up inside him like his stomach after a meal of bad fish. He clamped his mouth shut and swore he would not open it, that he would choke on the words before he allowed them to spill forth.

But his will was no match for that of the Most High, and he soon heard himself asking, "What happens when your patience has gone?"

"Then Vala will pay for her treachery in helping Galaeron escape," Telamont pronounced.

"That would certainly be a great waste of womanly flesh." As fond as Malik was of Vala, he was less worried for her than he was relieved at not hearing his own name. "But a waste that matters little to me, as I am quite sure the only thing I would ever find in her bed is a quick death."

"That might be preferable."

Again, Malik found himself asking a question he did not really want answered.

"Preferable, Most High? To what?"

"To taking her place," Telamont answered.

"Take her place?" Malik exclaimed. "But I am a man!"

"And if you want to stay that way, I suggest you make good on your plan."

Malik felt the blood leaving his head and knew he was close to fainting, which was hardly something that would inspire the Most High's confidence. Knowing from his long experience as a merchant and a spy that the best way to cover a weakness was to bluff, he forced himself to meet Telamont's gaze.

"You must know that in my service to Cyric, I have suffered a hundred injuries worse than that." It was as true a statement as any he had ever made. "If you wish to inspire me, you must do better than that."

The murkiness beneath Telamont's cowl stilled with shock.

"You dare demand a boon?"

"When the risks are great, the reward must be even greater," Malik said. "That is the first rule of business taught to me by my wise father."

Telamont remained motionless for several moments, staring at Malik in disbelief. Finally, the purple crescent of a smile appeared beneath his eyes.

"As you will, then," he said. "Bring me Galaeron Nihmedu, and you shall name your price. Fail . . . and I shall name mine."

CHAPTER SIX

16 Flamerule, the Year of Wild Magic

Even had there not been a giant-sized gap in the caravan between Galaeron and Ruha, the group of wealthy citizens holding a farewell party at the city gate practically announced that Aris of Thousand Faces was leaving town. The Arabellans had turned out in their finest splendor, many standing in silk-draped wagons beside their latest acquisitions—masterpieces in granite and marble, bought the day before at give-away prices. All eyes were fixed on the long line of riders and draft animals coming down the street, and as soon as the onlookers saw the unexplained space where the invisible giant was walking, they raised sparkling flutes of champagne in silent tribute.

"I'd say your idea worked, Ruha," Galaeron said quietly. "Had we hired a crier to stroll the streets all night, we couldn't have spread our 'secret' any faster."

"Yes, I have always found that the surest way to proclaim a thing is to say it should not be repeated," Ruha said. "I only hope it did not pain Aris to part with so many works so cheaply."

"Why should that pain me?" Aris whispered. "Their owners will enjoy the pieces all the more, and I don't have to carry so much gold."

"There are plenty of Arabellans who would've been happy to shoulder the burden for you," Galaeron said. "The way they hoard the stuff, one would think they eat it."

As the front of the caravan reached the gatehouse, the caravan master slipped out of line to pay the gate tax. The bursar held himself primly upright and made a show of tallying each draft animal as it passed through the gate. His guards stood at strict attention, their gazes fixed on the opposite side of the archway and their halberds posted at full-arm. Though Cormyrean officials were reputed to be generally honest—at least by human standards—they were no more prone to perpetual diligence than other men, and Galaeron realized that Aris's well-wishers were not the only ones who had come down to see them off.

When their turn came to pass under the archway and be counted, Galaeron glanced into the arrow loop behind the guards and found a familiar cascade of golden hair shining in the depths of the gatehouse. He dipped his head in acknowledgment. The hair moved closer, and Princess Alusair's familiar face appeared on the other side of the loop. Her eyes were red and glassy, though it was impossible to say whether from weeping or exhaustion.

"Thank you." Galaeron mouthed the words without speaking them aloud. "Your kindness has lit my heart."

Alusair smiled. "And your courage mine." She also spoke the words silently. "Sweet water and light laughter, my friend."

"Fare you well." Galaeron did not give the traditional

"Back soon" reply, for they both knew he would not be returning to Cormyr. "May your realm prevail and your people know peace."

Galaeron could not be certain Alusair saw enough of this last wish to understand, for she vanished behind the edge of the arrow loop as the caravan continued forward. They passed beneath the spikes of the iron portcullis and clomped across the drawbridge onto the beginning of the High Road.

Once they were outside the city walls, a small army of beggars—farmers and craftsmen rendered destitute by the ravages of the Goblin War—emerged from the tents and ramshackle huts of Pauper's Town to beg alms. Aris slipped sacks of gold to Galaeron and Ruha, who tried to avoid calling attention to their friend's generosity by proclaiming, "Here's a copper for you," and pressing the gift firmly into the supplicant's hand each time they passed out one of the gold coins.

The strategy proved even less effective than their "effort" to sneak out of town undetected. Whenever the astonished beggars—especially the children—opened their hands and saw what they had been given, they could not help crying out in delight. Soon, Galaeron and Ruha were surrounded by a moving throng, many of whom noticed the giant-sized gap between them and guessed the true identity of their benefactor.

They reached the small bridge that separated the marshaling fields from Pauper's Town, and the press of beggars brought the caravan's progress to a near standstill. The curses of drivers behind Galaeron and Ruha began to grow both in volume and vehemence but were drowned out by a steady chorus of, "Ilmater's blessing on the Generous Giant," or, "Thanks to the Tall One!"

It was in the middle of this madness that a slender hand wearing two silver rings reached up for a coin. Clasped around the wrist above the hand, hidden almost out of sight inside the cuff of a purple sleeve, was a silver bracelet bearing the skull-and-starburst symbol of Cyric, Prince of Lies. Galaeron ran his gaze up the sleeve to a silver-trimmed collar, where he found himself looking into the sunken eyes of a hollow-cheeked woman with ropy blond hair.

"I have had a vision," she hissed. "One you love—"

Galaeron pressed a coin into her hand and said, "Here's your copper. Take it and go."

She let the coin drop in the dust, nearly felling Galaeron's horse as a knot of beggars dived beneath its hooves to retrieve the offering.

"Listen to me, elf!" Her hand grabbed his reins and brought his progress to a stop. "You must return to Shade. I saw the Seraph in a dream—"

"I don't know what you're talking about," Galaeron said. He pulled his boot free of the stirrup and planted his foot in the center of her chest. "This caravan is bound for Iriaebor."

He started to push her off—and found the tip of a stiletto sliding up under the armor on his calf. The sensation of cold steel pricking his leg caused a dark fury to rise inside Galaeron. Leaving the half empty sack of gold to slide off his saddle and spill on the ground, he reached across his body and grabbed the hilt of his sword.

"Shade," the woman hissed. "Go, or she will die."

Galaeron's heart began to pound like a Vyshaan war drum. Though he desperately wanted to ask the woman about her vision, he held his tongue and drew his sword half out of its scabbard. Even had he thought he could trust a Cyricist, he would never have risked his plan by telling her that Shade was exactly where he intended to go.

"You have mistaken me for someone else, Madam," Galaeron said. "Now, step back or lose your head."

The woman's eyes turned black and sun-shaped, with long tongues of darkness wagging around the edges.

"Believe."

She sank her stiletto a quarter of an inch into his calf, and Galaeron's blade rasped free of its scabbard almost of its own will. The woman raised her chin and waited with eerie calmness as it arced toward her collarbone.

"Believe!"

Galaeron's attack came to a sudden end as his forearm struck a huge, invisible hand.

"No," Aris's voice rumbled down from above.

"Leave her be, friend," Ruha called from the other side of Aris. "The mad cannot be blamed for their madness."

"Nor the messenger for the message," the woman added. Her voice was gravelly and multifold, as though there were a hundred people speaking at once. "Go."

The black suns faded from her eyes. Leaving her stiletto hanging from Galaeron's calf, she stumbled back and fell into the throng of beggars fighting over the coins he had let fall. Aris's grasp slackened, and Galaeron lowered his blade, his hand trembling so badly he could barely slip the tip into its scabbard.

"My friend, what is it?" Ruha asked. "Why are you so frightened?"

"More startled than frightened," Galaeron said. He reached down and plucked the woman's dagger from his calf, then displayed the bloody tip. "A message from our friend the cuckold. He wants to see us."

Ruha's dark brow rose, and Galaeron tossed the dagger over the beggars into an empty place in the field. When he turned to urge his horse forward he saw that it was hopeless. The road ahead was blocked by at least a hundred paupers—all with their hands out, praising Aris's generosity—and the little bridge was occupied by two dozen caravan guards on their way back from the marshaling fields.

Once they were clear of the bridge, the guards began shouting at the paupers to clear the road, using their shields and the shoulders of their big war-horses to enforce their demands. Galaeron did his best to remain patient. Whether or not the message had truly come from Malik, it only served to heighten his concern for Vala. His feelings for her were not as spiritual as the love for Takari that he had denied all those years on the Desert Border South, but only because a human and an elf could never come together like two elves could.

Nevertheless, Galaeron did love Vala—if not as deeply as Takari, then at least as strongly—and it had tormented him to remain comfortable in Arabel while she served Escanor as a bed-slave. Not a day had passed that he did not dream of returning to free her. If only she could hold on until he got himself captured.

When the guards began to grow impatient with the paupers and slap at them with the flats of their blades, Aris hit upon a helpful solution and began to fling handfuls of gold away from the road. It took two throws before the beggars realized what was happening and fled, all yelling Aris's praises and pleading for him to throw a handful their way.

Once the road was clear, the guards moved quickly to secure the caravan, thundering past on both sides and barking orders to get moving. Five of their number peeled off and came up beside Galaeron and Ruha, placing themselves so that any beggars returning for more handouts would have to go through them first.

The largest, a hatchet-faced woman in a helmet and dusty fighting leathers, came alongside Galaeron and waved them across the bridge. The guard's voice was as familiar as it was biting.

"Well done, elf. I doubt there's a deaf man or blind woman within a league of here who doesn't know you're sneaking out of Arabel."

Galaeron took a closer look. The speaker's gaunt features softened into those of Storm Silverhand, the hair that looped out from beneath her helmet turning silver and silky, the thin-lipped mouth growing full and shapely.

"This wasn't part of the plan." Fearful of betraying the identity of his guards, Galaeron was careful to avoid the honorific one usually showed the Chosen. "The gratitude of the paupers took us by surprise."

"Oh, well that's fine then," growled the rider behind her. "How comforting to know things just *slipped* out of control."

They started across the bridge. Galaeron glanced over his shoulder to find the visage of an old horse-faced guard yielding to the black beard and frowning features of a man who could only be the renowned elf-friend, Khelben Arunsun.

Galaeron decided not to mention the message from Malik. The Chosen appeared less than enthusiastic as it was, and the last thing he wanted was to give them an excuse to change their minds.

"I apologize for the mistake," he said. "I should have realized how gold would affect—"

"Galaeron is not to blame," Aris said, his voice booming down out of the empty sky. "I am the one who wanted to give them the gold."

"Will you be quiet up there?" Khelben demanded. "At least *pretend* you're trying to sneak out of here unnoticed."

"I apologize," Aris said, his voice a low rumble that made the bridge planks quiver beneath the horses' hooves, "but you mustn't blame Galaeron—"

"There's no need to blame anyone," said a third guard. Riding opposite Galaeron on Ruha's far side, she had only one arm and a voice similar to Storm's. "No one should be condemned for sharing with the hungry."

As she spoke, Galaeron began to see through the illusion guarding her identity and realized that this had to be Khelben's consort, Laeral Silverhand. There was a tiny arm growing from the stump of the one she had lost in the Shaeradim, but even this did not detract from her beauty. She was, if anything, even more lovely than her sister, with a warmth and charm alien to Storm's brusque manner—or perhaps it merely seemed so to Galaeron because Storm never bothered to hide the dislike she bore him.

Khelben was silent a moment, then said, "You're right, of course." He sighed heavily. "Again."

This drew a laugh from the last two guards, and Galaeron recognize the same silver in their voices as in Laeral and Storm's. He hazarded a glance in their direction, and as he began to see through the illusions, he recognized in their sparkling eyes and silver hair two more of Storm's sisters. The slimmest of the two, and the most feminine in her carriage and manner, could only be the celebrated Lady of Silverymoon, Alustriel Silverhand. The other, a more imposing figure as powerfully built as a man, had to be the mighty Dove Falconhand—Harper, Knight of Myth Drannor, and friend to the elves.

The Chosen had not only answered Galaeron's call for help, they had answered it in strength. If Khelben seemed tense, it only made sense. With Elminster still missing with the Simbul, and ghostly Syluné more or less confined to her farm in Shadowdale, the only available Chosen they had not brought was the Dark Sister, Qilué. Given his limited experience with drow during his days in the Tomb Guard, Galaeron was just as glad.

They left the bridge and rushed to catch the head of the caravan, which was stopped in the marshaling field while the captain of the guards grouped the draft animals by swiftness and burden and assigned personnel to watch over them. He placed Galaeron and Ruha with a group of lightly burdened riders, and at Storm's magically enhanced suggestion, assigned the five Chosen to watch over them.

Once the captain had moved on, the Chosen gathered their horses in a tight circle around Galaeron, Ruha, and the still invisible Aris.

"Here's my plan, Galaeron," Khelben said. "We're going to make a few—"

"Darling?" Laeral interrupted. "Aren't you forgetting who thought of this in the first place?"

Khelben scowled but said, "All right." He turned back to Galaeron. "Your plan's a sound one, but we're going to—"

"Pardon me," Alustriel said. "But I'd prefer that someone

who's actually been inside the city does the planning."

Khelben rolled his eyes. "Very well." He turned back to Galaeron and said, "We all like your ideas."

"Very impressive," Dove said.

Khelben nodded almost reluctantly then continued, "But there are some things we should bring to your attention."

He stopped to check for the others' approval.

Storm whirled her hand to urge him on. She glanced back toward the rear of the caravan, which was already coming across the little bridge.

Khelben looked irritated but he said, "First, you won't be able to eat until we're inside the city."

Galaeron raised his brow and said, "I hadn't thought of that."

"We didn't think you had," Alustriel said, "but I'm sure you understand. The journey will be unpleasant enough as it is."

"I don't think I could ride for more than a few days without eating anyway," Galaeron agreed. "We'll put that part off as long as we can."

"My thoughts exactly," Khelben agreed. "Second, you may have noticed there are five of us."

"I can do it instead," Aris said. "I'm larger."

"Actually, we were thinking of splitting the group into two teams," Laeral said. "As insurance."

Though Galaeron was reluctant to ask Aris to assume any more risk than he already was, he knew better than to argue. The giant had made his feelings on the subject clear when he smashed the table in their courtyard.

"Splitting is a good idea, if Aris is willing," Galaeron said.

Khelben smiled. "Good," he said, "then we're all agreed."

"Not quite." Galaeron raised his hand, and avoiding Ruha's gaze, said, "Ruha can't come with us."

"That is not your decision," Ruha replied. Her tone was angry, though not surprised. They had spent most of the night arguing the point, finally letting the matter drop only because the time had come to join the caravan. "This has nothing to do with Evereska."

Galaeron ignored her and fixed his gaze on Storm.

"The Shadovar need me," he said, "and they value Aris, but Ruha is nothing to them but a problem. If she comes with us, there's every chance the Shadovar will put her to death."

"That is my risk, not yours," the witch said, running her gaze from one Chosen to the next. "He is trying to protect Malik. Malik saved his life, and now the foolish elf believes they are friends."

"That is true," Aris said, "but it is also true that Hadrhune believes you broke his command and tried to kill Malik. If you return, it will be just as Galaeron says."

The five Chosen gazed at Ruha expectantly.

When the witch merely looked away, Dove Falconhand said, "I think you should stay behind, Ruha. Your presence might endanger the mission."

"Or save it," Ruha argued. "You cannot know that yet—and what will become of Malik? I have hunted the dog too long to let him live like a Sheikh in their palaces."

"If we are successful, there may no longer be a Malik to concern yourself with," Storm said. "If we fail, he will come out sooner or later. Cyric is too cruel to leave him there in comfort for long."

Ruha said nothing more, but the angry look she flashed Galaeron left little doubt about whose life she thought he had just saved. A dark voice inside whispered that she was an ungrateful hag who deserved the death she would find in Shade, but Galaeron closed his mind to those shadowy thoughts and reminded himself that she had good reason to hate the little man. He was a remorseless killer who had single-handedly saved the Church of Cyric and restored the mad god to power, and he was undoubtedly working to spread his god's influence throughout the city of Shade. That he had saved the lives of both Galaeron and Aris many times while they traveled together mattered not at all. That had been an alliance of convenience, and Galaeron knew as surely as Ruha did that Malik would not hesitate to betray them in the name of his god.

Galaeron considered again whether to tell the Chosen about the message he had received from Malik but was deterred by the fury in Ruha's eyes. Given the number of Chosen who had come and the courtesy they had shown him in the strategy session, he felt sure that they intended to follow through on the plan no matter what. But Ruha would seize on any suggestion of betrayal by Malik as an excuse to accompany them into the city. Galaeron had no doubt at all about what would become of her if she fell into Hadrhune's hands. For the witch's own good, it would be better for him to keep the secret.

Or so Galaeron told himself.

CHAPTER SEVEN

16 Flamerule, the Year of Wild Magic

Once the captain had the caravan arranged to his liking, he gave the order to depart. Like some thousand-legged millipede, the line came alive and began to snake its way westward along the High Road. Galaeron and Ruha rode in silence on opposite sides of their invisible friend, Galaeron struggling to ignore the dark thoughts continually welling up in his mind, the witch glaring at him over her veil.

Aris, suffering from the fatal honesty that was the curse of his race, tried several times to reason with her, to make her see they were trying to protect her as much as they were Malik. Ruha heard only the part about protecting Malik and chastised the giant for serving an evil god. That was the end of any conversation for the rest of the day. They ate their lunch in cold silence, Khelben urging Galaeron and Aris to gorge themselves and build up what stores of fat they could. They did as the archmage suggested, and though the giant's presence was a very open secret in the caravan, Storm renewed the invisibility spell on him. They spent the rest of the day feeling lethargic and uncomfortable, until the caravan master finally called a halt. It was already late in the afternoon, with the sun sinking low over the Storm Horns and the road ahead vanishing into its golden glow.

No wonder, then, that no one sounded the alarm before the dragons were on them. The creatures came straight out of the sun, the big one in the center sweeping low over the center of the caravan, its mere presence panicking mounts and men alike, sending guards diving for roadsides and horses crashing headlong into the woods south of the road. The great beast did not breathe fire, gas, or anything else, nor did it devour any horses or snatch screaming men in its claws. It did little more than swing its long neck from one side of the road to the other, its great head passing slowly over each knot of cowering riders.

Blinded as he was by the brilliant ball of the setting sun, Galaeron did not realize for a moment that the dragon had no flesh or hide. It was all bone, with an empty cage of ribs large enough to hold Aris, and blue stars burning in the depths of its hollow eyes.

"Malygris!" Galaeron gasped. "They're coming for us *now*!"

"Into the woods!" Khelben shouted as he reined his horse into Galaeron's and forced him to turn toward the forest. "Aris, duck and run!"

The invisible giant went thumping toward the woods, his big feet flattening the brown grass as he ran. Ruha and the others led the way after him, and soon they were galloping away from the road in a loose circle.

They had traveled no more than thirty paces before the low *whumpf* of pulsing wings sounded over their heads, then a wall of blue scales dropped out of the sky to block their way. The dragon was an old one, close to two hundred feet from nose to tail, with fangs as long as swords and claws that could grasp a war-horse around the withers. It swung its head in their direction and opened its jaws to display the ball of lightning crackling in its gullet, then did nothing at all.

That was the frightening part, at least to Galaeron. The thing knew who they were or they would have already been dead.

"Back!" Khelben ordered.

As one they wheeled their mounts around and started back toward the road—only to stop an instant later when the third dragon crashed down in front of them. As long as the one behind them, it was perhaps a ton or two lighter, with a long, sinuous body and a bristly fence of spines down its back.

Like the other one, it opened its mouth to reveal the ball of lightning crackling in its gullet.

Surrounded as they were by Mystra's Chosen, some part of Galaeron realized they were in no trouble. Any single one of his companions could have slain both dragons with little more than a word and a flick of the wrist, but that was a hard thing to remember while staring into a mouthful of fangs as tall as an elf. Knowing there was a second dragon coming up from behind made it all but impossible to remain calm.

Drawing his sword, Galaeron turned to the closest Chosen—it happened to be Storm—and yelled, "Do something, you useless scold!"

"What would that be, milord?" asked Storm, who had already drawn her own sword. She pushed the weapon uselessly into the air. "I'm not here to fight dragons."

She set her heels to her horse and raced off. No sooner had she gone than the rest of the Chosen scattered, behaving more or less like typical caravan guards. Galaeron started after Khelben, and the dragon bounded in front of him. He wheeled around, his mount stumbling as it bounced off Aris's invisible leg, and started after Alustriel.

The other dragon landed on its haunches a hundred feet ahead, one claw stretching in Galaeron's direction. Black fear welled up inside Galaeron. He felt the Shadow Weave flowing into him and found his hand dropping the reins so he could cast a spell. In his terror, he almost didn't stop himself.

But the beast was only trying to capture him, and the dread he felt was only its natural aura of panic. If he allowed himself to succumb, his plan would fail. Evereska would fall. Vala would die. Galaeron forced his hand down again and fumbled for the reins, but he was already turning the horse by pressing a knee against its shoulder.

Ruha streaked past beside him and called, "Keep going!"

The witch flung sand into the air and shouted in the Bedine tongue. A thick cloud of dust whirled up to engulf the dragon's head, and its talons closed on air. Galaeron caught the reins and jerked the panicked horse back toward the mountain of blue scales ahead.

The dragon let out a crackling bellow and sweeping its long neck around in great serpentine arcs tried to shake free of the swirling dust. The cloud followed wherever its head went.

Ruha galloped under the undulating neck and streaked for the woods. The beast roared in frustration, sent a blue bolt of lightning cracking over her head, and swung back in Galaeron's direction.

A tremendous bang echoed across the plain, and Aris appeared beside the dragon's dust-swaddled head, his largest stone-shaping hammer grasped in both hands. He brought the tool down again, staggering the beast and sending a ripple rolling down its neck.

Galaeron dodged past a wildly lashing claw. He saw the giant raising his arms for another blow.

"Enough!" he called. "Run!"

Aris brought the hammer down anyway, this time drawing a dull thud as it cracked the dragon's skull. Galaeron ducked under a madly undulating neck and was nearly unhorsed by the edge of a flailing wing. He glanced back to see Aris vaulting over the dazed beast's back. The giant shouldered aside a wing-buffet and rushed after Galaeron.

The dragon's dust-engulfed head bobbed uncertainly around, and Galaeron heard a telltale sizzle rising from the thing's throat.

"Watch your—"

A blinding fork of energy danced out from the dust cloud, but Aris was already diving for cover beneath the dragon's wing. The bolt struck half a dozen paces behind the giant, spraying dirt and burning grass fifty feet into the air. Aris emerged beneath the other side of the wing and rolled to his feet, then raced for the woods in great booming strides.

Galaeron looked forward again to find the forest looming ahead like a wall. Ruha and two of the Seven Sisters had already dismounted and were crouching down among the drought-stunted leaves. He angled toward them. The witch rose and pointed at the sky behind him. Not waiting to see whether she was casting a spell or shouting a warning, he broke hard in the opposite direction. He felt a deep throb in his stomach as a pair of huge wings beat the air behind him.

A pair of enormous rear claws tore into the ground beside him, then the second dragon crashed to its forefeet and spun after him. Galaeron heard the shriek of Ruha's magic bolts and the twang of a couple of bowstrings, but knew the attacks would not even distract the beast. He pulled his feet free of the stirrups and hurled himself from the saddle, flinging his sword off to the side and tucking into a forward roll.

At that speed the impact felt like it would break bones clear down to his ankles, but Galaeron came up on his feet and somehow ran two steps before falling victim to his momentum. He tumbled headlong across the meadow. The dragon's scaly belly flashed over his head twice then there was only dusky sky and dusty ground.

Galaeron came to a rest sprawled on his back and gasping for breath, staring back overhead at a wall of blue scales. He heard his horse scream and saw its body spin through the air off to his right, then he felt his own body erupt in pain as he began to slide across the ground. He raised his chin and saw Dove and Storm dragging him by his ankles.

"Well acted, elf," Storm said. "I thought that 'do something, you useless scold' was an especially brilliant touch."

Galaeron was in too much pain to tell whether she was mocking him or actually believed he had been performing for the dragon. They reached the forest, where the undergrowth added to Galaeron's humiliation by slapping him in the face with leaves and twigs. The sisters dragged him another fifty paces to where Ruha was waiting. Finally, they stopped and pulled him to his feet, drawing a series of wheezy groans as he struggled to return the wind to his lungs.

Khelben Arunsun burst through the trees on his horse, then dismounted and sent the beast on its way with a slap.

He took one look out into the field, and asked, "Can you run, elf?"

Galaeron glanced behind him. The second dragon, the one that had just missed snatching him from his horse, did not seem to realize where he had escaped to. It was spinning in a slow circle, ripping up huge tufts of grass and sending small boulders bouncing across the ground as it searched for his hiding place. Still engulfed in Ruha's dust cloud, the other one had gone mad with rage. It was feeling its way down the road on all fours, smashing and shredding any living thing it touched. Already it was smeared to the elbows with blood, and it was closing fast on a screaming tangle of horses and handlers.

Seeing the situation, Galaeron nodded to Khelben and managed to croak, "Perhaps not fast . . . but I can run."

"Sure you can," Storm scoffed. "You can't even talk."

Taking his far arm by the sleeve, she bent down and hoisted him onto her shoulders. Khelben nodded his approval, then led the way deeper into the forest.

"Wait!" Galaeron wheezed.

The archmage didn't even slow down. "What is it?"

Though the pain was starting to subside, being slung across Storm's shoulders was doing nothing to put the air back in Galaeron's chest.

"The . . . caravan!" he said. "It's . . . it's being shredded."

"Yes, and it's our fault," Khelben said. "Very unfortunate."

"I think Galaeron is asking if you couldn't do something," Ruha said.

Dove glanced over at Galaeron and asked, "You really aren't asking if we could slay those little lizards, are you?"

"This is no time for ridiculous questions," Storm added. "Maybe you've noticed we were taken by surprise?"

"I noticed," Galaeron replied. Either his breath was returning, or his rising anger was giving him strength. "We can't just let them die."

Khelben stopped and said, "I thought you wanted to destroy Shade." His voice was sharp with impatience, but there was a softness in his expression that seemed to indicate he understood what Galaeron was asking—and why. "I thought you wanted to save Evereska."

"I do," Galaeron said, "but you can save those people, too."

Seeing that he had finally recovered his breath, Storm dropped him to his feet. Khelben stepped over, eyes burning with anger, and glared down at him.

"The Chosen cannot save everyone on Toril." His tone was as anguished as it was resentful, as though it pained him to state this obvious fact. He waved a hand in the direction of the screaming caravanners and continued, "You chose, elf. Those few, or the thousands in Evereska and the dozens of thousands across the rest of Faerûn who will perish if we reveal ourselves and your plan fails."

"But it's our fault," Galaeron said. He was beginning to feel very small and naive. "There must be a way without you revealing yourselves."

"If there was, don't you think we would have done it?" Storm demanded. "You insult me, elf. I wouldn't do it again."

She turned and started through the woods, more or less toward the last place Galaeron had seen Aris.

Khelben lingered long enough to explain, "The deed itself would betray us. How many caravan guards do you know who could defeat Malygris and two old blues?"

"None."

"That is the problem," Khelben said. "I assume you are choosing Evereska?"

With the screams of the distant caravanners ringing through the trees, Galaeron could barely bring himself to nod, but he did.

"I thought as much."

Khelben cast a last glance in the direction of the road, then turned and started after Storm. Dove motioned Ruha after him then took Galaeron by the hand and followed.

"It is a hard lesson," Dove told him, "but one you must learn if you ever hope to live with the power you carry." Though they were running at a near sprint and taking care to do it without rustling leaves or cracking twigs, Dove's words came as easily as if they had been strolling in the gardens of her house on Evermeet. "Babes may be born into this world innocent as rain, but they have blood on their hands 'ere the end of their first year. We all do."

"A comforting . . . thought," Galaeron said. Though he was as accustomed to running long distances as anyone, he had to concentrate to remain silent in both breath and step. "Are you trying to make me glad I have no children?"

"I am trying to help you. Even if you eat only fruit and never set foot on the ground, you cannot live without killing. Something dies that you may live, even if only the worm that will never hatch in the apple you ate."

"I understand the laws of nature," Galaeron said. "I am still that much of an elf."

"But not a wise one," Dove replied. "And wise you must become, lest you smother Faerûn in evil through your good intentions."

She could not have distracted Galaeron more had she sank a dagger into his chest. He caught his foot on a root and crashed to the ground, causing the entire group to stop and whirl around. Khelben cocked his brow, Storm scowled and shook her head, and Galaeron could not read Ruha's expression behind her veil.

"I beg your leave," Galaeron said as he scrambled to his feet. The others resumed their run, and he grabbed Dove's hand to hold her back. "I am listening."

Dove's expression turned to one almost of pity.

"And still you do not hear," she said as she squeezed his hand until something popped inside. His whole arm erupted into pain. "You have a lot of blood on your hands, Galaeron. The powerful always do."

Galaeron raised his throbbing hand. Though he had not seen Dove cast any spells or felt her use any magic, it had turned the color of an open wound. He was so shocked that he barely noticed the broken bone sticking up under the skin behind his index finger.

"I . . ." Galaeron did not know quite what to say. He was still too confused to be angry, and even his shadow seemed too stunned to react. "I don't understand."

"No?" Dove shrugged, then started after the others, adding, "When you do, the hand will heal."

Galaeron took a moment to set the break then, bones still throbbing, he set off after the others.

The injury proved a useful distraction. As he grew accustomed to the pain, his ire began to rise, and with it his shadow. It took only a dozen steps before he grew so consumed fighting the darkness inside that he no longer heard the screams coming from the road. The thought occurred to him that this was what Dove had intended, though he doubted the pain of a simple broken bone could ever make him forget the anguish of those they were abandoning.

A few hundred steps later, they came to a small stream where Aris was waiting with Alustriel and Laeral. The two sisters had filled five small vials with water and set them out on a flat boulder along the bank. Four of the vials were already gleaming with a silver aura of magic, and Alustriel was saying a spell over the last. Khelben and the rest of the Chosen went to the boulder and waited for Alustriel to finish.

Aris noticed the way Galaeron was holding his hand and frowned in concern.

"You hurt yourself. Maybe I can—"

"Quiet!" Dove hissed. "The dragons are coming."

Aris peered up into the forest's darkening canopy and said, "I don't see—"

Ruha held a finger to her veil and whispered, "Listen."

Aris fell silent. Galaeron listened and heard nothing but the distant murmur of panicked caravanners crashing through the dusky woods. It took him a moment to realize that Dove was talking about what they *couldn't* hear. There were no chirping crickets, no hooting owls, no more screams from the road.

A faint rustle drifted down through the treetops. Galaeron thought at first that a breeze was coming up, but the rustle continued to grow and soon became the distinct hiss of air rushing over scales. A dragon-shaped darkness appeared to the north and came sweeping through the woods toward them. Galaeron and most of the others scrambled for cover, Alustriel lingering to complete her spell and Aris kneeling beneath the boughs of a great oak. The hissing grew louder, and the darkness came nearer, meandering back and forth, as vast as a lake, swallowing everything in its path.

Alustriel finished her spell in a hushed whisper, then took up the last vial and lay down in the shadows along the stream bank. Galaeron kept his gaze turned upward, but the canopy was too thick for him to see anything except a tiny smear of sky and a handful of the evening's first stars. The hiss swelled to a whooshing, then the edge of a wing blocked even that small light.

They were plunged into darkness, and Galaeron waited in frozen silence, the throbbing of his broken hand forgotten. He counted one heartbeat, two, a dozen, then two dozen. Finally, the rushing faded to a hiss, and the darkness swept away to the south. He started to breathe again without realizing that he'd ever stopped, and a lone cricket began to chirp somewhere beyond the creek.

Khelben emerged first, going straight to the boulder to pick up a potion. By the time the others had arrived, he already had the cap off and was raising it to his lips.

Before he could drink, Alustriel caught him by the wrist and said, "Hold there." She took the vial from his hand and passed it to Laeral. "Perhaps you have no care whether you drink a man's potion or a woman's, but we do."

Khelben raised a brow. "There's a difference?"

Alustriel nodded and said, "A pair of bosoms would look as strange on you as a beard would on me."

She selected another vial that looked just the same and gave it to him. Once Alustriel had passed out the rest of the potions, Khelben raised his hand as though making a toast, and the Chosen drank the magic down.

The effect was swift, but not instantaneous. By the time they finished their potions, the Chosen had shrunk to the size of elves. They continued to diminish before Galaeron's eyes, their fingers growing so small they had to grasp the vials in their whole hands. Alustriel produced two green pills from somewhere within her cloak. Though they could not have been much smaller than peas, in her fingers they looked more the size of Cormyr's purse-hogging gold lions.

"Swallow this when you are ready to be rid of us," she said. "There is no hurry except that imposed by your hunger ... but in the Lady's name, don't eat! There are some ways I never wish to pass."

Galaeron reached down to take the pills and said, "Have no fear of that. I doubt Aris and I will be dining at any banquets."

Galaeron turned to pass the pill along and found the giant staring south into the forest, his brow drawn into a deep furrow.

"Aris?"

"The dragon—it's coming back," the giant whispered. "Ten seconds, perhaps twenty."

Galaeron passed Aris's pill up—he had to tug on the hem of the giant's tunic to get his attention—then looked back to the Chosen. They were still waist-high.

A faint hiss drifted down through the treetops, and a familiar darkness appeared in the woods ahead.

"We're not going to make it," Galaeron whispered.

Khelben looked up at Ruha. The witch paled—at least what little could be seen above her veil—but nodded and began to rub her hands together. Galaeron started to protest, but was reminded of the difficult decisions they had already made when his hand started to throb again.

By the time he turned to say his good-byes, Ruha was already racing away from them. She murmured a word of magic, and the sound of her whispering feet began to reverberate through the forest. A soft pulse sounded down through the leaves as the dragon flapped its huge wings, then its black shadow abruptly turned and swept off in pursuit of the fleeing witch.

"Fare you well, my brave friend," Galaeron whispered.

"You won't be rid of her that easily, elf," Storm said. She stood only about as high his knee, and her voice was little more than a tinny hiss. "Ruha spent her childhood dodging blue dragons. She'll be there waiting when Shade falls."

"I pray so," Aris whispered. He looked down, then kneeled and extended a hand. "I think I can do it now, if you're ready."

"I don't think we'll ever be ready for something like this,"

Khelben said, stepping onto the giant's palm, "but if you can do it now, the sooner the better."

Aris tipped his chin back, then dangled Khelben over his open mouth.

"And remember not to chew!" Khelben ordered.

Aris dropped him headlong into his gullet, then made a sour face as he struggled to swallow without closing his mouth. For a moment, Galaeron thought his friend would choke and send Khelben flying through forest, then the archmage's black boots finally vanished into the giant's gaping mouth.

Aris made a loud gulping sound, then lowered his hand again.

Laeral and Storm exchanged uneasy glances, and Storm waved her sister forward.

"By all means."

"You're too kind," Laeral said with a grimace, then she stepped onto Aris's palm.

She had grown just enough smaller that the giant was able to gulp her down without gagging, and Storm went down even easier. That left only Alustriel and Dove, who—at ankle height—were still too large for Galaeron to swallow.

While they waited, Dove turned to Alustriel. "You're sure we won't suffocate?"

"That's what the water breathing magic is for." She looked up at Galaeron and added, "You will remember to drink lots of water."

Recognizing it as an order and not a question, Galaeron merely nodded.

"And we won't be digested?" Dove pressed.

"We're Chosen," Alustriel said. "A little stomach acid isn't going to hurt us. And I *do* have protection—"

The flicker of a far-off lightning bolt flashed through the forest, followed almost instantly by a muffled crackle. Galaeron glanced over and saw the distant glow of a burning tree.

"What now?" he asked. At about twice the size of his

thumb, Alustriel and Dove were still too large for him to swallow—at least without chewing first. "It has to be coming this way."

"There's only one thing *to* do." Alustriel waved a tiny arm, and the five vials shattered into sparkling dust. "If you wait here, the dragon will know you want to be caught."

The steady throb of wings beating air sounded from the direction of the burning tree and began to grow rapidly louder, and the dragon's dark shadow sailed through the forest in their direction.

Galaeron snatched both Chosen up in his good hand and shouted, "Run, Aris!"

The giant spun and crashed off to the west. Trying to keep hold of the shrinking Chosen without suffocating or crushing them—in his panic to escape the dragon for a few moments longer, the absurdity of that concern did not strike him—Galaeron turned southward and sprinted along the bank of the stream. He was making it more difficult to capture them both, but he had to try as hard as he could to escape. A dragon that old would know if he tried to make it easy.

The dragon's shadow arrived to the terrific rushing of leaves as the trees shuddered beneath the buffeting of its wings. Galaeron stopped—more from terror than conscious will—and dropped behind a fallen log. The beast passed overhead so closely that he could smell the odor of fresh lightning still clinging to its scales and hear the high branches scraping its belly. He thought for a moment that it would take him before he could swallow the Chosen, but it continued on westward, chasing the crashing steps of Aris.

Galaeron opened his mouth to sigh in relief and found himself panting for breath. The dragon plunged into the forest with a horrific sound of crashing and splintering, and Aris bellowed in shock. The cry changed to one of pain and fear, then rose into the air.

And that was all. The giant was gone, just that fast.

Galaeron remained motionless, half-expecting to hear Aris's body come crashing back into the trees when the dragon realized it still didn't have him. When the giant's cries only grew more distant, he finally stood and looked down at Alustriel and Dove. They were about half the size of his thumb now, small enough that even an elf could swallow them.

"Aris was taken," he reported, "but I think it missed—"

The leaves shuddered with a sudden rushing as something settled in the treetops, then the trees began to groan and creak beneath some great weight. Galaeron was seized by such an aura of cold terror that his shadow rose inside him and set his mind whirling in a black tornado. Slowly, he raised his eyes, and above the treetops he saw what looked like black, bare limbs curving across the few visible wedges of starlit sky.

Galaeron stood there, frozen in terror and confusion, trying to understand what he was seeing. An enormous black cord of bare vertebrae snaked across a smear of open sky a dozen paces to his right, bringing into view a fleshless, horned skull as large as a rothé.

The skull slowly rotated around until Galaeron found himself looking into the burning blue star of a huge, lifeless eye.

Galaeron! Alustriel's voice came to him inside his head, slicing through the black fog of fear that was clouding his mind. *Now!*

Even in his dragon-inspired panic—and this was the worst he had ever experienced—Galaeron knew better than to raise Malygris's curiosity by swallowing the Chosen in front of him. Instead, acting as much by instinct as by plan, he spun on his heel and fled, bringing his hand to his lips as he ran and sucking the pair into his mouth.

A huge claw crashed down above him, bringing with it a torrent of leaves and splintered wood and trapping him in a cage of bony talons.

"Not so fast, elf," Malygris said. "You are the one I have been searching for."

Galaeron swallowed and felt the Chosen sliding down his throat. With any luck, he had remembered not to chew.

CHAPTER EIGHT

16 Flamerule, the Year of Wild Magic

Keya Nihmedu stood in the first rank of the Company of the Cold Hand, trembling in the rumble and the flash of the attack, her head tipped back as she watched sheet after sheet of crimson blast magic roll across Evereska's flickering mythal. The city's archers answered by darkening the sky with their arrows, and elf battle mages stood spaced along the Meadow Wall, barraging the demolished terraces of the Vine Vale with crackling bolts and arcs of acrid flame.

But, aside from the wall of bugbear mind-slaves behind which the phaerimm were hiding, nobody was dying. The thornbacks themselves were hovering at the edge of spell range, defended from Evereska's assaults by missile guards and spell shields, and they were even more careful to keep their ragged army of beholders and illithids scattered far up the vale where no arrows and few spells could do them harm. The elves were just as safe behind their mythal. While it stood, no attack—magic or otherwise—could cross the Meadow Wall to harm anyone inside.

For perhaps the thousandth time in the past two days, Lord Duirsar strode by in front of the Company of the Cold Hand, his wrists crossed behind his back and his gaze fixed on the distant rank of phaerimm. The events of the last months had aged him as elves do not age, turning his long hair more gray than silver and stooping his shoulders beneath the weight of his worries.

"I see what they're doing, Lord Commander," Duirsar said to a tall moon elf—the acclaimed Kiinyon Colbathin—who was striding along at his side. "It's going to work."

"The mythal has held all these months, Lord Duirsar, even when it was cut off from the Weave." Attired in the battered but once-elegant armor of an Evereskan high noble, Kiinyon looked as care-worn and stressed the high lord himself. "It will hold until Lord Commander Ramealaerub arrives."

Duirsar spun on Kiinyon, wagging a bony finger in his face.

"*If* Ramealaerub arrives, Lord Commander—if," he said. "Even if he does, it may not be in time."

Kiinyon did not argue the point. At last report, Ramealaerub's army had still been camped in the Vyshaen Barrows, awaiting guides from Evereska. Unfortunately, sending guides by foot was impossible, and those who tried to teleport made it only as far as the vale's boundary before falling to ground in a bloody spray, no doubt intercepted by the same phaerimm magic that prevented inbound supplies and reinforcements from entering Evereska via its translocational gates.

Duirsar turned and studied the phaerimm.

"They are wearing us down, Lord Commander, draining our defenses."

"They are *trying*, milord. That is not the same as doing."

Kiinyon glanced back at the long line of young runners bringing casks of fresh arrows down from the city and said, "It would take a decade to deplete Evereska's supply of arrow wood, and with the Weave available again, there is no need at all to worry about our magic."

"You know what I am worried about, Lord Commander— and it is not arrows or lightning bolts," Duirsar replied, glancing up at the flickering mythal. "I think the time has come for the lion to leave his den."

Kiinyon scowled in Keya's direction, and she realized she was nodding in agreement. She stopped but held his gaze until duty compelled him to turn his attention back to Lord Duirsar.

"Milord, that's what the enemy wants," Kiinyon said. "They are trying to draw us out where we will be vulnerable to their attack."

"Or exploiting our temerity to exhaust the mythal." Duirsar continued to study the sheets of magic crashing across the surface of the mythal and said, "In all my centuries, I have never seen it waver like this. The mythal needs our help, Kiinyon."

The lord commander looked up, shielding his eyes against the flashing magic, and said, "We are doing all we can. At least our archers and our battle mages are holding them at a distance. Imagine the damage the thornbacks could do, were they free to stand beside the mythal itself."

Keya had to bite her tongue to maintain the silence expected of a soldier in the ranks. Kiinyon Colbathin was one of the greatest spellblades Evereska had ever known— almost the equal of her own father, who had fallen saving the life of Khelben Arunsun—but he was an under-confident, and therefore timid, general. It would be wrong to blame Kiinyon for Evereska's inability to break the siege, though he had certainly not hesitated to blame her brother Galaeron for prompting it, but it was no exaggeration to say that his only clear strategy seemed to be holding out until someone from outside arrived to save them.

Lord Duirsar remained silent for a long time after Kiinyon spoke. Keya thought he might actually be trying to imagine what possible difference it would make if the phaerimm *were* standing at the mythal.

When he lowered his gaze she saw more anger in his face than uncertainty, and she knew that he was growing as frustrated with his lord commander as she and the rest of Evereska. Duirsar stared at the ground and seemed to be debating something, then raised his gaze and looked straight at her.

"What say you, Keya?" he asked.

Keya knew better than to let her astonishment show, or to hesitate for fear of offending Kiinyon. Khelben Arunsun had been her house guest for much of the siege, and during that time she had spent enough time in the company of both elves to know that Lord Duirsar expected an answer when he asked a question and that Kiinyon would only hold her reply against her if he thought she was being less than honest. Cautious though the lord commander might be in his strategy, he was faithful in his duty and loyal to his city, and if that meant being embarrassed in front of the High Lord, then so be it.

Keya took all the time she dared to consider her answer— thinking fast was no easy task with the battle thunder crashing overhead—then she inclined her head in deference.

"If Evereska's army crosses the Meadow Wall to meet the phaerimm spell to spell, it will not return," she said. "Milord Colbathin is correct in this much. Our losses were heavy enough when we had an army of Shadovar and two Chosen fighting at our sides. Without them, our casualties would be total."

Though accustomed enough in matters of state to hide his feelings behind a mask of indifference, Lord Duirsar was too exhausted and nerve-racked to conceal his surprise. He studied Keya as he might a crouching wolf, his eyes narrowed and his brow raised.

But it was Kiinyon himself who demanded, "And in how much am I mistaken, Swordlady?"

Keya dipped her head in the lord commander's direction and said, "In fighting not to lose, milord. We cannot break the siege by conserving our forces. We must summon our resolve and fight to win."

Seeing the look of apprehension that came to the lord commander's eyes, Keya turned back to Duirsar, whose wry smile suggested that he understood exactly what she was saying.

"Continue, Lady Nihmedu."

Keya felt a secret thrill at being called by her hereditary title. At just over eighty, she was still a decade too young to assume the title formally, and being addressed by it by Evereska's high lord was a token of his respect.

Daring to raise her head and speak more forcefully, she said, "For too long we have been trusting others to do what we must do for ourselves. No one can break this siege but us."

"Then we are doomed," Kiinyon said. "Without help, we are no match—"

"When are you going to understand, Lord Commander?" Keya interrupted. "There *is* no help."

"Mind your tone," Kiinyon ordered. "Lord Duirsar asked for your opinion. He did not give you leave—"

"I have heard you calling to Khelben and the others," Keya continued, growing ever bolder. "Have they come? Have any of the Chosen?"

Kiinyon frowned at her insolence, but said, "They will."

"Before the mythal falls?" Duirsar asked. "I have been calling to the Chosen, as well. Only Syluné answers, and just to send word that the others cannot come."

The despair that came to Kiinyon's face almost sank Keya into despondency as well.

"Our situation is not hopeless," she said, as much to herself as to Kiinyon. "We have resources and have only to use them."

"How?" Lord Duirsar asked. "Until you tell me that, you have told me nothing at all. If we dare not cross the Meadow Wall to meet them, and we cannot win by standing behind it, what are we to do?"

"Make them pay," Keya said. "If they want to attack the mythal, we must make them pay to do it."

"Again, I ask how?"

"With these," said Kuhl, one of the two humans flanking her in the company's front rank. Burly and black-bearded, he was about as big as a rothé and woollier than a thkaerth, with a swarthy round face and hands the size of a plates. He stepped forward holding his glassy darksword in hand. "We sneak out there with the Cold Hand and start cutting them down, one at a time."

"And we keep doing it until they all leave or they're all dead," added Burlen, the human standing to her other side. "Or until there aren't any more of us to go back."

"That's the way we do it in Vaasa," Kuhl said.

Keya smiled up at her mountainous friends, then nodded to Lord Duirsar and said, "We teleport out there in small strike teams, hit hard, and come back."

Duirsar smiled. "And we see how determined *they* are, for a change."

"Risk the darkswords?" Kiinyon asked, shaking his head. "Every one we lose out there is one we won't have in Evereska if they—"

The lord commander was interrupted first by the crackling roar of an erupting fireball, then by a chorus of anguished screams. Keya and the others spun toward the sound and were astonished to see a battle mage and his escorts rolling on the ground in flames, a wagon-sized ring of smoke above them rapidly contracting around a breach in the mythal.

Before the hole could close, a crimson sphere came streaking across the Meadow Wall in their direction. Lord Duirsar flung up his hand, raising a spell-guard with enough speed to convince Keya that the rumors about him being one of Evereska's secret high mages were true. The fireball flattened against the mystic shield and crackled into nothingness, leaving only a faint orange glow to mark where it had struck.

Duirsar watched only long enough to be certain that the mythal had sealed itself again, then turned to back to Kiinyon and said, "I would say that decides the matter, wouldn't you?" Without waiting for a reply, he turned to Burlen and Kuhl. "Teams of six? Four warriors and two battle mages?"

Unhappy at being left out of the planning and quite sure she was the only one who understood why the high lord was suggesting those particular numbers, Keya said, "That will be fine, milord—one mage to teleport and one to cast a decoy."

"Decoy?" Burlen asked.

"So you have time to attack," Duirsar said, nodding his approval to Keya. "Otherwise the phaerimm will be on you before you can recover from the afterdaze."

"Recover?" Kuhl scoffed. "We aren't going to be there that long. Just give us mages who can get us out as quick as they get us in—and the teams should have three warriors, not four."

"Only three?" Duirsar asked. "I don't understand."

"I do," Kiinyon said.

He flashed a smile at Keya—as close to an apology as she would ever receive from the great hero, she knew—then he set about organizing the Company of the Cold Hand into trios. Though the company had less than twenty darkswords borrowed from the Vaasans who had fallen when the phaerimm escaped their prison, Kiinyon had close to a hundred of Evereska's finest spellblades to choose from. The darkswords had been forged by the archwizard Melegaunt Tanthul over a hundred years earlier and passed down from parent to child for four generations, and they would freeze the hand of any wielder not of the owning family. To get around the problem, for each sword, the Company of the Cold Hand had five warriors who passed the sword from hand to hand as their fingers grew too numb to hold onto it.

For these attacks, there would be only one wielder for each sword, so Kiinyon was free to chose the most experienced and powerful spellblades available. When he came to Keya and the two Vaasans, the only three members of the company who could hold their darkswords as long as they wished, the lord commander at first assigned Burlen and Kuhl to separate trios. When Keya insisted on being assigned to a group as well, they insisted on teaming with her.

"Dex is already mad as a dragon about her taking his darksword," Burlen explained.

As Dexon's lover—or more precisely, the mother of his unborn child—Keya had become a member of his family and able to hold his darksword without freezing her hand. With Dexon still struggling to recover from the wound he had received in the last big battle, she had taken his sword and rushed off to join the fight when the phaerimm began to attack. Dexon had chased her down Treetop and halfway across the Starmeadow screaming for her to bring it back and stay there were he could defend her. Keya half expected to see him come hopping out into the meadow at any moment, dragging his spell-withered leg along and yelling all the time that they had to protect her. Humans were strange that way, believing they could hoard what they loved like gold and keep it safely hidden away in their vaults.

Lord Duirsar returned with seven of Evereska's most powerful battle mages, most of them instructors in the Academy of Magic—when there had still been such a thing. Kiinyon explained the plan, then arranged five of the teams into a triangle, with the wizard in the middle and the three warriors ringing him, facing outward. The sixth team—Keya's—he arranged in a square, taking the fourth side himself.

"You're sure this is going to work?" Kiinyon asked.

"Like grease on ice," Kuhl answered. "When we get there, just keep hold of my belt with your free hand and swing with your sword hand."

"Very well."

Kiinyon drew his borrowed darksword and signaled the attack. Keya heard the battle mage start his spell, then there came a dark eternity of falling. Her stomach rose into her chest, and she grew weak and dizzy and cold. A dead silence filled her ears, and she felt nothing but her own heart hammering fast and hard in her chest—and she was somewhere else, the ground rumbling beneath her feet and her eyes and nose burning with the brimstone stench of Hell.

"Swing!" shouted a familiar gruff voice.

Reminded of the sword in her hand, Keya swung even as her mind struggled to make sense of her smoky, fire-blasted surroundings. She hit nothing, but heard off behind her shoulder the wet slap of a sword cleaving flesh and spun instinctively toward the sound, bringing her darksword around in a vicious backhand.

This time, Keya hit something and felt her blade bite deep. Blood, hot and sour-smelling, splashed her across the jaw and throat. A squealing whirlwind filled the air with dirt and ash, then golden bolts of magic appeared from nowhere and began to ricochet off her spell-turning bracers. Some of them came bouncing back past her head, deflected by identical bracers worn by all the warriors in the Company of the Cold Hand.

Keya glimpsed an expanse of thorny scales and finally recalled where she was and what she was doing there. She reversed her blade and brought it back across the phaerimm's body, this time stopping at the end of the stroke to plunge the tip in deep.

The creature screamed again in its windy language. Its tail

came arcing up at her face, the barbed tip already dripping with its paralyzing poison. Kiinyon reached past her shoulder, catching the attack on his borrowed darksword and flicking the barb away before it could strike. Keya thanked him by bringing her own weapon, still plunged deep into their foe, down the length of its serpentine body.

The phaerimm pulled itself off her blade by floating a few feet backward. Keya thought it would teleport to safety, until Burlen's darksword came tumbling past and split the thing the rest of the way through. It fell to the ground in a pile of blood and entrails.

Burlen extended his hand toward the sword. It rose out of the gore and tumbled back into his grasp, then Kuhl's big hand grabbed Keya by the belt and pulled her back into position.

"Time to go."

Realizing that she had released her own grip, Keya started to reach back for Burlen's belt—then heard someone cry out from above.

"Keya?" The voice was so weak and hoarse as to be unrecognizable, but it was speaking Elvish. "Can that be you?"

Keya looked up the vale, and two terraces above, saw a half-starved wood elf scout peering through a gap in a wrecked wall. Over her shoulders and head, she had a makeshift camouflage tarp covered with withered grape vines, but Keya could see enough of the scout's face to tell that her red-rimmed eyes were as sunken as a banshee's and her lips cracked and bloody with thirst. A hundred paces behind her, a mixed company of beholders and illithids were rushing down the vale to investigate.

"It's time!" Burlen urged. "Grab hold."

"Wait!" Keya called as she started toward the elf. "She needs help."

"No time," Kuhl said. Still holding her by the belt, he lifted her back into the fighting square. "We kill and run."

Keya tried to break free, but the Vaasan's grasp was too powerful.

"I can't just leave her!"

"And you won't help her by getting yourself killed," Kiin-yon said. To the battle mage, he added, "Get us there and I'll—"

The battle mage cast his spell, her stomach rose into her chest, and there came that cold eternity of falling. A dead silence filled her ears and she began to feel queasy, then she was someplace not too different, the ground still shaking beneath her feet and the stench of brimstone still burning her nostrils.

Keya felt the weight of the darksword in her hand, and recalling the last time they had teleported, she began to swing.

Her sword hit nothing, but a familiar elf voice cried out, "What are you doing, you bear-stinking oafs? Hold your blades!"

The Vaasans had picked up enough Elvish to realize that they were being addressed, and Keya glanced over her shoulder to find an exhausted wood elf glaring up at them. Even as haggard as the elf was, Keya recognized the brown eyes and cupid's bow smile as those of her brother Galae-ron's favorite scout, Takari Moonsnow. Lying on the ground and covered to the shoulders in dirt and withered grape vines, it looked as though Takari was crawling up out of the ground, a sight that only added to the confusion of Keya's afterdaze.

"Takari?" Keya gasped. "What are you doing here?"

A rumbling cloud of black fume appeared two terraces down and began to rain tiny spheres of magic. As the balls struck the ground, they exploded into crackling sprays of fire, lightning, or hissing green fog. Keya felt her knees weaken as she realized how close the strike had come—how close *she* had made it come—to the spell sprays.

"Good thing you moved!" Takari said.

The withered grape vines rolled aside and Takari emerged from beneath the camouflage tarp. She was protected by little more than a ragged suit of leather perforated in so many places it could no longer be called armor. Nor was she wearing any magic—not the boots of secret passing given to all rangers who served Evereska, nor even a pair of spell turning bracers or one of the mind-shielding helms Evermeet had sent to equip the elven army.

Keya motioned Takari into the group as a rosy glow fell over them. She turned to see the pink cone of a magic-killing ray illuminating them from the great central eye of a beholder on the next terrace. With the beholder were another half-dozen of its kind and twice that number of mind flayers.

"Lolth's fangs!" Kiinyon cursed. "Over the wall!"

Keya had no chance to obey. Kuhl was already lifting her by her belt, wrapping her into an arm the size of a thkaerth and diving over the wall. Keya barely had time to turn the blade of her darksword away before they came down on the other side, Kuhl crashing to the ground like a magic-felled rothé and Keya landing atop him as light as a feather. Burlen flashed past overhead and smashed down beside them in a heap of clattering armor.

"Stay low!" Kiinyon yelled from somewhere beyond Keya's feet. "Ready your magic bolts."

"Magic bolts?" the battle mage gasped. "We need to leave . . . and now!"

"Do it!" Kiinyon ordered. "Kuhl, Burlen, watch our backs."

It sounded to Keya like the lord commander was preparing for a holding action instead of a fast retreat, but after coming so close to causing a disaster just moments earlier, she knew better than to question the order. She slipped off Kuhl barely in time to avoid being crushed as he rolled to his stomach and crawled off across the terrace.

The pink radiance of the magic-killing beam vanished, and the mordant smell of rock dust began to fill the air as the beholders swept their disintegration rays back and forth across the wall. Keya readied her magic bolts, then lay listening to the sizzle of dissolving stone as she awaited Kiinyon's order. He seemed to take forever, though perhaps it only felt that way because she knew the phaerimm who had assaulted their previous position would know where they were and would be moving up to attack.

Finally, in a surprisingly calm voice, Kiinyon said, "Beholders only. Three, two, now."

Timing her move so she came up behind the sweep of the disintegration ray, Keya peered over the top of the smoking wall and loosed her spell at the second beholder in line. Three golden bolts streaked from her fingertips, striking the central eye and causing it to erupt in a bloody spray. The creature screeched in pain and began to spray the beams of its remaining eyes haphazardly along the length of the wall.

Rising alongside Keya, Takari fired five bolts into the first beholder in line and dropped it on the spot. Kiinyon and the battle mage destroyed the rest of the creatures, the wizard spreading his attacks among three of the eye tyrants and leaving nothing but starbursts of red gore, Kiinyon's magic splitting both targets cleanly down the center.

"Cover!" the lord commander ordered.

Keya and Takari dropped behind the wall side-by-side, then heard the heart-stopping rip of a fire storm erupt behind them. Recalling that Takari had no magical protection, Keya turned to throw herself in front of the wood elf. She found herself looking down the throat of a fiery spray of tiny red spheres. A handful of the flickering spheres—it could have been three or thirteen—came arcing in her direction, then encountered the magic of her spell-turning bracers and ricocheted off in a smoking meshwork of flame.

Keya landed lightly on her side and knew instantly by the stench of burned leather and charred flesh that she had not prevented all of the fiery balls from getting through. She sprang to her feet facing the direction of attack, trying through smell and guesswork to place herself in front of the wounded wood elf.

"How are you back there?"

On the terrace below, she saw a pair of phaerimm moving behind the half-ruined wall opposite her, floating away from each other with only their arms and toothy mouths exposed. There was no sign of Burlen or Kuhl, though Keya knew better than to worry about that. The Vaasans had an uncanny knack for remaining unseen, even in the barest ground, until they attacked. Keya thought it had something to do with the darkswords, but if so, it was a trick Dexon had not yet taught her.

When Takari did not answer, Keya asked again, "You alive back there?"

"Do I sound dead?" Takari's voice was thin with pain. "How are you doing that?"

"What?"

A wave of ash and dust began to roll up the terrace toward them. Keya knew that, whatever was coming, she could not shield Takari from it by standing in front of her.

Keya started, "On my—"

Way ahead of her, Takari landed on Keya's back and slipped an arm over her collar to hold on. Keya could feel the other arm hanging limply against her back.

"The darksword," Takari said. "How come it isn't freezing your hand?"

Keya glanced down at the weapon in her hand but was spared the necessity of explaining her circumstances as the wave arrived with a low, barely audible rumble.

"Jump it!" Kiinyon yelled.

Keya took three running steps and leaped.

Though Takari was small for a wood elf and Keya's muscles were hardened by half a year of military service, she was still not strong enough to carry them both over something that was nearly as high as her chest. At the last minute, she decided her only hope was to dive.

The wave caught Keya just below the hips. Though her bracers protected her from the magic itself, the momentum of the impact numbed her legs and flipped her high into the air. Takari's arm slipped free, and the Green elf went tumbling away. The world flashed past in a whirling kaleidoscope of blue sky and blackened ground, gray terrace wall and flickering orange mythal. Keya felt the darksword fly from her hand, then she crashed down flat on her back and felt the air leave her lungs in a single pained howl.

A deafening boom sounded from somewhere above her. Keya craned her neck around and saw the wall she had just left erupting into the air. She watched in dazed fascination as the dry-laid rocks—each the size of an elf's head—separated from each other and flew off in their own directions.

As the stones finally reached the top of their arcs, it occurred to her that what went up usually came down—and that the gray shapes rapidly growing larger in the air above were going to come down on her. Keya rolled to her side and wrapped her arms around her head, then counted one, two, three nearby thuds before the first crashing thump struck her pauldron.

Keya's shoulder exploded into limp agony, and only the fingers clasped behind her neck prevented it from flopping away and leaving her head exposed. Her thigh went sore and useless as a stone struck it. Another glanced off her back and sent bolts of throbbing fire shooting into her temples and down to her feet. She tried—unsuccessfully—not to scream and told herself that the pain was a good thing, that as long as she could feel she could still walk—or run, given where they were.

Keya took two more strikes—one on her rump and another in the ribs—before the stones finally stopped raining down. Her father had managed to drill enough tactical sense into her that she knew the phaerimm would not have launched a shock attack if they did not intend to follow it up with a rapid advance, so Keya allowed herself only one attempt to draw the wind back into her chest—it was as unsuccessful as her effort to leap the wave—before she rolled to her hands and knees and spun toward her attackers.

She found them halfway across the terrace, their barbed tails dripping poison and their jagged teeth showing in the smiles atop their slug-shaped bodies. Dexon's darksword was nowhere in sight, but Takari lay a dozen paces farther down the terrace, twisting about in a pained daze, one shin canted at a wrong angle and the bones of her shoulder showing through the hole the first phaerimm attack had burned in her armor.

To Keya's astonishment, the battered wood elf somehow managed to draw her sword and swing herself into a kneeling position. The phaerimm paid Takari no attention whatsoever, but the sight inspired Keya to extend a hand and call to the darksword as Dexon had taught her, by imagining the feel of the hilt in her hand.

A moment later, the darksword came tumbling into Keya's hand from somewhere behind her. Only six paces beyond Takari, the phaerimm stopped and began to whistle to each other in their strange language of winds.

"Takari, I'm right behind you," Keya called. She did not advance toward the wood elf for fear of prodding the phaerimm into action. "If you can drag yourself back to me."

"Yes . . . I can do that."

Takari's voice had assumed a strange distance, and Keya cursed silently, knowing that one of the thornbacks had taken control of the Green elf's mind. Where were the Vaasans? They were supposed to be protecting the rear . . . and what were Kiinyon and the battle mage doing?

The last question, at least, was answered by a string of mystic syllables and the deep knelling that always accompanied the summoning of a large amount of iron. Keya turned and saw what looked like a rusty square cloud fluttering down on the terrace above. She did not even notice the charging illithids until they saw the shadow and looked up and began to screech in panic. The wall slammed down an instant later, so close that Keya felt a rush of displaced air and heard the crackle of bursting illithid skulls.

A handful of the fastest illithids escaped being crushed and spun on the battle mage, their tentacles flailing in his direction as they attempted to stun him with their mental blasts. The attacks were no more effective against his helmet's magic mind guard than would have been a phaerimm's attempt to make a mind-slave of him. As the battle mage leveled his hands in their direction, Keya glanced back at Takari and found her half a dozen paces away, sword in hand and still dragging herself up the terrace. Behind her, the phaerimm continued to float, content to let the wood elf do their work for them.

Disturbed by their calm, Keya hazarded a glance in Kiinyon's direction and found him surrounded by lemure corpses, no doubt summoned by the phaerimm to prevent him from casting his escape magic. Another trio of the little devils appeared as she watched. With the darksword now stored securely in its scabbard, Kiinyon felled two with a kick and a dagger slash, but the third escaped and circled around to attack from behind.

Keya had little doubt that the renowned spellblade would be able to drop that one as quickly as the others, but the phaerimm strategy was working. Translocational magic was too complicated—even for someone of his skill—to cast while fighting hand-to-hand, and the thornbacks had more beholders and illithids rushing in from all sides. They had to do something, and fast.

Keya started forward, stretching a hand out as though to help Takari to her feet. The wood elf's gaze was still blank as she reached out to accept Keya's hand, but her sword remained down by her thigh, ready to strike.

Takari's grasp felt cold and clammy as it closed on Keya's. Something like alarm flashed in the depths of her brown eyes, then her hand clamped down hard. With surprising strength for one so battered, Takari jerked Keya down. The wood elf's blade came up in a smooth arc that, had it not met

Dexon's darksword on the way, would have come down on Keya's neck.

As it was, the darksword sliced through Takari's blade as smoothly as it did phaerimm scales. The blade tumbled away harmlessly, flashing like a trout in a forest stream. Keya planted a foot in Takari's chest and pushed her to the ground, then stepped forward and sent her darksword spinning toward the nearest thornback.

A trio of screeching lemures appeared in front of the phaerimm. They were instantly sliced in half by the tumbling blade, but served their purpose by absorbing enough energy to send the darksword spinning to the ground. Both phaerimm turned to rush for the sword—and Burlen and Kuhl appeared behind them, rising from behind the far terrace like thieves stepping from an alley.

They hurled their swords as one, taking the astonished phaerimm so completely by surprise that Keya doubted the creatures ever knew what had killed them. The thornbacks simply sank to the ground half a dozen yards shy of Keya's sword and lay there with the Vaasans' weapons in their back.

"It's about time," Keya said. "What took so long?"

"An argument," Burlen answered. "Kuhl doesn't think we ought to be using you for bait."

He summoned his darksword back to his hand, and Kiinyon finally yelled for them to come running. Keya turned to see the black rectangle of a dimensional gate flickering in the air beside him. She summoned Dexon's darksword to hand, then cautiously removed her foot from Takari's chest and looked down to find the elf studying her with a look of utter astonishment.

"Are you all right?" Keya asked. "Ready to go home?"

Takari nodded, but seemed unable to take her eyes off of Dexon's darksword.

"You've got to tell me how you can do that!"

CHAPTER NINE

17 Flamerule, the Year of Wild Magic

Even for dragons, the flight to Shade was a long one. Galaeron hung in Malygris's grasp through the night and all the next day. At dusk he finally saw the city, a distant diamond of umbral murk floating low over the purple mirror of Shadow Lake. As always, it was swaddled in wisps of black fog, giving it the appearance of a lone storm cloud or a mirage. The swirling specks of a hundred or so vultures wheeled beneath it, in constant pursuit of the garbage that fell like rain from its refuse chutes. There were also larger specks, shaped like tiny crosses and circling the city in the tight formations of veserab patrols.

Malygris raised his head, and Galaeron's skin suddenly began to prickle and his hair stood on end. A deep crackling erupted a few yards above his back, and the air began to dance with silvery flashes. He craned his neck around and saw an enormous ball of blue lightning blazing inside the dracolich's empty cage of ribs. Malygris opened his jaws, and the lightning shot up his throat in a blinding white fork of energy that left Galaeron struggling to blink the glow from his eyes.

As Malygris announced his triumphant return to Shade, a terrible sense of fear and loneliness settled over Galaeron. His plan was a sound one, or the Chosen would never have agreed to the attempt, but it was also one that demanded more strength than he was sure he possessed and sacrifices that were not his alone to make. The last time he had glimpsed Aris, the giant had been hanging by his shoulders, chin resting on his chest and his captor's talons sunk deep into his flesh. Given Anauroch's heat and the dragons' refusal to stop for water, there was every reason to believe that Aris would be suffering from sun stroke in addition to whatever injuries he had endured during his capture.

Not for the first time, Galaeron cursed himself for listening to Storm. He was beginning to question just how much Aris's absence would really have raised the Shadovar's suspicions. Having seen how callously the Chosen spent mortal lives, it was easy to believe they were risking his friend's life for only modest benefit. If Aris were to die on behalf of the plan, Galaeron's resolve would be so weakened by guilt he would succumb to his shadow self.

In fact, he was starting to think that this was exactly what they wanted, that they had some other secret plan to save Faerûn that did not involve saving Evereska. Wouldn't that be just like the Chosen? Maybe they had quietly struck a bargain with the phaerimm to subvert the city defenses from the inside, so the thornbacks could attack from the outside and destroy their mutual enemy. It was just as well, then, that Galaeron had remained silent about the message from Malik. The little man might prove useful yet.

As they crossed Shadow Lake, Shade swelled from a tiny

diamond of murk into a more nebulous form that might have been a solitary thunderhead on the verge of bursting, or a plume of ash drifting across the sky from some nearby volcano. A patrol of veserab riders came out and took flanking positions to either side, their jittery mounts hissing and spewing black fumes as they felt the fear aura that surrounded all dragons. Paying the escort no attention at all, Malygris continued onward until the black haze filled the entire sky ahead, then he dived to the bottom of the cloud and entered the dark murk there.

Once inside the cloud, the enclave itself grew visible, a huge capsized mountaintop honeycombed with utility passages and ventilation shafts. Malygris began to circle the crags of the overturned peak in an ever-growing spiral, his fear aura keeping the ever-growing colonies of bats and birds at a cautious distance. Even the jewel-eyed sentries who stood constant watch from their hidden crannies shrank back out of sight as the dragon passed.

Though the city could be departed in any number of the usual mundane ways—flying, translocational magic, even jumping—circling up from the bottom was the only way to enter. Even then, those seeking entrance had to come only at dusk, when the hidden city grew briefly visible. Any other approach would lead the unfortunate traveler through the plane of shadow to any one of a thousand planes it touched. It was, Galaeron knew, a defense the Shadovar considered unbreachable by any army on Faerûn and one that made them feel invulnerable enough to treat the rest of the world as no self-respecting lord would his dogs.

At last, they neared the top of the mountain, where the great Cave Gate already hung open, its huge mouth an ebony hollowness opening into an even darker wall of black stone. Malygris seemed to take great delight in extending his wings and clacking both sides of the portal with the yellowed bone tips. A properly awed murmur rustled through the depths of the cavern as he swooped to a stop at the rear of the vast

Marshaling Plaza and banged down with Galaeron pinned to the floor beneath his huge talons.

A pair of similar crashes from nearer the mouth of the cave confirmed that the dracolich's companions had landed behind them.

Holding Galaeron down so tightly that his face scraped along the floor, Malygris pushed him forward.

"I bring gifts fitting to my splendor," Malygris said. His tone was surprisingly deferential, at least for a dracolich. "Here are the warmbloods you have been seeking."

"So I see." The voice was sibilant and pervasive, like a whisper rolling into the cavern from some distant passage. "It should not surprise me that dragonkind has succeeded where my own princes have failed. You are to be complimented, Malygris. This is most excellent."

The speaker was Telamont Tanthul, Most High of Shade and father of the Thirteen Princes. But even had the shadow lord not spoken, Galaeron would have sensed his presence in the chill stillness of the air—and in the cold fear that held the cavern in its grasp. Even Malygris, who as the Blue Sovereign of Anauroch need not bow to any other, lowered his skull in respect.

Without being audibly prompted, the dracolich spoke again. "Matters went as I knew they would, of course. The two-legs cowered in my shadow, and the ones we sought fled into the forest." The dracolich pricked Galaeron with the tip of his talon and added, "Though these mammals thought to hide their giant with their pitiful wizardry, they were fools. Their magic is nothing to mine, and the mere attempt revealed to us who we were seeking."

Galaeron's stomach suddenly went cold and queasy, and it had less to do with the Chosen being carried inside it than with simple fear. If Telamont's willpower could master even that of a dracolich, what chance did Galaeron have of hiding his betrayal? When the Most High's attention turned to him, the truth would become a breath held too long, and the harder he tried to keep it inside, the more desperate he'd grow to release it. His only chance was to confess all and claim the plan had been Storm's idea, that the Chosen had forced him to—

No.

That was his shadow speaking. The idea had slipped up on him so smoothly, felt so natural that he had almost accepted it as his own. But if he betrayed the Chosen, he would also be betraying his loyal friend Aris, and that one thought served as a lifeline back to his true self.

The Most High remained silent, and more words spilled out of the dracolich's mouth.

"My worshipers have spies in every city of Faerûn," Malygris continued. "When they informed my priests that the giant was selling all of his stone whittling, I knew the ones you desired would soon leave the city."

"As did we," Telamont replied. His voice was cold and calm. "Yet you acted while my sons planned and fretted. Shade is in your debt."

"Indeed," said a silken voice Galaeron recognized as that of Yder Tanthul, the Sixth Prince of Shade, "but one wonders at how easily this 'secret' was discovered. Our agents were watching as they left Arabel. Starting a beggar's riot does not seem a very secretive way to leave a city."

"You challenge me, shade?"

There was an alarming crackle in Malygris's voice, and Galaeron was almost crushed as the dracolich shifted his weight forward.

"As a courtesy to your lord," the dracolich continued, "I will suffer your insult this once. But your stink offends me. Be gone."

"Be *gone*?" Yder fumed.

Galaeron wished he could reach the little pill Alustriel had given him. Even a dracolich did not speak to a prince of Shade in such a manner, and he thought the coming clash might provide just the diversion he needed to disgorge the Chosen and escape into the city.

But Yder said no more, and after a moment of staring across the floor through Malygris's talons, Galaeron realized that the prince had indeed gone.

"Yder means no offense, Mighty One," Telamont said in a tone that was soft, and almost hypnotically soothing. "He is only a few centuries old and not yet capable of appreciating the full depth of a dragon's cunning. He stands in awe of your magnificence."

"Then it pleases me to let him live," Malygris replied. "Consider it a gift."

"You honor me too much, my friend. Is there a gift you desire in return?"

The air grew as cold and as still as ice. The hem of Telamont's dark robe—all Galaeron could see of the shadow lord—drifted forward.

"There is nothing," Malygris said. "The honor of your friendship is all I seek."

"That you have."

An expectant silence descended between the pair, then Malygris finally said, "But Techora is making demands on me."

"And Techora is?"

"The new one sent by the Cult of the Dragon," Malygris explained. "I mention this only because her petitions often interfere with our friendship."

"This is the seventh in as many tendays," the shade replied. It was a statement of fact. "One might think you are simply trying to escape the bargain you struck with the Cult of the Dragon."

"It is hardly my fault that the priests they send are all rude and foolish," Malygris rumbled. His talons tightened until Galaeron let out an involuntary groan. "Should I tolerate ineptitude among my servants?"

"No more than I." Telamont's tone was almost resigned. "Yder will see to her. That shall be his atonement gift to you. What defenses does this one bear?"

"Only the usual protection amulets," Malygris said as he raised his claw, freeing Galaeron, "and the mammal is not even as powerful as the others. The cult is beginning to run out of priests."

"That would be good," Telamont said. "Not that I have ever been displeased with the splendor of *your* gifts, Malygris."

The dracolich spun around in a great clatter of bones, nearly crushing Galaeron with a carelessly placed rear foot and upending a dozen of Telamont's bodyguards with his long tail.

"How could you? They came from a dragon."

Malygris sprang into the air and departed the Marshaling Plaza over the heads of his two assistants. Telamont motioned for Prince Clariburnus to keep watch over Galaeron, then exchanged gifts with the other two dragons, promising to undermine the walls of an annoying castle for the one that had captured Aris and to reroute a caravan trail closer to the lair of the other.

As the agreements were made, Galaeron had a chance to see that while Aris had suffered no wounds worse than the talon punctures in his shoulders, the heat and thirst had taken its toll. The giant lay on the floor half conscious, with glassy eyes, a flushed face, and limbs as white as chalk. His hands were trembling and his breath was coming in fast, shallow pants.

"Aris needs water," Galaeron said. He was surprised to find his own throat swollen and raw from thirst. "We haven't had any since last night, and the desert—"

"He can wait," Clariburnus replied. "After the trouble you two caused us, I hope he chokes on his tongue."

"I am sure that would make the Most High very happy," mewled a familiar voice. "Especially after he has waited all this time for you to recapture them."

The dumpy form of Malik el Sami yn Nasser pushed between the waists of Clariburnus and Brennus and stepped into view. Dressed in a gray tunic with a tabard of black shadow over the top, he seemed an unwitting parody of the imposing forms of the two princes—especially with his weary, bloodshot eyes and his cuckold's horns proudly displayed atop his head.

Malik turned and called back between Clariburnus and Brennus, "Go and fetch a few barrels of water, and hurry. If the giant is harmed, I will see to it that the Most High has your heads."

To Galaeron's amazement, half the troop turned and scurried to obey. Any doubt that Malik had meant his message to lure Galaeron into a trap vanished at once.

"I see you've come up in the city," Galaeron said.

"No thanks to you."

The little man came forward, and brushing aside the black pike Clariburnus put out to keep him from getting too close, stood over Galaeron.

"How could you leave Vala to suffer so long? Your cruelty nearly got me killed!"

Putting aside for the moment how one might be connected to the other, Galaeron asked, "Then she's still alive? Your message said—"

Clariburnus used the pike to push Malik away. "It is not this lizard's place to discuss the slave of a prince."

Malik shrugged, spread his hands, and said, "He is right. Perhaps, if you please the Most High, he will intervene and let you see for yourself all the terrible things that Escanor has been visiting upon her at night."

Galaeron would have smiled at Malik's cleverness, had the answer itself not filled his head with so many terrible images. The bones in his broken hand began to throb, and he thought of the crimson stain Dove had placed on it and how he would explain that to Telamont Tanthul.

The water arrived, and without leaving any for Galaeron, Malik led the soldiers carrying it over to his friend Aris. Clariburnus seemed to take delight in watching Galaeron lick his lips as he watched the little man trickle it down the giant's throat. Finally, Telamont Tanthul returned from his gift-making, and seeing where Galaeron's attention was fixed, motioned him to his feet.

"Come, you must be thirsty as well—and curious about your friend's condition."

He waited for Galaeron to rise, then placed an icy sleeve across Galaeron's shoulders and started toward the giant.

"I'm sorry for the difficult journey," Telamont continued. "It was my intention to bring you here in a more pleasant fashion, but you know dragons . . . I fear Malygris and his consorts may have been somewhat rougher on you than necessary. That young blue you killed in the Saiyaddar?"

Galaeron nodded, scarcely able to believe that the Most High was speaking to him as though he had just returned from a short trip outside the enclave.

"It was one of theirs," the Most High explained, just as they reached Malik and the water barrels and stopped. "To tell you the truth, you're lucky you made it here at all. They kept giving us beholders and asabis and demanding that we help hunt down the murderers."

Galaeron's throat grew even drier. Blue dragons were not particularly family oriented, but he had talked to enough of them while serving along the Desert Border South to know that it offended their sense of magnificence to have a warmblood kill a wyrm of their own line.

"Then I'd say we were very lucky," he said.

"We arranged something," said the Most High. He lifted an empty sleeve and pulled an ebony dipper out of the shadows, then filled it with water and passed it to Galaeron. "They really can't tell the smell of one moon elf from another, and it was a simple matter to sneak the hide into a camp one night."

Galaeron found the water going down the wrong passage and choked, spraying it out in a cone of silvery droplets.

"You didn't!"

"What choice did you leave me?" Telamont said. His voice

had assumed that cold levelness it acquired whenever he struggled to contain his temper. "They kept bringing gifts, and I could hardly tell them it was you."

Galaeron looked at the empty dipper and wondered if he dared fill it again. Having tasted water, he could think of little except his thirst, but he had seen Telamont in moods like this and knew how risky it could be to presume in his presence.

On the other hand, what was the worst the Most High was going to do? Certainly not kill him, and angering him might make it easier for Galaeron to resist his will. He refilled the dipper and drank.

Telamont watched, platinum eyes burning with fury, but his empty sleeves folded calmly in front of him.

When Galaeron had finished, he asked, "Good?"

Galaeron met the shadow lord's gaze and smacked his lips.

"Have another." Telamont took the dipper and refilled it, then passed it back and said, "I insist."

Galaeron found himself gulping the water down like a drunkard breaking a long abstinence. Once the dipper was empty, Telamont took it and refilled it.

"You left Arabel with a caravan bound for Iriaebor, did you not?"

"That's so, but we were bound for Evereska." Galaeron told the lie quickly, trying to get it out before Telamont's will began to press down on him and force the truth. "To join the fight against the phaerimm."

Telamont passed the dipper back to Galaeron, and again he found himself gulping the stuff down as though it might evaporate before he could finish.

"That is what our agents suggested, and yet Yder's point troubles me. What was it he said?"

Before Galaeron could answer, a pair of yellow eyes appeared in the darkness behind Telamont.

"That starting a beggar's riot does not seem a very good way to sneak out of a city."

Yder's gaunt face took form around his golden eyes, then he emerged from the shadows and stood at father's side.

"I also thought it strange," Yder added, "that they announced their departure by selling all of the giant's work."

Yder glanced over at Aris, who lay stretched out on his back, unaware of his surroundings, with Malik kneeling astride his chest dribbling dippers of water onto his cracked lips.

Telamont refilled Galaeron's empty dipper, and Galaeron began to gulp it down. He was no longer thirsty—he could already feel Alustriel and Dove sloshing around inside, banging off the walls of his stomach—but he could not stop himself from gulping it down as he had all the others.

"Had they needed the coin for their journey," Yder continued, "I would put this down to necessity."

"But if they needed the coin, why give it all to the beggars?" Clariburnus asked. "Something here stinks like the sulfur pits of Carceri."

Telamont refilled the dipper. Though Galaeron's stomach was already so bloated it ached, he found himself reaching for it.

"It does sound odd, does it not?" The Most High pulled his hand away and asked, "Perhaps you care to explain it?"

Again, Galaeron forced the lie out before Telamont's will had a chance to compel the truth. "The statues earned more than we expected."

His fingers touched the dipper's handle, but Telamont did not let him take it.

"Is that so?" Telamont asked.

He released the dipper, and Galaeron began to pour more water into his swollen stomach. He was already in pain, but his mind insisted that he was as thirsty as before. Stopping was out of the question.

Telamont waited until Galaeron was finished, then refilled the dipper and held it in front of him. Though Galaeron felt like he might vomit up what he had already swallowed at any moment, and spill Alustriel and Dove on the Most High's feet, he wanted that water. He ached for it in the way he ached to touch the Shadow Weave, in the way a suffocating man aches for air.

"There was too much," Galaeron said. "We couldn't carry it."

Telamont continued to hold the dipper away, but remained silent. His will began to press down on Galaeron, and this time Galaeron could think only of how thirsty he had been crossing the desert and how much he wanted that water, of how badly his stomach hurt already, of how good it would feel when he drank that last dipper and finally grew so full he had to bring up everything he had swallowed.

He heard himself saying, "Besides, Prince Yder is right. We wanted to be captured."

This drew a smirk from Yder and a flash of interest from the Most High. Telamont allowed Galaeron to take the dipper, then watched with the purple shadow of a smile as the contents vanished down the elf's throat. Galaeron felt water sloshing in his throat, and his jaws began to ache.

Telamont took the dipper and refilled it, and Galaeron found his hand reaching for it yet again. Telamont held the handle away and remained silent. The weight of his will was crushing, and Galaeron could think of nothing but his aching jaws, his bloated stomach, and his overwhelming thirst.

"We came to rescue Vala," he said.

"You see?" Malik was up and sliding off Aris's chest, flinging water in all directions as he gestured with his dipper. "My excellent plan worked!"

Telamont remained silent and continued to hold the dipper out of reach. Galaeron felt the shadow lord's will crushing down on him, trying to force out the rest of the truth. He clenched his jaws and thought only of Evereska and his loyal friend Aris, of how the giant and the Chosen were risking so much to help—and there was his mistake. A dark voice arose inside him, reminding him of the blood on the Chosen's hands, telling him they could not be trusted, whispering of necessary trade-offs and secret bargains with the phaerimm.

Galaeron's mouth began to open, and it seemed to him that it belonged to someone else, to the dark being inside—

And Malik was at the Most High's side.

"Anything I want," he said. "That was our bargain."

"If *you* brought me Galaeron Nihmedu," Telamont said. "As I recall, Malygris did that."

The weight of his will diminished, and Galaeron's mouth became his own again.

"It was *my* message that lured him out," Malik said. "If I had not sent word telling him to come and save Vala, he would still be hiding from your magic in his Arabellan bolt hole."

"Be careful who you argue with, little man."

Telamont grew distracted enough to let the dipper drift into reach. Still possessed by his thirst, Galaeron snatched the handle and began to drink . . . and knew his stomach had reached its limit. Even as he drained the last of its contents, he began to gag.

"This is not some back alley flea market," Telamont continued, paying no attention to Galaeron's discomfort. "And I am no trader in trinkets."

"Nor am I some idiot dragon who can be bought off with your unkept promises," Malik retorted.

This was too much for the Most High. Telamont's sleeve lashed out in Malik's direction, and the little man tumbled away into the shadows. Three heartbeats later, a loud thud sounded from the gloom high up in the vaulted ceiling. A long breath echoed down afterward, and a softer thump from a dark corner.

Galaeron drained the last drops in the dipper and felt the contents of his stomach starting to rise. Realizing there was no fighting his own body's reflex, he flung the dipper aside and covered his mouth with both hands, then began a frantic search for someplace he could expel the Chosen where the Most High and his princes would not see.

The blow that Telamont had struck Malik would have been enough to kill most men, much less the impact against the wall that had followed, or the long fall that had followed that. Yet even as Galaeron was pushing past Clariburnus with both hands over his mouth, Malik was limping out of the darkness, one impossibly twisted arm raised in Galaeron's direction.

"Ask him," Malik said. "Ask him if he did not receive a message from me that Vala's life was in grave danger, and if he did not allow himself to be captured so he could save her life."

There was an instant of silence then Telamont said, "As you wish . . . but I warn you, my patience is at an end."

Galaeron felt a familiar burden settling over him, but this time, the Most High would need to be patient. By then, Galaeron was leaning over Aris's leg, ejecting a watery torrent down between the giant's knees. He saw a pair of silvery flashes come splashing out and disappear into the shadows beneath Aris's huge thighs. He continued to vomit a foul-smelling bile, and the weight of Telamont's will vanished.

"I think we will leave the question unanswered for now, Malik." The Most High sounded a little queasy himself. "The fact of Galaeron's return matters more than who is responsible. Name your price—but do not presume too much."

"Me? Presume too much?"

Malik's delight was evident even over sound of Galaeron's continued retching.

The little man thought for a moment then said, "I am not the type to ask for much, er, much more than I think I can get. All I want is my friend Aris."

"The giant?" Telamont asked. "You wish me to spare his life?"

"Yes, that is what I wish," Malik said. "And to have him as my slave, since I am very sure you do not want him running loose in your city again . . . and since his statues will bring an even greater profit if I have no need to share."

"I see." Telamont began to chuckle. "You may have the giant—and with him, the responsibility to see that your slave does Shade no harm."

Galaeron finally stopped retching. Wiping his mouth, he turned to see a very battered Malik standing a few paces away, examining the giant from head to foot.

A cold sleeve settled on Galaeron's shoulder, and he turned to find Telamont standing beside him.

"Come, Galaeron, let us return to the Palace Most High," Telamont said as he guided the elf toward the Marshaling Plaza's gloomy exit. "After such a difficult journey, I am sure you must be starving."

CHAPTER TEN

1 Eleasias, the Year of Wild Magic

No hammer had ever felt so heavy in Aris's hand, nor any stone as unyielding—nor any work more forced. He was standing at the Black Portal inside his master's new church—Malik's Temple of the One and All—cutting a three-level relief of Cyric's sun-and-skull sigil above entrance. It was a perfunctory piece without heart, and given the egg-shaped corona surrounding the skull, badly flawed. He told himself that this was what came of slave labor, of forcing an artist to execute someone else's vision, but he knew better. The truth was that he lacked strength. With not a single opportunity since his arrival in Shade to expel Khelben, Laeral, and Storm from his stomach, he had refused to eat, and the long fast had left him too dizzy, weak, and blurry-eyed to do a good job.

Aris's guards—three of a dozen Shadovar warriors

hired by Malik to keep constant watch over him—made approving noises from below. Like most of their fellows, this trio acted more like assistants than keepers, passing him tools and running to fetch water kegs whenever he grew thirsty. They also heaped praise upon everything he did, even on the shape studies he made before beginning a new work. Aris did not know whether this was something they genuinely felt or that Malik had instructed them to do in the hope of keeping him happy and productive. In any case, the adoration had grown so ludicrous that the shape studies had to started to disappear when he was finished with them. He had started to shatter the roughs before discarding them, lest the guards—or, more likely, Malik—sell them as Aris originals. Even slaves had their standards.

Finally, he stepped back into the narthex to study his work and banged his skull on the rib of a ceiling vault. His head began to reel, and he had to brace himself against a column. His hammer, which he had not even realized he had dropped, clunked to the floor and sent a flake of marble as large as a vulture skittering down the arcade.

A guard peered out from around the column behind which he had dived for cover, his sapphire eyes shining like blue stars in his dark face.

"Aris?" The wispy voice belonged to Amararl or Gelthez—Aris could never tell one Shadovar from another. "Are you all right?"

Aris nodded but continued to lean against the column.

"You're sure?" This guard was bold enough to step over beside Aris's knee and ask, "Do you need a keg of water?"

"No, I am well." He flicked his free hand in the direction of the sun-and-skull relief and said, "Though it would be hard to tell from that."

"What are you talking about?" asked the first guard. "It's not beautiful, exactly, but compelling—*very* compelling. And those empty eyes . . ." He shuddered. "I can almost see the dark suns burning in them."

Aris pushed off the column and leaned forward, studying the eye sockets.

"You do not think the left eye is pear-shaped?" the giant asked."

The guard craned his neck to study the dark sigil.

"Maybe a little."

"Or the other one too large?" asked Aris.

"Larger than the other one," said the third guard. "But it only adds to the effect—and places it firmly in period."

"In period?" Aris scowled down. "What period?"

"Your Slave Period," the first guard said. "While your excellence of detail has slipped under Malik's output pressures, it's widely acknowledged that under bondage, your work has raised grimness to a level of the sublime."

"There's quite a debate raging among the princes as to whether this is your best work or your worst," said the second guard. "The Most High has yet to decree."

"What do you think?" asked the third. "It would be interesting to hear the artist's opinion."

"My opinion is that your princes know nothing about art," Aris grumbled. He started to retrieve his hammer, then suddenly realized there was a reason his keepers behaved more like assistants than guards. Trying to suppress a smile, he placed his hands on his knees and stooped down so he could speak quietly. "But I am flattered to know you think so highly of my work."

"Indeed," said the first. "Were it not for the chance to watch you, do you think anyone would work for what Malik is willing to pay?"

Now Aris *did* smile. "Is that why you were taking my shape studies?"

"Not exactly." The guards cast nervous looks at each other, then the second one continued, "We took a handful for ourselves—it's the only way someone less than a lord can afford your work—but Malik claimed most."

"He was offering them as gifts to anyone who joined his church," said the third guard.

"Why am I not surprised?" Aris growled. "After all I taught him, he knows better than to show a rough!"

The Shadovar shared smiles, then the first one said, "He certainly knew you would not like what he was doing. You should have seen his face when we told him you had started breaking them."

"I thought his eyes would pop out of his head," the second chuckled. "He actually lay on the floor beating it."

"Yes, I would have liked to see that."

Of all the betrayals Malik had perpetrated on him, Aris considered distributing his shape studies to be the worst. But he had more immediate problems to worry about, namely finding a few moments of privacy so he could swallow Storm's pill and free the Chosen—before he starved to death. Kneeling on the floor so he could speak even more softly, he fixed his gaze on the first guard, who seemed to be more or less the leader of this trio.

"Gelthez, it is not fair that Malik profits so much from my work," Aris said, "while he pays you a starving wage."

"Amararl," the guard corrected. He shrugged. "There are many things in this world that are not fair."

Aris winced inwardly and forced himself to continue in a casual manner. "That's so, but it's also true that friends must do what friends can to make the world better for each other. I think I'll make a piece for each of you, if you would like that."

The mouths of all three dropped open.

"There's nothing I would treasure more!" gasped Amararl.

"It's true what the Arabellans say," the second guard added. "Your heart is as big as you are."

The third guard was not so enthusiastic.

"What would Malik say?"

"Malik may own me, but my work is mine to give."

"I am certain he would feel otherwise," said the third guard. "And the Most High would agree. Whatever a slave makes, a master owns. That is a law as old as Shade itself."

"How unfortunate." Aris sighed heavily. "That is a strange law. No giant would ever honor it."

Aris left the statement to hang and retrieved his hammer, but continued to kneel on the floor and pretended to study his work. Just as he taught Malik the basics of sculpting, Malik had taught him the principles of negotiation. If his plan was to succeed, he knew that the guards themselves would have to suggest the critical illicit step.

It took only a moment before the first guard, Amararl, turned to the third. "Malik wouldn't have to know, Karbe."

"Of course he would have to know," Karbe said, his amber eyes flashing in anger. "He is the Seraph of my lord Cyric, the One and All! We could no more deceive him than the Most—"

The objection came to a strangled end as a dagger tip—it belonged to the second guard, Gelthez—erupted from Karbe's chest. Aris cried out in shock, but Amararl reacted by clasping his hand over the mouth of the dying Shadovar and pushing him back onto his attacker's blade. Gelthez finished the murder with a quick back and forth flick, then withdrew the weapon and let his victim collapse to the ground.

"I was so tired of listening to all that babble about 'The One,'" Gelthez said. "He was about to drive me as mad as his god."

Amararl kicked the corpse to be certain it was dead, then nodded and looked up at Aris and said, "I think we can work something out."

Aris could not stop staring at the corpse. Though he had seen plenty of death in battle, this was the first time he had ever been present at—no, been *involved* in—a murder.

"You killed him!" Aris gasped.

"Don't worry about him, Aris." Gelthez knelt over the body and wiped his dagger on its cloak. "He converted. It is no less than he deserved."

"Converted?" Aris asked. "From what?"

"That is not important. Now, what is it you want?" Amararl asked. "We may not have—"

They were interrupted by the muffled voice of someone approaching the Black Portal.

"As you can see, Prince," Malik was saying, "all of the sculpting is being done by my slave Aris—when he is not busy on his statues, of course."

Amararl and Gelthez looked to each other, their jewel-colored eyes sparkling with alarm.

"*Prince*?" Gelthez mouthed.

Their gazes dropped to the corpse between them, and Amararl mouthed some curse Aris did not understand.

"And should you decide to become a member of Malik's Temple of the One and All," Malik continued, "you will receive a discount of a quarter of the price on any of Aris's works you purchase."

The sound of Malik's feet scuffing the stairs came through the portal. Aris glanced outside, but saw only the murky facades of the buildings across the square.

"A discount?" It was the wispy voice of Prince Yder. "That does not seem much of a gift for the prestige I would bring by converting."

Gelthez grabbed Karbe by the arms and started to drag him away, but the spreading pool of blood made vain any hope of concealing the corpse. Aris pushed the body back to the floor, then motioned the two Shadovar aside.

"Of course, the discount is only on purchases made *after* you become a worshiper of the One." Malik's voice grew more distinct as he neared the top of the stairs. "Once you have announced your conversion, it will be my pleasure to make a gift to you of any work you desire."

"You are too kind." Yder's voice was even colder and more sibilant than usual. "I shall look forward to touring Aris's studio."

Outside, the crown of the prince's head was just rising into view. Aris stood and dropped his hammer on Karbe. It hit with a resounding thud, obliterating all evidence of the murder in a spray of blood and bone.

The conversation outside fell silent.

Aris dropped to his rump with a crash far louder than the sound the hammer had made, then braced his head in his hands. There was no need to pretend he was dizzy. His head was already reeling from rising and coming back down too fast.

Malik rushed through the Black Portal. On his heels followed Yder, with a dozen gold-armored escorts close behind him. All eyes instantly fell on the mess beneath Aris's hammer.

"What is this I see?" Malik gasped.

Gelthez was quick with the answer, "Aris did it!"

Aris glanced over and saw the Shadovar, trembling in fear of Yder, drawing his sword.

"Yes, that's what happened." Amararl stepped to Aris's other side. "He grew dizzy and dropped his hammer. It happened to land on Karbe."

"Is that so?"

Malik studied the mess beneath the stone hammer and the pool of blood spreading across the dark floor. When he saw the chip Aris had dislodged earlier, he marched across the narthex, his eyes bulging and his finger wagging.

"Look what you have done to my floor, you clumsy giant!" He stopped and stood in the divot. "If you would eat as I have commanded, you would have the strength to keep hold of your tools!"

Yder and his escorts followed Malik across the narthex.

"Aris is not eating?" asked the prince.

Malik cringed at his slip, then turned to face the prince. "It is nothing to concern yourself with." He tried to stop speaking there, but his face twisted into the bitter mask it made whenever Mystra's curse forced him to clarify a lie of omission. "He will certainly perish if he does not eat soon, but that will only increase the value of the pieces you purchase before he is gone."

Yder stepped past Malik to where Aris was sitting. Tall even for a prince of Shade, he barely had to tip his head back to meet Aris's gaze.

"Aris, why are you starving yourself?"

Afraid the prince would force an answer with the same magic Telamont used, Aris looked away and said the first thing that came to mind—well, the second, since the last thing he wanted to do was admit the truth.

"The food is not to my liking."

"What?" Malik said. "Have I not offered to prepare anything your heart desires? Have I not brought whole boars from your own home in the Greypeak Mountains and roasted them under your nose, only to see the entire beast vanish down a rubbish chute when you could not be enticed to eat one bite?"

Aris's mouth watered at the mere memory of the smell.

"I have never been fond of swine." His stomach growled its protest of the lie, but he added, "I am more fond of yaddleskwee."

"For the thousandth time," Malik demanded, "how can I serve yaddleskwee when you refuse to say what it is?"

This drew a sharp-fanged grin from Yder.

"I see," he said. "I think I know what this 'yaddleskwee' is."

Aris gulped, sincerely hoping the prince did not. A favorite of fire giants, yaddleskwee was the food he most hated in the world. Somehow, he had just never developed a taste for pickled beholder brains.

"You do?" Malik asked.

Yder nodded. "It is not that difficult to figure out." He raised his gaze back to Aris and said, "You refuse to eat because you are unhappy with Malik as a master."

Aris breathed a sigh of relief, and nodded. "He was once a friend—"

"As I am still! Had I not asked the Most High to make you my slave, who knows what would have become of you?"

Malik paused there, fighting against his curse, then continued, "Though I doubt your fate would have been much worse, for Shade values your art too highly to execute you out of hand."

Aris ignored the protest and said, "But now he betrays me at every opportunity." Aris glared down at Malik, and allowing the bitterness of his tone to give voice to his very real anger, said, "And he betrays my art."

"Betray your art? Ungrateful giant! How many times must I save your life before you show thanks?"

Malik met Aris's glare with a fierceness born of his own injured feelings—then he seemed to recall the prince he was trying to impress and grimaced, no doubt mortified at how badly matters were going. He took a breath and composed himself, then turned to Yder.

"Pay no attention to the prattling of a temperamental artist, Prince Yder. I will deal with my slave later—and I assure you he *will* eat." Malik shot Aris a look of pure venom, then dared to touch the prince's elbow and gestured toward the nave. "For now, however, allow me to show you the rest of the temple."

Yder remained where he was and said, "I think not." He glared down at the hand on his arm until Malik removed it, then looked back to Aris. "It pleases me to hear you are unhappy in Malik's service."

Malik's eyes widened in alarm and he said, "If you think you can steal my slave—"

"Silence." Yder's hand was on Malik's throat, squeezing until it appeared the little man's eyes would pop from their sockets. "When I wish to hear your obscene voice again, I will break something and let you scream."

Given the shade of purple Malik's face was turning, Aris doubted the seraph could have protested had he dared try.

Aris asked, "Why should a slave's feelings interest a prince of Shade?"

Yder's yellow eyes glimmered in amusement.

"Because it would have been a great waste to eliminate you," he said, "and now I know you will not—"

The sentence ended in a screech as Malik drew the dagger he kept hidden beneath his robe and brought the curved blade up into Yder's wrist.

The prince's hand opened, and Malik wasted no time gathering his wits or getting his breath back. He fled through the nave and vanished into the darkness between two columns.

Yder flung his arm forward, and showing no apparent concern for the hand flapping at the end of his bleeding wrist, cried, "After him!"

Yder's escorts swept past in a dark rush, leaving Aris alone with his two guards and the prince. It was only a moment before the temple was filled with shouted commands and the chime of blades probing beneath black pews. Though Aris could not decide whether he was glad for Malik's escape or sorry for it, he was not worried about what happen to the little man once he was caught. The seraph had an uncanny—Ruha insisted god-given—ability to vanish the instant he was out of sight.

Still trying to figure out *why* Yder was chasing Malik, Aris asked, "You did not come here to convert?"

"Hardly."

Finally paying attention to his injury, Yder grabbed his flopping hand and pressed it back to his wrist. The bleeding ceased immediately, and black shadows began to swirl over the wound.

Yder continued, "It was bad enough when the worm stole the ear of the Most High, but this—" he rolled his eyes across the temple's vaulted ceiling—"this could not stand. It is good you were not a part of it."

Aris glanced up at the relief he had been working on and wondered how much the prince really knew about what he had been doing.

"You're no Cyricist, I mean," Yder said. "Your disappearance would have been difficult to explain."

Aris asked, "And Malik's won't?"

"No one will notice. You will finish his temple, but Malik will become a recluse, never to be seen by anyone except his personal servants—personal servants who are loyal to the Hidden One."

Aris did not have to ask who the Hidden One was. Though Shar had no temples in Shade—at least none he had ever noticed—the Mistress of the Night was popular enough in the city that Aris, gifted with the acute ears of most giants, seldom went more than a few hours without overhearing a whispered prayer to her.

At length, one of Yder's escorts emerged from the nave and dropped to a knee.

"High One, the blasphemer has vanished."

"Vanished?"

Yder glanced over to Aris's guards, who, already trembling in fear of their own fates, could only shrug and shake their heads. His golden eyes deepened to stormy brown, and he looked back to his escort.

"You have used the Hidden One's Gift?"

"We have, and still we could not find him," the warrior said. "He must have escaped."

"Escaped?" Yder's voice was cold and level. "How did you let that happen?"

The escort's gaze remained fixed on the floor.

"It is a mystery—" this was a favorite phrase of Shar's worshipers—"the exits remain blocked, and we've searched every vestibule and chapel."

Yder cursed under his breath, and it dawned on Aris how much the prince was risking. Malik had bragged many times about his relationship with Telamont and how his strategy to lure Galaeron back to Shade had earned the Most High's undying gratitude. If only half of what the seraph claimed was true—and Aris knew that Mystra's curse prevented him from telling a lie—then all Malik need do to save himself was reach the Palace Most High and report what had happened.

If Yder survived Telamont's wrath at all, his political base would be greatly weakened.

Having learned the hard way from Malik's treachery, Aris thought he saw a way to turn the situation to his advantage. He could not volunteer the information too readily. Malik had taught him that the surest way to manipulate someone was to remind him of his problem, then let him think you knew a way to solve it.

"I may know where he went," Aris said.

Yder spun on him. "And you remain silent?"

"It didn't occur to me that you would want the opinion of a slave."

"You are a slave by the Most High's decree," Yder said. "There is nothing I can do about that."

Aris shrugged. "It was also his decree that Malik be my—"

In a movement as smooth as a sliding shadow, Yder leaped into Aris's lap and had the tip of a black sword pressed to his throat.

"If I am to be suffer once for defying the Most High, I may as well suffer twice."

"There's a trapdoor under the altar." Aris began to wonder if he had played the game a little too well, and added, "Gelthez can show you."

Yder turned his yellow eyes on the guard.

Gelthez's jaw fell. "T-t-trapdoor?" He continued to stammer for a moment, then finally seemed to understand what Aris was doing to him. "He's lying!"

"Go look. You open it by pressing on the left corner of the base stone."

Aris had no idea whether this was where Malik had fled, but having built the secret door himself, he did know that Yder would find the passage.

"If Gelthez refused to open it for you," the giant added, "perhaps it's because he has converted."

"Converted?" Gelthez gasped. He reached for his sword and spat, "Liar!"

Yder's escort caught the guard's arm before it could reach his scabbard, then slipped behind him and pressed a dagger to his back.

Gelthez turned to Yder with a look of desperation.

"You cannot listen to him, my prince. He is a murderer! He killed Karbe."

Yder stepped off Aris's lap and said, "I thought that was an accident."

"No, it was—"

"I wasn't talking to you," Yder said.

When he turned to Amararl, it was all Aris could do to keep from smiling. Amararl had no choice except to back up Aris or admit that he had lied earlier.

"The hammer was dropped, my prince," he said. "It did not look intentional to me."

This was enough for Yder, who nodded to the escort and said, "Take him and see. If he shows you how to open the door, spare his life."

The escort bowed, and still holding his dagger at the man's back, turned to leave.

"Send a company to the temple treasure vault," Yder said. "I'll join you there after I see to the giant."

"The treasure vault, my prince?" the escort asked.

"Where else would Malik lay a secret tunnel?" Yder said.

Aris's heart fell. He had Amararl in his hold just as Malik had taught him, but that would do him no good with a prince of Shade standing there.

Yder glared at Amararl and said, "Why did you not tell me about this trapdoor, guard? Are you also a Cyric-worshiper?"

"Never, my prince!" Amararl spat on the floor and said, "That is all I have for the Mad One."

Yder remained silent, awaiting his answer.

"I—I knew nothing about the door," Amararl said. "I was not guarding the giant when he built the altar."

The prince looked to Aris, who confirmed the claim with a nod.

"Gelthez was with a different group that day," Aris lied. He was beginning to think he had spent too much time in Malik's temple; the lies were beginning come as easily as his own breath. "That was when Malik converted them."

"You will give me these names, giant."

Aris shrugged noncommittally, then finally saw how he was going to get what he wanted.

"If you like, but they will be no good to you if you do not beat Malik to his treasure vault."

Yder's eyes brightened in alarm.

"He has escape magic there?"

"He doesn't need it," Aris said. "He has a blessing from his god that helps him hide. That's how he—"

Aris had no need to finish. Yder was already rushing into the nave, calling back over his shoulder for Amararl to stand watch on the slave.

No sooner was the prince out of sight than Amararl braced himself against a black column and sank to the floor, his legs trembling and his brow dripping with sweat.

"Well done, giant," he said. "What is it you want?"

"Nothing that will get you in trouble," the giant replied. Feeling nearly as relieved as the guard, Aris started for a dark corner. "Only a few minutes alone."

CHAPTER ELEVEN

1 Eleasias, the Year of Wild Magic

Malik pulled himself up inside the false coffer in his treasure vault and kneeled there in the cramped darkness, his breath coming heavy and fast, his throat raw and aching where Yder had nearly crushed it. An alarming rasp and rattle was building behind him as his pursuers scurried up the tunnel, and even with the gifts of stealth and endurance bestowed on him by the One, he would need to hurry if he wished to stay ahead of them. It would not be easy, not when every gasp of air fanned the anguish burning in his crushed gullet, but he had to reach the palace before Yder and inform the Most High of the prince's treachery. In circumstances such as these, a ruler's findings were always dictated by the one who arrived first.

Voices began to whisper up the tunnel, and

Malik knew he would be doing well to gather even the bags containing his most valuable gems before they entered the vault behind him.

"Accursed giant!" he hissed. Only Aris knew about the secret tunnel, as Malik had made him construct it secretly at night, when everyone assumed he would be sleeping. "Why am I vexed with friends who never think of anyone but themselves?"

Vowing that the giant would pay for his selfishness, Malik released the latches that held the coffer closed. Using his back to lift the lid, he rose to a crouch. The vault was dark, quiet, and enormous. Save for perhaps two dozen coin boxes and gem bags, it was also mostly empty. Building a temple was expensive—even when wealthy converts donated much of the material in exchange for Aris's statues—but Malik had no doubt the investment would prove worthwhile. Once the interior frieze work was completed, he planned to start charging a hefty fee to come and stand in the narthex. Any who wished to see the sublime work in the rest of the temple would be required to convert—a process that would require a substantial offering as proof of the novice's sincerity.

A Shadovar helmet thunked into the low lintel where the tunnel crossed the treasure vault's foundation. Reminded of the urgency of his situation, Malik slipped out of the coffer and lowered the lid as quietly as possible. The latches clicked softly as they reengaged, and he began to fumble for the magic lamp he kept on the floor at the corner of the coffer.

Instead of the smooth loop of a lamp handle, his hand found what felt like the scuff-roughened toe of a veserab-hide boot. Malik's mouth went instantly as dry as dust, and he reached for the curved dagger hidden inside his cloak. A strong hand caught him by a horn and lifted him off his feet. A second hand, still shaky because of the tendons Malik had slashed but more than strong enough to hold him motionless, clamped hold of his wrist.

"Not this time, my behorned friend," said Yder's hissing voice. "Not even you surprise me twice."

The prince bent Malik's hand back until he screamed and let the dagger fall free.

"The One will not stand for this!" Malik warned. He thought for a moment that Mystra's curse might actually permit the threat to stand, but soon heard more words tumbling from his mouth. "He will certainly punish me terribly for allowing you to interfere with the completion of his—"

The prince released Malik's wrist and brought his fist up. The blow drove Malik's jaws together with a tooth-shattering crack, and he had just enough time before sinking into darkness to wonder what would have happened to him had Yder hit him with his good hand.

Wet, pale, and tiny, the Chosen looked like a trio of newborn whelps—like a trio of *stillborn* whelps, as motionless and silent as they were. Worried that the fall to the vestry floor might have been too long for such small creatures—even on his hands and knees, the distance was more than six feet—Aris reached down and nudged Khelben with the nail of his index finger.

Nothing happened, except that Khelben flopped onto his back.

Aris placed a fingertip on Khelben's chest and felt nothing. Of course, given their size differences, searching for a heartbeat was akin to a human feeling for the pulse of a locust.

"Wake up," he whispered. "You *must* be tougher than that—you're Chosen!"

When Khelben remained motionless, Aris sighed and rolled first Storm, then Laeral onto their backs. When neither moved, he placed them side-by-side and checked for signs of life as he had with Khelben.

"Hey—watch those fingers!" warned a tiny female voice.

Raising his brow in surprise, Aris put his hands down and lowered his head to within a yard of the floor, now squinting in an attempt to keep the Chosen in focus at such a close distance.

"My apologies," he whispered. "I was only feeling for a—"

"We know what you were feeling for," chuckled a second tiny woman. "And I thought an artist would be different!"

Aris turned his head from side to side, trying to get a better view of the three figures stretched out beneath his head. None of them seemed to be speaking or moving, but considering that they were Chosen, that meant very little.

"Up here, big fella," said the first voice. "Beside you."

Aris turned in the direction of the speaker and found himself looking into a pair of tiny, ivory-colored blurs. He leaned away, and the blurs slowly resolved themselves into the beautiful faces of Alustriel Silverhand and Dove Falconhand. Still only half the size of his thumb, the two Chosen were dressed in flowing black cloaks that, as they hovered beside him, gave them the appearance of some sort of shadow sprites.

"Where did you come from?" Aris gasped.

"We've been keeping an eye on you," Dove said, chuckling at his surprise.

"This is no time to play games," Aris complained. He glanced down the passage to make certain that his guard, Amararl, was still out in the nave as he had promised—and to be sure that there were no other Shadovar approaching the vestry. "Yder is here with a small army."

"I'd call it more of a strike team," Alustriel said. "When we realized where it was going, we thought we'd better tag along and see what was happening."

"A good thing we did, too," Dove said. "This is the first time we've found you alone."

"It's the first time I've *been* alone—as you can see." Aris waved a hand at the motionless Chosen on the floor. "Was it too long? I didn't eat anything, but I don't think anyone expected it to take this long."

Alustriel's voice grew reassuring. "They'll be fine, as soon as I wake them."

She flew down to the floor and kneeled beside Khelben, then began to slap his face and whisper his name into his ear.

"They went into a magical hibernation." Dove explained. She hovered near Aris's head, watching down the passage with him. "After the third or fourth day without food—earlier, if they refused to drink water you'd already drunk—their bodies would have started to draw on the Weave to sustain them. Even a giant could not have withstood that much magic flowing through him for very long, so they used a spell to shut down."

"Like bears when the snow comes."

"Something like that. Except there's still been a little magic flowing through your body. It gave you the strength to work at Malik's tempo, but it's also done some damage—affected your coordination and perception, made it difficult to do things that should be easy." Dove pointed at a lopsided likeness of Cyric on the wall. "As soon as you burn off the last of that energy, you're going to fall asleep for a very long time. Before that happens, you should eat. Eat as much as you can keep down."

"As much as I can keep down?" Aris's mouth began to water at the prospect. "When can I start?"

"Soon," Dove laughed. "but first, keep watch while I remind the Blackstaff where he is."

She gestured at the floor, where Khelben's eyelids were fluttering and his chest rising at regular intervals. Alustriel had moved on to Laeral.

Khelben's eyes opened. He took one look at the images of madness decorating the vestry and scowled in alarm.

"You had better hurry," Aris said. "One look at these walls, and he's liable to think he's gone to the Nine Hells."

Dove was already dropping to his side. She pulled her

hood back and let her silver hair spill free, then took Khelben's arm.

"Now don't start hurling spells around," she said. "There's nothing to worry about."

"Of course there's something to worry about—" Khelben pushed himself into a seated position—"can't you see what Aris has been carving?"

Out in the nave, Amararl peered into the vestry passage with a beetled brow.

Aris looked down at the five Chosen, gestured in the direction of the nave, and said, "My guard's patience is coming to an end."

"Let's risk a few moments longer, in case we have need of your knowledge," Khelben said. He turned to Dove and Alustriel. "What progress have you made? Given that the city still floats, I take it you have not destroyed the mythallar."

"We haven't even found it," Dove confirmed. "Asking Galaeron's help is out of the question. He's been locked inside the Palace Most High since we arrived, and we can't go inside."

"Dare not go inside," Alustriel corrected. "It seems to be a nexus in the Shadow Weave. The closer we approach, the weaker our connection to the Weave. If we were to enter. . . ."

"No use in getting ourselves killed," Khelben agreed.

"But we have made this," Dove said as she produced something from inside her cloak. It was so tiny that it took a moment for Aris to recognize it as a folded sheet of parchment. "This shows most of the city, save for what's within the walls of the Palace Most High."

Khelben took the parchment and began to open it.

"Maybe Aris can help us," he said.

"I fear not. I've never been to the mythallar." Aris peeked out into the nave and found Amararl starting toward the vestry passage. "I should go, before—"

"I said *help*." Khelben spread the parchment on the floor and continued, "Even if you don't know where it is, you have a better idea of where to search than we do."

Aris regarded the parchment dubiously. Though it had opened to the width of Khelben's arm, it was little larger than a thumbnail to him.

"How can I read a map I can barely see?" he asked.

"Try," Dove said.

Aris glanced back to find Amararl coming down the side aisle toward the vestry, then he sighed and stooped down to obey. The instant his eyes fell on it, the image floated off the parchment and began to expand, growing so large he could barely take in all he could see.

Amazed, Aris diligently studied the map, systematically running his gaze along each street and down every service passage. It didn't take him long to realize that the image was adjusting itself to his scrutiny, sliding past beneath him to keep centered the object of his attention, growing larger or smaller depending how long his eyes remained fixed on a certain area.

Amararl's voice came down the passage, "Aris?" He sounded more worried than demanding. "What are you doing in there? What's that light?"

"Our bargain was for privacy!"

Though the voice that boomed this sounded like Aris's, it was from Alustriel's tiny mouth that the words came.

"Our bargain was for a few minutes of privacy," Amararl corrected. "It has been ten—and I heard voices."

"Echoes," Alustriel retorted. "The temple is filled with Yder's warriors."

Amararl considered this a moment, and said, "Warriors who will be returning soon. If you're not here, I'll say you ran off."

"And I that you allowed me to," Alustriel said. "Therefore, I suggest you return to your post. Tell me when you hear someone coming."

"I'm your guard, not your servant!"

"There is no difference, now," Alustriel shot back. "Unless you wish to meet the same end as Gelthez or Karbe."

She raised her tiny hand and flicked her fingers in a spell, then said in her normal voice, "Never mind him, Aris. We can still hear if he sounds an alarm, but now he can't hear or see anything in this room."

Aris spent another five minutes studying the map, then finally looked through the translucent image at the Chosen below.

"I just don't know," he said. "If I had to guess, I'd say it was inside the Palace Most High."

"That was our first thought too," Dove said, "but during the battle Galaeron described, the phaerimm were using magic. Unless they've learned to tap into the Shadow Weave—"

"We've seen no sign of that," said Laeral, who was standing with her sister Storm at Khelben's side, "but it still doesn't mean you don't have to go through the palace to reach it."

"Yes, it does," Storm said. "The phaerimm got there."

"With the aid of a malaugrym," Dove pointed out. "It might have been able to sneak them through the palace."

"Would *you* trust your life to a Malaugrym?" Storm countered. Without waiting for a reply, she continued, "If the phaerimm can get there, so can we."

"If we can find it," Laeral said. "If Galaeron can't help us—"

"We'll have to ask Vala," Khelben finished.

"Her, I can help you find," said the giant.

Aris shifted his scrutiny to the great plaza of gloom sculptures that surrounded the Palace Most High, then slowly moved his gaze along the edge until he came to a huge, many-spired mansion with a procession of flying buttresses and a long tunnel of barrel vaults.

"You will find her here, somewhere inside Escanor's palace."

The Chosen studied the map from below for a moment then Khelben said, "It would be nice if any of us had actually met her. The Shadovar were obviously trying to lure

Galaeron back with all those rumors about her being Escanor's slave. What if they're just that—rumors?"

"A good point," Storm agreed. "Vala and her men *were* in service to Melegaunt, and I have it on good authority that she slew three phaerimm for them in Myth Drannor."

"Vala and her men served Melegaunt in order to keep an oath their ancestors had sworn," Aris said. "Their duty was discharged when Shade returned."

"But that does not mean she is Escanor's slave," Storm pressed. "Ruha said that it was her choice to remain with the prince."

"So Galaeron would escape before his shadow took him," Aris said. Storm's aspersions were beginning to irritate him, and he let it show. "She loves Galaeron as a crane loves its mate. If she is with Escanor now, it is not by her choice."

Storm raised her brow at his tone, but shrugged and gave a little nod.

"If you say so, Aris."

"I do," he said. "If you wish her help, all you need do is say you are friends of Galaeron's."

"Good," Khelben said. He began to fold the parchment, and the map went dark. "That's just what we'll do. My thanks for your help, Aris. We'll try to fetch you before the city falls, but that may be—"

"We are all risking much," Aris interrupted, "but only Galaeron's sacrifice is certain. If you value that, save Vala first. The rest of us are here by choice."

"If that is what you wish, my friend." Khelben met his eye and nodded. "We will do what can be done."

Malik awoke to the sound of snakes hissing into both ears. Judging by how he felt, they had bitten him a dozen times, a hundred times. His head throbbed and his back ached. There were pins of light piercing his eyes and rivers of fire coursing through his veins, and he had a bladder that felt like two gallons of wine in one gallon of space. The snakes were about to draw him into quarters. They had him by each wrist and each ankle, and they were all pulling in opposite directions. His arms were ready to pop from his shoulders and his legs to divide what no man ever wished to have divided.

As Malik's head began to clear, the hissing grew softer and more distant, and he realized it was not snakes hissing into his ears. It was voices, the whispering voices that filled the throne room of Telamont Tanthul.

If he was in the presence of the Most High and in so much pain, there could only be one explanation.

Yder had beat him to the palace.

"It is not true!" Malik screamed. "Whatever the prince says, it is all a terrible lie!"

For once, his curse did not compel him to say more, and the whispering quieted. A strange sloshing sounded beside him. Malik opened his eyes and saw white fire in his brain. He closed them again, and the fire went away.

"Why do you torment me like this?"

He tried to turn toward the sloshing and found his head held motionless by a strap across his brow.

"I have done nothing wrong!"

"Oh, but you have, Seraph," hissed a cold voice—a familiar cold voice. "You have stolen from the Hidden One."

"Stolen?" Malik cried. "What have I stolen . . . aside from a few dozen coins from the pockets of worshipers in my own temple?"

"The worshipers themselves," the voice said. "You have stolen the Lady's faithful."

Malik was greatly relieved to recognize the voices as Prince Yder's. If Yder was doing the speaking, then they would not be in the Palace Most High, and it could not be Telamont Tanthul who had ordered the terrible punishment.

A pair of cold fingertips pulled Malik's eyelids open. The

brilliant fire returned, but this time the white fire was only a silver light as blinding as the sun, and there was a chasmal darkness in the center—with two blazing eyes and a heart of cooling embers.

"The Lady is angry, Malik."

As Yder spoke, Malik's eyes grew accustomed to the pain, and he discerned a pair of huge hooked horns crowning the head of the dark figure above him.

"In-d-deed," Malik stammered. "I can see that for myself . . . though in truth I must say she does not look very lady-like to me."

This caused a strange murmur of gasps and chuckles to spread outward behind Yder. There followed a moment of silence, and Malik had the sense that his captor had turned away to glare at his followers.

"Make a joke of your own god if you wish, little man," Yder said, "but when you make fun of the Hidden One, it is the Lady who laughs."

The prince's fingers pressed down until Malik thought his eyeballs would burst.

"Who was joking?" Malik cried.

The murmur that followed this was even louder than the first. Yder's hand came away from Malik's head.

"Silence!"

The command was muffled, as though the prince had turned his back when he spoke it. Malik blinked the spots from his eyes and again found himself staring at the dark figure overhead. It was a ghastly demon as large as Aris and as black as night itself, with long curving talons at the end of outstretched arms.

Yder returned his attention to Malik and said, "Mock the Hidden One again, and I shall pull your brains out by your own antlers."

The prince grabbed Malik by one of his horns, and a dark hand appeared on the hooked horn of the figure overhead.

Malik bit his own cheek, lest he cry out in astonishment

and give the prince an excuse to do as he threatened. The monster above was certainly his own shadow, but that gave him no hint of relief. Melegaunt Tanthul had once summoned the wretched being to serve as a guard, and the accursed thing had made clear it would like nothing better than throttling Malik with its own hands.

"You are learning, Seraph," Yder said. "Perhaps this will not be as difficult as I feared."

"Not difficult would be good," Malik agreed. "I am a captive in the temple of Shar the Ni—?"

Yder struck him a blow that returned his thoughts to their muddled state.

"Do not speak the Hidden One's name!"

"I am only trying to be certain," Malik complained. "How do you expect to convert me, if you will not tell me who it is I am to worship?"

For the first time, Yder's face came into view. He was wearing the black skullcap and purple mask of the high priest.

"You would convert?" he asked.

Malik's chest began to grow cold and tight, as it had when Fzoul Chembryl had asked a similar question in the hidden temple of Iyachtu Xvim. At the time, he had been weak from torture and assured only of a life of impoverishment in servitude to a mad god, and nothing would have pleased him more than to find protection in the church of some other deity. But that had been before he understood how impossible it was for him to betray the One, and before he had established what promised to be—in addition to the altar that would give Cyric control over the Shadow Weave—the wealthiest temple in all Faerûn.

"Convert?"

The tightness in Malik's breast became a smashing weight. The heart beating—slurping—in his chest was not his own, but a rotting mass of curd that, in a fit of the deranged genius of the mad god, the One had plucked from his own body and traded for Malik's mortal—though far healthier—heart. Since that day, the mere thought of betraying Cyric brought crushing agony. It was all Malik could do to continue speaking.

"Certainly I will convert." His chest felt as though someone was standing on it. "I will convert you and all of your followers to the Church of Cyric, the One and All!"

The weight vanished.

Yder's fist came from nowhere, catching Malik in the side of the mouth. Two teeth came loose and got caught in his throat. Malik began to choke.

"Trifle with me all you wish," Yder said. "The goddess relishes your blood on her altar."

Malik's only answer was a cough. He grew dizzy from lack of breath, and the world started to close in around him. He fought to stay conscious, summoning his anger by imagining his wealth in the hands of Prince Yder and his filthy Sharists.

"Nothing to say?"

Yder struck him again, and Malik's mouth grew so full of blood that it bubbled over his lips and spilled down his cheeks onto Shar's altar.

"That is good, Seraph," Yder said. "You are learning to please the Lady."

Unable to do anything else, Malik stared at the monstrous shadow hanging above him. A purple crescent appeared where the traitorous thing's mouth should have been—a smile. It thought he was going to choke to death.

Malik continued to cough.

"You *will* convert, Seraph," Yder said. "All you control is how long it takes."

"The Hidden One rules all," said someone behind the prince.

A chorus of whispers filled the chamber as Shar's worshipers repeated the paean. Had he not been so busy coughing and choking, Malik would have laughed. He might die upon Shar's altar or even rot upon it, but he would never convert. That was the one thing he did not control at all.

Malik's vision narrowed to a black tunnel, then went completely black. Yder's voice came to him from far away, demanding that he pay attention and not insult the Hidden One by closing his eyes upon her. The prince's cold fingertips settled on his eyelids and pulled them open, and that was the last thing Malik felt before sinking into a soft bed of unconsciousness.

The next thing was the heel of a large hand slamming him between the shoulders, and the icy fingers of another one dangling him upside down by his ankle.

"Breathe, you craven little ranag!"

The hand struck Malik again. The teeth upon which he had been choking flew from his lips, along with a mouthful of blood and bitter-tasting bile. He started to gasp and cough at the same time, two conflicting actions that left him helplessly hiccuping for breath.

"Did you really think you could escape that easily?" Yder demanded. "The Hidden One will not be deprived of her pleasure."

Malik opened his eyes and was blinded by the same painful radiance as when he had returned to consciousness before.

"And I am most thankful for that," Malik said, "though I know it is likely to cost me a month of terrible agony!"

Knowing Yder would interpret his gratitude as progress toward a conversion, Malik would have liked to stop there and enjoy the reward any good torturer would bestow on him as incentive for further progress—but Mystra's curse would not allow it.

"Now I can finish what I have started by converting you and your followers to the Church of Cyric—" Malik tried to bring his hands up to cover his mouth, but found his wrists manacled together behind his back. The words continued to spill out—"so that I may spare my soul the danger of having to present itself at the Shattered Castle after I have failed to seize control of the Shadow Weave for the One, as he instructed."

Yder shook with such a rage that the chains binding Malik's wrists began to jingle. Malik cringed and tried to guess whether he would lose fewer teeth by clenching his jaw or leaving it to hang slack, but the blow never came. Instead, the prince remained silent and continued to hold him upside down, allowing Malik a few precious moments to study his surroundings.

They were, as Malik had guessed from the altar, in a temple to Shar—though it was certainly far from what he had imagined such a place would look like. While the walls were covered with the expected images of mysterious women and dark disks limned in purple flame, the chamber itself was blindingly bright, so much so that the shadows dancing on the walls seemed more real than the worshipers standing motionless in long rows of pews. There were easily a thousand Shadovar there, all submerged to their knees in a glimmering pool of mirror-bright fluid. As thick and viscous as quicksilver, the liquid was slowly flowing out toward the edges of the chamber, where it gathered at the walls and vanished down the drainage pits in lazy whirlpools.

Malik recognized the liquid instantly. It was the same thing that he and his friends had found inside the Red Butte in Karsus, spilling out of the Karsestone that Galaeron had used to summon Shade back into the world.

The prince hoisted Malik by the chain between his manacles, forcing his arms up and back until he thought his shoulders would break.

"In my centuries," Yder said, "I have learned a few things about pain."

Malik felt sick to his stomach. Though the One had blessed him with the ability to suffer any amount of agony and still have the strength to perform his duties as Seraph, that did not mean he was immune to pain. Quite the contrary.

It seemed to him that he always felt pain more acutely than those around him—and usually a great deal more of it.

As Yder turned back toward the altar, Malik was not all that surprised to find himself looking at a luminous white boulder about the size of a horse. There was a jagged fissure down the center, and from this crack poured a steady flow of the silvery liquid that had filled the temple.

The stream was, Malik knew from his earlier adventures in the Red Butte, the last whole magic in the world. Seventeen centuries earlier, a mad Netherese archwizard named Karsus had tried to steal the godhead of Mystryl, the goddess of magic at that time. It had been a terrible mistake. The Weave had filled Karsus to bursting and killed him on the spot, and it had split into the Weave and the Shadow Weave. The luminous white boulder was Karsus's heart—all that remained of the mad archwizard—and the silver magic pouring from it was all the remained of the original, unsplit Weave.

Though Cyric's rancid heart began to slush so hard that Malik could barely hear himself think, he forced himself to remain calm. The Karsestone, as they had dubbed the boulder, was undoubtedly an artifact of untold power, but it seemed to Malik that for Shar's worshipers to tolerate its bright light inside their hidden temple, it had to be something more—something much more.

"The Karsestone!" Malik gasped as though he had just realized what he was looking at, for it was important to his plan that Yder did not realize how much Malik understood about what he was seeing. "That seems an odd altar for followers of the Nightsinger."

"Shadow is born of light," Yder said.

The phrase was repeated by a thousand whispering voices as Yder hoisted Malik onto the stone and laid him facedown.

"All the same, so much bright light must be a great insult to your goddess . . . unless the Karsestone is the source of the Shadow Weave, of course." Malik swore a silent oath, for it been Mystra's curse that compelled him to add such a clumsy probe, then he hastened to add, "Or the one you worship here is not really Shar, but some other Hidden—"

Malik's face smashed into stone as his tactic succeeded in angering the prince and distracting him from the gaff.

"I told you never to call the Hidden One by name."

"My apologies," Malik said. His voice sounded rather nasal, for his nose had been shattered and was pouring blood down over the Karsestone. "I only meant that this is certainly the last place the Most High would look for his stolen Karsestone."

"What makes you think it is stolen?" Yder asked, not quite able to keep the smugness from his voice.

Ever wary of the Seraph's ability to escape, the prince pinned Malik's neck to the stone with one hand while he removed the chain from the manacles and attached it to a ring hanging from an iron post alongside the altar. Malik didn't know whether to be glad his plan had worked or ashamed it had taken so long for him to see the true nature of things.

For the Shar worshipers to tolerate the Karsestone's brilliance in their temple—and, more importantly, for the goddess not to strike dead the ones who permitted it to be there—the boulder had to be of inestimable value to the Nightsinger. Malik no longer doubted that much—it was the source of the Shadow Weave, as Mystra's curse had caused him to blurt out, or something that she wished to keep hidden from the other gods.

More terribly, if Shar considered Shade a safe place to hide such a thing—and if Telamont Tanthul truly had given the Karsestone to Yder for the Hidden One's temple—then she had to feel secure in her control of the city. For Shar to feel secure in her command of the Shadovar, she had to control the Shadow Weave itself.

"The spiteful hag!" Malik cried. "She has commanded it all along!"

"Curse her now all you wish, Malik."

Yder spun him around then flipped him onto his back and fastened another chain to his second manacle.

"Before this is done," the prince added, "you will sing her praises."

"And you will lick the offal from my boots!" Malik shot back. "The Shadow Weave is Cyric's by right! Am I not the one who saved the life of that fool Galaeron so he could betray his word to Jhingleshod and steal this stone?"

It was his own anger that compelled him to say this and not Mystra's curse, but he knew it was a mistake the moment the words spilled from his mouth. Yder's yellow eyes turned as bright as the sun. He bared his ceremonial fangs and bent so low that Malik feared the prince would bite his nose from his face.

"Is that why you came here?" he demanded. "To steal the Hidden One's crown?"

Malik said nothing and looked away.

"Answer!" Yder commanded. "Answer, or I will feed you to your own shadow."

The prince pulled his head aside so that Malik could see his shadow's hateful eyes glaring down at him. No longer did the monstrous thing seem dependent on Malik for its form. It looked as thick and as solid as any giant he had ever seen. Malik looked away on the pretext of meeting Yder's angry gaze.

"Do you think I am afraid of my own shadow?" he demanded. "I am favored of the One. I have seen a thousand things that were a hundred times worse . . . though never any who know all the wretched things I have done in my life."

"Look!" Yder grabbed Malik's aching jaw and forced him to stare up into his shadow's angry eyes. "You have seen the trouble Galaeron's shadow has brought on him. What do you think yours would do, were I to let it inside you?"

"Why should I fear such a thing?" Malik squeaked. "If a shadow is all the things I am not, this one is undoubtedly as charitable as I am selfish, as trustworthy as I am corrupt, as brave as I am craven. My shadow would only make me all the things that women desire and men admire."

"What of Cyric?" It was the shadow that asked this question—and that flashed a brutal purple smile as it did so. "How would he feel about a Seraph who was all those things?"

The blood went cold in Malik's veins, and he swung his gaze to Yder.

"What was your question again?"

CHAPTER TWELVE

1 Eleasias, the Year of Wild Magic

In the dim light of the cell, the link was easier for Vala to feel than to see, even with skin numbed by cold and calluses. She worked her foot up the chain until she felt pit-roughened metal, then pinched the loop between her toes and lifted it toward her mouth. Even flexible as she had grown over the past couple of months, she could not bring it all the way to her face. Once the chain went taut, she used her leg muscles to pull herself closer. She let her toes slide down one link then spit a mouthful of saliva onto the pitted surface.

Vala had her doubts about whether she could actually spit her way to freedom, but with her hands manacled behind her back and no other tools to work with, it was the best she could do, and it gave her something to focus on when she was not being abused by Escanor or his retainers. She could not just sit there in the dark, waiting between sessions. She had to keep trying, to know she was at least attempting to escape.

Besides, when she had started, there had been no pits in the link at all. Vala let the chain go slack, then wrapped her toes into it and began to jerk downward against the eye hook that secured it to the wall. A hundred times, then find the link and spit. If she just kept working at it, something would give. The hook would loosen in the wall, or the link would grow rusty and break, or a guard would think she had lost her mind and grow careless enough to let her kill him. *Something* would happen. It had to, if she was ever to see her son again.

A voice whispered, "Vala?"

Vala hit the end of the chain and was back on the floor before she realized she had jumped. She spun on her seat, her legs cocked for thrust kicks, and found no one there.

Great, she thought. Something *has* happened. I've started to hear things.

"We're not going to hurt you," the voice said.

Vala squinted toward the voice and saw nothing but murk, then a tiny man in black robes hopped onto her foot. She wasn't just hearing things. The man—the *delusion*, she corrected herself—had an unruly black beard and dark eyes, but his face and arms were too light to be Shadovar.

"No need to cower, my dear," he said. "We're friends of—"

Vala flicked the figure off her foot and heard it hit a wall with a real-sounding thud. She *was* cowering, frightened of her tortured mind's own phantasms.

"I won't let this happen," she said to herself. Vala straightened her shoulders and raised her chin—but she did not lower her leg. "Go away!"

"Softly, child!" This time the voice was female, and it came from over near the door. "Mind the guard."

Another voice, on her other side, began what sounded like a spell. The bearded figure returned, this time flanked by two female figures with flowing silver hair, and Vala realized that, phantasms or not, they were all around her. There could be hundreds of them out there in the dark, swarming over the floor. Thousands, maybe, an army of dark little shadow faeries come to feast now that her flesh was suitably battered and bruised. She screamed. She could not help herself, the sound just erupted as she let out her next breath.

The shadow faeries cringed and looked toward the door, and in the next moment Vala was silent. Her mouth remained open and her throat continued to vibrate, but there was no more sound.

The male faerie looked toward the door and asked, "The guard?"

"Still thinking about it," the female voice whispered. "He's curious, but not alarmed."

Vala could see her, another silver-haired faerie down on the floor, peering around the corner of the archway.

"Keep an eye on him," the male said.

Followed by the two silver-haired females, he circled toward Vala's head. They were joined by a third female, which fluttered over from behind Vala and settled on the floor next to them. Vala tried to spin around to bring her feet toward them but one of the females made a motion with a sliver-sized wand, and she found herself unable to move.

"I'm sorry we frightened you," the male said. "Clearly, your ordeal has taken more of a toll than we imagined."

Had Vala been able to talk, she would have suggested that they change places and see what kind of toll being a Shadovar slave took on him.

"Can you stop screaming?" asked one of the women. "We have some questions."

Vala grew aware of her aching jaw and realized that her mouth continued to gape open, that her throat was raw from screaming. She clamped her mouth shut and glared at the black-clad faeries beside her. They certainly looked solid enough.

The woman nodded, made a dismissive gesture, and a whimpering, rasping sound came to Vala's ears. It took a moment to identify the source as her own throat.

"Good," the man said. He held his hand out and moved it in a placating motion that made Vala want to kick him. "We're friends of Galaer—"

"Galaeron?" Vala finished for him.

She brought her breath under control. Phantasms or not, she could not have these faeries telling Galaeron that she had whimpered when they came for her.

"He sent you?" she asked.

The women looked at each other. They looked uncomfortable.

"What's wrong?" Vala demanded. "Is he hurt?"

"We wouldn't know," the man, whose manner was gruff, said.

One of the faerie women stepped in front of the male and said, "Galaeron is on a mission of the utmost importance to all of Faerûn."

"As are we," said the second woman, also stepping in front of the male. "Perhaps it would help if we introduced ourselves. I am Storm Silverhand."

"I'm Dove Falconhand," said the woman at the door.

"I am Alustriel Silverhand," said the woman who had cast the spells. She motioned at the last woman, who was still standing beside the black-bearded man. "This is our sister Laeral."

"And that would make me Khelben Arunsun." The faerie man pushed his way between the two women who had stepped in front of him. "Now that you're properly awed, maybe you'd care to answer a question or two and help us save the Heartlands."

Vala scowled down at the male, quite certain that she had lost her mind.

When she didn't say anything, Khelben rolled his eyes and turned to the one who had introduced herself as Alustriel.

"How can she not know who we are?" he asked. "Is Vaasa so backward?"

"We know of the Chosen even in Vaasa," Vala said. "We also know the difference between flesh and phantasm. Why would the five of you show up in my cell, the size of dolls, unless I were mad?"

"Because we need your help," Alustriel said. She stepped over and placed a hand on Vala's jaw. Her touch felt real enough, solid and warm. "We must find the mythallar, and you're the only one who can help."

"Trouble!" hissed the woman by the door. "The guard's coming."

The faeries vanished as quickly as they had appeared, leaving Vala alone in her cell.

"Wait!" She felt more isolated than ever—and more certain that she was losing her mind, more frightened. "Don't!"

The guard appeared in the doorway, a hulking shadow lord with ruby eyes and filed teeth. Vala thought he was Feslath, one of Escanor's favorites.

"Don't what?" Feslath demanded. "Who are you talking to?"

Though his Shadovar eyes could see in the dark as easily as Vala could see in daylight, he did not even bother glancing around the cell. He knew as well as she did that there was no one in the room, that her mind had finally snapped.

"I asked a question, slave."

Vala glared at him and refused to answer. She was not worried about revealing the presence of her visitors—the delusions were hidden safely inside her mind—but she could not obey, not even in this. Once she started to surrender, it would grow easier and easier, until she finally belonged to them in spirit as well as body.

"You defy me?"

Feslath grinned and took the whip off its hook. He did not even need to look to find it.

"As you like. Assume the position."

Vala was supposed to turn her back and bow her head so her eyes would be protected.

Instead, she glared straight into Feslath's eyes and said, "Go suckle a veserab."

The whip caught Vala across the chest almost before she had finished the curse. Refusing to give him the satisfaction of a scream, she clenched her jaw and took the next strike in silence as well, but the third caught her across the ribs and forced an involuntary gasp. Feslath, in particular, was a master of the technique and delighted in forcing her body to emit the sounds her mind held in check.

The next lash caught her across the previous one, and Vala began to grow dizzy. The assault would not end until she fell unconscious. Praying that he would keep landing his strikes on top of each other, she glared into his eyes and watched his arm draw back.

A dark-cloaked figure rose behind Feslath and caught his arm by the wrist. Feslath's eyes flared red, and he spun around to find the butt of a large black staff crashing into the side of his head. His knees buckled, and he melted to the floor like a suit of empty silks.

Khelben Arunsun, standing fully six feet tall, kicked the shadow lord in the ribs—hard—to make certain he was unconscious, then came to kneel beside Vala.

"You could have answered him," he said.

Vala shook her head, and vaguely aware of her gaping jaw, gasped, "You *are* real."

Khelben nodded, but made no move to undo her manacles.

"Does that mean you'll help us?" he asked.

Vala shook the chain by which she was attached to the wall.

"Does that mean you'll get me out of here?" she asked in return.

Khelben's face grew impatient.

"We'll come back for you, but our mission depends on secrecy and surprise. We can't take you along now without the risk of drawing attention to ourselves."

Vala considered this a moment then pointed her chin at Feslath's fallen figure.

"You're already running that risk," she said. "And no offense, but if you're going after the mythallar, I don't like your chances of getting back here to rescue me before this rock hits the ground."

"The fate of Faerûn itself hangs in the balance!" Khelben's voice was deep and righteous. "You would bargain for your own life?"

"I have a son who needs a mother." Vala didn't flinch at Khelben's angry scowl, but added, "I am not the one who is bargaining."

"She has a point, Khelben."

Dove and the other three Chosen appeared on the floor between them, still no more than a hand high.

Dove continued, "We promised Aris—"

"We will keep our promise," Khelben insisted, "without risking our mission."

"You're sure our mind wiping magic will work on a Shadovar?" Alustriel asked. "They are not beings of the Weave."

"Even if it does, there will still be the lump on the guard's head to explain," Storm said. "He'll wonder how he got it, and that in itself might give us away."

"I know a way it won't matter," Vala said, seeing her chance.

Khelben looked to her and raised his brow.

Vala explained her plan, and when she finished, Khelben continued to study her with narrowed eyes.

"This will work," Vala said. "It stands a better chance than your memory-stealing magic."

"Alustriel's memory-stealing magic," Khelben corrected. "That's not what worries me."

"Then what does?" Laeral asked.

"Vala," he said plainly. "It's not as though she's helping us out of the goodness of her heart. If Galaeron couldn't tell us where to find the mythallar, how do we know Vala can? She might be lying so we help her escape."

"Galaeron returned to the Palace Most High via Telamont's magic," Vala said. "I *walked* home."

Khelben continued to look doubtful.

"What if I were lying?" Vala asked. "Would you leave me here to fall with the city?"

"Of course not," Alustriel said. "We promised Aris we wouldn't."

"Then why should I lie?"

Finally, Khelben smiled and said, "I suppose you're right at that, aren't you?"

Khelben dragged the unconscious guard over to Vala and laid him at her feet. While she used the heel of her foot to make it look as though *she* had knocked him unconscious, Khelben removed the keys from his belt and undid her manacles. Once she was free, Vala wrapped the chain around his throat and began to choke him. None of the Chosen watched this part. They clearly wished there had been another way.

Not Vala. She had only to think of the beatings she had suffered at Feslath's hands for this small vengeance to seem not nearly enough. The thought sent a chill down her spine, and she found herself wondering if it was only magic-users who could let their shadows inside.

Once the guard was dead, Vala took his equipment and dressed herself in his clothes, and Khelben shrank himself back to the size of the others. She stuffed all five of the Chosen into her pockets, and aided by spells of invisibility and silence, crept down the stairs to the base of the confinement tower. Here, she had to kill two more guards, the first when he turned toward the opening door, the second while he was struggling with the dying body she had shoved into his arms. Leaving the bodies inside the stairwell behind the locked iron door, she used the second one's cloak to wipe the blood off the floor, then tossed it into a garderobe and left the area.

From there, it would have been a simple matter to descend the back stairs and vanish into the city. Instead, Vala entered a servant's passage and traversed the back of the great palace. Though she passed a constant stream of maids, pages, and butlers, she remained concealed from both eye and ear, for the magic of the Chosen was powerful enough to remain effective even after combat had been joined.

A quarter hour later, Vala emerged from the servant's passage into the dusky lobby outside the prince's private wing. The great anteroom doors were closed and guarded, as they had been since his return from the battle on the High Ice, and for a moment she despaired of making her plan work. There was no other way into the wing—at least that she had ever seen—and even invisible, she could not best a dozen of Escanor's shadow lords.

But, as Vala had hoped, the prince's duties could not be ignored even when he lay half-dead in his bed. It was not long before a courier approached the great doors bearing a shadow-filled message bottle. Vala fell in on his heels, following so closely that when a guard ordered him to stop three paces from the doors, she had to dodge around his side to keep from running into him. The guard took the message bottle and dismissed the courier, waiting until he had vanished down the corridor before he turned and knocked softly on the door.

Vala stood at the guard's side for a seeming eternity, barely daring to exhale lest her breath tickle the hair on his arms. Finally, a steward opened the door just far enough to lean out and take the message bottle. It would probably have been wise to wait for a serving maid or some other domestic whose duties would require opening the door more than a shoulder's width, but there was precious little time to make the decision, and Vala knew that the deaths in the confinement tower would not go unnoticed for long. She dropped to her haunches, pivoting around in front of the guard, and duck-walked sideways through the narrow opening, trying so hard not to step on his heels that the closing door caught her foot.

The guard called something to the chamberlain, who was already a step away, then shoved with his shoulder. Vala's foot seemed to fold along the length, but the heavy door bounced back enough for her to pull her foot into the room after her.

The door clicked shut, and Vala dropped to her seat, at once sighing in relief and opening her mouth in an unvoiced scream of pain. It would have been nice to set aside one of the weapons in her hand and check for broken bones, but such indulgences killed more warriors than they saved. She rolled to her knees and came up facing the interior of Escanor's large anteroom, where half a dozen clerks sat attending to the prince's private business.

Vala started across the chamber on her hands and knees, angling for the dark corridor that led deeper into the prince's inner sanctum. There, she had to slip under the crossed glaives of another set of guards.

Once inside the murky passage, she rose and put some weight on her foot. The pain was dull and general, more like a bad bruise than a break. She took a few steps. Finding the foot would support her, she continued through Escanor's private study into his dressing room, and passing another pair of guards and a small clique of servants at each stage, from his dressing room into his large and opulent bedchamber.

Escanor lay alone in his bed, little more than a man-shaped shadow cleaving to a cage of black ribs. His beating heart was visible inside, still glowing faintly with the light of the Weave flames that had nearly consumed him. He was attended on one side of the bed by a servant and on the other by a black-robed priestess wearing the purple mask of Shar. Two of Escanor's battle lords were standing at the foot of the bed. Vala's darksword was on display in a rack above the prince's headboard, locked behind a pair of crystal doors.

Vala! Khelben's voice came to her inside her head. *In the name of the Weave, what are you doing?*

Vala did not answer. She had not told the Chosen about this part of her plan, but it was as necessary to their success as finding the mythallar. She stepped over to the foot of the bed, and in a single spinning stroke, slashed the throats of both guards.

The men had barely fallen before the priestess raised her hands and began a wispy prayer to her hidden goddess. Vala cut this short by lashing out with the whip in her other hand. The cord wrapped itself tightly around the woman's throat, and the prayer ended in a strangled gasp as Vala jerked the priestess off her feet. The servant started for the door, his jaw working in shock, but emitting only strangled gasps. She spun past the end of the bed, bringing her sore foot up in a hook kick that caught him square in the nose with the hardest part of her heel. He flew off his feet so hard that the back of his head hit first and made a sickening crack on the stone floor.

Giving up on her spell, the priestess charged blindly forward, using one hand to pull against the whip around her throat and the other to slash her dagger blindly through the air. Vala waited for the next stroke to sweep past then she stepped forward and snapped the outside of her hand into the hinge of the woman's jaw. The priestess went instantly limp, her eyes rolling back in her head and the dagger slipping from her hand.

Vala dropped the whip and turned back to the bed. In Escanor's shadowy eye sockets were a pair of copper flames, faint and flickering as he struggled back to consciousness.

Vala! If you're counting on us to help you kill—

"Quiet."

Though Vala spoke the word aloud, she heard the word only in her mind. She started forward toward the display case. The flames in Escanor's eyes brightened, and she knew the prince was returning to his senses. She hurled her sword, reached for her dagger, and leaped onto the bed.

A wisp of shadowy arm rose through the covers. Her

tumbling sword ricocheted upward and smashed a crystal door, and something hit her in the chest like one of Aris's hammers. She fell off the bed backward and landed face-down on the floor.

"Guards!" Escanor's voice was barely a croak, but a croak loud enough to cause a stir out in the dressing room. "Help!"

Vala raised her hand and called silently to her darksword. She heard the tinkling of shattered crystal, and the weapon came sailing over the foot of the bed. The hilt slipped into her palm like the hand of an old friend. The blade was trailing a wisp of shadow where it had brushed Escanor's body.

You have your sword—time to go! Storm urged. *Out onto the balcony.*

Vala rolled sideways to her knees and came up with her arm cocked to throw. When she saw Escanor swinging out of the opposite side of the bed, she did just that. The blade caught him between the shoulder blades, slicing through two ribs and the faintly pulsing heart.

The prince died without a scream. His ribcage simply dropped to the floor in two pieces. The guards from the dressing room rushed into the chamber to find the cleaved heart dissolving into a cloud of shadow.

"*Now* it's time to go."

Again, Vala heard her words only in her own mind. As the guards rushed to their dying prince, she called the dark-sword back to her hand. She would have liked to stay and find the magic ring given to her by Corineus Drannaeken in the catacombs beneath Myth Drannor, but a search of that magnitude was out of the question. She raced toward the double doors and leaped into the air—then barreled into two more guards as they came rushing in.

Vala planted one foot on each of their shoulders—she was aiming for their throats, but had not jumped high enough—and she managed to drive enough of a seam between the startled Shadovar for the rest of her body to pass through. She thumped down on her side with her head barely a sword's length from either one, then she gathered her feet beneath her and dived forward, rolling across the balcony in a series of somersaults. The guards shouted the alarm and blindly clinked their swords on the stone only inches behind her.

At last, Vala came to the end of the balcony and found the balustrade blocking her path. She finished one more somersault, gathered her feet beneath her, and sprang over headlong.

Vala was within a dozen feet of the street before a magic hand finally reached out to stop her fall.

Next time, young lady, we won't catch you, Khelben warned. *That was nothing but a vengeance killing.*

"So it was," she said, "and if I hadn't done it, no one would have believed my escape was my own. Not after the things that devil did to me."

Vala's feet touched the street, and she started toward Shade's lower warrens at a sprint.

The Vaasans sat together on one side of the table, laughing and dribbling and whacking each other on the back mightily as they ate and drank and described the day's combat to their jealous comrade, Dexon. To listen to the men talk, battling phaerimm was no more dangerous than stalking forest rothé, save that the phaerimm made it all much more exciting by hunting back. Had Takari not been along and seen for herself the humans' deadly effectiveness that day—and many others—she would have believed the wine was stretching their tongues.

But it had all happened just as they described, and they had indeed added three tails apiece to their belts. Armed with Dexon's darksword, Keya Nihmedu had claimed two for her own growing collection. Takari had taken only one, but that was with nothing but her own elven steel. Had she been wielding a darksword of her own, she would have killed more phaerimm than anyone.

Takari took the ewer and refilled it from the wine cask in the scullery, then stopped in the doorway and eyed the two healthy Vaasans from behind. With their massive shoulders and braided black hair, they looked more like thkaerths to her than humans, but she had spent enough time fighting at their sides to know that neither man was entirely the brute he seemed. She had seen Burlen risk his life several times to protect Keya without ever allowing her to notice, while Kuhl had returned from one patrol with a litter of orphaned raccoons tucked inside his cloak.

After a moment of deliberation, Takari settled on Kuhl and came up behind him with the ewer. They always stopped to wash the blood and soot off in Dawnsglory Pond before returning home to Treetop, so she knew that Kuhl was both a little leaner and less woolly than Burlen. It was still going to be like wrestling a bear, but she saw no reason to make it any more distasteful than it had to be.

"More wine, Kuhl?"

Without waiting for an answer, Takari pressed herself to Kuhl's burly back and reached around his shoulder to refill his goblet.

She was wearing only the thinnest of shifts, so she knew he could feel her as well as she could feel him, but he only nodded and voiced his thanks without so much as a glance in her direction. Seeing that Dexon's goblet was almost empty, Takari took the opportunity to make her point more clearly by plastering herself to Kuhl's shoulder as she stretched forward to refill it. Lingering there rather longer than was necessary, she turned and smiled.

Kuhl looked away, a crimson flush rising up his cheeks.

Burlen pushed his goblet toward the ewer and said, "I'll take another swallow myself, if you don't mind."

Takari banged the ewer down and peeled herself off Kuhl's shoulder.

"Why should I mind? I'm sure you can pour."

This drew a roaring laugh from Dexon and a hurt expression from Burlen. Kuhl's face grew even redder. Takari wondered whether all humans were as dense as the one she had picked, or if there was something about Kuhl she did not understand. She had seen him casting hungry looks her way as they bathed.

Takari circled around to Kuhl's other side and found Keya Nihmedu studying her with a thoughtful frown. After learning how Keya had acquired the ability to hold Dexon's darksword—by allowing him to get a child on her—Takari had made the mistake of asking whether the other Vaasans had families at home. Keya seemed to have guessed her plan.

Takari ignored the condemnation she sensed in the younger elf's gaze and pulled a chair close to her quarry.

She ran a finger up Kuhl's forearm, and his brow grew shiny with human-smelling sweat.

"I'd like it if you showed me how you did that rollover on the bugbear today," she said.

A expectant silence descended over the room, and Dexon and Burlen studied Kuhl with wolfish grins.

"It was a good move," Keya broke in. She kept her gaze fixed on Takari. "Maybe you could show us all tomorrow."

"Now would be better for me," Takari said.

She had spent a tenday and a half praying to the Winged Mother to make her ready, and she could sense by the warmth in her womb that she was. It had to be this evening. She rested her fingers on the inside of Kuhl's meaty elbow and applied a little pressure.

"You can show the others tomorrow," she whispered.

Kuhl seemed to melt under her touch, but was somehow still oblivious to what she was suggesting.

"I can show you now. It won't take long," he said, rising and gesturing at the floor. "Lie down and be me, and I'll get on top and be the bugbear."

Dexon cringed and said, "I don't think this is something I want to see."

"Nor I," Keya agreed. "Takari, this isn't fair—"

"*Fair*?" Takari interrupted. "Galaeron made his choice when he left me in Rheitheillaethor and ran off with Vala. If I decide to try a human, too, that's no business of his—or yours."

Keya's mouth fell open, and Takari could see by the confusion in the younger elf's eyes that she had succeeded in muddling the issue. Whatever Keya had guessed, she could not know whether Takari was using the human for pleasure, revenge, or access to a darksword.

"Uh, Takari?" Kuhl asked. "What do you mean, 'try a human?' "

"What do you think I mean?" Takari rolled her eyes and said, "I've seen the way you stare at me when we bathe."

Kuhl looked guilty. "You have?"

"It's hard to miss," Takari said.

"It's all right?" Kuhl gasped. "I thought it bothered elves when we peeked."

"It is a little unsettling, to tell the truth," Takari said. Seeing the look of confusion that came to Kuhl's eyes, she decided that it would be best to state the matter as plainly as possible. "I'm giving you a chance here to do more than stare, Kuhl. Are you interested or not?"

"Interested."

"Good."

Takari took him by the wrist and started for the contemplation, but they were quickly intercepted by a disapproving Keya Nihmedu.

"Kuhl," she said, "you do realize she's using you?"

A grin the size of the crescent moon spread across Kuhl's face and he said, "I sure hope so."

He picked Takari up and slipped past Keya at a near charge, and a moment later Takari found herself wrestling the bear. The experience was not as unpleasant as she had feared, in large part because it was over so quickly.

The second time lasted a little longer. She was surprised to find that she was no longer disgusted at all, save for near the end when he really did start growling like a bear.

The third time, she actually started to enjoy it, and that was when Lord Duirsar's messenger flew in through the open window. Oblivious to what was happening, the snowfinch began to flit around their heads, chirping and tweeting as though the world were coming to an end.

"Manynests," Takari gasped. "Not . . . now!"

The bird landed on her shoulder and shrieked into her ear. The mood vanished instantly, and Takari extended a finger.

"Bird, this had better be good."

Manynests broke into a long series of whistles.

"What?" Takari asked. "When?"

She freed herself of Kuhl's embrace and swung her feet onto the floor. The snowfinch peeped in reply, then chirped a query.

"Of course!" Takari said, rising. "Tell him we'll meet them at the Livery Gate."

Kuhl propped himself on an elbow and asked, "Meet who?"

She snatched Kuhl's weapon belt off the floor and tossed it to him without touching the darksword's hilt. She didn't want Kuhl to know why she had bedded him, not until she knew the seed had been planted.

"The phaerimm," Takari replied. "They've breached the mythal."

Somewhere in the Palace Most High, Galaeron hung swaddled in velvet murk, immobile, able to breathe and scream but no more. Shadovar voices hissed in the distant gloom. Shadow seeped into his pores, permeating him with every breath, doubt and suspicion and anger steadily darkening his heart. How long he had been there was impossible to say. No one ever came to feed him or give him water or attend to his broken hand, or even to ask if he was ready to cooperate, but he never seemed to grow hungry or thirsty, or have need to answer nature's call. He hung there suspended in the moment, a throbbing pain-filled moment without beginning or end, without limit of any kind.

It seemed to Galaeron that the mythallar should have been destroyed long before, that the Chosen should have found it and sundered it, and brought Shade crashing down into the desert. Maybe they had. Trapped as he seemed in a single moment, how would he know? Or maybe he had been there only an instant after all. Maybe all his thoughts since Telamont hung him there had rushed through his mind in a single instant, and Khelben and the others were still awaiting their chance to escape into the city.

Or perhaps the Chosen had abandoned him, wherever here was, content to believe the shadow inside him would never escape to darken Faerûn. That would be just like them, to sacrifice an individual for the sake of the many—as long as that individual was not one of *their* number. Galaeron thought back to his capture and recalled how quick they had been to abandon the caravan, how cleverly they had arranged things so that none of them had been called upon to make the ultimate sacrifice. The cowards would not hesitate to leave him there alone to suffer for all eternity.

And that was exactly what Galaeron—the *real* Galaeron—would want, he reminded himself.

His shadow had all but taken him. Every thought contained a hidden doubt, every emotion was colored by suspicion. It would not be long before he yielded. He had only to grab a handful of shadowstuff and use its dark magic to cast a spell, and he would be free to seek his vengeance on all who had wronged him. Telamont had said as much when he'd imprisoned him, had promised that that was how Galaeron's struggle would end, that all Galaeron controlled was *when* it ended.

Galaeron believed him. If the timing was all he could control, then control it he would.

The hissing of the distant voices faded to silence, and the air grew heavy and chill. Galaeron's heart climbed into his throat, and he began to search the darkness ahead for the burning disks of Telamont's platinum eyes.

The air only grew colder and more still.

"You are stronger than I thought, elf," the Most High's wispy voice hissed into Galaeron's ear. "You are beginning to anger me."

Galaeron smiled. He tried to turn toward the voice, but his whole body seemed to pivot with him, and Telamont remained just beyond his peripheral vision.

Galaeron had to settle for speaking into the shadow.

"At least there's that," he said.

"Oh, there is more," Telamont said. "Much more. My son Escanor is dead."

Galaeron started to say something spiteful then realized that to express such malice to a grieving father—even *this* grieving father—would be to invite his shadow in.

"I'm sorry to hear that."

A deep chuckle sounded beside Galaeron's ear.

"Lies are of the shadow, too, elf."

"It was compassion—not a lie."

Galaeron's thoughts were racing. Had the city fallen and Telamont come to take vengeance? Did he see a way to use his son's death to force Galaeron completely into shadow? Or was he simply there to take out his anger on Galaeron?

"Whatever I may have thought of Escanor," the elf said, "whatever I would have liked to do to him myself—I'm sure you loved him."

Telamont was quiet for a moment, not using his will to press for an answer as usual when he fell silent, but genuinely seeming to contemplate Galaeron's words.

"Perhaps I did, at that," the Most High said. "What a pity Vala was not so charitable as you."

A cold knot formed in Galaeron's stomach. Telamont's cold presence pressed closer to him.

"She escaped her cell," the Shadovar said. "She killed him in his sick bed."

The knot in Galaeron's stomach grew as heavy as lead.

"Did his guards . . . ?" He could barely bring himself to voice the question, "Is she dead?"

"That would make you angry, would it not?"

A cloaked form coalesced in the murk before Galaeron. With the Most High already whispering into his ear, it took Galaeron a moment to realize that the figure in front of him also belonged to Telamont.

"I could tell you she is, and you would fly into a rage." Telamont's eyes grew bright and angry, but his voice continued to whisper into Galaeron's ear, "And with rage would come your shadow. It would claim you for all time."

"Then she's not dead." Nor had the mythallar been destroyed, Galaeron realized. Had Shade fallen, Telamont would be more interested in killing him than claiming him. "You don't know where she is."

"And with hope comes strength," hissed the disembodied voice. "The strength to defy me. What am I to do?"

He fell silent, and the air grew heavy with expectation.

Fearing that one answer would lead to another and another until he betrayed their plan, Galaeron tried not to answer. Telamont remained silent, and his will pressed down on Galaeron all the more fiercely. Eventually, he could resist no more, and the words tumbled out of their own accord.

"Tell me the truth."

The purple crescent of a smile appeared in the hood beneath Telamont's eyes.

"The truth? What is 'truth,' really?" Telamont's voice whispered into Galaeron's other ear. "The truth is that she will be."

The lump in Galaeron's stomach began to grow lighter. Vala was still alive.

"If you catch her."

"*When* we catch her," Telamont corrected. "Where can she go? It's a thousand feet to the ground."

He paused, and Galaeron feared for a moment that Telamont meant to force an answer that would betray the attack on the mythallar, but Telamont had something else in mind.

"She will be caught. My other sons are tracking her even now."

Galaeron fought not to smile. He had said nothing about the Chosen yet, and if the princes were busy searching for Vala, they would not be watching the mythallar. Perhaps they had even helped her escape to create a diversion. That would be just like those cowards, to sacrifice a helpless woman so they wouldn't have to risk their own lives. It occurred to Galaeron that he might save Vala's life by warning Telamont about their plan. That was what those traitors deserved.

"You do not care?" Telamont asked. "I thought you loved this woman. I thought she was the reason you betrayed us."

Telamont grew quiet, and again the weight of his will slowly crushed Galaeron's resolve.

At last, Galaeron admitted, "That's true. I do love her."

"A pity, then," Telamont said. "The things that will happen when we recapture her. . . ."

He fell silent, leaving Galaeron to imagine the horrors that would be visited on her. Given the punishment Vala had suffered just for aiding in his escape, he could not bear to think of the death she would meet after killing a prince of Shade. He began to feel Telamont's will pressing down on him, compelling him to speak what he was thinking. Time and again, Galaeron found himself ready to blurt out his plan, to reveal how he had tricked Telamont into bringing the Chosen into Shade.

Somehow, he resisted. Deep down inside, part of him wanted to believe it was honor that stopped him, that something inside him was strong enough to resist the will of the Most High of Shade. But the truth was that he had again fallen into the grasp of his shadow self, and it simply did not believe Telamont could be trusted.

Every time Galaeron started to say he would trade Shade's life for Vala's, or that he could deliver five Chosen in exchange for her freedom, his shadow refused. It reminded him that Telamont had once offered to teach him how to control his shadow—as if that could be done—and of how badly that bargain had turned out. It reminded him of how powerful the Most High was. Galaeron had only to hint at the attack on the mythallar and Telamont would begin to pressure him for answers. The Shadovar would know everything within minutes, Vala would be condemned to a lingering death anyway, and Galaeron would be left with nothing for his betrayal.

For once, Galaeron's shadow self was right. Telamont had done nothing but betray him. Telamont deserved what was going to happen to his city. All of the Shadovar did. And Vala? He wanted to save Vala, but he could not do it by yielding to Telamont.

Finally, Telamont said, "Love is not as strong as I imagined." The pressure did not relent, but his voice came from the hooded shape before Galaeron's eyes. "You do not wish to save Vala?"

"I would do anything to save Vala," Galaeron said, "but I am no fool."

"No?" Telamont's voice sounded like cracking ice. "Then you know she will not escape."

"And you know I can help you."

A dark voice inside Galaeron screamed for him to hold his tongue, that he was a fool if he thought he could bargain with Telamont Tanthul.

Galaeron ignored the voice and continued, "The phaerimm continue to trouble you. Take me to the world-window. When I see her at home in Vaasa, I'll help you with them again."

Telamont drifted closer, until Galaeron could see nothing

in front of his face but two platinum eyes. He forced himself to hold the gaze, and eventually he saw that the eyes were silver coronas burning around two disks of shadow blacker than darkness. The pressure of his will grew crushing, and still Galaeron did not look away. Finally, the shining coronas flickered with something like amusement, and Telamont drew back a little.

"Love is not as strong as I imagined."

The Most High's eyes resolved themselves back into disks, and his dark form began to melt back into the darkness.

"But hope . . ." the shade said. "That is so much stronger."

The crushing burden of his will remained. Galaeron waited, expecting the compulsion to answer some unspoken question to arise inside him at any moment. There was only the intangible weight—and a different pressure, rising from inside, a feeling that was closer to fear and uncertainty, perhaps grief. Finally, when the shape of Telamont's body had dissolved back into the darkness and there was only the pale light of his fading eyes, it was this pressure that forced Galaeron to break his silence.

"Wait!" Galaeron said. "What about Vala?"

"I accept." The eyes vanished, but Telamont's voice hissed from the darkness all around, "If you wish to save her, you have only to grasp the shadows and free yourself."

Before Galaeron could object, voices began to hiss again in the distant gloom, and the crushing weight of Telamont's will was gone. Galaeron found himself torn between pride in having matched wills with the Most High and apprehension over his comment about hope. What had he meant about hope being so much stronger? Probably, it was just some ploy to make Galaeron yield to the Most High's will, to surrender himself to shadow, but there had been something about the way it was said that made him feel otherwise, a note of revelation in Telamont's voice that suggested a flash of insight. His tone in agreeing to trade Galaeron's cooperation for Vala's life had been one of ridicule, as though he knew the offer would never be accepted.

A dark voice whispered that Telamont was playing him for a fool. There was only one way to escape, and Galaeron refused to use it. Half the Shadovar in the enclave had to be laughing at him at that very moment. Galaeron resisted this line of thought by reminding himself of what happened the last time he used the Shadow Weave, of how he had alienated Vala and nearly gotten Aris killed. If Telamont had provided an easy escape, it was because it was no escape at all. Galaeron had sworn an oath never to use shadow magic again, and it was an oath he intended to honor.

Galaeron occupied himself for what seemed the multiverse's next eternity, arguing back and forth with the dark voice inside his own head, knowing there was only one escape and knowing as well that a fate worse than death awaited him if he took it. Had he been confident that he would know when the Chosen shattered the mythallar and the city fell, perhaps he would have had the fortitude to wait.

As it was, the uncertainty was more than he could bear: the fear that Shade would crash into the sands of Anauroch and be fifteen centuries buried with him still there in that dark moment wondering if his plan would ever succeed, wondering if Vala would live to see her son again, wondering if Takari had ever forgiven him for the selfish fear that had made him turn her away. The image of a black, drop-shaped body appeared his mind and began to grow larger. The thing had three bulbous protrusions that, considering the fang-filled mouths at the end, might have been heads. A trio of arms, each ending in three hands with a single eye in the palm, sprouted from its body in three unlike places. The phantasm—for he had no doubt that that was what it was— reminded Galaeron vaguely of the sharn he had freed when they destroyed the first lich Wulgreth.

I have been looking for you, Elf.

Galaeron's jaw dropped. For once, his shadow self seemed

too stunned to take advantage of the situation, and he experienced a moment of internal silence that he had not enjoyed since making the mistake that had allowed his shadow to invade him in the first place.

What, no "hi ho, old friend?" the sharn asked. *No, "well met, Xrxvlayblea?"*

"W-hat, uh, how . . . ?"

"That will do, I suppose."

The sharn—Xrxvlayblea—was floating in the shadows before Galaeron, all ton and a half of him, or it, or them, or however one referred to a blob of three-headed . . . stuff. It waved the eyes in several of its palms over Galaeron.

"Y-you're real?" Galaeron stammered.

One of the heads shot up close to Galaeron's face and spewing drool from its fangs, snapped, "Did I not say I would return to repay the favor you did me in Karsus?"

"You did," Galaeron gulped.

"Now is when you need me most, is it not?"

Galaeron managed a nod.

"Of course it is," another head spat. "Or I wouldn't be here."

Galaeron shook his head and wondered if he had begun to hallucinate.

"There you have it, then," the third head said. "You're ready now. Favor repaid."

The sharn turned and started to float away into the shadows. Galaeron tried to pull an arm free and found that he was as stuck as ever. He debated the wisdom of talking to a hallucination. A dark voice asked what could it hurt, and he decided nothing.

"Wait!"

The sharn stopped, but did not turn.

"Ready for what?" Galaeron asked.

"Ready to do what you were not ready to do then," the sharn replied.

Galaeron frowned. "But I'm still caught."

"Whose fault is that?" asked one of the heads—from behind, it was impossible to see which. "You'd better get unstuck."

"You don't understand," Galaeron said. "I can't use the Shadow Weave. I swore an oath."

"An oath?"

The sharn swung back around and shoved two palms in Galaeron's face so it could stare at him eye-to-eye.

"Why'd you do a witless thing like that?" it asked.

"I've been having a shadow crisis," Galaeron explained. "When I use the Shadow Weave, my shadow self takes over. The next time, it may be permanent, so I vowed not to cast any more shadow magic."

"Breaking a vow is bad business." The eyes in the palms blinked, and it said, "But don't be angry with the Shadow. That's what he wants—and it's not his fault, anyway. You made a promise you can't keep."

The sharn turned and started to float away again.

"That's it?" Galaeron cried. "That's your big favor?"

One of the heads twisted around to glance back over its body.

"Look, I'm not here to tell you how to live your life. You can do it now, or you can do it later, when it doesn't matter. Your choice. Favor repaid."

"One more question," the second head added, "and you owe me."

"You don't want that," the third head said. "Really."

"No," Galaeron said. "I'm sure I don't. My thanks, and fare you well."

"No doubt of that," the sharn said, and it vanished into the whispering gloom.

More than a hundred heartbeats passed before the dark voice inside suggested that maybe they should ignore the sharn, that maybe it had been an illusion conjured up by Telamont Tanthul to trick him into using the Shadow Weave. Maybe, after all, they should hang there in the murk for a while longer. Galaeron realized that maybe his shadow self was saying the opposite of what of it truly wanted, that maybe it really wanted him to escape and was just suggesting the opposite because it knew he would do the opposite of *that* . . .

"Maybe," Galaeron said. He closed his eyes, then grasped a handful of shadow and closed his fist as well. "And maybe not."

CHAPTER THIRTEEN

2 Eleasias, the Year of Wild Magic

To Aris's dismay, elegance had not returned with strength. With Malik gone, the giant found himself secretly in the service of Prince Yder. He stood over the High Altar in Malik's Temple of the One and All, cutting a relief of Shar's Black Moon around the oblong skull-and-starburst he'd done when the temple still belonged to Malik.

He could hardly ask for better working conditions, even were he a free giant. He had only to ask, and whatever he wanted to eat or drink would be brought from any far corner of Faerûn. A company of assistants attended to his every need, and he worked at his pleasure and was free to do whatever he wished at other times. He was not even much of a captive, as he was free to wander the city of Shade at will—so long as he did not mind an escort of several armed shadow lords.

His tool control had returned to normal after he'd slept off the effects of hiding the Chosen in his body, and the Dark Moon was cut shallowly enough so that it did not draw attention to itself. Still, there was something intrinsic to the goddess's hidden nature that he was not quite conveying. A viewer had only to look at Cyric's skull-and-starburst to see that it floated inside Shar's Dark Moon, and that would not do at all. She was more subtle than that, more mysterious.

Aris stepped away to gain some perspective, barely noticed as he sent a dozen attendants scrambling for cover, and decided he would have to rethink the whole thing. He dropped his hammer and chisel into the tool bag on his belt and backed out of the chancel area.

"Go to my workshop," he said, motioning the attendants toward the door in the north transept. "Bring a stack of sail canvases and a barrel of sketching charcoal."

The attendants rushed to obey, leaving only four shadow lord guards who did their utmost to remain quiet and out of sight. Yder had apparently ordered them to avoid reminding Aris that he was a captive, but it made no difference. He always knew they were behind him. He could *feel* them there, just out of sight.

A throaty rasp came up the nave's center aisle as someone pushed open the Black Portal. Aris waved an absentminded hand in the direction of the sound and kept his attention fixed on the object of his frustration. A pair of guards rushed off to send the visitor away. There followed the hiss of whispered conversation, then a scuffle, a few syllables of magic, and the clatter of armored bodies hitting the floor.

"What's wrong with you oafs?" Aris snapped, too absorbed in aesthetics to register anything but an annoying disturbance. "Can you not see I'm trying to think?"

The other two guards were already stomping down the aisle to intercept the intruder. This time, the incantation ended in a sharp crack. The flash of lightning lit the chancel, and at last Aris saw the solution to his problem. The entire High Altar would become the Dark Moon, with the upper hemisphere forming a semicircular back panel at the rear and the lower hemisphere descending down into the choir. The trick would be to get the right foreshortening where the level changed, and to find a way to round the staircase toward the bottom. Growing ever more excited, Aris dropped to his knees and began to search his belt bag for a nubbin of sketching charcoal.

"Difficult to tell who's the slave here and who are the guards." The voice registered vaguely as a familiar one. "You weren't this difficult back in Arabel."

"Do you have something to sketch with?" Aris lowered a hand without looking. "I must get this down while I still have it in mind."

"Aris!" the voice barked. "Leave it. You're done here."

"Done?"

Scowling at the interruption, Aris shook his head and found Galaeron standing at his side. The elf looked much as he had when they were separated at the Cave Gate, save that his face was lined with fatigue and his eyes veiled behind a glossy darkness.

"Galaeron . . ."

Aris could feel the details of his idea slipping away even as he spoke, but he was so happy to see his old friend alive that he didn't care . . . much.

"What are you doing here?" he asked.

"What do you think?" Galaeron retorted. "I escaped."

"Escaped? From the Palace Most High?"

Galaeron nodded. "I had to use the Shadow Weave," he said, looking back down the main aisle of the nave, where Aris's four guards lay in various forms of death. "I'm sorry."

Aris's heart went out to his friend.

"You have not failed anyone." He laid two fingers on the elf's shoulder and said, "I am proud you did not yield before this."

"I didn't yield," Galaeron said. "I chose. Telamont is after Vala."

Aris went hollow inside.

"Then he knows?" asked the giant.

"Knows?"

"About the Chosen," Aris said. "They couldn't find the mythallar, so I sent them to Vala."

A shadow descended over Galaeron's face.

"The Chosen must have freed her," he said. Galaeron motioned Aris to his feet and turned toward the Black Portal. "I gave them away. That's what he meant."

Aris rose, but made no move to follow.

"What who meant?"

"The sharn," Galaeron answered as he continued down the aisle. "He appeared to me in the Palace Most High. He said he had come to repay the favor he owed us, and told me I had a choice to make."

"And?"

"And he left, and I made my choice," Galaeron replied. "I couldn't bear the thought that Telamont would capture Vala again, but now I see he was talking about more—much more."

Seeing that Galaeron was not going to wait, Aris caught up to him with a single step. He plucked Galaeron off the floor and held him at head height.

"The sharn from Karse came to you in the Palace Most High?"

"Isn't that what I just said? Put me down. We need to go find Vala and the Chosen."

Aris continued to hold Galaeron and said, "The sharn left you there to free yourself? He left you and told you to use the Shadow Weave?"

If Galaeron saw the reason for Aris's alarm, he showed no sign.

"The sharn was warning me," the elf said. "Telamont had just been there, trying to convince me to use the Shadow

Weave to save Vala. When I refused, a strange look came over him. Telamont said hope was stronger than he had imagined and left."

"That was what the sharn was warning you about?"

Galaeron shook his head and replied, "I think Telamont knew I was defying him because I expected something to happen soon. It must have dawned on him that Vala had help escaping, because he left in a hurry. We have to find the Chosen and warn them."

"All very plausible," Aris said. "But the sharn left you there with no way to escape except to use the Shadow Weave."

Galaeron shrugged and said, "I had to accept the inevitable, and I'm the stronger for it."

He peeled Aris's thumb back and slipped free, landing on the floor in an easy crouch.

"Who is stronger?" Aris asked, a little frightened by how easily Galaeron had broken his grasp. "How can you be certain it was the sharn you saw and not some trick of Telamont's?"

"Because we beat him," Galaeron replied, starting toward the Black Portal again. "My shadow and I matched wills with Telamont Tanthul, and we beat him."

"Galaeron, listen to yourself," Aris said. He stepped over the elf, then spun and stooped down to block his way. "Telamont Tanthul has been trying to trick you into yielding to your shadow since the day we arrived in Shade. You finally do it, and suddenly you're stronger than he is?"

"Yes," Galaeron said simply. "The Shadovar thrive on deception and subterfuge, I know that, but the biggest fraud they ever committed on me was when Melegaunt tricked me into fighting my own shadow. He filled me with doubt, and doubt made me weak."

"And now you are sure," Aris said, filling his voice with mockery and mistrust. "Now you are strong."

"Now I am whole," Galaeron snapped back. "That makes me strong. I have no time to explain it now."

He whispered a mystic word and waved his hand at Aris's foot, and the foot started to slide across the floor.

"I am going to the mythallar," Galaeron said, stepping under Aris toward the Black Portal.

"Wait!" Aris turned, growing ever more suspicious, and said, "Back in Arabel, you told me you didn't know how to find the mythallar."

"Not on this plane."

Galaeron pressed a palm to the Black Portal and spoke a few words in ancient Netherese. The door dissolved into shadow mist.

The elf turned to Aris and said, "I hope you'll come with me. One way or the other, I don't think Shade will be safe for you very much longer."

Aris's mind was whirling with suspicions, foremost among them the fear that Telamont was using Galaeron to reveal Vala and the Chosen to the Shadovar. But for that to be so, Galaeron could not be under the Most High's sway, for if he were Telamont would have only to ask to learn what he wished to know.

"I'll come," he said, stepping toward the shadowy portal, "but first you must promise that when this is done, you will never touch the Shadow Weave again. You can still be saved."

"I was inviting you, Aris, not begging," Galaeron said in a voice that held both scorn and patience. "I don't need to be saved from anything."

Galaeron turned and stepped through the Black Portal, leaving Aris alone in the Temple of the One and All, alone and feeling angry and abandoned. He could not decide whether it was Galaeron who had just departed or Galaeron's shadow—or someone Aris did not even know. The elf's parting rebuke had left him feeling both resentful and hurt, and such rudeness simply was not like his friend. It made Aris want to retreat into his work, but of course that was foolish. If Galaeron's plan worked, it would all be rubble in a few minutes anyway, and if the plan failed, the last thing he wanted to do for the next few hundred years was devote his talent to hiding Dark Moons in the sacred sculpture of other deities. Besides, whether or not he still knew the elf, Galaeron was his friend, and no matter how strange they became, one did not desert one's friends as they went off to fight Telamont Tanthul and the Princes of Shade—at least stone giants did not.

Aris followed Galaeron through the Black Portal and into the shadow mist. The air grew frigid, and the floor turned as soft as snow.

Aris called into the blackness, "Galaeron?"

He took another tentative step, doing his best to continue in a straight line.

"Where are you?"

When no answer came, Aris decided he had waited too long. The shadows were no place to become lost. He turned around and retraced his steps exactly.

Three steps later, he remained in the dark.

Perhaps his first two steps had been longer than he thought. Holding his arm before him, Aris took another step forward.

"Galaeron!"

A small hand pressed itself to his kneecap and the elf whispered, "Quietly, my friend."

Aris's sigh was anything but soft.

"I thought you'd left me behind."

"I have too few friends to leave them wandering around the Fringe alone," Galaeron replied. He pulled on the leg of Aris's trousers, guiding him forward. "We must be careful. I don't know who else might be watching."

"Watching?" Aris whispered.

Galaeron stopped, and the black mists ahead slowly grew translucent. Aris saw that they had stopped just inside the Shadow Fringe. Ahead lay a large crater lined in obsidian, with no apparent seams and a surface as smooth as the interior of a glass bowl. Standing near the bottom, spaced at equal intervals along the inner wall, were Khelben and the four sisters. They held their arms outspread, fingertips pointing toward their comrades to either side, so that they formed a great ring around the interior. Within this circle lay a disk of gray opalescent light, which they were slowly walking toward the bottom of the basin.

Vala was nowhere in sight. Nor were Telamont and his princes.

Aris kneeled at Galaeron's side and stooped down to whisper, "Perhaps they did not find—"

Galaeron made a motion, and the rest of Aris's sentence vanished into silence.

The mythallar is beneath that dimensional portal, Galaeron's voice said inside his head. *Vala is here somewhere, you may be sure.*

Aris was about to ask whether Telamont was also there when, about a quarter of the way around the crater, the dark figures of all ten surviving princes emerged from the Shadow Fringe. They did not step from the obsidian lining so much as they peeled themselves out of it. They began to slide silently down the wall. Aris reached for his tool pouch for something to throw and started to rise, but Galaeron put out a restraining hand.

The Chosen will have foreseen this.

The princes were almost upon the Chosen when they struck an invisible barrier and came to an abrupt stop, tiny forks of golden energy crackling outward around each impact point. They leaped to their feet, wailing in pain and shock, and scrambled a few steps up the wall then stopped there, bleeding dark mist into the air. Three of them collapsed again almost immediately and melted back into the Fringe. The others hurled globes of shadow magic toward the bottom of the crater. The balls hit the barrier and erupted into huge black sprays, then rained back down in tiny beads of darkness that skittered across the invisible surface like drops of water on a hot frying pan.

While the others continued to assail the barrier, the gaunt figure of Prince Lamorak conjured a shadow disk. He and his brother Malath stepped aboard and floated out toward the center of the crater, their fingers working madly as they twined strands of shadowsilk into the shape of a small hand axe.

Aris grabbed one of his chisels but before he could pull it from his tool bag to throw, a bolt of golden magic streaked down from the opposite crater rim to blast Lamorak's shadow disk into shards. Malath pitched headlong into the invisible barrier and fell instantly limp, his body first melting into a black puddle, then coming apart and skittering across the surface in steaming black globules. Lamorak hit on his back, screamed once, and managed to bounce himself into the air. He vanished with the sharp crackle of a teleport spell.

Aris looked across the crater toward the source of the golden bolt and glimpsed a swirl of Vala's golden hair as she dropped out of sight behind the rim. Though he had never seen her cast a spell, it was not a wild guess to think that one of the Chosen might have loaned her a ring or wand capable of hurling the magic bolts. Unfortunately, Aris was not the only one who had spotted her. Yder and Aglarel scurried after her, their lanky limbs oddly spiderlike as the princes ascended the slick wall.

Aris glanced down and was relieved to find his friend staring after Vala, his elf brows arched high in concern. Still, Galaeron made no move to go after her. Recalling how, while facing a similar situation under the influence of his shadow self on the Saiyyadar, the elf had nearly gotten him killed by using him to bait a dragon into an ambush, Aris grabbed Galaeron's shoulder and urged him after her.

Galaeron pulled free of Aris's hand.

They would have foreseen that. We must wait here in the Fringe for what they did not foresee.

Aris started to ask angrily what that might be, but Galaeron's spell kept him silent. He could only wait and watch as the Chosen, ignoring the princes' ever more frantic efforts to penetrate the mystic barrier, continued to walk the dimensional portal toward the bottom of the basin. Yder and Aglarel reached the rim of the crater and disappeared over the top. The basin began to tremble and fall away beneath them.

Aris's jaw dropped. The Chosen had done it—Shade was falling. He snatched Galaeron up. Determined not to become separated from the others whatever the elf said, he jumped into the basin—but landed in the same place he had been, with the basin continuing to fall away below him.

When we are needed, Galaeron hissed. *Not before.*

How long he had lain chained on Shar's altar, Malik could not say. All he knew was he had grown so weak with hunger that his belly had lost the strength to rumble, that his tongue was so swollen with thirst he could not have drunk if someone had given him water, that his ears had become so inured by the constant hissing of the Hidden One's worshipers that the sudden silence left him feeling deafened and dizzy.

He had the sensation of floating—a sensation that only grew stronger when his shadow on the ceiling started to shrink and loom ever darker, when the stream of silver magic pouring from the stone began to swirl around him in beads as large as his head, and especially when the confused forms of Shar's worshipers began to tumble through the air and bounce along the shadow-stained ceiling.

So weakened by thirst and hunger was Malik that for a few moments, he was too confused to comprehend what he was seeing. Had he finally died and begun his journey to the Shattered Castle, or had the harlot Shar suddenly granted all her worshipers the ability to fly? Or perhaps it was an hallucination. Perhaps all the hardships he had endured on behalf of his god Cyric had finally taken their toll, leaving him as demented and mad as once his god had been.

Then Malik hit the end of his chains and felt his withered hands nearly slip free of one of the manacles, and he knew what had happened. The One had answered a prayer. Finally, Cyric had taken mercy on his poor servant and raised a finger to help in the impossible mission he had assigned him, and soon the Sharites would pay for all of the torment and abuse they had heaped upon him while he lay chained to their goddess's stolen altar.

"Your doom is upon you!" Malik yelled through the floating swirl of silver beads. "Cyric has come for me at last, and he shall take a terrible vengeance on you."

"Fool!"—the voice that hissed this came from his own shadow, lying flat upon the ceiling not a dozen paces above him—"Nothing could be farther from Cyric's mind than your misery."

"You cannot know that!" Malik said, more for his own comfort than because he believed his shadow needed to know. "You are nothing to him." He meant to stop there, but felt more words welling up as Mystra's curse compelled him to speak the full truth. "Except another torment for me!"

This drew a purple smile from the shadow, which said, "The one service I am happy to perform for your lying god, but that does not change the truth of what is happening. The city is falling."

"Falling?" Malik shrieked. He noticed that other voices were beginning to join him. "With *me* in it?"

"A pity, is it not?" the shadow asked.

"More than you know."

In this, Malik was telling the truth, for Cyric was fond of telling him the fate that awaited him if he ever failed in one of the divine missions assigned to him. It took only an instant for the thousand promised torments to flash through his mind, for in his infinite wisdom, the One had made Malik memorize them until he knew them all as well as his own name.

But there was no way to avoid it. The city was going to crash into the desert, and he was going to die along with everyone else, no doubt crushed beneath the Karsestone, since he was still chained to it . . . and that was when Malik saw how he would save himself.

Once before, when Cyric had sent Malik to fetch a sacred book from inside the Keeper's Tower at Candlekeep, the One had told him he had only to call the name of the One and All three times once he had succeeded in his duty and he would be rescued. Given that Yder had called the Karsestone the crown of his goddess Shar, and given that it was also the only remaining source of the ancient whole magic in all of Faerûn—perhaps even Toril itself—it seemed reasonable to suppose that he who controlled the Karsestone might also control the Shadow Weave.

The stone might be, Malik realized, just like a crown. If not actually the source of Shar's power over the Shadow Weave, it was at least a symbol of it, and he had learned in Calimshan that he who controlled the symbol soon owned the power.

When the city's true caliph had lost his crown to a ring of thieves, the master of the thieves had audaciously set the crown on his own head and challenged the caliph to take it back. Try as he might, the old man never succeeded, and it was not long before the city revered the thief as the new caliph.

And so it would be with the Karsestone, Malik believed. No—he *knew*. There could be no other reason the goddess of shadows would permit an artifact of such blazing light to serve as the High Altar in her holiest of temples.

Seeing that he had floated to within five feet of the ceiling— and that his shadow was little larger than he himself, but as black as obsidian—Malik closed his eyes. He had no idea how long it would take the city to crash into Anauroch, but they had been falling for a full five or ten breaths, and they had to hit soon.

"I have it, Mighty One! I have the Shadow Weave chained right here on my back!"

When Mystra's curse did not compel Malik to add anything more, or even to clarify that it was just a symbol, he decided his plan was going to work and called, "Cyric, the One, the All!"

Nothing happened. He floated so close to the ceiling that he could not see anything except his shadow's smirking face.

"How pitiful you are," it said. "It shames me to know I spring from your image. Even if Cyric could hear you, do you think he would answer?"

"*If* he could hear me?" Malik screamed. "What do you mean *if*?"

"What do you think I mean?" the shadow retorted. "This is the temple—"

The explanation came to an abrupt end as Malik touched the ceiling and came into contact with his shadow. The red eyes winked out and its shape grew more squat and less monsterlike. Malik experienced a rush of cold magic as it reattached itself to his body.

"Thish is justh what you desherve!" With his face pressed against the stone ceiling, it was impossible to speak clearly. "You will be with me when I fathe the One'sh anger!"

The ceiling lifted away from his face, and Malik thought for a moment that his shadow had been wrong, that Cyric had come for him after all. Then he heard splashing, and screaming, and all around him he saw Shadovar flailing their arms and beads of silver magic assuming teardrop shapes as they plummeted back toward the temple floor.

Closing his eyes, Malik yelled again, "Cyric, the One, the All!"

Nothing happened, except that a steady roar began to build beneath Malik. No sooner had he identified the sound as the Karsestone's steady stream of magic pouring into the pool below than the roar exploded into a thunderous splash, and the air shot from his lungs as his back slammed into the Karsestone. He bounced once and felt his legs come free as the shackle bolt holding his feet came out, then he felt bones snapping in one hand as it was pulled through the closed manacles.

For a moment, Malik thought it would end there, that everything would go black and he would awaken on the Fugue Plain, abandoned to the rough mercy visited upon all the faithless wretches who displeased their holy masters by the thieving god of the dead, Kelemvor.

But that was not to be. Still attached to the Karsestone by his one unbroken hand, Malik rolled off to the cracked side and caught the spray of magic full in the face. Before he could close his mouth and twist away, he swallowed three huge gulps, and of course they went down the wrong passage and immediately filled his lungs.

Malik expected to drown—and quickly—but this was magic. It coursed through his lungs into the rest of his body, filling him with renewed vigor. The weakness brought on by his hunger and thirst vanished, and the hand he had just broke began to heal—though with the fractured bone still unset, it felt like Aris had driven a chisel through it. Malik gathered his legs beneath him and turned to find the temple filled with battered Shadovar, some floating facedown in the silver magic and some sloshing toward the exit arches as fast as their dark legs would carry them.

A pair of fanatical Shar worshipers saw him standing beside the Karsestone and started to rush it, yelling that this was the doing of the infidel thief. It was at that very moment that the ceiling vaults gave way beneath the strain of the sudden stop and began to shower down into the temple. The largest worshiper was crushed beneath a section of a stone rib as long as Aris was tall, and the other vanished behind a screen of falling debris.

Making good use of his Cyric-given ability to vanish, Malik ducked beneath the surface of the silver pool to hide. The surviving fanatic arrived a moment later, hacking into the water with his black sword and swearing that he would mount Malik's horned head on his wall. Though it would have been a simple matter to follow the last manacle chain down to Malik's hand itself, the One's magic prevented the worshiper from seeing this. Malik came up behind him, reaching around to draw the Shadovar's dagger from his belt. He used the worshiper's own weapon to open his belly.

A long section of wall collapsed behind Malik. The whole temple tilted, and he found himself being dragged along behind the Karsestone as the current carried everything in the room toward a huge whirlpool in the corner. He had just enough time to realize that he was about to be dragged down one of the drainage pits he had noticed upon his first awakening in the chamber.

Malik felt for a moment like the city had begun to fall again, but then his manacle chain went slack, tight, and slack again as the Karsestone hit something, bounced, and began to roll. He found himself first flying wildly through the air, then watching the stone fly past over his head, then being jerked along behind it before he finally slammed into it face first and came to a rest.

Compared to the crash and roar of the initial fall, the chamber seemed eerily quiet. That did not mean silence. The air was filled with the wailing and groaning of the injured, the staccato splashing of debris and people falling into viscous pools of magic, and the steady gurgle of the magic stream still pouring out of the cracked Karsestone. Malik slowly picked himself up, and discovering he had survived more or less intact, he turned to see where he had landed.

He lay propped against the wall of one of the workshop caverns where the Shadovar made their shadow blankets. To his right lay the huge, comblike loom they used to weave the shadowsilk into cloth, and to his left lay the hundred-yard slit they used to provide the light they needed to create shadow. Most interesting to Malik, however, was the shallow tin pan directly in front of him. Tipped at a steep angle because of the city's tilt, the pan was easily a hundred paces square, but no more than a fingernail's thickness in depth. At the far side—several dozen yards higher than Malik's head—was a long collection trough still containing some of the silver magic that had once distributed evenly across the trough.

A tremendous rumble shook the loom cavern, then it slowly righted itself. The silvery magic from the Karsestone spilled into the tin pan and began to spread toward the far corners of the room. The sun drifted briefly across the mouth of the light slit, then vanished behind the top edge and sent a narrow wedge of shadow shooting across the pan. Where the shadow came into contact with the spreading sheet of whole magic, it bonded instantly into a wafer-thin triangle of shadow blanket.

"They use whole magic!" Malik gasped, suddenly understanding what he was seeing. "They need the Karsestone to make their blankets."

The city continued to tilt, going a little past center and tipping in the opposite direction. Realizing that whatever he had learned, it would do him no good if he did not survive to tell Cyric, Malik leaped to his feet. Sometimes pushing, sometimes pulling, and sometimes being swung along himself, he began to guide the Karsestone toward the sun slit along the right side of the room.

Given his usual luck, Malik thought he would probably manage to push the Karsestone out into the desert just before the entire Shade Enclave came crashing down upon them.

Dark as Galaeron's heart had grown, it had nearly torn apart as he and Aris watched Aglarel and Yder vanish over the basin rim in pursuit of Vala. After the abandonment of the caravan at Eveningstar, he had no illusions about the Chosen's willingness to risk one for the good of the many. That he was also willing to take the same risk—and with someone he loved—struck him as neither good nor evil, only necessary. That events had proven him right made him feel neither vindicated nor culpable, only sorrowful. He finally understood what Dove and the others had been trying to tell him that day—or so he believed, as his hand had finally healed and returned to its proper color—that the Chosen already carried their shadows inside, that it was not possible to bear so much responsibility and power without darkening one's own spirit.

"Ready yourself, Aris," he said. Galaeron spoke normally, for there was no longer any chance that the Shadovar would overhear him. "We are needed."

Through the thickening shadow fog rising from the battle below, the Most High was barely visible, a ghostly figure standing at the edge of the Chosen's melted defense barrier. He was staring down into the bottom of the basin, where the mythallar sat amid the fuming tatters of the dimensional portal Khelben and the others had been lowering over it when he finally revealed himself by spraying a wave of shadow fire across their overhead protection.

The battle after that had been as fast as it was furious, with the five remaining princes diving straight through the black flames to attack. In the few moments it took for the barrier to burn away enough for Galaeron to see what was happening, the dimensional portal was destroyed, the Chosen were engaged by the princes, and the city stopped falling—at least temporarily. The obsidian mythallar was a truncated sphere no more than a hundred feet high, but with ghostly shapes gliding about inside and the same dark aura as the first time Galaeron had seen it.

The fight raging around the mythallar was both fierce and wild, with shadow balls and lightning bolts crashing against spell shields, silver blades clanging against black, feet and fists flying too fast for an eye to follow. Fearful of creating more dimensional rifts like the one that had sucked Elminster into the Nine Hells, both sides were avoiding the use of pure magic. Even so, in half a dozen places there were alarming whirls of shadow-filled air, two of which seemed to be drawing spells into their spinning hearts and growing larger as they fed on the magic.

Galaeron pointed at the broad-shouldered figure of Prince Clariburnus, who was being steadily beaten back by a blinding flurry of blade and foot attacks from Dove Falconhand.

"See if you can take Clariburnus from behind," he told Aris, "and tip the balance in our favor."

Aris hefted his giant hammer and replied, "I'll distract him at least, but it worries me that we see only the princes and the Most High." The giant gestured at Telamont, who was holding his palms out toward the damaged mythallar, no doubt controlling the flow of the Shadow Weave to steady the city, and asked, "Where is their army?"

"Anywhere but here," Galaeron replied.

It didn't take a wild guess to know that the Shadovar would not want to run the risk that one of their soldiers would meet a stream of the Chosen's silver fire with a shadow bolt. The resulting tear in the world fabric might well suck the entire enclave into a plane more hellish than the one they had just escaped.

Aris grunted, and asked, "Do I want to know what you will be doing?"

Galaeron pointed at Telamont and said, "I'll be keeping the Most High busy."

Aris's eyes went wide.

"Has your shadow made you insane?" he gasped. "You're no match—"

"A bloodfly is no match for a rothé, but which one does the biting?" Galaeron motioned Aris forward and said, "You will emerge behind Clariburnus."

Aris regarded Galaeron with a skeptical expression.

"Be careful, my friend. I have not yet given up on you."

Galaeron smiled and said, "Then it must be true, what the Sy'Tel'Quessir say—there is nothing more stubborn than a Stone Giant." He laid a hand behind Aris's knee and pushed.

"Hurry, before those fools open another hell mouth."

Aris lurched forward, stumbling out of the Fringe. Galaeron remained behind long enough to see him emerge from the basin's obsidian wall a few paces behind Clariburnus, his great hammer already arcing down toward his target's head. The prince sensed the attack at the last instant and twisted away, but the distraction was all Dove Falconhand needed to drive her own attacks home. Flinging magic with one hand and swinging steel with the other, she first dispelled the Shadovar's blade guard, then sank her magic sword to the hilt in his abdomen. He stumbled back under Aris's legs, letting out a throaty howl that was audible even above the battle din. The prince took his vengeance by slashing his black sword behind Aris's leg.

The giant's knee buckled, and that was as long as Galaeron dared watch before leaping out of the Fringe. He came out directly behind Telamont, kicking with both feet, calling a bolt of black lightning with one hand and swinging his stolen sword with the other.

The Most High did not flinch. He did not even look. He merely stepped out of the way. As Galaeron sailed past, he swung the sword and flung the lightning. As soon as his black blade touched Telamont's robe, it shattered. The lightning bolt fizzled an inch from his hand, then Galaeron found himself hanging motionless before his target, staring into a pair of flickering platinum eyes.

"Elf!" the Most High barked. In his anger, Telamont almost balled one of his wispy hands, and the city trembled as his control over the mythallar slipped. "How did you get free?"

Galaeron smiled—it seemed the Most High did not know all that happened in his palace.

"In the most unexpected way possible . . ."

Galaeron opened himself to the Shadow Weave and felt its cold magic come flowing into him from every direction.

"I took your advice."

Galaeron turned his palm outward and unleashed a bolt of pure shadow magic. The attack seemed to take Telamont by surprise, if only because he had not been prepared to see Galaeron calling upon the Shadow Weave. Unfortunately, it also had next to no effect, casting only a short-lived cloud over the Most High's face before it vanished into the darkness beneath his cowl. The city seemed to fall once more—for just a heartbeat—then the Most High caught it again.

"You have yielded to your shadow, I see," Telamont said. "It will not be long before you are able to return the information Melegaunt worked so hard to collect."

"I can recall it now," Galaeron said, "but you wouldn't be wise to count on me for favors—and 'yielded' is not the word I would have used. I have joined with my shadow, but my will remains my own."

Telamont's platinum eyes flashed, and Galaeron's limbs spread outward. He spun around until he was hanging upside down over the battle. Aris lay on the floor of the basin, bleeding from three different wounds and writhing in pain. The Chosen were faring far better. Though both Dove and Storm were pouring blood from rents in their armor, only three princes remained in the basin. Prince Mattick was giving ground under a furious assault of blade and spell.

All Galaeron had to do was keep Telamont's attention focused on him instead of the fight. He tried again to open himself to the Shadow Weave, but all he felt this time was a spongy presence through which no magic would pass.

"Is something wrong, elf?" Telamont asked. "Perhaps your will is not your own, after all?"

In the basin below, Prince Mattick had dropped to a knee beneath the furious onslaught of magic coming from Alustriel and Laeral. Dove and Khelben were driving his brother Vattick away from him and would soon be in a position to finish him with a blow from behind.

"My will is enough mine to vow you shall never have the

knowledge Melegaunt passed to me," Galaeron said. "And if you doubt I have the strength to keep my oath—"

"Your strength I do not doubt. You resisted your shadow far too long." Telamont's voice was wispy and cold. "A pity, really. Had you surrendered to it as I urged, I could have saved you as I did Hadrhune. Now, you are useless to me. I will be forced to wring the knowledge from your worthless mind . . . just as I have your foolish hope for defeating my princes."

As Telamont spoke these last words, the princes Aglarel and Yder emerged behind Alustriel and Laeral. Aglarel caught Alustriel from behind with a vicious overhand strike that cleaved her a foot and a half through the shoulder blade before she could teleport away in a wailing spray of crimson blood.

Khelben glimpsed Yder from the corner of his eye and aiming his black staff over Laeral's shoulder blasted him with a storm of meteors that sent him tumbling halfway up the basin wall.

That left Mattick free to counterattack. He rose, wielding an oversized black sword in one hand and flinging a spray of winged black spiders from the other. The spiders swarmed Khelben's head in a droning black cloud, but it was the sword that proved most deadly, hacking Dove's leg off at the knee. She fell cursing and saved herself from a deadly second blow by unleashing a long ribbon of silver fire.

Mattick escaped a certain death only by flinging himself off to one side and bowling Khelben over by rolling into his legs. In the meantime, Dove's silver fire was burning through the shadowy fog above the basin, and Galaeron glimpsed a curving sweep of a sandy lakeshore far below. It took him a moment to register what he was seeing, and he realized why the mythallar was so difficult to find except through the shadows. The basin was in what had once been the the top of the mountain but was now the bottom of the city, resting upside-down and looking straight down upon the desert below.

The hole in the clouds closed as quickly as it had opened, and Dove teleported to safety as well. Only Khelben, Laeral, and Storm remained, with the five Shadovar princes closing in around them and relentlessly herding the trio toward a whirling cyclone of shadow-filled air. There was Aris, too, still writhing on the floor, slowly sliding toward the middle of the basin on a sheet of his own crimson blood. No one was paying him any attention, and Galaeron quickly looked back to Telamont, lest the Most High sense the hope growing in his heart and do something to stop the clever giant.

Galaeron found even that strategy fraught with peril. Sliding down the basin wall behind Telamont was Vala, holding one hand clamped into a fist so she could point a star-shaped ring at the Most High's back. In the other she carried her darksword, her arm cocked and ready to throw at the first sign that he knew she was there.

Desperate to keep his mind on something else—and terrified that Telamont had already sensed his thoughts—Galaeron looked back to the Chosen.

"Use the silver fire!" he shouted. "It is the only—"

"Silence, you fool!" Telamont said. "Would you destroy Faerûn rather than let us have a place—"

He too fell silent as, to Galaeron's amazement, Khelben raised his hand and loosed a stream of the shimmering magic fire at Telamont. Crying out in rage and disbelief, Telamont had no choice but to lift both hands and raise a spell shield before him. Freed of the Most High's grasp, Galaeron plummeted toward the bottom of the basin and barely had time to cry out a spell of soft falling before the air erupted into whistling white sparks and cracking lances of black lightning. He brought his legs around beneath him and landed atop the mythallar itself—just in time to turn and see Vala come tumbling into Telamont from behind.

What happened next was impossible to say. He saw Telamont's shadowy feet fly, Vala's sword arc, and a black arm whip into the crackling air. All of them dissolved into shadow.

The blow of a tremendous hammer shook the mythallar, and Aris cried out in triumph. Something like a volcano exploded beneath Galaeron's feet, and he found himself tumbling through air as black and as thick as tar.

He smashed into an obsidian wall and tumbled to his feet only to have his legs fly out from beneath him as the basin swung up beside him. He went somersaulting down toward the edge then came to a sudden stop, then went cartwheeling back toward the center. Three times he glimpsed the mythallar, chipped and pouring shadow fume out into the basin, with Aris wedging his legs beneath one side and still hammering at it with his sculpting hammer, before he hit it and stopped.

"Aha, Galaeron!" Aris cried. "It is an unworkable stone, but not too hard to flake!"

"I think—" the basin pitched wildly in the other direction, and Galaeron barely kept himself from tumbling away by grabbing hold of the giant's tool bag—"you have done enough!"

Aris stopped hammering long enough to ask, "What else is there to do?"

Galaeron saw Vala go tumbling by—and sweep Vattick off his feet to leave a severed Shadovar leg in her wake—before she vanished into the black mist and began to scream a savage Vaasan war cry. Galaeron plucked a handful of shadowstuff from the blackening air and shaped it into a pair of spiders. One of these he passed to Aris with instructions to swallow, and the other he gulped down himself. Two quick incantations later, and they were both scrambling across the basin on all fours, their hands and feet sticking to the slick surface as though coated with paste.

They found Vala and the last three Chosen in desperate straits, unable to keep their feet and caught inside a ring of Shadovar princes. Aglarel hurled a shadow ball at Storm, who barely managed to swing her legs around in time to take the attack in the thigh instead of her chest. The orb drilled a fist-sized hole through muscle and bone that clearly left her unable to fight, yet she did not teleport away as had the other Chosen when they grew too wounded to fight. Khelben leveled his staff at the prince who had wounded her, but the only thing that shot from the end was a laughable drizzle of yellow light.

Galaeron touched a finger to his temple, then used his shadow magic to speak to Aris in his thoughts

They're helpless! he explained. *The shadowstuff is smothering their magic.*

Aris nodded then pointed to Aglarel and Yder, and hefted his hammer.

Good, Galaeron sent. *Go.*

They sprang forward together, Aris catching the two princes by surprise, smashing their helms and sending them somersaulting across the basin floor before they vanished into the black mists. Galaeron caught Mattick from behind with a shadow bolt that sent him tumbling headlong into the Chosen's midst, where Laeral and Khelben quickly proved that they were not entirely helpless by planting their daggers at least twice in every unarmored inch before the prince beat a hasty retreat by dissolving back into the shadows.

That left Brennus, Clariburnus, and Dethud attacking from behind. A pair of dark bolts caught Khelben in the shoulders and sent him sliding across the basin toward Aris, while a shadow claw extended from Dethud's forearm to close around Laeral's throat and start dragging her back toward the Shadovar's ranks. Galaeron leaped forward to attack, but Vala was already hurling her darksword into the prince's chest. The weapon sank to the hilt, then dropped to the floor as Dethud retreated into the shadows.

Vala called the weapon back to hand and started to charge Brennus but was knocked from her feet as that basin made another wild swing. Her hip had barely touched down before she was back on her feet and starting forward.

Galaeron caught her by the arm and said, "It's done."

"Not yet." She turned and pointed up the basin wall into the black mists and said, "I got one of his arms, but Telamont's still up there."

A pair of dark disks came hissing across the basin and would have slashed their heads off, had Aris not knocked them off their feet before it arrived. Galaeron rolled to his knees and counterattacked with a flight of shadow arrows.

Brennus blocked them easily and sent the dark shafts streaming back in their direction. Aris took two in his arm, and Vala one in her shoulder, and three more nicked Galaeron along one side of his neck and arm.

"It's done," Galaeron said. They were the most difficult words he had ever been forced to say, and also the surest. He took Vala's arm and shoved her back toward the three battered Chosen. "We aren't going to win this."

Aris refused to retreat.

"But the mythallar—"

"Is cracked," Galaeron said. "Perhaps that will be enough to bring the city down."

Aris turned and hurled his hammer at the heart of mythallar.

Clariburnus waved his hand and sent the tool somersaulting away, then Brennus sent a bank of black fog rolling toward them. Galaeron raised a wind spell that he hoped would send the fog rolling back toward the princes, but Brennus dispelled it with a gesture. Storm began to choke on the fumes, and it occurred to Galaeron that he was learning something else about power, that sometimes the most difficult part of wielding it was knowing when it was not enough.

"We've done as much as we can."

Galaeron motioned for the wounded giant to gather up Storm and the other Chosen, then he grabbed hold of Vala and shoved her into the others.

"Well said, elf," Khelben replied. He stretched a hand behind Vala's back to clasp Galaeron on the shoulder. "You're learning."

Another shadow bolt came hissing into the group to catch Storm square in the back. Laeral's arm lashed out to catch her sister under the arm, then the basin tipped precariously in the opposite direction. Only Aris's sticky appendages and long reach kept the group from tumbling across the basin and becoming separated again.

"All right!" Laeral cried. "Galaeron, will you please get us out of here while there's still something left to get out of?"

CHAPTER FOURTEEN

2 Eleasias, the Year of Wild Magic

Ruha sat wedged in a shady cleft high in the Scimitar Spires East, watching the Shade Enclave slowly sink toward the purple waters of Shadow Lake. Enormous as it was and swaddled in black shadow-stuff, the enclave resembled a storm cloud crashing down from on high, complete with sheets of silver lightning illuminating jagged sweeps of misty curtain and mysterious, half-heard roars rumbling out from its hidden heart. Veserab riders were descending from the city in masses of swirling wings, and hordes of shadow walkers were beginning to emerge from dark places all across the nearby hills. This increased the likelihood that she would be forced to flee before she found her friends—and Malik—but Ruha was glad to see so many Shadovar escaping alive. As terrible as were the calamities they had unleashed on Faerûn with their shadow blankets, she had no thirst for vengeance. The death of an entire city would do nothing to bring back the hordes who had already perished.

The enclave—or rather, the black cloud surrounding the enclave—dropped an abrupt five hundred feet, sending scores of veserabs tumbling through the air and bringing the city approximately level with Ruha's hiding place. Though it was difficult to see much through the billowing murk, every so often she glimpsed a crag of stone cliff sweeping past, or an expanse of black wall plummeting down out of the shadows only to suddenly reverse direction and vanish back into the gloom.

Shade was wobbling, Ruha realized, as though someone were struggling to keep it aloft. She could only guess what that meant for her friends, but it could not be good. Certainly, they were not the ones attempting to save the city.

"Storm?" Ruha said aloud. "How fare you? I am here."

Knowing the Weave would carry no more than a few words to Storm's ear, Ruha stopped there. Several more times, a craggy cliff emerged from the black mists and swept past. Each time, the stony face seemed a little hazier and indistinct, as though she were looking through a denser fog—or more of it. Despite this, she quickly began to recognize the features of the cliff and realized that the city was no longer sinking.

Someone was saving it.

"Storm?" Ruha called again. "Khelben? Are you there?"

When no response came she tried Laeral, then Alustriel, and finally she received an answer.

The battle went badly, and I cannot contact them either. Even coming to Ruha through the Weave, Alustriel's voice sounded weak and full of pain. *I was wounded and forced to leave. Is Shade still . . . ?*

It stopped sinking, Ruha replied using Alustriel's spell. *What that means, I don't know.*

Dove was injured as well, Alustriel reported. *I hesitate to ask, but—*

I'll learn what I can, Ruha offered.

The rumble of a collapsing building—or perhaps several of them—sounded somewhere inside the enclave, then a huge cascade of rubble tumbled out of the cloud and splashed into Shadow Lake.

The situation here is unsteady, Ruha sent, *you may not hear from me for some time.*

Thank you, Alustriel said. *Be careful. Dove and I will return as soon as we are well enough to help.*

Ruha watched until the rubble had stopped splashing into the lake, then she drizzled a little saliva on her hand. She had not used her magic for fear of alerting a Shadovar patrol to her presence, but Alustriel's request rendered that fear irrelevant. The Shining Lady would never have asked for help, were she not worried that Galaeron's plan had gone terribly wrong. Ruha made a wiping motion in the air before her, at the same time using the elemental magic favored by desert witches to cast a spell of clear seeing.

The shadow mist grew transparent, so long as she looked straight ahead. For the first time, she saw Shade unmasked. The city of grand palaces and imposing edifices that had seemed so breathtaking was gone. In its place hung a jumbled mountain of shabby tenements and dilapidated mansions, collapsing one after the other as the enclave lurched about like a camel on the deck of a storm-tossed ship. Even the overturned peak upon which it rested was flaky disintegrating shale instead of hard granite.

Pouring down the face of the mountain was a stunning thread of silver liquid, not so much falling into the lake as stretching down through the surface. Whether it actually touched bottom or continued through it down into the heart of the Phaerlin was impossible to say, but Ruha knew by how the strand remained tight from top to bottom that it was not falling water. She followed its shining line up to the source and discovered that it came from a cleft in a red, heart-shaped boulder lodged in a horizontal fissure about halfway up the mountain.

Swinging about beneath the boulder, affixed to it by some means not apparent at that distance, was a pudgy little shape with a pair of tiny nubs rising from the top of his head. Ruha needed no more magic to recognize what she was seeing. She knew a pair of cuckold's antlers when she saw them.

It was Malik's accursed fortune that the Shadovar had to be the worst smiths on this plane or any other. He was hanging with his feet braced against the lower lip of the sun slit, trying to pull the Karsestone—which stood a full head higher than he was tall—through an opening that rose only to his chin. One of the links in his manacle chain had opened. The gap was not large, but given his strength and his pitiful condition even that much was a comment on the sorry state of Shadovar metalworking.

"Cyric!" he called.

He continued to pull, but kept a careful eye on the link.

"The One—"

The cleft swept upward as the city began another of its wild oscillations. For perhaps the hundredth time, Malik found himself tumbling down toward the opposite corner. He could think of nothing but the weak chain, of what would become of him if the link opened and he went tumbling into the lake below. Drowning would be the least of it. Thirsty as he was, it might even be pleasant. Afterward, though, the things that would happen to his spirit if he failed Cyric and died . . . that he could not even bear to contemplate.

The free manacle struck him in the head, and the chain jerked him along upside-down. He slammed into the upper lip of the sun slit and flipped down in front of the tumbling

Karsestone just in time to catch a long spray of whole magic straight in the face. He began to cough violently, then the boulder was rolling onto his chest. Ribs crackled, his breath left him in a scream, and the stone stopped. On top of him.

Malik cursed and kicked and shoved, but the thing would not budge. It was wedged in place against the ceiling of the slit, which meant he had somehow—at last—dragged it into the opening.

He craned his neck to the side, and through the cascade of silvery magic pouring down over his face, he glimpsed a ragged notch in the upper lip of the sun slit. Malik began to believe he might really succeed in stealing the stone. That he would no doubt be killed in the process was an unpleasant consequence, but in his service to Cyric, he had suffered many things far worse.

The pain was beyond belief, and it was impossible to draw breath, but Malik had long ago learned to ignore minor inconveniences such as those. He hooked his heels over the lip of the opening and pulled. The Karsestone slipped a little—and more weight settled on his chest.

Maybe that meant there would be more room at the top. Malik pulled harder with his legs. Something snapped in his chest. He pulled harder *and* shoved with his arms. Nothing moved, but he did grow dizzy from lack of air. Thus reminded that the stone was laying on *him*, he saw that if he could only get out from beneath it, there would be room for it to fall completely on its side and slide out into the empty air.

Lacking any other means of extracting himself, Malik straightened his legs and began to swing them back and forth in a widening arc, trying to work first his hips free, then the rest of his body as well. Behind him, the roar and crash of screaming Shadovar and tumbling stone rose and faded in time to the wild oscillations of the enclave. The Karsestone pressed more heavily as the slit swung downward. Malik's vision closed in, and stars began to appear around the edges of the darkening tunnel. The rush of oblivion filled his ears, then the slit reached the apogee of its swing and started back down.

The weight all but vanished. Malik flung his legs down in the direction they were traveling and felt his hips slip out from beneath the boulder. He rolled to his side and pushed, hard, and was free.

The Karsestone rocked toward him.

"Devil rock!"

Malik pushed off and pivoted on his hip, whirling out of its path and back into the loom chamber. The Karsestone settled on its side, rocked to the right, rocked to the left, and slipped over the edge.

The manacle stretched Malik's arm out full, and he thought his hand would pop free of his wrist. Instead, he flew out the sun slit after it and found himself following the Karsestone down through a swirling cloud of veserab riders. The boulder struck glancing blows to two beasts and sent them tumbling and hissing away, then finally caught one square between the wings. The impact slowed their fall just long enough for a little slack to develop in the chain that connected Malik to the stone. The rider slipped past, bloody and twisted on one side and the mount broken and screeching on the other, then the purple waters of Shadow Lake grew visible no more than a thousand feet below.

Malik smiled.

"Cyric!" he screamed. "Hear me now, Cyric, the One—"

When he cried the last word, no sound came from his mouth. The lake continued to come up beneath him, though with the ferocious wind filling his eyes with tears, it was all but impossible to see. He tried again and remained as mute as a tortoise. He cursed Shar, thinking she was only trying to protect her prize, then glimpsed a dark shape angling down to intercept him. Thinking it was only an alert Shadovar lord, Malik reached for his stolen dagger—and instantly found himself engulfed in a web of sticky magic strands.

In a web of sticky strands of *Weave* magic.

Malik stopped falling, and wailed more in frustration than pain as the Karsestone stretched his manacle chain taut—again—and jerked his shoulder out of its socket. He thought the terrible strain would tear off his arm. Instead, the boulder stopped falling, and he found himself staring out a small gap down his manacle chain to the open link. The gap was as wide as a dagger blade and growing before the one eye that could see it.

Malik tried to see who had captured him, but the magic web held his head too tightly for it to turn. It hardly mattered. He knew without looking who it was. She had a gift for arriving when he most needed her to be somewhere else. They turned and started across the lake toward the Scimitar Mountains.

"Where are your manners, Malik?" Ruha called. "Will you not thank me for saving your life?"

The opening in the link continued to grow, and in his fury it barely registered that Ruha had annulled the magic that had silenced him earlier. "Meddling Harper witch!" Malik cried. "Can you not see that I am robbing the Shadovar of their greatest power?"

"And giving it to Cyric, I am certain," Ruha surmised, relieving him of the compulsion to add this himself. "I think the rest of us will be better served with the Karsestone in the hands of the Chosen—and you standing before a Harper court."

"You may as well murder me here!" Realizing that he could speak again, Malik tried again to say, "Cyric, the—"

Again, his words began to spill silently from his mouth. They passed out from beneath the city's shadow, but Malik could see that the chain would never hold until they reached shore. The open link was straightening before his eyes. He tried to call out, hoping that if he could warn Ruha she would at least save the stone until he could steal it later, but the only thing to leave his mouth was his silent, anguished breath.

The link lost its last bit of curve, and the Karsestone

plummeted free. Malik and Ruha shot skyward, but only long enough for Ruha to regain control and start down after the falling stone.

"You heel-biting cur!" Ruha stormed. "What have you done?"

Even had he been able to speak, Malik would not have bothered to defend himself. He was too busy trying to mark the place the stone would enter the water. Flapping along behind the diving witch as he was, that was an impossible thing in its own right. He saw little more than flashes of dark water and streams of fleeing veserabs.

"Kozah's breath!" Ruha cursed.

She pulled up sharply, and suddenly. As Malik swung beneath her he had a view of nothing but water. A giant waterspout was rising up to meet the Karsestone, seven watery fingers stretching out to entwine it. Perhaps the One had heard after all. Or so Malik prayed.

The silvery fingers closed around the boulder and pulled it down into Shadow Lake, leaving behind a huge black whirlpool. Malik prayed that it had been Cyric's hand that had taken the crown of the Shadow Weave and that consequently he would not be left to languish forever in the hell of his god's displeasure.

But it was not to be. As the stone vanished into the lake's murky depths, a glistening purple eye appeared in the heart of the whirlpool and winked at him.

Malik knew better than to hope the eye belonged to Cyric. The One never sent signs, except when he was angry.

Head spinning with afterdaze, Galaeron arrived clasping Vala's hand, his other arm looped around Aris's knee, his eyes aching in the brilliant sun. Crackles, bangs, and half-muffled roars rumbled out of the sky while off in the distance an erratic din of booming splashes rolled across a broad expanse of water. There was trouble over there, and it slowly came back to Galaeron that he and his companions were the cause. Aris groaned, stumbling forward, and crashed to a knee, spilling an armload of bloodied humans as he put a hand out to catch himself.

A glimpse of black beard was all it took for Galaeron to recall where he was and how he had come to be there. Instead of turning to check on the injured Chosen, he looked back and was disappointed to see the murk-swaddled city still hovering a thousand feet in the air, engulfed in swirling clouds of veserabs and releasing a steady rain of debris down into the lake. There were no obvious signs of pursuit, though anyone powerful enough to recapture Galaeron and three Chosen would come by shadow, not air.

As Galaeron studied the enclave, he noticed a thin line of darkness running between the lake and the city. It was near the shore and so faint as to be almost invisible but also straight and unwavering. As he watched, the lower end moved out toward deeper water, slicing through the purple waves without leaving a wake. Shade itself remained where it was. Galaeron spent a few moments observing, trying to puzzle out what he was seeing. Veserabs circled around it, and debris bounced off it as though it were a solid rope, yet it was as transparent as a pale shadow. Through it he could see passing Shadovar, falling boulders, and even the mountains on the lake's far shore.

Galaeron finally gave up guessing, and seeing that the enclave was not going to sink any lower, he turned back to his companions. Laeral was handing Aris his third flask of healing potion, and the wounds Khelben and Storm had suffered were already closing. Khelben held a vial out to Galaeron and motioned at the gashes in his neck.

"You may as well take care of those before we return."

"Return?" Aris asked. The flask Laeral had given him slipped from his hand and shattered on the stony ground. He appeared not to notice. "To Shade?"

"That's where the mythallar is," Storm replied. She stood and tested her wounded leg. It nearly buckled beneath her, but that did not stop her from nodding approvingly. "I'll need a quarter hour, no more."

In what seemed another life, Galaeron would have been impressed by how quickly the Chosen healed. Having seen what he had seen and knowing how quickly any Shadovar warrior—especially the princes—could heal themselves, he knew his companions to be woefully overmatched.

But it was Aris who objected.

"Has that silver fire melted your brains? We can't return to Shade without Galaeron's magic, and look at him!" Hardly seeming to notice the two shadow arrows still lodged in his shoulder, the giant waved a huge arm in Galaeron's direction. "He's going to have a terrible time getting back to normal as it is. You can't ask him to use more shadow magic."

"Aris, there's no 'normal' to get back *to*. I've told you that," Galaeron said, wondering how he would ever make the giant understand that shadow and light were only illusions. Once one accepted the truth of that, everything became light . . . and everything became shadow. "I was not all good before, and my shadow was not all bad."

"You could have fooled me," Aris said. "Or perhaps you have forgotten what happened in the Saiyaddar?"

"Of course not, but that happened because of the struggle, not because of my shadow. It's the refusal to yield that causes the crisis."

"It was the crisis that Telamont was trying to exploit," Laeral surmised. "He wanted to make you fear your shadow so you would keep struggling and remain unbalanced until he could take control."

"To some extent, yes," Galaeron agreed, "but the struggle *is* necessary. You need to build strength. The shadow is very strong, and I think it would overwhelm you if you accepted it too soon."

"I understand—better than you can know." Laeral said. She cast a private glance at Khelben then looked back to Galaeron. "Once you're ready, accepting your shadow will make you stronger and better."

"Stronger, yes, but better?" Galaeron asked. "I don't know. Strength overcomes weakness, so the strengths in my shadow have overcome some weaknesses in my character, and the strengths in my character have overcome most of the weaknesses in my shadow. So I feel whole—but that hardly makes me a paladin. The world is a darker place than I knew before, and I'm the darker for seeing that. It's not something I'd describe as better."

Sympathetic expressions came to the faces of all three of the Chosen, and Khelben said, "We can't know what you're going through, Galaeron, but I'm sure we share this much. There are times when we all wish we could go back to, uh . . . the way we were before, but the door only opens one way."

"And even were it possible to go back, I would still use any magic necessary to return us to the city," Galaeron said. As thankful as he was for the understanding and comradeship the Chosen were extending to him, he was also convinced that it was folly to do as they asked. "If we return now, we accomplish nothing but our own deaths. The princes heal as fast as the Chosen, and there are more of them than of us."

"Which is why we must strike now, and quickly," Storm said. Her eyes were locked on Galaeron, fixing him in place like a snake pinned beneath an eagle's claw. "This is your plan. Will you see it through or not?"

"Not if it means losing three of Mystra's Chosen," Galaeron said. "Impotent though you may be, you are the only hope Faerûn has, and I will not—"

"Impotent?" Khelben grumbled. He stepped closer, all trace of his earlier camaraderie vanished. He raised his famous black staff as though he meant to rap Galaeron on the brow with it. "I will teach you impotent!"

Galaeron stood unflinching, ready to take whatever blow

the wizard cared to deliver, if that would make him and the other Chosen listen.

Laeral spared him the necessity, catching Khelben by the arm and dragging him back a step.

"He has a point, my love. Telamont will not have failed to notice our helplessness once the mythallar was cracked."

"All the more reason to strike now." Khelben's glare slid from Galaeron to Laeral as he said, "Before he expects our return. If we are as 'impotent' as the elf claims, surprise may be our only chance."

"And if we fail, we have no chance," Aris countered.

" 'We?' " Storm echoed. "I doubt there is any sense in your risking your life as well, my friend. Your size is nothing but a hindrance, and your strength will do us little good."

"Little good?" Aris boomed. "Did you not notice that I am the one who cracked the mythallar? You are not returning without me, I promise you that."

Though it did not escape Galaeron's notice how smoothly Storm had shifted the topic to *how* they would return from *whether*, he turned a deaf ear to the argument and glanced toward Vala. She had remained on the fringes of the argument, silent and withdrawn, watching him the entire time in the blunt Vaasan way. Her green eyes remained as enigmatic as the emeralds they resembled.

Galaeron would have given anything to know what she was thinking. Did she consider him weak for yielding to his shadow? Or was she under the misconception—as he had been—that it was a sacrifice necessary to save Faerûn? He considered it a given that she hated him for abandoning her to Escanor. After all that had befallen her—and Telamont had described it to him many times while he was a prisoner in the Palace Most High—he did not understand how she could stand to look upon his face without drawing her sword, but the choice had been hers. She was the one who had hurt him in order to save him, and if her plan had worked she had only herself to blame.

Galaeron knew what he saw in Vala's eyes: anger. She had given so much to protect him. It could only seem to her that he had thrown her sacrifice back in her face, that he had returned to Shade without a thought to what she had done and become the thing she had so desperately tried to prevent.

She was right. Though he had certainly hoped to free Vala, it was Evereska and Faerûn he had come to save. The Chosen would never have agreed to help him otherwise, and he could see how right they would have been. Vala was a mere afterthought, one even Galaeron would have forsaken for a slight increase in their chances of success.

None of that changed his love for her—or how he wished he had spoken to her about it when there was still a chance she would listen.

Galaeron grew aware of a heavy silence and realized the others were looking at him.

Without taking his eyes off Vala, he said, "You know the Shadovar better than anyone here. What do you want to do?"

"What I want is to end this and go home." Vala's gaze finally left Galaeron's. She turned to face Khelben and said, "What I think—"

Vala pulled her darksword and spun back in Galaeron's direction, her arm drawing back to throw.

Startled by just how badly he had underestimated her anger, Galaeron opened himself to the Shadow Weave. He swirled his hand before his body and hissed a wispy Shadovar spell, and a shadowy disk of protection sprang into existence between him and Vala.

Vala dropped her gaze and scowled, and it was only then that Galaeron realized she had been looking past his shoulder. Khelben took advantage of the distraction to slip to her side and catch her by the crook of the elbow.

"No need, my dear," he said. "It's Ruha."

Vala squinted into the sky above Galaeron and said, "So it is. She really should wear some other color."

Galaeron turned to see Ruha's black-cloaked figure sweeping down from the sky, her *aba* and veil flapping wildly in the wind and a familiar figure dangling from a manacle chain attached to her wrist.

"Aha!" Aris boomed, yelling in Malik's direction. "Let us see how you like life in bondage!"

Ruha circled them once, losing altitude, then let Malik slam down and dragged him half a dozen steps across the rocky ground before alighting gently herself.

She bowed in Storm's direction, and pinning Malik's neck to the ground with her foot, touched her fingers to her brow. "Well met, my friends. Have you conversed with your sisters?"

Storm cast a quick glance in the direction of the other Chosen then said, "Not since our defeat in Shade."

Thinking that no one was paying attention to him, Malik snaked his free hand out to reach for a rock. He found three throwing daggers—Galaeron's, Vala's, and Ruha's—planted in the ground around his wrist and quickly withdrew the offending arm.

Ruha continued the conversation without pause.

"I am pleased to say they both survived. When they could not reach you in the customary ways, Alustriel grew worried and asked me to investigate."

"How long before they're ready to attack the mythallar again?" Khelben asked. Turning to Galaeron, he added, "They'd make a big difference, especially if we're willing to risk the silver fire."

"Fight? In the shadow harlot's den?" Malik cried. "I will cut my wrist off before I allow you to drag me back there!"

"Your wrist is safe for now." Galaeron met Khelben's gaze and said, "There is no point in fighting on their ground. Better to attack the shadow blankets directly and draw them out as the phaerimm were doing."

"It hardly matters to you, Malik," Ruha said. She pulled him to his feet, jerking his hand away from Vala's dagger just as his fingers brushed the hilt. "If I am not needed here, I ask leave to return Malik to the justice of Twilight Hall, while I still have him chained to my wrist."

All three Chosen inclined their heads with expressions that suggested they would be just as happy to adjudicate the matter themselves and be done with it there.

Storm said, "An excellent plan, and I think enough magic remains here for us to see you safely sped along your way."

"To Twilight Hall?" Malik's fear was evident in the way his voice cracked. "I'll be murdered!"

"Only after you are found guilty of a few of your crimes," Khelben answered. "And the word is 'executed'."

"Executed or murdered, it is all the same!" Malik cast a plaintive gaze in Aris's direction and said, "Will you just sit by and let them do this to someone who has saved your life so many times?"

"I will be glad to describe how you saved me," he said, "and also how you enslaved me so you could use my shape studies to grow your church!"

For the first time, a look of despair came over Malik's round face. He seemed to consider his options for a moment then turned to Khelben with a wild-eyed gaze.

"I can tell you how to destroy Telamont Tanthul in a single strike!" He remained silent only a moment before his mouth began to twitch, and more words spilled out. "Of course, there is every chance that you will destroy all of Shade and half of Anauroch with him. . . ."

Even a prospect that terrible was not enough to keep Khelben from cocking his eyebrow.

"You know I can never lie," Malik reminded him.

"We're listening," Laeral said.

Malik's bulging eyes appeared to focus on the tip of Ruha's boot as he planned what he would say next. Given what he had already told them about the pitfalls, Galaeron could not believe the Chosen were even interested in hearing the suggestion.

Finally, Malik looked back to Khelben and said, "What good will it do me to save the world if I am not here to see it?"

Ruha dropped a knee into the middle of his back and used a cuckold's antler to pull his head up, then wrapped the chain connecting their manacles around his neck.

"What makes you think I would ever let you tell them something that would destroy Anauroch?" Ruha asked. "I would rather see you dead and stand before the judges of Twilight Hall myself!"

She tightened the chain until he began to gasp. "Ruha!" Khelben shouted. He seemed as surprised as Galaeron was by the witch's behavior. "Let him speak."

"Never!" she replied, pulling until Malik's eyes began to bulge. "If you want to know—"

Ruha's exclamation came to an abrupt end as Storm plucked her off Malik's back.

"Harper hag!" Malik croaked. "I ought to tell them just for spite!" Again, his face contorted into a conflicted mask, and he added, "Except that after what happened in Shadowdale, I know no Chosen would ever be foolish enough to fling a bolt of silver fire into a being of pure shadow essence."

Galaeron did not realize Ruha's threat had been a ruse until he saw her exchange congratulatory glances with each of the Chosen.

Laeral said, "Not very helpful, Malik."

"Actually, we've already tried silver fire," Storm said. She didn't explain that the attack had only been a ruse designed to buy time for Vala. "Telamont blocked it with a shielding spell."

"Though that hardly matters," Khelben added. "I no longer have much influence with the Harpers anyway."

"Harpers?" Malik screeched. "I am talking about Ruha."

"In exchange for revealing that Telamont Tanthul is pure shadowstuff?" Galaeron scoffed. He was beginning to understand the game the Chosen were playing. "You'll have to do better than that if you want me to set you free."

"There is no use listening to him, Malik," Ruha warned. "*That* will never happen."

The anger in Ruha's eyes was convincing, and it occurred to Galaeron that the others might not realize he had joined their game.

"Perhaps not while you live," Galaeron said, keeping his tone even. He dropped his hand to the hilt of his sword. "It makes no difference to me."

Malik's eyes lit like a pair of torches.

"Kill her?" asked Malik. He considered the situation for a moment, then grew doubtful. "You are too much of a coward. You would never do such a thing."

"To save Evereska?" Galaeron responded. "What do you think I *wouldn't* do?"

It did not escape Galaeron's notice that Khelben, Vala, and all the rest were inching in his direction—nor did it escape Malik's. He considered the proposal only a moment.

"You have already won!" Malik blurted. "There is no need to destroy the mythallar or even to slay Telamont." He would have stopped there, but for Mystra's curse. "They cannot make their shadow blankets without the magic of the Karsestone, and the Karsestone is gone!"

"What?" This from Vala, who was finally beginning to seem interested in the discussion. "Gone how?"

"Into the lake," Ruha explained. "It was attached to his other wrist and fell free. A waterspout reached up to take it."

"It was Shar's hand," Malik explained in a dismal voice. "She has had control of the Shadow Weave all along."

This was enough to make Galaeron draw his sword and press the blade to Ruha's throat. Storm and Vala drew their own blades and stepped over to defend the witch, and it was not clear to Galaeron whether they were warning him off or just supporting his act. In fact, he was no longer sure that he was acting. Doing his best to seem as though he might be worried about the possibility of fighting two of the best swordswomen in Faerûn, Galaeron kept his blade pressed to Ruha's throat.

"Before I set you free," he said to Malik, "tell me how you know all this."

Malik eagerly recounted how, while chained to the Karsestone in Shar's hidden temple, he came to the realization that it was the symbol of her control over the Shadow Weave. Then he told of how, when the city began to fall, the stone had pulled him down into one of the looming chambers, and of how hard he had struggled to steal the stone for Cyric so that he would one day rule the Shadow Weave—and perhaps the Weave itself, since if there was any god capable of putting the two back together, it was the One and All.

By the time Malik finished, Galaeron was not only sure that the seraph was telling the truth, but also that he had correctly interpreted everything he'd seen. Even Khelben seemed convinced.

"I'm willing to grant that Shar caught the Karsestone," Khelben said, "and even that the stone is the symbol of her control over the Shadow Weave, but if the Shadovar need it to create more shadow blankets, I don't see what's to stop her from returning it."

"Nothing," Galaeron answered. "Except that Shar is the goddess of *unrevealed* secrets. After Prince Yder allowed the seraph of an arch rival to not only discover the Karsestone's role and location, but to come so close to stealing it, I am sure she will find a safer place to hide it."

"And let the Shadovar suffer for their sins," Laeral said. "I agree."

This drew a broad smile from Malik, who looked up at Galaeron and said, "I am waiting."

"I would do many things to save Evereska," Galaeron said. "and one of them is lie."

"Lie?" Malik screeched. "The One will punish you for this—though I will surely be the one who suffers in your place! After the many times I have saved your life, how can you do this to me?"

"Because it is necessary."

Though Malik had never done anything to hurt Galaeron and it pained the elf to betray an old friend, he lowered his sword. He stepped back, and with the little man still hurling invectives at his back, he turned to Storm.

"It seems our plan worked for most of Faerûn, if not Evereska," he said. "I thank you for trying."

"As we thank you," Khelben said, slapping a hand on Galaeron's shoulder, "but we are not done yet. Did I not overhear you telling Telamont that you now have a complete understanding of the phaerimm?"

Galaeron nodded, not daring to believe Khelben would say what he hoped Khelben was going to say.

"You did."

Khelben glanced over his shoulder toward Shadow Lake, where the erratic torrent of debris falling from the gloom-cloaked enclave had finally dwindled to a sporadic rain. Instead of fleeing the city, most veserabs seemed to be trying to find a safe route back, and even the crash of collapsing buildings was growing more intermittent and muted.

"Laeral, Storm, what say you?" he asked. "Have we done enough damage here?"

"Not enough," Storm said, "but all we can."

"Yes," Laeral said. "I think it is high time we returned to Evereska."

She held out her arms, inviting Galaeron and the others to join hands with her for an instantaneous return to the Shaeradim. Aris kneeled down and extended a pinky for her to hold, but Vala made no move to join the circle. Galaeron was surprised—and perhaps just a little relieved—to discover he had a sinking feeling in his chest. If his heart was breaking, then sorrow could not be a weakness his shadow had overcome. He went to stand close to Vala.

"I know it's a lot to ask," Galaeron began, "especially after what I put you through, so I won't. If you want to come to Evereska with us, you and your sword are more than welcome."

Vala grunted what might have been acceptance, refusal, or simply an acknowledgment of the question, then said, "One thing. Were you watching when Yder and Aglarel chased me out of the mythallar?"

Galaeron nodded.

"And you didn't come after me?"

Galaeron shook his head.

"Why not?"

"Because I wanted to destroy the mythallar, and I knew our chances would be better if Aris and I remained in hiding until Telamont showed all of his tricks." Galaeron swallowed, then added, "And because I knew you could take care of yourself."

"*Knew*, Galaeron?" she asked.

"Hoped, anyway."

Vala pushed her upper lip into a half-hearted sneer, then shrugged and smiled.

"At least you're honest." She grasped his hand, stepped over to Laeral's teleport circle, and said, "Of course I'm coming. Do you think I'd dare go back to Vaasa without my men and our darkswords?"

CHAPTER FIFTEEN

2 Eleasias, the Year of Wild Magic

After Ruha departed for Twilight Hall with Malik chained to her wrist, Khelben used his sending magic to advise Lord Duirsar of their imminent arrival. The spell failed. Nor did he receive any reply when he tried to contact Kiinyon Colbathin, and when Galaeron tried to contact Keya, the only response he experienced was a fleeting impression of terror. The six of them wasted a few more minutes hazarding uninformed guesses as to how the phaerimm might be interfering with communication magic based on the Shadow Weave as well as the Weave. Able to imagine only dire scenarios, they finally concluded that they simply could not know what was happening and divided themselves into two traveling groups.

A few moments later, Galaeron was lying between

Vala and Khelben on a sooty terrace high in the Vine Vale, staring down a staircase wasteland into the crater-pocked pasture inside the Meadow Wall. The once-lush grass was gone, burned off or blasted away by battle magic or withering beneath the rotting corpse of one of the thousands of elf warriors scattered across the field. In the center of the meadow, the marble cliffs of the Three Sisters were speckled around the base with stars of soot and sprays of crusted blood. Atop the hills themselves, curtains of black fume were rising out of the great bluetop forest, coalescing into a single dark cloud that left visible only the lowest reaches of Evereska's majestic towers.

As Galaeron watched, a leaden light erupted in the woods beneath the Groaning Cave, and a deafening crack reverberated across the entire vale and echoed off the looming cliffs of the High Shaeradim. As Galaeron blinked the flash from his eyes, he noticed a ring of falling trees expanding outward, their crowns all pointing away from the center of the explosion. By the time the blast played itself out, the circle of destruction was more than a mile across.

"It is safe for Laeral and Storm to come ahead with Aris," Galaeron said. He spoke without turning to look at Khelben. "You can be sure there are no phaerimm within a mile of us."

"That's awfully quick to be so certain of their positions," Khelben observed. "We haven't been here a minute."

"A minute is all I need," Galaeron said. He rose to his knees and waved a hand in the direction of the burning city. "The phaerimm are down there, looting Evereska of its magic."

"And their servants?" Khelben asked. "All it takes to sound the alarm is a beholder or even a gnoll."

"The phaerimm think they have won," Galaeron explained. "They will have their servants with them, carrying their plunder and helping to claim and defend their new lairs."

"They have no fear of a counterattack?" Khelben asked.

"At the moment, they fear us less than they fear each other." Though the words were Galaeron's, the knowledge came to him in the form of a strange half-thought, closer to a premonition or a feeling than something he actually remembered. "They will know how preoccupied Faerûn has been with the problems caused by Shade, and how impossible it would be for anyone to send an army against them."

"True as that may be," Khelben said, "it does not always require an army to defeat one."

"They are certainly worried about the Chosen," Galaeron said, picking up on Khelben's meaning, "but I doubt they have a choice in the matter. It is not in the nature of the phaerimm to work together. Now that the prize is in hand, everyone must claim his share or watch another steal it from beneath him."

As Galaeron explained this, the tiny shape of a stick figure elf tumbled out of the smoke cloud, hit the edge of the cliff summit, and pinwheeled all the way down into the meadow. Had the mythal been functioning properly, it was not something that would have happened. A protective spell would have caught the victim and lowered him—or her—gently to the ground.

The death made Galaeron wonder what had become of his sister, Keya. The last he had heard, she was doing well with her pregnancy and also as a warrior, joining Vala's men on hunting forays and claiming half a dozen tails for her own belt, but that had been before the mythal fell. Could she be one of the bodies lying down in the meadow or perhaps the one he had just watched plummeting out of the smoke? He longed to try another thought sending, but knew that would be foolish. Assuming she remained alive, there was a good chance that she was fighting at the moment, and the distraction of an unexpected thought popping into her head might well prove fatal. Galaeron could only hope that the moment of fleeting terror he had experienced the first time meant she was still alive—and that his intrusion had not changed that.

"How long will the phaerimm remain at each other's throats?" Khelben asked.

"A tenday, at least," he answered, "but not much longer. Their internal squabbles are swift and deadly."

"A tenday." Khelben's discouragement was hard to miss. "What then?"

"By then, they will have settled matters and prepared their individual defenses." Galaeron did not like the drift Khelben's questions were taking. "They will be impossible to root out."

"The Shadovar did it at Myth Drannor," Khelben countered.

"At the cost of their other ambitions in Faerûn," Vala pointed out. "And there were only a few dozen at Myth Drannor. Here, there will be hundreds."

Khelben sighed and said, "We have lost Evereska." His fist thudded into the ground, raising a small cloud of ash and dust. "It will be all we can do to contain them in the vale."

Though Galaeron did not share Khelben's despair, he remained silent, ordering his thoughts and summoning to mind all he knew about the situation in Evereska. He had an inkling that matters were not as hopeless as Khelben thought, but whether that feeling was due to Melegaunt's wisdom or his own need to undo the terrible mistakes that had led to the fall of the LastHome, he could not say.

Vala laid a warm hand on his forearm and said, "I'm sorry, Galaeron. You did everything you could."

Galaeron started to say that he had not yet done everything, but he was cut off by the soft crackle of a teleport spell. He glanced over his shoulder to make certain the new arrivals were who they expected and saw a gray cloud rising two terraces above. Laeral and the others lay on the ground, spitting soot and blinking confusion from their eyes.

"Hold your spells, miladies," Khelben called to his fellow Chosen. "We're safe enough for now."

The sound of Khelben's voice seemed to draw Laeral out of her afterdaze. She glanced into the bottom of the valley, and her face fell.

"Goddess help us!" she gasped. "We're too late."

"I think not," Galaeron said, finally convinced that the inspiration he felt was more than his own desperation.

He rose and motioned for Laeral to bring the others down, then took a length of shadowsilk from his pocket and began to wrap it around his little finger, fashioning it into a small cone.

"We have come just in time."

Khelben rose to his knees and pulled Galaeron back down.

"Have patience, elf. We'll save as many Tel'Quessir as we can, but first we must plan."

"The best way to save my people is to kill the phaerimm in their city."

Galaeron went back to fashioning his cone.

Laeral and Khelben exchanged knowing glances, and Khelben said, "This isn't your fault, Galaeron. It was Melegaunt who freed the phaerimm, not you."

"That's right," Storm said. Having recovered from her afterdaze, she was jumping down onto the terrace with Galaeron and the others. "We know how the Shadovar think, now. They planned all along to make the phaerimm everyone else's problem. I'd bet my hair that Melegaunt breached the Sharn Wall where he did on purpose. What better way to lure the phaerimm out of Anauroch than to offer them Evereska's mythal?"

"If it was indeed an accident, it worked to the Shadovar's advantage," Galaeron agreed. He finished his cone and carefully removed it from his finger, then set it aside on a stone. "But I am no innocent in this. I was warned many times about Melegaunt, and still I brought Shade into the world."

"You can't blame yourself," Aris said. He was sitting on the back wall of the terrace, leaning over to cup a hand beneath one of the thousand springs that had once watered the terraces of the Vine Vale. "They would have found another way."

Galaeron raised a hand to forestall more forgiving words, and said, "I'm not seeking absolution . . . nor am I speaking out of guilt."

"Then out of vengeance." Laeral phrased this as a fact, not a question. She glanced at Storm, then added, "I know how I would feel, were my sister down there and I unable to contact her."

"If I was seeking vengeance, I would not want your help." Galaeron could see they were still afraid his shadow might be influencing him, and he had no doubt it was. That did not mean he was wrong. "I am talking about victory, not retribution. Hear me out. If you don't like what I say, I'll not hold it against anyone who chooses to remain behind."

Khelben scowled, clearly unhappy with having someone else assume the leadership. Still, he listened patiently. When Galaeron finished, his frown turned thoughtful, and he looked to the other Chosen.

"What do you think?"

"Simple plans are the best," Storm said. "This one is simple, I'll give it that."

"Perhaps too simple," Laeral said. "What's to stop the phaerimm from seeing through it?"

"The arrogance of the phaerimm themselves," Galaeron answered. "They won't believe anyone capable of defeating their spells of clear-seeing."

Leaving the others to consider the merits of his plan on their own, Galaeron started to fashion another cone out of shadowsilk. After a moment, Aris removed a stone from the terrace wall and shaped it into a small bowl with two quick strikes of his hammer, then filled it with soot from a charred log and used the spring to moisten it. When he began to smear the resulting paste up his legs in thick black stripes, Vala cocked a doubtful eyebrow.

"You're a little large for camouflage," she said. "Don't you trust Galaeron's magic?"

"I trust Galaeron," Aris replied. He glanced at Galaeron

and gave a grim nod. "But given who we are going to attack, I think it wise for one of us to use no magic. Besides, stone giant camouflage is better than you know. The number of times you have walked past one of us and not known it would surprise you."

"Nothing surprises me anymore," Vala said. She dipped her hand in the bowl and leaped up on the terrace behind Aris. "Bend down, and I'll do your neck before we go."

"Then you've decided to go as well?" Laeral asked.

"Have to. My men and our darkswords are down there." She peered around Aris, looked down at Galaeron, and added, "And I really need to see how this turns out."

Her words made Galaeron ruin the shadow cone he was pulling off his finger. She was probably alluding to the promise she had made to slay him if he ever fell completely under the sway of his shadow, but there was a warmth in her tone that made him hope that she might forgive him, that there might still be room in her heart to love him.

Continuing to hold Vala's gaze, Galaeron began to wrap the shadowsilk around his little finger again. At the same time, he whispered the incantation for a spell of thought sending and began to speak to her in his mind.

Vala.

Her jaw dropped, and her sooty hand came off the back of Aris's bald skull.

Before we go, I want to apologize for leaving you behind, Galaeron said. *I'd understand if you never forgive me, but I hope you can.*

Vala's eyes softened.

There's nothing to forgive. The choice was mine, and I knew what could happen. She returned to camouflaging the back of Aris's head, adding, *But I am torn up, Galaeron. Inside.*

Galaeron's heart sank. *I see. I didn't mean to intrude. Please forgive—*

There's that word again, Vala interrupted. *I don't blame you—that's not what I mean. But since Khelben and the others helped me escape, I've been filled with this . . . I haven't felt anything good. I just want to go home and drink mead in front of the fire. Alone.*

What about Sheldon? You must want to see him.

Galaeron felt ashamed of himself. He had allowed Vala's usual stoic bearing to lull him into thinking she had somehow emerged whole from her enslavement. He had been thinking only of how her ordeal affected him, not of what it might have done to her.

Not like this, she replied. *Not all broken inside.*

You won't always be broken, Galaeron said. *I'll stand by you for however long it takes. I wish I'd told you this before, Vala. I do love you.*

Vala gave him a wistful smile.

Now you tell me. Now that your shadow made you.

Galaeron didn't realize they had become an object of attention until Vala's eyes grew self-conscious and her gaze darted away. Khelben cleared his throat, and either ignoring the looks that had been passing between the two or pretending he had not noticed, he stepped in front of Galaeron.

"You are quite certain the phaerimm will not be able to detect or dispel your magic?" he asked.

"They would have to use the Shadow Weave," Galaeron said, "but we must be wary of beholders. They could undo us with their antimagic rays."

"Beholders we can handle," Storm said.

Khelben sighed, then said, "Very well. If you are determined to pursue this foolish plan of yours, it seems we have no choice except to come along to protect you. How soon can you be ready?"

In answer, Galaeron slipped the last cone of shadowsilk off his finger and pressed it to Khelben's chest.

"Hold that there."

Khelben did as instructed, and Galaeron drew on the Shadow Weave to cast a spell. The black cone expanded to a full ten feet in length, engulfing the Chosen in a stocking of darkness. Galaeron fashioned a barbed tail at the narrow end and four crooked arms at the wide end, added some teeth and other details to create the head-disk, and he found himself looking at what appeared to be a shadow-swathed phaerimm.

"An excellent likeness," Aris complimented. "Though the elbows are too far down the arms, and the tail barb should curve a little more."

Galaeron made the necessary corrections and a few more when Vala, Laeral, and Storm added their opinions. When everyone agreed the likeness was true, he stepped back and spoke a final word to set the shape.

"In Evereska, we should try to stay in the wooded areas where shadows won't seem out of place," Galaeron said. "I assume you can use your own magic to fly and speak the phaerimm wind language."

Khelben replied with a whistling gust of wind and floated into the air.

"Good," Galaeron said. "Avoid using your silver fire. If the phaerimm see it, they will know you are here."

"What about wands and rings?" Laeral asked.

"The shadow mask will conceal their use, as it will your voices and gestures," Galaeron said, "but you must careful not to fling any spell components outside your disguise. The phaerimm do not need components, so if they see you using them. . . ."

"Understood," Storm said, stepping forward. "Me next. I always like fighting with four arms."

Galaeron pressed a shadow cone to her chest and repeated the spell he had used to disguise Khelben, then did the same for himself and Laeral. Finally, he turned to Vala.

"Since you're not a spellcaster, it would be best to disguise you as a mind-slave."

Vala rolled her eyes and tried to make light of the suggestion, but the hurt was plain in her eyes.

"Don't enjoy it too much."

"Not at all," he assured her. "If you think you could hold a blank look—"

"Galaeron, just do it."

Galaeron flattened a small disk of shadowstuff in his hand and carefully molded it over her face. When he cast his spell, Vala's complexion darkened by half a dozen shades. Her eyes grew glassy and vacant, and her expression fell dead and still. It pained Galaeron to see her even in this counterfeit bondage. It reminded him of how selfish and deluded he had been during his shadow crisis and of all she had sacrificed to save him. How he would ever repay her, he could not begin to imagine.

"Are we all set then?" Khelben asked. "I've opened a door to the woods at the base of Cloudcrown Hill. Unless you've a better idea, I thought Lord Duirsar's palace the ideal place to open our campaign."

"There is no better idea," Galaeron said. He turned to find a magic door shimmering at the downhill edge of the terrace. "The phaerimm are sure to be fighting over the plunder there."

"I thought as much." Khelben waved a slender phaerimm arm toward the door. "Storm and Laeral have departed."

Not bothering to ask why Khelben had asked for an opinion if he had already sent the two sisters through, Galaeron started toward the shimmering door. He made it only one step before Vala caught him by his collar—she probably thought she was holding onto one of his disguise's four arms—and pulled him back.

"Wait."

She spun him around and stood there staring at him with her vacant eyes. Finally, she asked, "Where do I kiss?"

Galaeron leaned forward and pressed his lips to hers. It felt a little like kissing a zombie, at least until he closed his eyes, and even then it remained tentative and reserved—at least by Vaasan standards.

When they finally finished and Galaeron caught his breath again, he asked, "For luck?"

"Just in case," Vala corrected, drawing her darksword. "I wouldn't want a Shadovar's fist to be the last thing that ever touched my lips."

She stepped past Galaeron into the magic door and vanished with a crackle.

Galaeron followed Vala into the portal. He had grown so accustomed to teleport magic that he was no longer bothered by the breath-taking cold or the eternal instant of falling, but that did not prevent him from being dazed when he finally felt the ground beneath his feet again. The air was filled with sluggish rumbles and long, unintelligible howls. A crimson ball of fire was rolling toward him in slow motion, with orange tendrils curling out from its flanks in listless swirls.

Galaeron dived out of the way and found himself floating among the enormous trunks of a majestic bluetop forest, four spindly arms waving in front of his face. The sight reminded him that he was supposed to be impersonating a phaerimm, though exactly why still remained a mystery to him. While the open woods around him felt familiar, there was something that did not seem quite right, as though he turned a corner and found himself in an unexpected room.

The fireball was still coming, slowly. Behind it, a fork of lightning flickered into existence and slithered through the trees like a crooked white snake, then exploded through a bugbear's chest and twisted off in pursuit of a mind flayer. The attack was answered by ten golden bolts, flying along in a tight wedge formation that angled toward their moon elf target at about the speed of a flock of migrating geese.

Galaeron floated out of the fireball's path. Crouching behind a freshly split boulder about fifty paces distant, he saw a much-battered bladesinger still holding up the smoking hand that had hurled the spell. More offended by the attack than concerned about it, he pulled a few strands of shadow-silk from his pocket and hurled them in the bladesinger's direction, hissing an incantation. The elf was instantly wrapped in a cocoon of sticky black shadow.

Galaeron! the familiar voice of Laeral Silverhand sounded inside his mind. *There's no need to defend yourself. You can fly faster than that spell's coming.*

A pair of shadow-swathed phaerimm emerged from the trees behind him, Vala close on their barbed tails. As soon as Galaeron saw the emptiness in her eyes, he recalled their plan and saw that something had gone terribly wrong.

This isn't Cloudcrown Hill, he objected.

No—we're at the Groaning Cave, Vala replied. *I recognize it from when we came during my first visit.*

Galaeron looked over his shoulder and saw the cave less than a hundred paces up the hill. A small company of elf warriors was gathered on the entrance veranda, crouching behind the stone balustrades and using the high terrain to fire arrows and spells down on the bugbears and illithids in the forest below. Like everything else in this strange battle, their attacks seemed to be in slow motion, the arrows floating rather than flying to their targets and the spells less flashing across the sky than simply advancing.

Galaeron drifted out of the path of two arrows coming toward him, then heard a soft crackle as Aris arrived in the wood. The fireball had already passed by and was in the process of exploding into the hillside behind them. Galaeron grabbed the giant by his arm and pulled him forward so the back blast wouldn't burn him.

Khelben appeared an instant later, in the middle of a slowly wagging tail of flame. He floated there in the fire for a moment, afterdazed and no doubt finding it even more difficult than had Galaeron to adjust to his new surroundings. Galaeron shoved Aris's arm toward Vala, then he floated over and pulled the Chosen out of the fire.

"Where are we?" In his confusion, Khelben neglected to use thought speech. "This isn't—" He caught himself and switched. *Cloudcrown Hill!*

We came out on the other side of the city, Laeral informed him, *near the Groaning Cave.*

Worse than that, Galaeron said. *We came out in the past.*

How can that be? Storm demanded. She reached behind Galaeron and batted an arrow aside. *It can't happen.*

It did, Galaeron replied. *A little after we arrived in the Vine Vale, this whole wood was leveled by an explosion. And now—*

It's still standing, Vala finished. *I saw the blast, too. Somehow, we got here before the trees fell.*

A fork of lightning snaked down from the cave mouth and caught Storm square in the center of her phaerimm disguise. The blast drove her to the ground but seemed to cause her no injury. Khelben and Laeral lifted their head-disks toward the source of the attack, and that alone was enough to send several dozen elves scrambling away in slow motion.

These disguises have one drawback, Vala sent as she rushed to take cover behind a fallen bluetop. *They work!*

She vanished over the trunk. Galaeron and the Chosen followed, and a moment later they were taking shelter in the crook of a massive limb. Aris came and stood behind them, his camouflage working so well that had Galaeron not been directly under the giant, he would never have seen him.

I should have realized something like this would happen. Khelben's tone was apologetic. *We've already seen what comes of mixing Weave and Shadow Weave.*

We have, agreed Storm, *but not this time. If this had something to do with shadow magic, how could Aris be here? He has no shadow magic.*

That's true, Laeral said. *Whatever went wrong, it happened when Khelben opened his magic door.*

"The mythal!" Galaeron was so excited that he forgot himself and said this aloud. *It had a defense against teleporting!*

Not 'had,' Khelben replied. *Evereska's mythal still has a bite.*

So it sent us into the past? Vala asked.

Arrows began to sink into the trunk of the fallen bluetop at sporadic intervals.

And it relocated our exit portal, Laeral said. *We're lucky the mythal was weakened, or the displacement might not have been so minor.*

If this is minor, Vala said, *I don't want to see major.*

The comment brought to mind the strange blast that had leveled the woods around the Groaning Cave shortly after Galaeron and the first group arrived in the valley. He turned to look at Khelben.

Khelben? Do you remember that big blast we saw after we arrived?

The gray light? he replied. *Of course.*

Well, Galaeron said, *that happened here.*

It was impossible to say what happened beneath Khelben's disguise, but all four of phaerimm arms stopped moving, and his tail dropped to the ground.

Time! he gasped. *We're moving through it faster than everyone around us—*

And when we catch up . . . Laeral let the sentence trail off.

What? Aris asked. He had vanished so completely into the forest that Galaeron had forgotten he was there. *I don't understand.*

Trouble, Storm said. *Really big trouble.*

It seemed to Galaeron that the arrows were starting to thunk into their tree trunk more rapidly. He peered up toward the Groaning Cave and saw the archers moving a little less torpidly now, sending their shafts down the hill with a speed that could almost be described as flying rather than drifting. A battle mage caught sight of him and stretched out a finger to send a lightning bolt in his direction.

Galaeron used his shadow magic to send a thought message to the man.

Hold your attack! I am Galaeron Nihmedu, an elf and a friend.

The mage grabbed his head and stumbled back. *Ooouuu-uuuut offffffff myyyyyyy heeeeeeeeeeeeeeeeeaaaaaaaaaaaaaaaa-aaaaaaddd, monnnnnnnnnnssssssssssssssterrrrrrrrrrrrrrrrr!*

The mage followed his order by stumbling back to the

balustrade and completing his spell. The lightning bolt shot down the slope far faster than previous ones, almost too fast for the eye to follow. Galaeron barely had time to roll aside and cry a warning before the bolt was there.

Storm rose into its path and took the bolt full in the body.

Storm! Galaeron cried.

The bolt sank into Storm's body and vanished with no stench of charred flesh and not even much of a crack. She settled back behind the tree trunk and let out a satisfied belch.

Don't concern yourself, Galaeron, Laeral said. *Storm can eat lightning all day.*

A little gift from my sisters when I went to fight Iyachtu Xvim, Storm explained. *Now, don't you think we ought to get away from here? Far away from here?*

What could it hurt? Khelben replied.

For one of the Chosen, you don't sound all that confident, Vala observed.

It's not a matter of confidence, Laeral said. *It all depends on whether the temporal displacement wave is centered on us or our point of arrival.*

Huh? Vala asked.

She means run! Galaeron said.

He lifted Vala to her feet and shoved her into the woods in the direction opposite the elves who were attacking them. Khelben and the other Chosen rose into the air and floated along beside her, using their magic and their bodies to deflect the barrage of attacks that rained down from the veranda of the Groaning Cave. Before following, Galaeron took a moment to dispel the shadow web he had cast on the bladesinger.

Leave . . . this . . . place . . . now! he urged, spacing his words so the elf would be more likely to comprehend. *Big danger!*

The bladesinger pulled out of the dissolving shadow web looking more confused than alarmed but quickly took the advice when a beholder and his escort of bugbears came charging after him from the phaerimm side of the battle. Galaeron sent a similar warning to the elves on the veranda outside the Groaning Cave. Their only answer was a shimmering sphere of force that closed to within a dozen paces before Galaeron noticed it and fled his hiding place. A dull rumble sounded behind him a moment later, and he looked back to see the bluetop erupting into a spray of splinters. The ball expanded almost swiftly enough to catch him. Time was definitely moving faster.

Galaeron caught up to the others and followed close behind, dodging silver snakes of lightning and using his magic to turn arrows with wind spells or shadow shields. Aris ran alongside at a distance of twenty paces, slipping through the woods as stealthily as any ranger. As long as the companions kept moving, they had little to fear from their elf attackers, who clearly found it impossible to hit targets that must have seemed mere blurs. Though there were bugbears, illithids, and beholders aplenty in the wood, they were too busy fighting to pay any attention to a shadowy band of "phaerimm."

The companions had little trouble leaving the area of the cave, only to discover that the battle in the rest of the forest was just as fierce and twice as confused. There seemed to be no clearly drawn ranks or objectives, just random clusters of elves and mind-slaves and the occasional phaerimm attacking each other with spell and steel, sometimes from a hundred paces distant, sometimes standing toe-to-toe. All too often, the battles were between elves and elf mind-slaves, the former reluctant to strike killing blows and the latter all too eager. Whoever the combatants were, they seemed to be moving faster, their lightning bolts flashing through the wood faster than Galaeron's eye could follow, their arrows whizzing past too swiftly to deflect.

Whenever possible, Galaeron urged the warriors to flee and used his magic to free the elf mind-slaves. It was this last good deed that complicated their flight, when six phaerimm appeared behind a rank of advancing bugbears and began to whistle at them in Winds.

"Yoooou!" The phaerimm's challenge was slow and trilling, but not so slow it was difficult for Galaeron's speech magic to understand. "Explain yourselves."

Realizing no one else would understand the importance of responding with an accusation, Galaeron floated forward to confront the phaerimm.

"You stole . . . my slave." Though Galaeron had not intended it, the wind spell he was using to modulate his speech ripped through the forest like a cyclone, tearing leaves from the trees and assailing their challengers with sticks. "I . . . demand a gift!"

"A gift?" The six phaerimm drifted a few paces back, clearly buying the space to begin a spell battle. "Who are you? Why do you whistle so fast?"

"Who dares ask—"

That was as far as Galaeron got before three tongues of silver fire shot out to engulf the three closest phaerimm.

"No time!" Khelben yelled in Common, already flinging a handful of rainbow dust on the ground beneath the phaerimm. "We've got to keep going!"

Galaeron was already hurling a shadow ball at the nearest surviving phaerimm, while Vala had drawn her sword and was cocking her arm to throw. Though the forest time had nearly caught up to their time, enough of a difference remained for Khelben and Galaeron to unleash their spells before their foes reacted. The shadow ball caught its target at an oblique angle and drilled a head-sized oval through half the length of its body. The phaerimm collapsed in a limp heap, its life spilling out onto the forest floor in a steaming heap.

Khelben's prismatic wall was not so effective. It sprang up beneath the phaerimm as he had obviously intended, but the thing floated through its defenses in a spray of gem-colored flashes and counterattacked with a black disintegration bolt. Khelben took the bolt square in the chest and smiled, then stretched two of his arms in the creature's direction.

In the meantime, the last phaerimm had loosed a flight of magic bolts at Vala. To Galaeron's horror, she stood her ground and hurled her darksword at her attacker.

"Vala!"

Galaeron stretched out a hand to raise a shadow shield in front of her, but even with time on his side, he was not that fast. The bolts struck home.

"No!"

Vala staggered from the impact and dropped a foot back to brace herself. She raised her fist, pointing her ring in the phaerimm's direction and shooting the same flight of golden bolts back at her attacker.

The darksword arrived first, opening the thing from lip to tail. It trilled wildly and vanished in a silver dazzle of teleport magic. The golden bolts sizzled off into the forest to draw an anguished cry from some elf warrior Galaeron had not even seen. Vala opened the same hand and called her sword back without lowering her arm.

Khelben's phaerimm refused to retreat so easily. A wall of flames sprang to life between it and its attackers and set the forest instantly ablaze. Unable to see, Khelben elected to save his spell, and the whirling disk of shadow that Galaeron sent spinning through the barricade cut nothing down except a long swath of bluetops—and perhaps the half a dozen elves whose voices he heard screaming in panic and rage.

Balls of flame as large as a beholder began to sizzle off the fire wall in the direction of Galaeron and the Chosen. Galaeron barely managed to pluck his shadow off the ground and throw it up in front of him, and even then the heat was enough to singe his hair as the crackling orbs struck his silhouette and vanished into the shadow plane.

Unable to react quickly enough, Khelben caught one of

the spheres full in the chest and erupted into flame. He floated calmly to the ground, where he remained until Laeral, who caught two spheres in the chest without emitting so much as a wisp of smoke, covered his body with hers and smothered the fire.

As this happened, Storm was streaking headlong into the flames. She took three of the fireballs square in the head-disk and laughed, then plunged headlong through the burning wall . . . and was too late.

Aris had already emerged from the woods on the other side of the burning wall. He stooped down and wrapped his big hands around the phaerimm—it was at the near end of the fire barrier, not where Galaeron had expected at all—and squeezed until it popped. Storm was left with nothing to do but dispel the phaerimm's magic and extinguish the flames.

Galaeron rushed to Khelben's side and asked, "How bad—?"

"It isn't," Khelben growled. His disguise remained that of a shadow-swathed phaerimm, so it was impossible to see how badly he was hurt. "We don't have time. Those phaerimm were *fast*. The time streams must be converging."

"Right," Laeral said. "Let's go."

Aris and the three Chosen turned to start through the woods again, and Galaeron was about ready to start after them when he realized that Vala was neither ahead of them nor behind.

"Wait!"

Storm stopped and twisted her head-disk around to look at him.

"Wait? We don't have time to—"

Galaeron flew over to where he had last seen her and noticed a set of boot prints—a set of *big* boot prints—on the ground.

"They took her!"

"They?" The three Chosen gathered round and began to curse as one. "Of all the black fortune!"

"That's human," Galaeron said. "Male and large. Very large."

"Vaasan," Khelben growled. He looked into the woods, and in Common yelled, "Kuhl! Burlen!"

Their answer came in riotous motion as a dozen elf warriors sprang out from behind tree trunks, under logs, beneath piles of dead leaves, and rushed to attack. Only the slim advantage of their faster-moving time stream spared Galaeron and his fellow Chosen from being chopped into a dozen pieces each by the darkswords that had once belonged to Vala's slain company of warriors.

"Up!" Galaeron cried in Common. "Watch yourselves!"

As he yelled the warning, he was already rising above the reach of his attackers. Khelben and the other Chosen followed, but poor Aris found himself surrounded by half a dozen elves tossing their glassy black swords from hand to hand.

The elves below Galaeron and the Chosen drew their arms back to throw.

"Hold!" Galaeron cried, speaking Elvish. "I am Galaeron Nihmedu, a citizen of Evereska, once a Tomb Guard princep patrolling the Desert Border South, who resides in Treetop in Starmeadow, son to Aubric Nihmedu and brother to Keya Nihmedu of the Long Watch, friend to—"

"Strange how you do not look much like an elf," said a familiar—though much hardened—female voice.

A young moon elf of little more than eighty appeared from behind the trunk of a bluetop, her turquoise hair tucked up beneath an ostentatious battle helm that could only have been made by the Gold elves of Evermeet. Her gold-flecked eyes were shot through with red lines, and her cupid's bow smile had gone straight and grim with worry, but Galaeron would have known his sister had she looked a hundred times more drained. His heart drummed in joy.

"Keya! You're alive!"

Keya narrowed her eyes in suspicion and said, "So it seems, for now."

There was a slight drawl as she spoke, just enough to suggest the slower passage of forest time. She reached behind a tree and pulled Vala into view, and Galaeron was astonished to see that someone had actually taken Vala's darksword and bound her hands in elven rope.

"Where did you come by this mind-slave?" Keya asked. "Tell me that, and we will let you live—so long as you swear to leave Evereska and never return."

"You are not a very good liar, Keya." He dispelled the masking magic that made him look like a phaerimm, then drifted down toward the ground, adding, "But neither you nor Evereska has anything to fear from us."

"Hold there, you devil!" Keya ordered. "Any lower, and I'll give you the death you deserve for impersonating my brother."

This drew a snicker from Vala, which drew an angry glower from Keya.

"Keya!" Khelben snapped in Elvish. "He *is* your brother. Release Vala and flee this area—now!"

"Do you think I take orders from worms?"

To demonstrate that she did not, Keya hurled her darksword. Even with the faster speed of his time stream, Khelben barely had time to pivot out of the way and let the weapon tumble past. Two dozen archers suddenly appeared from their hiding places, arrows nocked and arms drawing their bows back to fire. Storm and Laeral were already casting spells of paralyzation. Keya's entire company froze where they were, bows half flexed and swords half raised.

Khelben retrieved Keya's darksword from the tree where it had lodged itself, then flew down to her. Burlen stepped into view from behind the tree where Vala had been held, his own arm rising to throw his darksword.

Galaeron stopped him with a shadow web.

Khelben nodded his thanks, then flipped the weapon around and shook the hilt in Keya's face.

"You are trying my patience, young lady. We have reasons

for our appearance, and no time to explain them to you now."

A loud crackle sounded from the direction of the Groaning Cave. Galaeron glanced back and saw a tiny brilliance flickering down through the bluetop boughs.

Khelben continued to lecture Keya, "When we release you and your company, you are going to take it on faith that I am telling you the truth and flee this area—"

"Uh, Khelben?" As Galaeron spoke, he was watching the tiny sphere of brilliance expand above the trees. "There isn't going to be—"

"Starmeadow!" Laeral yelled, already laying a portal on the ground in the center of the elven company. "Teleport!"

Storm was already shoving paralyzed elves into the circle. Khelben took one look at the expanding circle of light and cursed, then wrapped his arms around Keya, Burlen, and two more elves, and vanished. Galaeron sprang to Vala's side, grabbing her bound hands, and started back toward Laeral's teleportation circle.

Vala jerked him back, nearly pulling him off his feet.

"Not without my sword!"

Back near the Groaning Cave, crooked forks of light began to dance down through the trees, and the war rumble there fell into a sudden silence. Galaeron stepped around Vala and found her sword leaning against the tree. He snatched it up and cut her bindings—no other blade would have severed the elven rope—then handed the weapon back to her.

"*Now* can we go?"

Galaeron grabbed her wrist and turned toward the teleportation circle and ran headlong into a small wood elf with doe-brown eyes, an impish smile, and a bared long sword.

"Well met, Galaeron," she said. "*Still* rescuing Vala, I see."

Galaeron's jaw fell. "T-Takari?"

Takari smiled and said, "So you *do* remember."

Galaeron surprised her with a heartfelt embrace, and she surprised him by returning it just as warmly.

"I was afraid I'd never see you again," he said.

A long, deafening crackle sounded from the direction of the Groaning Cave, and a column of leaden light appeared in the forest in front of the veranda.

Vala appeared beside them.

"Break it up, you two!" She slid an arm between them and used a deft elbow to force Takari back, then said, "No offense, but we've got to go."

Takari glanced at the offending elbow as though she might remove it, then smiled sweetly and said, "No offense taken."

She glanced back in the direction of the brightening column of light, then turned and waved at what appeared to be a pile of leaves.

"Come along, Kuhl! We'll let Galaeron teleport us out of here."

CHAPTER SIXTEEN

2 Eleasias, the Year of Wild Magic

Galaeron arrived in a tangle of arms both human and elf, Vala clasping his shoulders on one side, Takari tucked against his ribs on the other, Kuhl standing opposite, encompassing them all in a great bear hug and glaring down as though he wasn't quite convinced that Galaeron's transformation from phaerimm to elf was a return to true form.

The air reeked of brimstone and charred flesh, and it resounded with booms and cracks and wails. Still struggling with teleport afterdaze, Galaeron recalled he had been somewhere else trying to flee some impending cataclysm. The air had smelled the same there, and the battle din had been just as loud. He began to fear they had not escaped after all, that they were about to suffer the consequences of whatever terrible event they had been fleeing.

Galaeron glanced up at the canopy of a bluetop forest and cringed at the familiarity of it.

"I think the mythal rebuffed—"

He was about to say "my teleport spell" when a leaden brilliance filtered through the wood. He was jolted by a tremendous concussion—a concussion that erupted in the pit of his stomach and blasted outward. His palms and soles went numb, his eardrums thumped, and pain filled his head.

He found himself on his hands and knees with Vala, Takari, and Kuhl, thinking they were all going to die and wondering why the mythal had interfered with his magic when it normally deflected translocational spells only when they crossed its perimeter. Of course, Galaeron had used shadow magic. Months before a healthy mythal had prevented Melegaunt from touching the Shadow Weave, but in its weakened state, it had not obstructed any of the shadow spells Galaeron cast outside the Groaning Cave.

This was as far as Galaeron's thoughts went before it occurred to him that he had already survived the shock wave. The roaring in his ears was actually a deafening silence, he realized, and the ground beneath him had not shuddered once with the impact of a falling bluetop. He rose to his knees, glancing around, and saw that while the wood was familiar, it was not the one beneath the Groaning Cave. The undergrowth had been allowed to offer shelter to the birds and animals, and the terrain was not as steep.

Perhaps they had reached Starmeadow after all. Galaeron started to rise . . . and was pulled back down by Kuhl's meaty paw. The Vaasan used fingertalk to call for silence, then slipped back into the underbrush as stealthily as any elf. When Vala and Takari did the same, Galaeron dropped to his belly and followed, then turned and peered through a bush.

Starmeadow lay directly ahead, its small expanse layered in acrid fume and its lush grasses blackened from battle. At the far end, Dawnsglory Pond had turned pink with spilled blood and was still boiling from some blast of magical heat. Bodies both elf and otherwise lay strewn along the far side, where the Chosen and the Company of the Cold Hand had been attacked while still dazed. Like Galaeron and his companions, those out on the battlefield were already starting to recover and rise. Both sides seemed to have been unprepared for the fighting, with the elves and their allies caught out in the open and the phaerimm and their mind-slaves strewn haphazardly along the meadow edge adjacent to Galaeron and his companions.

An elf in tattered armor picked up a darksword and used it to lop off the tentacled head of a mind flayer. A phaerimm floated up and countered with a black ray that left a melon-sized hole in the warrior's chest. Another elf sprang up, catching the sword before it hit the ground, and charged the killer. The battle burst into full rage, silver bolts and white flashes tracing brilliant streaks through the air, flames bursting up from the blackened ground, heads and chests and bodies rupturing from no visible cause. Even the mythal exerted itself to join in, pelting Evereska's enemies with a hail of slushy pellets that dissolved on their shoulders and had no effect except to make the elves fight harder.

Galaeron thought of Keya and wanted to charge out onto the field to find her, but the calmer part of him—the darker, more cunning part—held back. Foolish heroics would accomplish nothing except a foolish death, and Keya needed him alive. The entire Company of the Cold Hand needed him, as did Khelben and the other Chosen, as did all of Evereska. He was the only one who understood the phaerimm, who knew how to defeat them. He had to work toward his purpose and trust his sister to keep herself alive. To do anything less was to betray the warrior spirit in her . . . and that of Evereska herself.

Galaeron found the Chosen near Dawnsglory Pond, still in their phaerimm disguises and hurling spells back into the main body of the Company of the Cold Hand. At first, he thought they were just trying to protect their identities and escape until they could execute his plan. It took a moment of careful observation before he realized that their spells were all flash and thunder, and that they were carefully positioning themselves to catch the phaerimm in a flanking attack. Seeing they could do even better, he backed deeper into the underbrush, then motioned for the others to arm themselves and follow.

Kuhl moved more like a forest cat than the cave bear he so resembled, and the four companions slipped around the phaerimm flank guard. Galaeron sprang out of a bush behind an illithid, and the thing's heart stopped beating before it realized someone had driven a sword through it. As Galaeron was dropping back out of sight, Takari's death arrow droned past his head and killed the illithid's beholder partner, then Vala and Kuhl charged out of the underbrush to attack four astonished bugbears. The closest pair raised their battle-axes to block. The Vaasans' darkswords slashed through the thick oak shafts like bread, then opened the throats of both creatures. The second pair of bugbears, alarmed as well as stunned, thought better of fighting and turned to roar the alarm.

It was a bad mistake. Galaeron hurled a dark bolt, Takari fired two more death arrows, and the Vaasans threw their darkswords. Only Vala targeted the nearest one, but her black blade sank to the hilt between the monster's shoulder blades. He took three more steps, then crashed to the ground in a lifeless heap. The other bugbear fell where he was, head lost to Galaeron's magic, heart burst by Kuhl's darksword, legs shriveling around Takari's black arrows.

The first sign of a counterattack came when a huge blue-top trunk burst into flaming splinters. A terrific cracking echoed down through the boughs, and Galaeron looked up to find what seemed an entire sky of leaves and trunk crashing down toward him. He flicked a wad of shadowstuff up at it and shouted a word in ancient Netherese. A web of dark strands appeared overhead, anchoring itself to surrounding trees to catch the falling bluetop.

The swirling crackle of meteor stones reverberated through woods from somewhere ahead. Galaeron dived behind the nearest bluetop and glimpsed a smoke trail bending toward him as the pebbles adjusted course. They struck the tree with a series of staccato bangs. He scrambled forward and peered around the other side of the trunk and almost lost his head to a black ray. He rolled back in the other direction and was flash-blinded by a fork of oncoming lightning.

Galaeron dropped flat and bit dirt as the bolt cracked past overhead. With time passing at the same rate for everyone, he was no match for a phaerimm. He pulled back, readied a shadow shield, and barely had time to raise it before the undergrowth parted a dozen paces away and a thornback head rose into view.

Vala emerged behind it, ran her darksword down the length of its back, and disappeared back into the brush just before a beam of green radiance disintegrated the foliage where she had been standing. Takari's bow sang, and the ray vanished. Vala leaped up, waving a severed phaerimm tail in Galaeron's direction, and started through the forest again.

Before following, Galaeron said, "Khelben, they're trapped between us. We're coming from the opposite end."

By the time he rolled out from behind the tree, Kuhl had already killed a second phaerimm rushing to aid the one that Vala had slain. Galaeron returned to his place in the battle line, and they sneaked through the undergrowth, slaying several more bugbears and two more illithids before Takari threw her voice into the trees overhead and gave a warning bird whistle.

A conflagration of fireballs and lightning bolts streaked up toward the sound, setting two bluetops ablaze and showering the forest floor with burning boughs and broken limbs. Galaeron followed one of the spells to its source and spied what appeared to be a cone-shaped log standing suspiciously upright in the heart of big honey bramble about twenty paces ahead. He sent a flight of shadow arrows streaking toward the log, then dived for cover and started rolling. He was helped along the way by several concussion waves and a wall of magical heat.

By the time Galaeron stopped, the forest ahead was disintegrating into splinters and flame. He came to his knees and found an illithid stumbling in his direction, its tentacled head looking wide-eyed back over its shoulder. Galaeron barely had time to draw his sword before the thing ran onto the point and impaled itself. He finished the job with a few blade flicks, then shoved the illithid away.

The situation was much the same along the rest of the battle line, and Galaeron had no doubt that it was because the Chosen were behind the enemy, attacking. The phaerimm mind-slaves were blindly fleeing the inferno, running headlong into Vala and Kuhl. The Vaasans were taking a terrible toll, spinning and whirling, cutting in two any monster that came within reach of their darkswords and using their pommels to knock unconscious the occasional elf mind-slave.

But there were only two of them and easily a hundred mind-slaves. Dozens slipped past and crashed off through the brush. Takari did her best to stop the monsters, emptying her quiver into their backs and slowly working her way forward so she could conserve arrows by plucking once-fired shafts out of dead bodies. Galaeron used shadow bolts to cut down a pair of bugbears and a beholder angling toward her back, then Takari felled a fleeing illithid, and there were no more enemies.

The patter of falling rain sounded behind Galaeron. He turned to find a small torrent deluging the battle line, dousing the fire and filling the wood with billowing steam. The storm would do nothing to save the trees already burning, but it would at least prevent the flames from spreading.

When a trio of phaerimm emerged from the steam cloud, Galaeron found himself preparing a shadow bolt. He knew by how the forest murk seemed to cling to their bodies that they were the Chosen, but that didn't prevent him from cringing. The disguise was more convincing than he had realized, and he suddenly understood why it had been so hard to convince Keya of his identity back at the Groaning Cave.

"A sad thing to lose so many bluetops," Khelben said, twisting his head-disk around to look back toward the battle line. "Most are older than I am."

"Evereska has been invaded," Galaeron said. "The trees must pay along with the rest of us."

Takari's jaw dropped in outrage. She started to rebuke him for saying such a thing, then reconsidered and simply cast an accusing look in Vala's direction.

Vala shrugged and said, "Don't look at me. I'm not the one who told him to embrace his shadow."

"I'm not saying we should let the forest burn," Galaeron retorted. "Only that we should remember what will become of Evereska's forests if we let the phaerimm take Evereska."

"Sometimes the lesser of two evils is the only good possible," Laeral agreed. She started toward the edge of the meadow. "Let's see if Keya needs help, shall we?"

But the Company of the Cold Hand had the situation well in hand. Without their phaerimm masters to guide and intimidate them, most of the mind-slaves had already lost interest in fighting and started to withdraw. It required only a couple of thunderbolts from the flank to turn the retreat into a rout, and Evereska's forces were alone in the field only a few minutes later.

Keya gave orders to gather the wounded and retrieve the darkswords, then waved Aris out of his hiding place on the opposite side of the meadow and came over to join Galaeron and the others. With a battle-jaded face and worry lines in her brow as deep as field furrows, she looked immeasurably older and grimmer than when Galaeron had last seen her, but stronger as well. With Burlen at her back, she stopped and gave Vala a warm—though weary—embrace, then stepped back and studied her brother.

There was a hardness in her eyes that made Galaeron worry she blamed him for what had happened in Evereska, and he began to fear their reunion would be less than a joyful one. He was more than willing to accept responsibility for his blunders, but the thought that his mistakes might drive a wedge between him and his sister was more than he could bear. It was bad enough that the war he started had taken their father from them; that it should also destroy the little that remained of his family would be a punishment worthy of Loviatar.

Finally, Keya dropped a hand to her protruding belly and said, "You heard, I suppose?"

Wondering what her pregnancy had to do with his mistakes, Galaeron replied, "Storm told me."

"Well, what are you waiting for?" Keya moved her hand back to the hilt of the darksword hanging in her scabbard and said, "You might as well say it and be done with it."

Galaeron frowned, puzzled.

"What is there to say?"

Keya cringed, but tightened her lips and visibly began to gather herself.

"I know this isn't something you expected, but I'm over eighty years old. I can make my own decisions—and it's not like there was anyone here to ask."

"Ask," Galaeron repeated. "About what?"

Vala nudged him the back with her elbow. "The baby."

"You rothé!" Takari hissed. "Have you gone completely human?"

Finally, Galaeron realized that Keya did not blame him for what had happened in Evereska, that she was not even thinking about the war. She was frightened, not angry, and she only wanted the same thing from him that he wanted from her. He started to laugh, which only made Keya set her jaw.

"Is that all you're worried about? What *I* think?" Galaeron asked. He took her by the shoulders. "I can't tell you how happy that makes me!"

Now it was Keya who looked puzzled.

"Why wouldn't I care what you think?"

Before Galaeron could answer, Takari interposed herself between the two.

"Galaeron is very happy for you," she said, "and he thinks Dex will make a wonderful father . . . for a human. Right, Galaeron?"

"Of course," Galaeron said. "I only thought—"

"And Keya is happy to have you back," Takari said. "No matter what the Golds say, she knows this isn't your fault. Isn't that true, Keya?"

"Even the Golds know the Shadovar tricked you," Keya said. "They've been planning this for centuries."

Takari nodded to Burlen and said, "Let's get out of here before the phaerimm come back to finish the job."

"Come back?" Galaeron repeated. "That's the one thing we don't have to worry about. No phaerimm survivor is ever going to admit he was defeated."

Keya and Takari exchanged looks, then Keya said, "Galaeron, they *always* come back."

"They're determined to wipe out the Company of the Cold Hand," Takari added, "but we're making them pay."

"Determined?" Galaeron did not like the sound of that. "You mean they're still fighting an organized battle?"

Burlen scowled down at Galaeron and grumbled, " 'Course they're organized. You want to kill a wolf pack, you'd better be more organized than they are."

"So they're *all* working together?" Galaeron asked. This felt wrong to him, contrary to all Melegaunt had learned about the phaerimm during his century of spying. "None are fighting over Evereska's magic? None are trying to claim the best lair?"

Keya said, "They're too busy hunting us." She turned to Burlen and said, "Have the war mages lay some death wards. We'll rendezvous at the Floating Gardens to plan our next strike."

Burlen had barely turned to pass the order along before the Company of the Cold Hand began to melt into the woods. Keya took Galaeron by the hand and, motioning for the others to follow, started through the forest toward the back side of Dawnsglory Pond.

"Glad homeagain, brother—such as home is these days." Keya threw a disgusted scowl in the direction of the Chosen, then quietly asked, "Why the phaerimm costumes? We almost killed you."

"My idea," Galaeron said. "I expected the phaerimm to be at each others' throats by now. We were going to fan the flames, make it look like they were killing one another and stealing each other's plunder. We'd hoped to start an all-out battle between them."

They reached the near bank of Dawnsglory Pond. Keya paused to send Takari to scout ahead with Kuhl and Burlen, and Vala decided to go along. As they had vanished into the undergrowth, Keya looked back to Galaeron.

"What made you think they'd fall for something like that?"

"I was wondering the same thing," Khelben said, speaking over their shoulders. He and the Silverhand sisters remained disguised as phaerimm. "Clearly, Galaeron's source was mistaken."

"No. The information was correct. That's why Telamont wanted me back."

"It would not be the first time the Shadovar have fooled you—or me," Laeral said, laying a pair of spindly phaerimm hands on his shoulders. "They are never playing the game we think. That's what makes them so hard to defeat."

"Or maybe something's changed," Storm added. "Whatever.

But these disguises have served their purpose. If the phaerimm are coordinating their efforts, I doubt we're going to fool them again—and, to tell the truth, I'm tired of dressing like an overgrown slug."

"As am I," Laeral agreed. "The next time I'm attacked, I'd rather it not be by elves."

Galaeron dispelled the disguise magic but remained convinced that the information Melegaunt had worked so hard to gather would not simply grow outdated. There was something about the situation he did not yet understand.

They started through the forest after Takari and the other scouts, and Galaeron said, "Keya, hunting the Company of the Cold Hand can't be the only thing the phaerimm are doing in Evereska. What else are they doing?"

"That we know about?" Keya replied. "For one, they're keeping Lord Duirsar and Kiinyon Colbathin trapped in the palace on Cloudcrown."

"Alone?"

Keya shook her head. "Lord Duirsar has a circle of high mages from Evermeet, and Zharilee is there with what remains of the Long Watch."

"How do you know all this?" Khelben asked, walking along on Keya's far side. "I've tried to reach both Lord Duirsar and Kiinyon with magic and heard nothing back."

"The phaerimm have besieged the palace with an antimagic shell," Keya reported, "but Manynests comes and goes as he pleases."

"They're holding Lord Duirsar prisoner?" Galaeron asked.

"Isolating him," Keya corrected. "They couldn't breach the palace wards, so they prevented him from leaving."

"More likely the High Mages," Laeral observed. "If the Company of the Cold Hand is giving them trouble—"

"That's it!" Galaeron burst. "The high mages!"

"What about them?" Khelben asked.

Instead of answering, Galaeron stopped and took his sister by the shoulders.

"You said 'for one thing,' the phaerimm were keeping Lord Duirsar trapped," he said. "What are the other things?"

"Aside from the fighting you'd expect in any battle, there's really only one other thing," Keya said. "About ten of them have gathered at Hanali Celanil's statue. We haven't tried to penetrate their security perimeter, but Manynests says they're using a lot of magic."

"I'll bet they are," Khelben said.

Keya appeared perplexed by this remark, but Galaeron had a feeling he knew exactly what Khelben meant.

"That's where the mythal was cast?" Galaeron gasped. This was a secret so closely guarded that, aside from Lord Duirsar and the city's high mages, only Evereska's most loyal friend among the Chosen would be privy to it. "At the statue of Hanali Celanil?"

"I doubt there was a statue there when it was cast," Khelben said. "And I wasn't there, you understand."

"But that's what you've been given to understand," Galaeron concluded. Conviction and excitement began to well up inside him as half-formed thoughts raced through this mind, fitting all the pieces of the puzzle into place. "That would explain why they haven't fallen into quarreling yet."

"It does?" This from Aris, who had been creeping along behind them. "They're feeding off the mythal?"

"Not feeding," Galaeron said. "Feeding would cause fights."

"Dismantling, then," Khelben said, following the line of Galaeron's reasoning. "They're taking it apart spell by spell."

"So the magic will return to the Weave?" Keya asked. "Why would they do that?"

"Because the magic *won't* return to the Weave," Storm said. "It's not raw anymore. It can't."

"The magic will stay here, inside the boundaries of the old mythal," Laeral explained. "It'll infuse the whole area."

They came to the path that led from Dawnsglory Pond up to Starmeadow Tower. Hearing Takari's all-clear warble, they crossed to Goldmorn Knoll and traversed the slope, the woods more open and therefore more dangerous.

Once the entire group was safely across, Khelben looked down over Keya's head and said to Galaeron, "It seems the phaerimm have learned to share. That hardly sounds like the creatures you claimed you could have warring with themselves inside a day."

"It doesn't," Galaeron agreed, "but if they have learned to share, it's only because a leader has emerged who is strong enough to dictate terms."

"If a strong leader has emerged among the phaerimm," Laeral said, "we dare not let them have Evereska."

Storm nodded and made a fist, which she touched lightly to Galaeron's shoulder.

"Not if we value the rest of Faerûn, we don't."

The snowfinch was up in the tree again, peering down through the bluetop boughs at the ring of phaerimm hovering around the statue of the elf goddess. It did not peep either in alarm or complaint and in fact seemed to be spying on their progress, but Arr did not dare blast the feathered nuisance. The SpellGather had finally found a thread of loose magic and was about to pull the first spell from the mythal, and the last thing she wished to do was disrupt their concentration.

Even with Zay and Yao, and eight more of the finest spell artists of her race—or any other—working nonstop since they entered the city, her plan had yet to yield a breath of magic. Already, two young softthorns had violated the War-Gather's edict against plunder-taking, and she had been forced to promise Tuuh a service gift to hunt them down and pin their skins to the GatherStone as a warning to others. And now there was talk of four longbarbs at the Cave-that-Taunts attacking their own kind shortly before the killblast.

The members of the WarGather were beginning to doubt her plan, especially her ability to prevent loot-taking. She could sense that much in their frequent inquiries about the SpellGather's progress and in the gusts with which they warned one another away from the great armory at the Academy of Magic. Her plan had to start freeing the mythal's magic soon, or the WarGather would dissolve around her. Arr had no illusions about what would befall her then. She had promised too many gifts, and forgiveness was not a virtue of the phaerimm.

Ryry emerged from the forest behind Arr and floated to her side.

"How goes it?" Ryry asked.

"You shall have your spell crown," Arr gusted. "What news from the Cave-that-Taunts?"

"After the killblast, now it is calling us flatworms," Ryry reported. "It claims the spell was its doing."

Arr found herself curling her tail. She forced it straight again, then decided that had to be a lie. Who had ever heard of a cave that could cast spells?

"Then I am certain," Arr began, "that you asked why it killed so many elves along with our dozen and a half."

"Of course."

Several of the SpellGather phaerimm began to work their four arms over each other as though pulling a long rope. Arr put a hand out to silence Ryry and went still as stone, praying that they finally had a thread, even a small one, to demonstrate the progress she had promised the WarGather.

The finch peeped.

The arms of the spell artists fell motionless one after the other, and they returned to pluck at the strand they had found. Arr gnashed her pointed teeth and checked again to see if there was any magic on the bird, but it seemed as null as a rock. Another peep like that, she vowed, and it *would* be a rock, and she didn't care how many days of concentration the spellcasting shattered.

Calming herself, Arr turned her attention back to Ryry and asked, "What was the cave's reply?"

"It had none," Ryry answered smoothly. "Its claim was a lie, I am sure."

"No doubt," Arr answered. It was almost certainly Ryry who was lying—to cover for her oversight—but Arr would only alienate a fellow member of the WarGather by making the accusation. "It is an insult that a hole in the ground speaks our language."

"Indeed."

"What of the four betrayers?" Arr asked.

"They are not betrayers."

Ryry's thorns bristled with pride. Arr waited in stillness, for she had learned the value of allowing allies their moment.

"They are impostors," Ryry said at last. "Impostors who escaped the killblast and fought with the blackswords at the Starmeadow."

"There was a fight at the Starmeadow?"

"Only just completed," Ryry said. "I have sent a killtroop, but you know how quickly the blackswords vanish after they attack."

Arr was still thinking about the betrayers.

"Impostors?" she asked, openly skeptical. "And no one saw through their magic?"

Ryry grew less proud of herself. "They may be shadow pullers," she said. "One of the softhorns who survived saw dark bolts."

"Dark bolts?" Arr repeated. "Did our spies not say Shade had fallen?"

"Nearly fallen," Ryry corrected. "The Chosen have some-how anchored the city over the north end of the lake, but Shade is now stable. It isn't going to fall, not until we bring it down ourselves."

Arr was so shocked she nearly let herself sink to the ground. Tricking the Chosen into destroying Shade for them had been a cornerstone of her plan, but somehow the

Shadovar had prevailed. Could it be true? *Could* the Shadow Weave be stronger than the Weave?

"Arr?"

Arr did not realize she had let herself sink again until she found herself looking up at Ryry. She used her tail to push herself back into the air.

"Why was I not told of this earlier?"

Ryry angled her thorns back in anger and replied, "If Xayn fails to abide by his promise, I am not to blame."

"Xayn?" Arr repeated, finally getting hold of herself. "The blackswords killed Xayn this morning. It is nothing to concern ourselves about."

Ryry's stillness was an accusation.

Arr gestured at the statue of the elf goddess.

"The SpellGather has loosened a strand," she said. "It would take all the princes of Shade to stop us now, and they sent only four."

Ryry brought her four hands together over her dished head and quoted Arr's oft-repeated refrain, "Together, all things are possible." She steepled her sixteen fingers into a single pyramid, causing the finch overhead to take wing and flee. "Is there a way I can be of service?"

"Yes." Though it would mean the promise of another service gift, Arr pointed after the bird and said, "Kill that finch."

CHAPTER SEVENTEEN

2 Eleasias, the Year of Wild Magic

"You're sure this plan will work?" Takari asked. "I don't think anyone was all that impressed with the last one."

"There are no sure things," Galaeron said, "but it has a chance."

"A *good* chance?" Vala asked.

They were hiding among the musty-smelling roots dangling beneath the Floating Gardens of Aerdrie Faenya, waiting in the mucky water of a knee-deep nourishment pond. Aris and the Chosen had already left for Cloudcrown Hill to rescue— fetch was more accurate—Lord Duirsar and the high mages. Galaeron had once again assumed the likeness of a phaerimm, and the entire Company of the Cold Hand had vowed they were ready to lose fingers—or even entire hands—to the cold of their borrowed darkswords.

Galaeron turned his head-disk toward Vala and held her gaze.

"A better chance than you had in Myth Drannor. That turned out well enough."

Vala rolled her eyes. "I only had to kill six phaerimm," she said. "We're talking ten here—all at once."

Manynests, just returned from his spying mission and perched on Keya's shoulder, chirped an urgent correction.

"Twelve," Keya translated for those who did not understand peeptalk, then frowned at Galaeron. "I don't see how you can do it."

"I don't have to," Galaeron explained. "I only have to kill the leader. After that, the WarGather will fall apart."

"That we understand," Vala said, taking Galaeron's four-fingered hand. "It's the part where you don't live I'm having trouble with."

"That *we're* having trouble with," Takari added.

She came around to Galaeron's other side and slipped her hand through the crook of one of his spindly arms. The Vaasans scowled—Vala at Takari, and Kuhl at Galaeron—and Kuhl rested a hand on the pommel of his sword. Their jealousy meant nothing to Galaeron. He loved Takari as much as he did Vala, and if that angered someone, it was no concern of his. He covered Takari's hand with his own.

"I'll be all right," Galaeron said. "You'll be right behind me."

"We have to fight through a ring of beholders and illithids," Vala reminded him.

"That's going to take time," Keya added. "Why don't you shadow walk a dozen of us in there—"

"Because we'd be lucky to last a breath," Burlen said, cutting her off. "*We* won't look like a phaerimm, remember?"

Though Galaeron knew Burlen was more concerned with protecting the mother of Dexon's child than assuring their success, he mouthed a silent thanks to the Vaasan. His plan depended on timing. The Company of the Cold Hand had to clear the defenses around the SpellGather before Aris arrived with the Chosen and the high mages. It would take time to do what Galaeron intended, and Keya and the others would need to set a defensive ring of their own before the phaerimm pulled themselves together to counterattack.

Khelben's voice sounded inside Galaeron's head, *We're in position, with a clear view of the statue hill.*

Good—we'll leave now, Galaeron replied.

He looked up at Manynests and sent the little snowfinch ahead with a tweet, then used his two free arms to wave the others forward.

They followed Manynests to the shore and left the dangling roots behind, stepping out from beneath the overhead gardens into a thick hedge of duskblossom. The snowfinch took his leave with a merry chirp and climbed above the hedge toward Cloudcrown Hill—then wheeled around and came diving back, squealing in alarm.

Thinking an owl or a hawk was after their courier, Galaeron flung a strand of shadowsilk into the air behind Manynests and spoke a two-syllable incantation. He realized his mistake when a silver lightning bolt cracked through the hedge crest and snaked its way out across the nourishment pond, leaving a mile-long tunnel of scorched root ends in its wake.

In the next instant, the phaerimm that had cast the spell came streaking over the hedge into the shadow net. The strands could not be broken, but Galaeron was not prepared for the shock—and was probably not strong enough to hold it even had he been—and the net slipped free.

The astonished thornback tried to swing around to see what had caught it, but lost control of its flight and rolled sideways into the mass of roots beneath the floating gardens. It tangled quickly and hung there in the air, howling gusts of frustration and stirring the water below into a froth. The three Vaasans reacted first, Vala and Burlen charging through the hedge to meet the oncoming attack, and Kuhl splashing into the pond to finish off the trapped phaerimm.

Keya sprang into action almost as quickly, ordering half her company southward in a flanking action and sending the other half through the hedge to support Vala and Burlen. As surprised as he was impressed by the commander his little sister had become, Galaeron prepared a dark bolt and turned to hurl it before the phaerimm teleported out of its predicament.

But this one had no intention of leaving. It thrust two hands through the shadow net, and a shimmering mirror of magic appeared before it and sent the black dart sailing back at Galaeron. He pivoted out of the way and heard a muffled crackle as the missile slammed into the ground behind him. A third hand waved in Kuhl's direction, and the Vaasan went tumbling across the pond. He slammed headlong into Takari, who had been trying to sneak around for a clean flank shot, and they both splashed into the water and did not rise again.

Galaeron was already flicking an obsidian sliver into the air. He yelled a word of command, and the sliver grew as long as his arm and began to spin, blurring into a large black disk. It shattered the phaerimm's mirror and severed one of the arms that had been holding the shield. Slicing a tunnel through the root tangle, it vanished.

When the injury did not cause the phaerimm to teleport away, a cold lump formed in Galaeron's stomach. He began to fear that the WarGather had somehow learned of their plans and was already mounting an assault to stop them, but if so, why send only one assailant over the hedge?

Galaeron rolled a thread of shadowsilk into a wad. Before he could speak the mystic word that would expand the tiny orb into a shadow ball, the phaerimm was pelting him with golden darts of Weave magic. When the bolts dissipated harmlessly against the spell-guard Laeral had placed on him, the thornback switched instantly to dispelling magic. The spell-guard began to flicker and flash.

Galaeron hurled his shadow sphere, only to see the phaerimm stick an arm through the net and open an extradimensional portal in its palm. The black orb grew

you must fly to Cloudcrown Hill. Khelben is expecting you, and he'll worry if you don't show."

Manynests peeped a question.

"I know I'm bleeding," Galaeron said, "but there's no need to worry him about that. The attack continues as planned."

Manynests peeped another question.

"Yes, I did see how fast you flew," Galaeron said, "but no, I don't think all the thornbacks are after you now. They have other quarry to hunt. Now, off with you."

Galaeron raised his hand and launched the finch, which vanished into the forest canopy.

"Takari!" an angry bellow erupted from the hedge behind Galaeron.

Galaeron twisted around to see Kuhl's burly form pushing through the duskblossoms. A steady cascade of blood was pouring out of his head wound, concealing his sunken eyes behind a red curtain and filling his bushy beard with thick, steaming crimson. Somehow, he saw through the torrent clearly enough to locate Takari, who was using his darksword to poke through the snarled stems of a giant bell-bramble.

"Thief!" Kuhl staggered forward, his hand rising to call his darksword. "My sword!"

Takari's knuckles whitened as she fought to hold the weapon.

"Let me use it a while. You can barely walk."

"Elven trollop!" Kuhl continued forward, not seeming to realize that in the case of a wood elf, at least, that was a little like calling a snake a reptile. "It was never me you wanted. I see that."

"That's not true." Takari wrapped her second hand around the hilt. "I wanted you, too, sometimes."

She began to back away. Though it looked like she was retreating, Galaeron was astonished to see Takari holding the darksword tip down, grasping the hilt in a double-hand stack and keeping a half-open stance. She was *trying* to look helpless and unprepared, inviting Kuhl to charge.

And charge Kuhl did, leaping forward with all the power and speed of a wounded rothé. Even flying, Galaeron knew he would never intercept the man in time to save his life. Instead, he flicked a strand of shadowsilk in Kuhl's direction and spoke a quick incantation, catching him in the same shadow net he had used to tangle the phaerimm.

The net appeared around Kuhl a mere three steps from Takari, and his momentum carried him forward another two before he crashed to the ground. Worried that Takari would go ahead with her plan anyway, Galaeron used the trailing line to pull the kicking Vaasan safely out of harm's way.

Kuhl rolled around so he could face Galaeron.

"And *you* are her panderer!" the Vaasan shouted. "This was your—"

Galaeron pinched his fingers together and uttered a spell, and the Vaasan fell silent. He handed the trailing line to the warrior who had addressed him as Lord Nihmedu with instructions to keep Kuhl safe but bound, then turned to deal with Takari.

Vala was already handling the matter. She had crept up behind Takari—no easy feat—and plucked the wood elf off the ground. Vala wrapped a burly arm clear around her body and grasped her sword arm just above the elbow. With her feet off the ground, Takari had no way left to defend herself except drop the darksword and cast a cantrip, and she was not dropping the sword.

Vala wrapped her thick fingers around Takari's wrist and slowly twisted it back toward the thumb, and the darksword dropped free. She passed her captive to Burlen with instructions to choke her unconscious at the first sign of trouble, then she picked up Kuhl's sword and used it to slash open the shadow net holding Kuhl.

"Here's your sword," she said, returning the weapon. "Put it away and get that cut attended to, and don't even *look* in her direction."

"But she—"

"Kuhl! I'll take care of it." Vala shoved him toward the hedge, then turned granite-hard eyes in Galaeron's direction and said, "We need to talk."

None to happy to see Kuhl free and Takari restrained, Galaeron dipped his head-disk in agreement.

Vala led the way to a small hollow where they could speak privately.

"I should have known this would happen." Her tone was angry, but not accusatory. "You'll have to take one of them with you."

"Why?" Galaeron asked. He was still unhappy with—and a little suspicious of—her decision to free Kuhl and restrain Takari. "Because you're jealous of her?"

"You think this is about you?" Vala rolled her eyes. "Get over yourself. Takari is carrying Kuhl's baby."

"I realize that," Galaeron said, "but I am not enough of a human to be jealous—"

Vala brought a hand up and managed to find Galaeron's head through his disguise and cuff him—more or less gently—above his ear.

"Are you listening?" she demanded. "We can sort that out later, if we live long enough. We've got a problem with Takari and Kuhl."

"That much was apparent," Galaeron said, finally overcoming his initial reaction to how she had handled Takari. "Perhaps you should explain the rest."

"Thank you," Vala said.

Before she could begin the explanation, Keya appeared at the edge of the hollow and came down to join them.

"I sent Burlen to watch Kuhl and put an elf in charge of Takari."

Keya was informing, not asking permission, and Galaeron was again impressed with the commander she had become. Her arrangement was both more secure and likely to raise less resentment in the rest of the company.

"I think they're really ready to kill each other," Keya

continued. She turned to Galaeron. "And you're not helping matters. I know you and Takari have a past, but do you have to rub Kuhl's nose in it?"

"That's not the real trouble," Vala said. Even she did not question Keya's leadership; she simply turned to include the young elf in the conversation. "Kuhl's darksword has a history."

"A history?" Galaeron asked. "They all have histories."

"Not like this," Vala said. "Most of our darkswords have passed through the hands of five or six warriors, eight at most. Twenty-two have carried Kuhl's sword."

"Twenty-two?" Keya gasped. "That's one every five years."

"The bearers are lucky to carry it that long," Vala said. "The first was Yondala, who took the weapon up to defend her child from a flight of saurians. After, her husband began to grow jealous of the power she wielded. One morning, we found her floating in the marsh, and Gromb had the sword. When it was determined that he had killed her in her sleep, he tried to escape Bodvar's justice and used the darksword to slay two more warriors. The weapon was given to their eldest son, but he died a year later when a rock fell on his head while he was playing with his brothers."

"And Bodvar let the family keep such a sword?" Keya gasped.

"It was not his to take, and it would have come back the instant some relative of Yondala's stretched a hand out and called to it."

Nor would they have dared destroy the weapon, Galaeron realized. Even he could not say what would happen if one of the blades was broken—nor how Melegaunt would have reacted. He nodded to Vala.

"You're right, we can't have them together—especially not during the battle."

"I'll dismiss Takari from the Cold Hand," Keya said. "She can go back to the Hidden Caves to help Dexon guard the children."

"If you dismiss her from the Cold Hand, you can't tell her to do anything," Galaeron said. "Do you really think she'd stay away from the battle?"

"Not likely," Vala said. "One of them must go with you."

"That's almost a death sentence," Keya objected. "Galaeron will be lucky to survive with his shadow magic."

"We will all be lucky to survive, no matter where we are," Vala replied, "and one of them is sure to die if we do anything else."

Keya considered that, then nodded.

"Galaeron should choose." She turned to him and continued, "Whoever it is will be fighting at your side. You should choose the one who will help the most."

Galaeron knew that Keya's suggestion—no, her order—made sense, but it felt like she was asking him to choose between Takari and Vala. He had already done that once, during the battle with the second Wulgreth, when he had been forced to chose between saving Vala's life and protecting Takari. He had saved Vala, and Takari had been terribly injured, and he did not ever want to make a decision like that again.

If he took Takari, he stood a good chance of losing her forever. If he took Kuhl, Vala would know he was saving Takari's life at the expense of one of her followers. While Vala had already made clear she would consent to the decision, he doubted she would ever forgive him for it.

Galaeron looked back to Keya and asked, "Who's doing was this situation? Did Takari pursue Kuhl, or Kuhl—"

"That has nothing to do with your decision," Keya said. "Choose the one who'll be the most use to you."

"Kuhl's wound is not serious," Vala said, "and he will have his darksword."

"But Takari has fought at your side for twenty years," Keya said. "She will know what you are going to do before you do it."

Keya's argument made clear which choice she believed

he should make—and Galaeron knew she was right. Even without Kuhl's darksword, Takari would be better at watching his back, and he would be better at watching hers.

"Keya, you've grown too wise for one so young." Galaeron closed his eyes, then said, "Takari."

Keya laid a hand on his arm. "She's the best choice, Galaeron."

"We'll start the shadow walk from here," he said. "It will give us time to prepare."

"As you wish. I'll send her along."

Before leaving, Keya stretched up to kiss his cheek, but missed because of the phaerimm disguise and got his chin instead.

"Soft songs, my brother."

"And light laughter, my sister," Galaeron said. "Father would have been proud."

"Of both of us."

Her eyes grew glassy and wet. She turned away and wiped them, then disappeared over the rim of the hollow.

Vala grabbed hold of Galaeron's ears, no doubt misled by his magic disguise into thinking she had taken him by his hands.

"No need to worry about your sister, Galaeron. Dexon has Burlen and Kuhl looking after her. I'll be there, too."

"Then she'll be fine, I have no doubt," Galaeron said. "As long as my plan works."

"It will—*I* have no doubt."

Vala leaned in, finding Galaeron's lips the first time, and kissed him long and hard—Vaasan hard. He wrapped his real arms around her waist and held her there until he began to grow dizzy from lack of breath.

When he finally let go, she stepped back and studied Galaeron with a raised brow.

"Never thought I'd do that."

Galaeron frowned in confusion, then realized she could not see his expression and had to ask, "What?"

Vala made a sour face and said, "Kiss a phaerimm."

She started after Keya, but stopped atop the hollow to look back over her shoulder.

"But I'm glad I did—and I'd have done it anyway, even if you had chosen Kuhl."

"Would you have?"

The question slipped out before Galaeron realized he was truly asking it, but he did not try to attenuate the doubt it implied. When it came to offending others, even those he loved, his shadow had made him fearless.

Vala's tone grew serious, though not angry. "I understand about Takari—I truly do."

Galaeron felt as though a knot in his chest had come undone.

"I'm glad," he said. "Thank you."

"No reason to thank me. I'd never want you to do something that cold for me. I know I wouldn't for you."

Vala drew her sword and turned toward the Company of the Cold Hand.

Soot-starred and smoke-shrouded though it was, Cloud-crown Palace was the finest example of Evereska's naturist architecture that Aris had yet seen. From the slope below, where he was hiding in the trees at the edge of what remained of the forest that had once covered all of Cloud-crown Hill, the palace resembled a stand of bluetops packed so closely together that the huge boles had grown into each other. The scaling on the bark was so expertly done that even his practiced sculptor's eye would not have known it was stone, save for the handful of places where an enemy spell had actually penetrated the defensive magic and cratered one of the ancient towers.

The antimagic shell the phaerimm had erected around the palace was functional but artless, a bell-shaped dome of shimmering translucence that soared up from beneath the ground and vanished from sight a thousand feet or more overhead. Aris knew it had to continue far higher and curve inward to cover the tower pinnacles, but even his eyes were not keen enough to see a variation so subtle at such a great distance.

The thornbacks themselves were standing watch on the slope above, hiding among the tangles of blast-toppled trees that covered the hillside. So far, Aris located only three on this side of Cloudcrown, spaced at even intervals in a semicircle just out of arrow range. Their mind-slaves—and more than a few of their fellow phaerimm—lay scattered over the killing zones beneath the palace's hidden arrow loops, a decomposing testament to the ferocity of the battle that had ended in stalemate.

The undulating speck of a tiny finch rounded the palace wall at what would have been treetop height, had there been any trees still standing, then disappeared in the direction of the statue of Hanali Celanil. Though Aris had not yet visited that particular work, he had been assured by everyone who had that it was among the city's finest. Rumor had it that it was also as old as Evereska itself, which would make it one of the few surviving examples of high elven religious art from the Pre-Netheril period.

Something sharp pricked his knee, and he looked down to see Storm Silverhand slipping her dagger into its scabbard. She did it without looking, for she was scowling up at him with a worried expression.

Red eye? Her fingertalk was as fast as Galaeron's, which made it difficult to follow. *That's the sigil.*

Sigil? With his long fingers, Aris suspected his reply seemed to Storm like he was drawling or stuttering. *There's a sigil?*

Fur the tackle!

Storm pointed at the palace, and Aris finally realized what she was trying to remind him of. Manynests' departure was the *signal*.

Sorry, he signed. *I'm a little nervous.*

What's to be nervous about? Storm replied. *This plan has to be better than the last one.*

That should make me feel better?

Aris removed the two largest hammers from his tool belt, and fixed his eye on a nose-shaped burl about twenty feet off the ground. The hardest part of his job would be keeping that knot in sight. If he went to the wrong one, Galaeron's plan would fail.

An immense roar erupted on the opposite side of the hill, and fans of gold and crimson blast magic spread across the sky behind the palace. The three phaerimm rose from their hiding places and stirred the air into a tempest as they hurled questions back and forth, but none of them showed any sign of departing their posts. Heart rising into his throat, Aris raised his hammers and prepared to make a run he knew he could not survive.

Storm laid a restraining hand on his knee.

Aris looked down to find her shaking her head. She raised a single finger, then looked back up the slope.

The battle continued to rage on the other side of the palace. The hill shuddered beneath their feet and sheets of flame licked around the walls of the palace, and still the phaerimm remained on post. Aris cocked his brow. They had only a minute or two before the thornbacks realized that all of the noise was being made by just two Chosen. After that, it would be only seconds before they realized the attack was a diversion and returned to his side of the palace.

As the largest target on the hill, Aris knew what would become of him if he was still on the battlefield then. He wouldn't even mind—not much—except that would mean that Galaeron's plan had failed. Evereska's art would be lost forever.

Storm took her hand from Aris's knee. Aris nodded, she nodded back—and two of the phaerimm flew off toward the other side of the hill.

Storm's jaw fell. She closed it, then flashed the quick fingertalk sentence: *Told you so!*

She pointed at the last phaerimm, her finger darkening to black as she whispered an incantation so softly even Aris couldn't hear it.

The last phaerimm left his hiding place and raced after his fellows.

For a moment, Aris was too shocked to react. There was nobody between him and the burl. All he had to do was run up there, reach through the antimagic shell, and knock a hole in the wall. Then Lord Duirsar and Kiinyon Colbathin and the High Mages and the Long Watch would start pouring out on their ropes, leaping across the antimagic shell into the battle-torn meadow, where Storm would by then have laid a teleport circle that would take them straight to the statue of Hanali Celanil that Aris wanted so desperately to see.

"What are you waiting for?" She pulled a packet of amber dust from inside her cloak, raised her arms so Aris could pick her up and carry her up to the palace, and said, "Plans don't work any better than this."

CHAPTER EIGHTEEN

2 Eleasias, the Year of Wild Magic

Galaeron and Takari arrived at the statue of Hanali Celanil to find a small circle of phaerimm using all four hands to pull golden strands of magic off the hem of the goddess's gown. They were feeding the threads out behind them, filling the air with a shimmering snarl of loops and whorls so dense and bright that it was difficult to see the thornbacks themselves. Where the tangle touched the ground, it passed through the paving stones as sunlight passes through water, leaving the impression that the great statue stood upon the surface of a dark, still pond rather than a courtyard of granite cobblestones. Galaeron counted twelve phaerimm pulling thread, with a thirteenth watching from beneath a tree at the edge of the plaza.

"That's the one Manynests told us about." He did

not bother with fingertalk. Though the phaerimm could undoubtedly eavesdrop into the Shadow Fringe where he and Takari were hiding, they could not do it without using Weave magic—and in the Shadow Fringe, Weave magic would shine like a beacon light for Galaeron. "I'm fairly sure that's their leader. It's the only one we absolutely have to kill, so if something goes wrong—"

"Nothing's going to go wrong, now that you've come to your senses and decided to bring me along." Takari let a hand drop the hilt of her borrowed darksword. "I only wish Keya would've given me Kuhl's sword. That one I can hang on to."

"Kuhl's sword is not Keya's to give," Galaeron said. "And Kuhl has need of it himself."

It was the fifth or sixth time he had reminded her of that, and his patience was giving way to alarm. There was a dark familiarity in the way that simple fact kept eluding her, in how every conversation seemed to return to Kuhl's darksword.

"Our need is greater." She pointed at the phaerimm leader and said, "You said yourself we absolutely have to kill that one."

"That is what *we* absolutely have to do. Kuhl and the others have to destroy the defensive perimeter—absolutely. If they fail, our success means nothing."

As he spoke, Galaeron looked Takari full in the eyes. Though hardly veiled in darkness, the irises were shot through with tiny streaks of shadow. She had to be told; it was her only chance of controlling her hunger for the sword.

"Takari, I didn't come to my senses. We thought it best to keep you away from Kuhl and his darksword."

"What?" she asked. "Why would you keep me away from something that is mine by right?"

"Because it isn't yours by any right. You only think it is because you've been shadow touched."

"Shadow touched!" Takari objected. "I *earned* that sword!"

"It's an heirloom. How could you earn . . ." Galaeron let the question trail off as he realized what Takari was saying. He looked at her stomach, which had not yet begun to bulge, and asked, "You did that on purpose?"

Takari raised her chin and said, "Of course it was on purpose. Do you think I would lay with that rothé by accident?"

"Of course not, but neither did I think you had done it to steal his darksword."

"'Steal' is such a human word," Takari said, rolling her eyes. "I just wanted to use it and maybe keep it after he died."

"After you killed him," Galaeron corrected. He turned to keep an eye on the tree branch. Manynests would be arriving soon. "You always meant to keep it."

"How do you know what I meant—"

"I know a shadow when I see it, Takari," Galaeron said.

The phaerimm leader sent an angry gust whirling across the cobblestones, and the SpellGather began to pull threads twice as fast. That would be word of the attack on Cloud-crown Hill. Galaeron did not have much time to convince Takari of her peril. The way she was thinking, once the battle started she would run down to take the darksword from Kuhl.

"There's a shadow in your eyes," Galaeron continued. "You wanted a darksword for yourself, and Keya showed you how to get what you sought."

"That doesn't mean I was going to kill him," Takari retorted. "Humans have short lives—especially around here—and I'm patient."

"Maybe that was what you intended, before you touched the sword, but you were going to kill him at the Floating Gardens."

"He was charging me!"

"You could have scrambled up any of a dozen trees. I saw how you were standing, Takari—and the way you held the sword. It was a double-hand stack."

"You don't know how quick Kuhl can be," Takari said. "I had to defend myself."

Galaeron risked turning his attention from the phaerimm long enough to lock gazes with Takari.

"When he grabbed for the sword, you were going to fall and let the blade swing up in his groin." There was no accusation in his voice, only insistence and certainty. "It would have looked like an accident."

Takari met his gaze for only a moment before her eyes flicked away, her defenses finally starting to crumble. She retreated to the edge of the Shadow Fringe and peered out through snarl of magic threads.

"Hanali's gown is starting to look ragged," she said. "If we don't attack the SpellGather soon—"

"You can't ignore this, Takari," Galaeron interrupted. "Think back to when you borrowed Kuhl's sword at the Floating Gardens. You took the time to turn him face up."

"I didn't want him to drown." She sounded as though she were remembering, not explaining. "He's not so bad, for a human."

"But after you borrowed the sword. . . ."

"I didn't *borrow* it. You can't borrow what's already . . ." Takari let the sentence trail off, then raised a hand to her mouth and turned to look at Galaeron again. "And now I want him dead!"

"It's the sword. That one carries a curse." Galaeron took her by the arm and gently pulled her away from the Fringe edge. "It opens you to your shadow."

"My shadow?" Takari gasped. It was the first time Galaeron could recall seeing true terror in her eyes. "Will I turn into one of *them*?"

"That will depend on how you react, I think," Galaeron said. "I'm not sure, but I do know you mustn't take Kuhl's sword from him again. If you fail in that, you'll have to kill him, and if you kill him, you *will* be lost."

"Great." Takari's eyes slid away from his, focusing somewhere beyond his shoulder. "Manynests. . . ."

Galaeron turned around to find the little bird flying into the tree above the phaerimm leader's head. In his beak, he carried something pointed and twice as long as he was.

"What's that he has?" Takari asked.

Galaeron twisted a few strands of shadowsilk together at the top, then uttered a spell and began to whisk himself with the brush end.

"I don't know," he said. "It's not part of the plan."

Manynests landed on the lowest branch over the phaerimm's head-disk. He stretched his neck forward, letting out a sharp chirp, and released what he was carrying. The pointed end dropped first, spinning slightly so that the long spine rising along one side of the shaft grew visible.

"It's a tail barb!" Takari gasped.

The barb hit the phaerimm on the rim of the mouth and bounced off its missile guard. The creature puffed in surprise and tipped forward to retrieve the barb. It held the thing over its open mouth for a moment, then raised its head-disk toward the branch where Manynests sat scolding it in peeptalk.

"*Ithinkthat'soursignal.*" Galaeron's words came out in a rush, for the spell of speed he had cast upon himself had already taken effect. "*Remembertheplan.*"

Without awaiting a response, Galaeron floated to the edge of the Fringe and sent two dark bolts hissing into the phaerimm leader. The first burned a fist-sized hole through the middle of its chest and sent it wobbling back into the tree trunk. The second clipped it along the rim of its mouth, gouging a long furrow along the side of its head-disk and lopping an arm off at the shoulder.

Takari's booted feet landed squarely in Galaeron's back as, executing her part of the plan, she caught him with a flying drop kick that sent him tumbling tail-over-arms out into the courtyard. He did not pass through the strands of Weave magic so much as they passed through him, burning like nettles and engulfing him in a crackling halo of green sparks. That was not part of the plan. He glimpsed the leader of the phaerimm wrapped around the base of the tree. Its three remaining arms rested limply on the ground and black gore oozed from the hole in its body. Galaeron brought himself to a halt and spun to face Hanali's statue.

The members of the SpellGather had stopped pulling magic and were already starting to drift away from the circle. Galaeron pointed two arms back toward the shadow from which he had emerged. Takari was already retreating into the shadows, her legs and the tip of her borrowed darksword just disappearing into the Fringe as planned. Galaeron gestured wildly in her direction, his arms throwing off huge sheets of green sparks as they sliced through the air.

"After her!" He used his magic to howl in Winds, "She's getting away!"

Whether it was his accent or the sweeping lines of green sparks, the phaerimm were not falling for it. They raised their arms in his direction, and even with his speed magic, Galaeron barely had time to raise a shadow shield before a hundred golden bolts came streaking in his direction. He huddled down behind the circle and tried not to scream. The hiss of the approaching bolts rose to a sizzle, and the sizzle to a roar, and the roar to a deafening crash as the missiles reached his shield and vanished down into the shadow plane. The crash disappeared into a ringing silence that left the ground shaking and Galaeron's eardrums throbbing, his nostrils tingling with the rainwater smell of spent magic.

Galaeron did not wait. He flipped the shield around and dived through it into the shadows, and even then he was very nearly caught by the storm of fire magic and disintegration rays that converged on the place he had been kneeling. He remained a moment to see if any of his attackers would be foolish enough to pursue him into the dark circle, then he closed it behind him and streaked through the shadows back to Takari's side.

"That plan worked about as well as a pixie ladder," Takari said. "I don't think they were fooled by your disguise."

She was peering out into the courtyard, watching two trios of phaerimm work their way toward the shadow where she and Galaeron stood watching. "It doesn't look like it," Galaeron replied, "but my plan did work."

Galaeron dispelled the illusion magic that made him look like a phaerimm, then took an arrow from Takari's quiver and began to rub it with shadowsilk.

"Really?" Takari sounded more than doubtful, she sounded distrustful. "I don't see that."

"They stopped attacking the mythal, didn't they?"

Galaeron plucked a death arrow from her quiver and rubbed the head with shadowsilk. He uttered a piercing spell and passed the missile back to her.

Takari nocked the arrow and raised her bow, but turned to Galaeron before firing and tipped her head back, lips slightly parted.

"In case this one doesn't work either—"

"It *will* work."

Galaeron took another arrow from her quiver, and Takari rolled her eyes.

"Same old Galaeron." There was genuine disgust in her voice. "Won't ever give a wood elf a chance."

She set the tip of her arrow on the closest phaerimm, which was no more than twenty paces away, and pulled the bowstring back.

Galaeron laid his free hand over her draw arm.

Takari turned, her expression one of irritation.

"I do love you," Galaeron said.

Takari's jaw dropped. Had Galaeron not tightened his grasp, she would have let slip the arrow.

"You're only saying that because we're about to die."

Galaeron shook his head, then looked back to the approaching phaerimm. They had closed to fifteen paces. He cast another piercing spell on the arrow in his hand.

Takari ignored the thornbacks and continued to study Galaeron.

"You always did have a lousy sense of timing," she said, "but I'll take what I can get."

She loosed her arrow, and the shaft took its target square in the body. Galaeron's shadow magic allowed it to penetrate the phaerimm's missile guard and sink to the fletching. The thornback squalled in pain and teleported away, though not so quickly that Galaeron failed to notice the black disintegration crater forming around Takari's arrow.

The five survivors attacked with a veritable spell-storm of flames, meteor stones, lightning, and half a dozen other kinds of magic death. As the spells entered the shadow where Galaeron and Takari were hiding, they were funneled through a shadow door that opened on the opposite side of the courtyard, and the phaerimm were blasted from behind by their own spells.

Two died instantly, and two more teleported away to safety. Galaeron handed the death arrow to Takari. She nocked and loosed it into the remaining thornback even as it flicked its fingers at their hiding place. Galaeron's dimensional door shimmered once, then crackled out of existence. By then, the phaerimm who had dispelled it lay motionless on the ground, a black hole expanding around the arrow buried in its head-disk.

Galaeron grabbed Takari's hand and guided it to his belt.

"Hold tight," he said.

"You can be sure."

He turned and raced into the deep shadows. Though his power was great enough to keep at bay most of the lesser creatures they were likely to stumble across on such a short journey through the Deep, Galaeron was careful to keep moving and moving fast. Shadow-touched though she was, Takari was still enough a creature of the Weave that Galaeron could feel her radiating heat against his back . . . warm and distinct . . . and if he could feel it, so could the shapeless mouths that preyed on the hapless visitors who wandered too far from the Fringe.

They had traveled about a dozen heartbeats when a terrible gurgling growl erupted in the distance behind them. Takari stopped, her hand pulling on Galaeron's belt as she turned to look over her shoulder.

"Keep moving!" he warned. "Or it'll be us next."

"What is it?" Takari asked.

"Its guarding our back trail," Galaeron answered. "That's all that matters."

A lightning bolt crackled in the distance and fell silent. There was no flicker of light, not even a faint one, and Galaeron knew that had they been looking straight into the bolt, they would have seen nothing. So deep in shadow, light vanished almost at its source. The shadow monster growled again, then died with an agonized wail.

"That can't be good," Takari said.

"We can do our own dirty work," Galaeron said. "The attack will slow them down. The sound will draw things that even phaerimm don't want to run into."

"What about us?" Takari asked.

"We don't want to run into those things either." Galaeron pulled her toward the Fringe and added, "That's why we went first."

Once they were out of the Shadow Deep, Galaeron came up behind the tree where Manynests had alighted. He stopped in the Fringe. Though they could not see into the courtyard from the their vantage point, any phaerimm still lurking in the area were less likely to come poking around in the shadows. He cast his piercing magic on another death arrow and returned it to Takari.

"Use that only if a phaerimm comes for us," he said. "Let me borrow the darksword."

Takari unhooked her scabbard, but did not hand it over.

"Where are you going?" she asked.

"To surprise our pursuers," he said, drawing the darksword

from the scabbard. "This shouldn't be difficult, but you know what to do if I don't come back."

Though the hilt began to chill his hand, the cold no longer caused him any discomfort. Like Melegaunt, Telamont, and Hadrhune, he was part of the shadow.

"Yeah," Takari said. "Die."

"I meant check the leader," Galaeron said. "Be certain it's dead."

Takari shook her head in mock despair and said, "I know what you meant, Galaeron." She started to turn away, then changed her mind and grabbed Galaeron behind the neck. "First, you prove you weren't lying. First you prove you love me."

She pulled his head close to hers and kissed him long and hard, a kiss born of two decades of longing, a kiss that would no longer be denied. Though he knew their pursuers would be coming up fast, Galaeron let himself melt into it, let his spirit and his lips and his tongue touch Takari's as he never had before. They joined as only elves can join, and Galaeron felt what she had always known, that they were spirit mates, that they belonged together no matter what the heartache and loneliness and sorrow brought down on them by their destiny. Nothing remained to keep them apart—nothing except their human lovers.

Takari sensed this as soon as Galaeron did, of course, and she was the first to pull away.

Galaeron would not make her ask.

"I still love her," he said.

He was not admitting anything Takari did not already know, but he had to say it aloud. He owed her that much—and himself, too.

"I'd have to be blind to miss that," Takari said. She smiled—a little sadly—and glanced down at her belly. "I have a few entanglements of my own."

Galaeron kissed her again—briefly—and slipped back into the shadows. Once he was alone, he had no fear whatsoever of the unseen creatures who haunted the Deep. He was as much a part of the darkness as they were, and anything powerful enough to find and stalk him would also be intelligent enough to sense the power he bore. This wisdom was also born of the gift Melegaunt had passed to him, as was his knowledge of the phaerimm, and the ways of the Shadow Deep, and the lore of shadow spells, and who knew how many other dark Shadovar secrets. As far as Galaeron could tell, the only part of Melegaunt's experience that the old archwizard had failed to pass along was what to do with so much power and how to wield it wisely. Melegaunt likely had never known or—if he had—cared.

Twenty steps later, the Fringe lay well out of sight. Galaeron stopped to wait. There was no need to hide, nor anyplace to do so had he wished. In the Deep, there was only shadow, and in the hands of those who knew the art, shadow could be shaped into whatever was needed or desired.

Soon, Galaeron sensed a fiery presence approaching along the path he and Takari had taken. Though it was impossible for an elf—or any creature enclosed within a skin—to perceive shape, he felt by the intensity of the thing's heat and its apparent size that it was a phaerimm. He waited long enough to be certain only one creature remained, then he raised a wall of shadow in front of himself and waited.

While far from lost, the phaerimm was obviously frightened. In the vain hope of keeping shadow monsters at bay, it was talking softly to itself, using its powers to stir the shadows into a constant whirl. The thornback also had half a dozen spells prepped and ready to cast—Galaeron could feel the scorching nodules of Weave magic hanging from its body. He allowed it to pass, then dismissed his shadow wall and stepped out behind it.

The nervous phaerimm reacted quickly, encasing itself in a cocoon of fire and launching a volley of magic darts. The blow caught Galaeron in the shoulder and sent him tumbling back head over heels—not a safe way to travel in the Shadow

Deep, even for him. A pair of jaws opened beneath him and tore into his calf, trying to drag him down into some hidden lair. He brought his darksword down alongside his leg. It felt like cutting air, but the mouth opened and he pulled free.

The phaerimm was faring worse than he. Galaeron could feel it a dozen paces ahead and off to one side, stirring the silent shadows into a froth as a pack of shadow creatures—some flying and some slithering—manifested all around and pulled in six directions at once. The thornback was defending itself as well as it was able, but its teleport spells would not work and its other spells were ineffective. No matter how many creatures it destroyed, more formed to take their places. No matter what kind of armor it covered itself in, their shadow fangs and dark claws tore through. An arm came off, then the tail, and finally a long strip of thorny hide.

Galaeron would have left the creature to its fate, save that Melegaunt's wisdom had taught him better than to count a phaerimm dead until it lay disemboweled and burning on the ground. Moving back toward the tree where he had left Takari to avoid attracting a pack of his own attackers, he prepared a volley of shadow arrows and sent them hurling into his entrapped foe.

The impact caught both victim and tormentors by surprise. The phaerimm literally came apart, pieces flying in the dozen different directions that it was being pulled. The angry shadow creatures—those that had not been pinned in place by a dark arrow—melted back into the darkness and came undulating in Galaeron's direction.

Galaeron opened a shadow door and stepped through, emerging into the relatively safe world of the Fringe. For a moment, he was lost to the afterdaze and did not know where he was. Then, as the flash and flicker of war magic began to filter up through the trees from the slope below, he recalled that he was in the middle of a battle and that it was his job and Takari's to make certain the statue of Hanali Celanil was free of phaerimm when Khelben and the Chosen arrived with the High Mages, and that Takari should have been waiting for him right there in the Fringe.

"Takari?"

Galaeron glanced around the Fringe, finding nothing, and limped out onto the hillside. He was dizzy and sore, his arm so weak he could barely lift it.

"Takari!"

The only answer came in the form of a series of excited peeps from the tree above his head. Galaeron raised his chin and found the familiar white face of Manynests peering down at him.

"She did what?" Galaeron gasped. Takari was not the type to leave her post, not even when she was shadow touched. "That can't be right."

Manynests answered with a sharp chirp, then pointed his beak down the hill.

"What about the leader?"

Manynests chirped a question.

"The phaerimm leader," Galaeron said. "The one you dropped the barb on."

The finch peeped angrily.

"All right, the one you *attacked*," Galaeron said. "What did she do about that phaerimm?"

The bird's answer caused Galaeron to limp around the tree as fast as he could move. There were no phaerimm in the courtyard surrounding the statue—at least at first glance—and there was nothing where the leader should have been, save for a puddle of steaming black blood.

"She let it go!" Galaeron cried. "Takari left her post!"

Manynests dropped out of the tree. He landed on one of the darts still protruding from Galaeron's shoulder. He twilled a long question, then cocked his head and looked down the hill toward the battle.

"No," Galaeron growled. "I really don't think Kuhl needed her help."

CHAPTER NINETEEN

2 Eleasias, the Year of Wild Magic

Whether the caustic taste in her mouth was ash or fear, Keya Nihmedu could not say. She knew only that her tongue had gone as dry as a flame, that it had become impossible to tell the shuddering of the ground from her own trembling, and that the child in her belly would be lucky to see the world with its own eyes. Burning bluetops were crashing all around her, horse-sized boulders were tumbling down the slope in a ceaseless cascade, and the air was hot enough to bake acorns. The Cold Hand's objective had sounded simple enough when Galaeron explained it back under the Floating Gardens, but she was hoping he had a backup plan.

Crawling on her belly, Keya crept along beneath the upper slope of the trail cut to where Vala was taking shelter with Kuhl and Burlen. Unlike her elves, who were either lying flat on their bellies keeping a watch up the slope for tumbling boulders or blindly arcing arrows up in the general direction of the enemy, the Vaasans were sitting with their backs to the battle. They were sharing sticks of jerked thkaerth meat and laughing and shoving each other in the shoulder, though they had made concession enough to the fighting to remove their swords from their scabbards and leave them lying at their sides within easy reach.

As Keya approached, Vala removed a stick of dried meat from their rations bag and offered it to her.

"No, thank you," Keya shouted to make herself heard over the battle roar. "I don't have much stomach for thkaerth lately."

Though she hoped the Vaasans would think this was because of her pregnancy, the truth was she simply could no longer stand the sight of cooked meat; it reminded her too much of the burned bodies that lay scattered and unburied throughout all of Evereska. Trying to look as unconcerned as the Vaasans, she drew herself up beside Vala and removed her sword from its scabbard.

"What do you think?" Keya asked. "Concentrate our spell-casters and try to mount a breakthrough?"

Vala replied, "That would only make them easy pickings for the phaerimm."

"What phaerimm?" Takari asked. "Manynests didn't say anything about phaerimm."

"Manynests is a bird. What he can't see doesn't exist for him. But they have one." Vala jerked her thumb over her shoulder and said, "Up there."

Burlen leaned in front of Vala, looking Keya over with a concerned expression, and held out a piece of jerked thkaerth.

"You sure you don't want one?" he said. "You need to keep your strength up."

Keya waved him off and continued to address Vala. "How do you know where the phaerimm is?"

Vala cast a pointed gaze in the direction of a line of charred bodies and said, "The best thing we can do right now is wait."

A sonorous rumble sounded from above and quickly began to grow louder. Keya started to roll to her stomach so she could crawl up the bank to see what was coming. Vala extended an arm and stopped her, pushing her flat against the slope before lying back herself. The rumble built to rhythmic crashing, then suddenly went silent. A rothé-sized boulder tumbled off the rim of the slope and sailed over their heads, bouncing off the far side of the trail and vanishing into the woods below.

"Mind-slaves aren't very bright," Vala said. "Sooner or later, the bugbears will run out of boulders, and the beholders will knock down the last bluetop. *Then* we attack."

"We don't have that long," Keya objected. "According to Galaeron's plan, we should be taking out the perimeter defense now, before Khelben and the others arrive with the high mages. Otherwise, the mind-slaves will turn and counterattack—"

"Then *that's* when we'll take them," Vala interjected. "Or maybe when Aris gets here. If he can hurl a few boulders back up the hill, we might be able to break their line."

"What we can't do is attack into the teeth of their defense," Burlen said. "We'll just get the Cold Hand wiped out, and who will there be to stop the counterattack?"

Keya glanced past Vala and Burlen to Kuhl, and asked him, "What do you think?"

Kuhl's expression merely darkened, and he looked away.

"He agrees with us," Burlen said. "Pay no mind to his manners. He's letting his sword do his thinking."

Burlen reached out and slapped his companion in the back of the helmet. Kuhl's scowl deepened, but he looked away and continued to remain silent.

"Plans are good," Vala said, drawing Keya's attention back to the matter at hand. "Once the spell-flinging starts, they aren't worth the breath it took to speak them. We have to wait for our opportunity—"

She was interrupted by a gusty howl they all recognized as the screech of a wounded phaerimm.

"There's your thornback!" Keya called. She rolled to her stomach and began to shimmy up the bank. "While we sit here talking, someone is killing it."

She stuck her head above the rim just far enough to look up the shattered hillside. Fallen bluetops crisscrossed the slope, blast craters pocked the ground, and curtains of fire poured gray fume into the air. Fifty yards above, a long rank of mind-slaves peered down from behind a meandering breastwork, hurling boulders and magic, anything they could down upon the company of the Cold Hand. There were dozens of bugbears and maybe ten beholders, reinforced by a trio of illithids and a handful of vacant-eyed elves, but the wounded phaerimm was nowhere to be seen. The instant it suffered a serious wound, it had no doubt teleported to safety.

The dark dash of an elven death arrow flashed out of a bluetop behind the enemy breastwork and disappeared into the trenches. A beholder rose briefly into view, its sharp-toothed mouth twisted into a grimace of pain. Keya had just enough time to identify the Tomb Guard's distinctive black-feather fletching on the butt of the arrow before the Cold Hand's battle mages blazed the creature into a red spray.

A thick human hand grabbed her by the ankle and pulled her back down the slope.

"Get down!" Vala snarled. "Dexon will have my head if I let some beholder burn that pointy-eared head off your shoulders!"

Keya was about to protest when a purple ray droned past above, cutting a deep furrow in the rim of the slope, coming within a finger's width of disintegrating her skull. Her heart hammered in her chest so hard that she thought it would break a rib, but she managed to retain enough control of her wits to point her darksword up the slope.

"T-T-Takari!"

"Takari?" It was Kuhl who growled, "Where?"

"In a tree," Keya gasped. "Behind the enemy. I saw her arrow—"

"Which tree?"

Kuhl crawled to the rim and peered through the furrow that had nearly cost Keya her life.

"I don't see her," he said.

"Kuhl, she isn't after your darksword," Keya told him. The last thing they needed was to renew the fight over his ancestral weapon. "Takari's trying to help us break through."

"She's coming for my sword!" Kuhl insisted. He glanced away from the furrow long enough to scowl in Keya's direction. "And you—you're a thieving vixen just like her. The phaerimm took Dexon's leg, but you're the one who's stolen his sword—and his manhood."

There was a time when the raw rage in Kuhl's voice would have sent Keya fleeing, but now it only filled her with cold anger.

"Kuhl, I will overlook the affront to me because it is easy to see how your sword might be more powerful than your mind," she said, "but insult my husband's manhood again, and you will die choking on yours."

Keya glared at the Vaasan until she saw enough of the anger fade from his eyes that she felt certain there would be no need to make good on her threat. She glanced over at Vala, who only shrugged and spread her hands. Keya frowned and nodded toward Kuhl. Vala looked away, thinking, then a veil of sadness seemed to fall over her face. She nodded and crawled up the slope next to Kuhl.

With the burly Vaasan safely under control, Keya turned her thoughts back to the battle. She hazarded a glance over the rim and saw that whatever Takari was doing up there, her attacks were having an effect. A patrol of a dozen bugbears that had been dispatched up the hill to hunt her down lay scattered across the slope, some lying motionless with smoking holes through their torsos, others flailing about trying to pull long elven arrows from their backs. Several beholders were sweeping the forest canopy with their disintegration rays, reducing the number of attacks coming down the hill above Keya as well as raining boughs and limbs on the slope.

Keya slid to the bottom of the embankment and used finger-talk to order the Company of the Cold Hand to assemble behind her, leaving only the archers and every third battle mage to hold their current lines. Within moments, a long stream of warriors began to crawl along the base of the embankment. Keya issued her orders to the first arrivals, along with instructions to pass them along, then she crawled back up to join Vala and the Vaasans.

Vala had her arm across Kuhl's shoulders and was whispering something into his ear that Keya could not hear.

"Another arrow!" Kuhl growled, pointing. "There she is."

Kuhl started to rise and charge up the hill, but Vala caught him by the belt.

"Not yet, Kuhl," she said, pulling him back down. "That's what she wants, isn't it?"

Kuhl considered a moment then nodded.

"Vala!" Keya gasped. "What are you doing?"

Vala whirled on her with an expression that could only be described as demonic.

"You want to use this or not?" she demanded. "Because Kuhl's the only chance we have to get there anytime soon."

As Vala spoke, Burlen continued to speak to Kuhl from the other side.

"She wants you to charge out there alone, doesn't she?" Burlen asked. "She wants you to get yourself killed."

"I won't," Kuhl replied. "She doesn't know. She'll never get my sword."

There was a darkness in his eyes that Keya had never seen there before, something cold, monstrous, and terrifying risen to mask the laugh-lined face she had come to consider that of one of her human brothers.

"What doesn't she know?" Keya asked.

"You'll see," Vala said. "It's Kuhl or Takari now. There's nothing we can do about that, except decide whether we're ready to use it. Are you?"

Keya glanced along the embankment in both directions and saw a long line of warriors in position to charge up the hill. To an elf, their faces were pale and their knuckles white from squeezing their sword hilts, but their jaws were set and their eyes fixed on Keya, awaiting the command to charge.

"Ready when you are," Keya said. "May the gods forgive us."

"It's not the gods we should ask," Vala replied.

She placed a hand on Kuhl's shoulder then raised her head and pointed into one of the bluetops still standing behind the mind-slaves' breastwork.

"There she is, Kuhl," said Vala.

"None of this is your doing," Burlen added. "The pointy-eared vixen seduced you."

"That's right," Vala added. "She let you get a child on her on purpose." As she spoke, Kuhl started to darken—not only his expression, but his face and hands, his eyes, and even the huge ranger's cloak Lord Duirsar had presented him. "All Takari wanted was your sword."

"Oh, she wanted the child, too," Keya said, catching on to what the Vaasans were doing. "The Sy'Tel'Quessir sell their half-human children to pay for wine."

Vala and Burlen dropped their jaws, and Keya thought for a moment she might have taken the fib too far.

Kuhl turned soot-black, blurring around the edges like a shadow or a ghost, and he let out an angry wail. He rose and did not bound over the embankment so much as soar over it, and the slope instantly above exploded into a roaring tempest of death as the defenders hurled all manner of missiles and magic down upon him.

Thinking it had been the Vaasans' purpose to goad Kuhl into drawing the first wave of enemy attacks, Keya raised her hand to call the charge. Vala caught her arm and pulled it down.

Wait. Vala spoke in elven fingertalk—the only speech that would not be drowned out by the crash and roar of battle. *Let him get a little ahead of us.*

Ahead of us? Keya retorted. *There can't be anything left of him.*

But when she peered over the rim of the embankment, she saw that there was. Through a wall of smoke and flame twenty paces thick, Keya saw Kuhl's black silhouette still weaving and twisting up the hill. Lightning blasts passed through his shadowy form without slowing him down. Magic bolts glanced off him, trailing long wisps of black murk. Disintegration rays struck his dark aura and dissolved. Boulders he always managed to duck or dodge, spears he deflected and slipped, arrows stuck only in the strongest parts of his armor. It was as though he had become half phantom and half rothé, a creature of the shadows that could be seen but never stopped. Keya watched in awe until he vanished into the thickening smoke, then turned to Vala and raised her own darksword—or rather her husband's.

Can this sword do that? she asked.

No!

And never try! It was Burlen who added the explanation, *He's given himself to his sword. It can't be undone.*

The roar began to abate as Kuhl continued his charge, and Vala looked up the hill and spoke a single syllable. She didn't shout or use fingertalk, but Keya didn't need words to understand her meaning. She brought her arm forward then rose and charged over the rim of the embankment.

From Takari's perch high among the rustling bluetops, the charge of the Cold Hand looked the stuff of songs.

Through the smoke and flame came a golden-helmed tide of elf spellblades, words of mystic power pouring out of their mouths, forks of silver and gold flashing from their fingertips, swords glinting in their hands and armor gleaming on their breasts. The mind-slaves met the onslaught with a tempest of ray and rock, hurling boulders, flinging death bolts, spraying fire. Still the elves came, bounding over blast craters, scrambling across fallen bluetops, leaping through fire curtains and falling by the dozens but never wavering, never dropping for cover, never slowing.

Leading the charge was a shadow-cloaked bear of a man, out ahead by twenty paces or more, twisting and turning, taking magic blasts full in the chest, eyes shining like bronze embers, darksword in hand, burly legs carrying him up the wrecked hill at a speed no elf message runner could match.

Kuhl.

Swaddled in murk though he was, Takari would have known the slope of those huge shoulders from a thousand paces distant, would have recognized among an army of men the grace with which her paramour carried his mighty frame. As humans went—as *males* of any sort went—he was a magnificent example, ferocious when there was need and kind when there was not, always brave and never boastful, a lover who knew how to give *and* take.

Takari could not be sorry for how she had used him—or she would never have known him as the gentle giant he was—but she was sorry for what had come between them, for the curse that had turned her simple plan into a deadly rivalry.

But the fault lay with Kuhl, not Takari. He should have warned her about the curse before he lay with her—and never mind that she had told him not to worry about children. She had not said there wouldn't be any, only not to worry about them. Even after the mistake had been made, all the stupid rothé had to do was share. Had he only been strong enough to lend her the sword, everything would have been fine and there would have been no need to—

Takari did not grasp what she was about to do until she found herself staring down the length of an arrow at Kuhl's chest. The shaft was marked with black fletching, of course, for she had only two death arrows remaining. The rest of her quiver she had exhausted trying to soften up the mind-slave defenses for Keya. But even had there been another choice, she knew better than to think she would have found anything else on her bowstring. It had been the curse that nocked the arrow, and the curse wanted Kuhl dead.

Takari released the tension on her bow slowly, but deliberately did not move her aim away from Kuhl. There had to be another phaerimm down there somewhere or the mind-slaves would not be fighting so hard, and Kuhl was in the most danger. Having seen how slyly the curse worked, she would be stronger than it was and protect Kuhl from afar. She was not some base human whose will could be dominated by a sword.

The shower of death ebbed as more mind-slaves fell to the onslaught of elven spells, and as they exhausted their supply of boulders and magic. The charge gathered speed, with an ever-growing number of Cold Hand warriors pouring up the hill from behind, pressing those in front onward and taking their places when they were struck down. Twice, Kuhl was attacked by spells powerful enough to have come from a phaerimm, but each time Takari traced the flash trail back to mind-slave mages. Through a break in the smoke, she glimpsed Keya dancing up the slope with Vala and Burlen pounding along at her heels, then a pair of beholders found her hiding place and began to attack the base of the tree with their disintegration rays. She slipped around the trunk out of their view, then raced along a limb and jumped into another tree.

By the time Takari found a new hiding place, Kuhl had crashed into the enemy lines and was whirling his way down the entrenchment, his darksword opening bugbear bellies left and right, his feet sweeping legs from under elf mind-slaves, his boot heels crushing the skulls of fallen illithids. Somehow, his free hand had tangled itself in a snarl of beholder eye-stalks, and he was swinging the eye tyrant around like a shield, catching bugbear axes and elven swords on its leathery body.

Takari was alarmed—and a little repulsed—to find herself feeling a secret thrill of delight. Though Kuhl showed no sign of slowing down, he had to be hurting. Even through the finest Evereskan armor, the bugbear blows alone would be powerful enough to snap bones and crush skulls. Kuhl would soon fall, and she would have only to stretch out her hand—

No.

Takari did not dare speak the word aloud—not with two beholders hunting her—but she did think it. She was stronger than the curse. She was a wood elf, who knew what was important in life (dancing, honey wine, and jolly company)—and what was not (power, wealth, and authority). She would help Kuhl—if only she could find a way—and they would share the sword.

Kuhl's helmet came flying out of the melee, its chinstrap broken and its gaudy gold brim buckled by the impact of a bugbear axe. Takari thought that it was done then, that Kuhl would fall beneath the feet of his attackers and vanish.

But the Vaasan bear fought on, reaching the back of the trench and scrambling out onto the hillside. He spun on a knee and lopped the heads off a trio of pursuing bugbears. He smashed a foot into the face of an elf mind-slave and sent him tumbling back into the breastwork. He was free, with no living enemies within a dozen paces of him.

Instead of turning along the back of the trench to attack the enemy's flank, Kuhl started up the hill into the forest. Takari thought he intended to slay her two hunters, but he ignored the beholders—who did not seem to realize she had escaped their attack and were busy searching for her body in the tree they had toppled—and he angled toward her new hiding place. Though it seemed impossible he could have seen her move when the beholders had not, his angry bronze eyes went straight to the bough on which she was perched. It had to be the darksword. The weapon could feel her desire for it, and it was leading him to her. Takari might be stronger than the sword's curse, but Kuhl was not. He'd kill her, if she didn't kill him first.

That was nonsense. Kuhl was too heavy to move through the forest canopy like a wood elf. All Takari need do was stay high in the bluetops, out on the bough ends where Kuhl could not follow. What was it that Galaeron had told her? That she had opened herself to her shadow, and that if she killed Kuhl, she would be lost to it. Takari believed him. It was already working hard to claim her, to trick her into murdering the father of her child.

Would it be murder if he died in battle?

The question came to her in her own voice, but so wispy and cold that it sent a chill down her spine.

No one would ever know.

So startled was Takari that at first she didn't see the illithid climbing out of the entrenchment behind Kuhl. She was preoccupied with the voice, wondering whether someone was eavesdropping on her thoughts or her shadow had already grown strong enough to speak. Of course, this distraction was exactly what the voice had intended. By the time she saw what was happening, the illithid had run a dozen steps toward Kuhl, and its mouth tentacles were extending in his direction. Angered by this manipulation, Takari did not think, hesitate, or even consciously aim. She simply drew her bowstring and let fly.

The angle was not a particularly difficult one, at least not for a Green elf ranger who had spent her whole life making exacting shots. The arrow zipped down in Kuhl's direction, passing a dozen feet over his head but still close enough to make him duck, and it planted itself in the center of the illithid's mouth tentacles. The creature flew off its feet backward and crashed to the ground as still as a statue and immediately began to shrivel inward.

How Kuhl reacted, Takari never saw. The deafening boom of a magic blast rumbled up from the forest floor behind her, and she knew without looking that something powerful had found her hiding place. She jumped for a clump of leaves low on the adjacent tree, her stomach rising into her chest and limbs spread to slow her descent, one hand still clutching her bow.

As Takari crashed into the boughs, she was slapped in the back by the giant hand of a blast concussion. It pushed her deep into the tangle of twigs and leaves facefirst, but she caught a fistful of a branch with her free hand and hooked her legs around another limb as thick as a Vaasan arm.

Takari thought her descent would stop there, but she felt the limb shudder and suddenly found herself falling, staring up at the splintered end of a branch. She had just enough time to wonder why she hadn't heard it break, then she slammed down on the forest floor and was instantly buried beneath a snarl of leafy boughs.

It took only an instant for Takari to realize why she had not heard the limb shatter and that listening for the enemy would do her no good. Her ears were ringing like a halfling dinner bell. She pushed out from beneath a log and found her last arrow still in her quiver. Takari cautiously climbed for the top of the tangle.

Her shoulders ached, and her legs felt half numb, but everything moved when she told it to. It was only a moment before she poked her head up to find Kuhl less than a dozen paces away, striding purposefully in her direction. Behind him were the two beholders that had been hunting her, making good use of his preoccupation to float up close for a sure kill.

Takari pushed herself up onto a somewhat steady branch and nocked her last death arrow. Kuhl narrowed his bronze eyes and broke into a sprint, cocking his sword arm to throw and inadvertently blocking her shot at the beholders. She found her aim drifting to his chest—then she jerked it up and away.

"No." More loudly, she yelled, "Kuhl, go left!"

Reacting perhaps by instinct or perhaps because he realized that the arrow would already be on its way if it was meant for him, he stepped left—and threw the sword anyway.

Takari cursed his human weakness, set the point of her arrow on the big central eye of the nearest beholder, and let fly. She watched only long enough to see her shaft pass beneath Kuhl's sword, then she dropped back into the tangle of boughs . . . and heard a sickly thump behind her.

A howling wind tore at the trees, and Takari knew before she turned to look that Kuhl had not thrown at her, but that he had found the phaerimm she had been hunting.

Ears still ringing, Takari scrambled out the back of the bough tangle and found the phaerimm lying motionless on the ground, opened down the center where Kuhl's tumbling darksword had split it open. The sword itself lay a few paces beyond the dead thornback, so coated in gore it was barely recognizable.

Takari stretched her hand out, preparing to call the darksword to her grasp. She thought of Kuhl, and waited. He would need the sword to meet the second beholder behind him, and if he had to fight her for it . . . but the sword did not fly to his hand. It did not even rise, or wobble.

Go ahead—it's yours now, the dark voice inside whispered. *The beholder is coming.*

"Be quiet!" Takari hissed.

She turned her palm up and called the darksword to her hand.

With the beholder coming, what choice did she have?

CHAPTER TWENTY

2 Eleasias, the Year of Wild Magic

The grim expressions on the high mages' amber faces as they examined the tattered hem of Hanali Celanil's stone cloak told Galaeron all he needed to know. The phaerimm had undone too many of the mythal's ancient spells for his plan to work. Before they could proceed, the circle would have to repair the damage—provided they were willing to make the sacrifice for a city that was not even their own.

Not waiting for the high mages to announce the conclusion themselves, Galaeron turned to Lord Duirsar and the others waiting with him in the shadow of the great statue, and said, "Milord, the phaerimm have done too much damage." To make himself heard over the battle roar coming from the slopes below, Galaeron nearly had to shout. "The high mages need time to do a high casting, and that means we must be prepared to defend them."

"If time is all we need, we have this battle won already," said Kiinyon Colbathin. Like Lord Duirsar and every other Evereskan in the courtyard, Kiinyon was dressed in a full suit of much-dented battle armor that—by the smell of him—he had not shed in the better part of a tenday. "Young Lord Nihmedu's plan has proven an excellent one. We have only to send the Long Watch down the slope, and we'll have the enemy trapped."

"For how long?" asked Storm. She was standing behind Lord Duirsar, towering over his shoulders with Khelben and Laeral. "Any victory here will be short-lived until we repair the mythal. The phaerimm have tens of thousands of their mind-slaves scattered across Evereska, and I'd bet my hair that most of them are on their way here right now."

"All the more reason to move swiftly," Kiinyon replied.

He turned toward the back of the courtyard, where the Long Watch was forming into battle ranks as they emerged from Laeral's teleport circle. He summoned the company commander forward, then turned back to Storm and said, "Once we seize the breastworks, it will not matter how many mind-slaves the phaerimm send against us. Galaeron's plan is an excellent one, and I'm confident we can hold long enough to see it through."

"Yes," Lord Duirsar said, making a point of casting an approving nod in Galaeron's direction, "you may well have saved us."

"Not so easily as Master Colbathin suggests, I fear," Galaeron said. "The mind-slaves below are not the danger."

"They are," Kiinyon declared. The commander of the Long Watch—a young Gold elf female named Zharilee—arrived at his side, and he turned and spoke to her. "When the Cold Hand drives the mind-slaves out of their entrenchment, they will have no place to retreat but here. The Long Watch will prevent that, descending through the forest to fall on them from behind. The enemy will be trapped between two of our companies, and it will be a simple matter to seize the entrenchment for our own use."

He nodded and waved Zharilee away to execute his order. Galaeron bit his tongue to keep from calling Kiinyon—a former commander who had spent two decades making Galaeron's life as a Tomb Guard as miserable as possible—a fool.

Instead, Galaeron said, "It's the phaerimm I'm concerned about. They can teleport into the courtyard as easily as we can."

"Didn't you say that they wouldn't do that?" asked Storm. " 'Without their leader, they'll be too disorganized and busy thinking of themselves to counterattack.' I'm *sure* you said that."

"I did." Galaeron felt the heat come to his face but continued in a sure voice, "And without their leader, that would be so."

Khelben winced, closed his eyes, and said, "Don't tell me—"

"The leader survived."

Galaeron did not explain what had happened, in large part because he didn't know. Takari might have ignored his order and gone straight after Kuhl's sword, or she might have gone around the tree to finish the leader off and discovered that he was already gone.

"But it was injured?" Laeral asked.

"Yes," Galaeron said. "Very badly. It was unconscious for a time."

"Then it won't return," Kiinyon said. He glanced over his shoulder and nodded approvingly as the Long Watch filed down the hill. "These phaerimm are cowards at heart. Hurt them once, and they run for cover."

"Normally, yes."

As he spoke, Galaeron's mind was racing. With Kiinyon having committed the Long Watch to battle, any attempt to recall them would be noticed by the enemy, and it wouldn't take the phaerimm long to puzzle out why. If Galaeron wanted to foil the counterattack, he would have to find a more subtle way.

"This one was the leader," he continued. "It will have too much at stake to give up. It'll be back with all the help it can muster."

Kiinyon shook his head and started to chide Galaeron for contradicting him, but Lord Duirsar raised a silencing hand.

"How can you know this?" he asked Galaeron. "You speak as though you've lived among the phaerimm."

"Not exactly," Galaeron said.

Though he knew the dim view his fellow Evereskans were likely to take regarding the source of his information, he explained without hesitation how Melegaunt had passed on his knowledge before dying—and how he had been forced to yield to his shadow before he could retrieve it. The tale evoked an expression somewhere between revulsion and pity from Lord Duirsar and plain revulsion from Kiinyon Colbathin.

"So you're telling us your information comes from the Shadovar?" Kiinyon asked. The last of the Long Watch was disappearing into the forest, and the sound of their first attacks could already be heard rolling up from the far side of the courtyard. "Milord, Galaeron's intentions have always been good, but his naivete has made him a pawn of the Shadovar from the start."

Khelben started to defend Galaeron, but Lord Duirsar cut him off by speaking directly to Kiinyon.

"Master Colbathin, did you not say just a moment ago that Lord Nihmedu's plan was an excellent one?"

Kiinyon scowled but nodded.

"Then I suggest we listen to him."

"Thank you, milord," Galaeron said. Though the relief he experienced was for Evereska, he did not try to hide the triumph he felt. "I'm sure Master Colbathin will find he was correct in his first assessment of my plan."

"I wouldn't be too impressed with myself," Kiinyon said. His eyes looked as dangerous as those of any beholder. "I'll recall the Long Watch."

Galaeron caught him by the elbow. "It's too late for that."

Kiinyon glared down at the hand on his arm as though he would bite it off.

Galaeron continued to hold it.

"This is what we must do now . . ."

He explained his idea, emphasizing how important it was that the Chosen save their silver fire until the mythal had been repaired, then he asked, "Any questions?"

"Only one," Khelben said. "What if we're not quick enough?"

"Then the high mages die and we continue the fight for Evereska without them . . . or the mythal," Lord Duirsar said, drawing his ancient sword. "So I suggest we be quick enough."

Lord Duirsar asked the high mages to begin their repair of the mythal at once, and Galaeron spent the next few minutes positioning his 'troops' in the shadows around the statue. He would have liked to have Aris there with them, but they had already decided the giant would be most useful supporting Keya and assigned him to join the Cold Hand after departing the palace. Galaeron thought he could hear Aris's boulders crashing into the enemy entrenchment already, but with the battle roar below, it was impossible to be certain.

Once the others were arrayed in their hiding places along the edge of the courtyard, Galaeron stepped into the shadow of the statue itself. He took one last glance around. Seeing that Lord Duirsar, Kiinyon, and the Chosen were all safely concealed within the Fringe, he descended into the shadows himself. The phaerimm were surely wary of such hiding places, but there would be a moment after they arrived when their caution would not matter. It was then that Evereska would be won or lost, Galaeron finally redeemed or forever vilified.

The high mages had already encircled Hanali's statue and begun their work. The two assistants stood to either side of the goddess, their palms turned down, drawing from the ground the golden strands of Weave magic the phaerimm had released earlier. Their dulcet voices were raised in intonation, each singing a separate spell of support, yet weaving their words together in musiclike harmony.

The leader stood behind the goddess, casting a protection spell so ancient the words barely seemed Elvish. As he sang, he was taking the Weave strands from his two assistants and plaiting them back into the hem of Hanali's cloak, slowly restoring it to its original flawless condition. With every fiber he restored, the mage grew a little wispier and more translucent, as though weaving himself into the mythal. Though Galaeron was hardly privy to the secrets of elven high magic, he had heard whispers of spirit-binding during his time at the Academy of Magic, and he knew what he was seeing. The leader would become a part of the mythal, watching over Evereska for all time.

The high mages continued their work for what seemed an eternity, slowly weaving the magic back into the mythal and restoring the statue to its original state. Galaeron concentrated on watching for phaerimm but found his attention drifting to their work more often as time passed. They wove in the most powerful magic first—the spells of imprisonment and foresight and meteor storms—and saved the simpler magic for last. By the time they had worked their way down to relatively minor magic like detection spells and dimensional locks, the leader was so translucent it was possible to look through him to the far side of the courtyard.

Only a few ragged edges remained to repair on Hanali's cloak, and the battle in the entrenchment was raging ever louder, suggesting that mind-slave reinforcements were already starting to pour in from the rest of Evereska. Galaeron knew Kiinyon and the others would be wondering if he had been wrong about the phaerimm counterattack after all, but the long wait only convinced him that the leader had more influence than he had believed. Even for the phaerimm, it took time to gather resources—and the longer they took, the more they were gathering.

The high mages were down to their last magic—simple spells of soft falling and true striking—when half a dozen phaerimm crackled into existence around the statue. Teleport-dazed though they were, they arrived attacking, spraying the courtyard with golden bolts of magic and long tongues of flame. Most of the attacks were blind and found no target at all, but one flurry did strike a supporting mage. Her spell shield flashed silver and dissipated, drained by the power of the attack, and one missile penetrated to burn a thumb-sized hole in her shoulder.

The mage continued her incantation without missing a syllable.

Galaeron and the other two elves were already leaping from their hiding places, each rushing to attack the nearest phaerimm and hurling his most powerful death spell at the next closest. Galaeron sent a dark bolt hissing through the torso of his first thornback and glimpsed Lord Duirsar's falling to a black death ray that could have taken a giant. Then he was on his second target, slashing his darksword down the length of its thorny body. The creature vanished in a twinkle of teleport magic, leaving behind a pool of black blood.

More crackles sounded around the courtyard as a second wave of phaerimm arrived flinging magic and fire. Galaeron raised a shadow shield to cover his back, then hurled a flight of dark bolts at the first thornback he saw and charged the second. A scything blade appeared out of nowhere and came swinging at him from the side. He blocked with the edge of his darksword, cleaving it down the center, and turned back to find Storm Silverhand stepping out of the shadows behind his attacker. Dispelling its blade guard with one hand and swinging her sword with the other, she lopped the phaerimm's tail off about a third of the way up its body—then came staggering in Galaeron's direction as an errant fireball ricocheted off her shoulder and went raging into the forest.

Eyes flashing, Storm whirled on her attacker and charged. The battle became a mad melee of spell, blade, and claw. A female voice shrieked in pain. Galaeron spun around to see the high mage who had been wounded earlier falling to the ground. Where once there had been a leg she had only a smoking wound, but she was still singing her alarm spell and feeding golden strands of Weave to the leader.

Galaeron rushed to help, but Kiinyon was closer. Hurling a flight of magic bolts at her attacker, the legendary spellblade sprang to her side and caught her under the arm. His bolts dissipated harmlessly against the phaerimm's spell shield, but by then Galaeron was flinging a shadow net over it from behind. The startled thornback tried to teleport away and exploded into a thousand fleshy cubes.

Kiinyon pulled the mage to her feet, holding her up so she could finish the spell and shielding her with his own body. A trio of lightning flashes streaked in from all sides, and Galaeron knew the phaerimm were recovered enough from their teleport afterdaze to mount a concerted attack.

The first bolt overloaded Kiinyon's spell shield and drew a startled curse. The second caught him square in the chest, melting through his armor and setting him on fire at head, hands, and feet. The third bolt caught the high mage square in the back and slammed her headlong into the side of Hanali's leg. Her body didn't even go limp; it burst into flames and flew apart.

The spell songs of the other two high mages fell out of harmony, and the leader's hands began to fumble as he struggled to continue weaving. Though they were also under attack, it was not as heavy as on Galaeron's side of the statue, and Laeral and Khelben were doing a good job of keeping it that way.

Racing the last five steps to Hanali's feet, Galaeron flung a shadow sphere into the head-disk of one of the mage's attackers and hurled his darksword through the torso of the second, then he stepped over Kiinyon's body and turned his palms toward the ground. He was no high mage, but the alarm spell was not difficult, and he had seen enough of how the circle harmonized to stand in.

Galaeron began to sing.

The surviving high mages faltered. The leader turned his translucent head toward Galaeron and studied him for a moment, then looked back to his weaving. Galaeron feared the two mages would not accept him into their circle but they adjusted their pitch to blend with his more sonorous voice and continued their spells.

Galaeron felt a slight impact as a flurry of spells struck him in the back and disappeared into his shadow shield. His heart raced with the knowledge that he was standing there motionless while a bevy of phaerimm hurled magic at him, but he forced the fear from his mind and gave himself over to the song he was creating with the high mages. He began to twist his fingers through the gestures of the alarm spell, drawing the magic up out of the ground as he had seen the dead mage do.

The strands came up dark and cold.

Galaeron's voice quavered, but when he hesitated to pass the shadow magic over, the leader reached over with a translucent hand and took the first black thread. As the mage plaited the strand into the hem of Hanali's cloak, his eyes darkened, becoming a pair of murky orbs floating in a transparent face. He reached over and took the next strand from Galaeron's hand.

A three-armed phaerimm flew up beside the statue where its attacks wouldn't be blocked by the shadow shield protecting Galaeron's back. It plunged its tail barb into his belly. So absorbed in the spell song was Galaeron that it barely registered that this was the leader or that it was pumping its poison into him. He felt his feet leave the cobblestones, but that troubled him no more than did the distant pain burning in his belly.

Lord Duirsar was there, beating the phaerimm back with spell and blade. Galaeron continued to sing. He was one with the high mages, concerned only with the casting. The leader reached up and took the next strand from Galaeron with an invisible hand. This time, when he plaited the thread into Hanali's cloak, he followed it in.

Galaeron came to the end of his song, and his belly erupted in pain. He did not realize that the casting was finished and he had been released from the spell until he saw Lord Duirsar below him, fighting the phaerimm leader toe-to-tail, driving it back with flashing steel and pelting it with bolt after bolt from a magic ring. Storm was rushing to the elf lord's side, one hand raised to hurl her own spells, the other still carrying her sword.

Galaeron reached for his shadowsilk but knew even as tried he would not succeed. The phaerimm's poison had left him paralyzed and floating helplessly above the ground. As he watched, two more phaerimm appeared at Storm's back, spraying fire and lightning blindly and lashing out with their tails. He shifted his eyes in the opposite direction and saw that the situation was much the same in the rest of the court-yard, with Khelben and Laeral standing back-to-back and wary phaerimm pelting them from a distance.

Newly repaired though it was, the mythal remained exhausted and starved from the abuse it had suffered since the start of the phaerimm invasion. It mustered itself enough to send a single golden meteor streaking down into the courtyard. The orb blasted only one of the phaerimm that had just teleported in behind Storm, leaving the other to tumble off smoking and teleport away.

The boom was loud enough to draw the attention of every-one in the courtyard. Lord Duirsar narrowly blocked a tail barb when he spun around to see what had caused the sound. Storm, who had been much closer to the explosion, was left picking herself up off the cobblestones.

"Storm!" Galaeron had to hiss the words between clenched teeth, but he knew that as one of the Chosen, she would hear. "The mythal is whole! Use the silver—"

The phaerimm leader gestured in Galaeron's direction, and even his muttering grew silent. Lord Duirsar took advantage of the opening to pour a flurry of magic bolts into the thornback's torso and send it tumbling away, then Storm turned and loosed a stream of silver fire into the base of Hanali's statue. Khelben and Laeral followed her lead an instant later, and the statue began to glow with a bright silver light.

The glow faded as quickly as it had appeared. The phaerimm leader hurled a black death ray at Lord Duirsar that the elf lord sent ricocheting off with a spell mirror. Taking a cue from their leader, the other phaerimm renewed their attacks, and Galaeron began to think that he had failed Evereska again, that his idea had been disastrously misguided and even the unadulterated magic of the Chosen's silver fire could not provide the burst of energy the mythal needed to defend Evereska. Fighting through his disappointment and pain, he opened himself to the Shadow Weave and prepared to loose a shadow blast. He had no control over his own movement, but if a phaerimm happened to pass—

A rain of golden meteors came streaking down from the sky, crackling, sizzling, and leaving a long trail of black smoke in their wake. The first one struck the phaerimm leader, blasting the creature into a spray of sparkling nothingness and laying Lord Duirsar out on the ground next to it. The next three landed in a semicircle around Khelben and Laeral, leaving the two Chosen slumped back-to-back, their eyes as round as coins and their jaws hanging slack. Two more crashed down behind Storm, who flinched a little and looked around to see if there was anything left to kill.

It took only four more strikes in half as many seconds

before there wasn't anything left to kill. The rest of the phaerimm—the few who had survived—teleported away, and the meteor shower began to spread outward from the statue, seeking targets in other parts of the city. Galaeron saw perhaps another dozen strikes before the rain grew erratic and dwindled away, leaving the sky streaked with the smoky trails of their descent.

No, not smoke. Smoke trails grew crooked and feathery as they dissipated in the breeze. The streaks remained straight, narrow, and dark.

"Are those what I think they are?" Storm asked.

Galaeron looked down to see Storm below him. She had a coil of elven rope she had taken from Kiinyon's belt and was busy tying a slip knot. He would have asked her what she thought the stripes were, except that he remained both paralyzed from the phaerimm leader's poison and silenced by its magic. It was probably just as well—he really didn't want to be the one to say they were shadows.

Storm finished her knot, then deftly tossed the loop up over Galaeron's feet.

"Well, Galaeron," she said as she began to pull him down, "when you save a city, you certainly leave your mark."

For the third time in as many hours, the Chosen poured their silver fire into the base of Hanali Celanil's statue. A silver blush rolled up the goddess's imposing figure, then slowly faded as the ravenous mythal drew the raw magic into itself. Moments later, a swarm of golden meteors crackled down from the sky, each streaking toward a distant part of the city where some enemy of Evereska's lay hiding from the mythal's justice.

Galaeron supposed that most of those enemies were still phaerimm, but the last time the meteors had fallen, he had seen them strike beholders and illithids, even a bewildered bugbear who looked more interested in fleeing the city than conquering it. Once the mythal might have shown mercy on a hapless mind-slave as much a victim of the phaerimm as Evereska's own citizens, but no longer. The renewed mythal concerned itself only with who was an enemy to the city and who was a friend, and it destroyed enemies and protected friends.

Considering the stripes of shadow that remained behind every time a meteor descended, Galaeron half expected the next golden ball to land on him, but the mythal had finished with the courtyard surrounding Hanali's statue, and even with the hill below. No attacks had fallen anywhere near the hill since the second wave, when its deadly barrage had broken the counterattack on the captured entrenchment and sent the phaerimm mind-slaves fleeing for the far corners of the city. With reinforcements pouring up the hill by the dozens, victory was only a matter of waiting and consolidating, of carefully expanding the areas of elf control each time the mythal struck.

Galaeron should probably have felt proud, but in truth he was simply restless. After the mythal's initial strike, Laeral Silverhand had attended to his stomach wound, and finding no phaerimm egg planted inside, pronounced him likely to survive but in need of rest. Storm had trickled a healing potion down his throat, then tied him down to a tree root to wait for the phaerimm's paralysis poison to wear off, and there he had been stuck, wondering what had become of Vala and Aris, of Keya and her Vaasan friends, and most of all, what had happened between Takari and Kuhl and their sword.

It was another quarter hour before Galaeron could move his fingers, and a quarter hour after that before he had control enough to untie Storm's torturous knots. By the time he succeeded, Lord Duirsar was holding a meeting with the Chosen, the commanders of the city's surviving companies, Aris, and anyone else likely to play an important part in the events to come.

Galaeron coiled the rope and hung it on his belt, then straightened his armor and started across the courtyard to join the others. Storm's healing potion had proven remarkably effective. Though he had felt the phaerimm's tail barb sink deep, the wound caused him little discomfort as he walked, and when he looked down, he was surprised to find the puncture already closed.

As Galaeron approached, his sister Keya was the first to notice. Without excusing herself from the circle kneeling in front of Lord Duirsar, and apparently not caring that she was bringing the meeting to a dead stop, she leaped to her feet and rushed across to him with her arms spread wide.

"Brother!"

Keya threw herself into Galaeron so hard that he stumbled back and would have fallen, had she not closed her arms around his shoulders and caught him.

"You're well?" she asked.

"Well enough," Galaeron laughed. He pried himself loose and held her at arm's length. "And you?"

"Not a scratch."

Keya did a twirl to demonstrate, though she was so crusted in dirt and blood that it was barely possible to tell she was female.

"I'll take your word for it. And what of the others?"

"We lost Kuhl," said Vala, coming to join them. She smiled grimly. "Everyone else made it."

"I'm sorry for Kuhl's loss." Galaeron took her hands, then said quietly, "And glad to see you still here."

"Then how about showing it?"

Vala kissed him deep and hard, drawing a hearty and somewhat astonished laugh from the others in the crowd. She held the kiss just long enough to be scandalous, then released him and nodded over her shoulder at Takari.

"And showing it not just to me," Vala said.

Not quite sure what to make of Vala's remark or Takari's unaccustomed meekness, Galaeron went to Takari. He was hardly surprised to find Kuhl's darksword in her scabbard, but when he looked into her eyes, the shadow was gone. There was sorrow and guilt, perhaps, but no darkness.

"Galaeron, I'm sorry," Takari said, hardly able to look him in the eye. "I didn't mean to leave my post, but it was already gone when I went around the tree, so when I heard the Cold Hand trying to attack . . ."

"It's all right."

"I thought I should go help," she continued. "It was probably just the curse. . . ."

"Whatever it was, Takari, you did the right thing," Galaeron said, taking her hands. He didn't know what had happened with Kuhl's sword and wasn't sure he ever wanted to, but he could see by the clearness in her eyes that she had not been taken by her shadow. "I'm just happy you're still here."

Takari smiled that carefree cupid's bow smile that he remembered from all those years on the Desert Border South.

Galaeron could not resist. He kissed her as hard as Vala had kissed him, though this time the crowd's astonishment took the form of a shocked murmur rather than a hearty laugh. It didn't matter to Galaeron. He loved Takari and Vala both, and he had made so many mistakes so much worse on the way to saving Evereska that he really didn't care what they thought. He would not curb his feelings to please anyone—he had learned that much at least.

"Ahem," said Lord Duirsar's familiar voice. "If I might intrude."

Galaeron and Takari parted—reluctantly—and he bowed to the elf lord.

"Thank you. Now that you seem to be feeling better—" Duirsar drew a nervous chuckle from the assembly by turning to them and arching one of his gray eyebrows—"it occurs to me that with the death of Kiinyon Colbathin, Evereska has need of a new Master of the Defenses."

"Galaeron would make a fine commander," said Laeral Silverhand. "He has already saved the city once."

"Hear, hear!" cried Dexon, limping up behind Keya on his still-withered leg. "I can tell you, your young cubs are already recounting the tales of how he lured the phaerimm to their deaths."

As the Vaasan spoke, Keya, Zharilee, and the other commanders of the elven companies were kneeling on the cobblestones. They drew their swords and turned the tips toward Galaeron, then touched them to the ground in a gesture of loyalty. Even the high mage from Evermeet, the one whom Galaeron had joined in repairing the last strands of the mythal, dropped to a knee and inclined his head.

It did not escape Galaeron's notice, however, that it was only the humans who were actually voicing their approval. With the exception of Takari and his sister Keya, the elves were reluctant to meet his eyes, and many of them seemed unable to keep their gazes from straying toward the shadow-striped sky.

"What say you, Galaeron?" Lord Duirsar laid a hand on Galaeron's shoulder. "Will you lead the defenders of Evereska—what few of us remain?"

"Milord, I don't know what to say."

Instead of kneeling to accept the appointment, Galaeron turned and looked into the eyes of the high mage. There he did not find even the uncertainty and apprehension that filled the eyes of the others—only revulsion, fear, and mistrust. Of all the elves there in the courtyard, the high mage had felt the touch of Galaeron's shadow most clearly, and it was in his eyes that Galaeron could read his future in Evereska. He inclined his head to the mage not in bitterness or anger, but acknowledgement and acceptance, then turned back to Lord Duirsar.

"Lord Duirsar, I will, of course, serve Evereska until we have seen the last of the phaerimm and their mind-slaves driven from the Shaeradim."

He glanced in Takari's direction and allowed his glance to linger there until he saw realization dawn in her eyes, then he turned to face Vala.

"But I have given my word to Vala that I would see the darkswords we have borrowed returned safely to their families in Vaasa."

Duirsar's jaw dropped, and a murmur of disbelief rustled through the assembly. No elf dared refuse Lord Duirsar—at least no elf who was a citizen of Evereska.

"Galaeron!" Vala hissed. "There's no need—"

"I am an elf," Galaeron cut her off. His eyes darted toward the high mage. "I keep my promises."

Even Vala could not miss the gratitude and relief in the high mage's expression.

"I hope you understand, milord," Vala said. "It is a matter of some importance to my people that the weapons be returned by the one who borrowed them."

Taken aback though he was by Galaeron's refusal, Lord Duirsar was nevertheless wise enough to recognize a graceful out when it was offered. He nodded courteously and smiled.

"It was rude of me not to think of that. I'm quite certain we'll be able to find someone else." He paused for a moment then turned to Keya and said, "And what of you, young Lady Nihmedu? Will we be needing to find a new commander for your company as well?"

Dexon limped forward, as completely oblivious to the proper etiquette as only a Vaasan could be, and growled, "With your permission, Milord, we'll be making our home here—as long as you can stomach me, that is."

Lord Duirsar turned to Vala and asked, "Would that be agreeable to the Granite Tower?"

"He's free to do as he pleases," Vala said. She reached out and pinched Dexon's swarthy cheek. "As long as he gives the baby a Vaasan name."

"At least the first one," Keya promised.

"Very well, then," Duirsar said, turning to Dexon. "Then it would be our honor to 'stomach you' for the rest of your life, my friend."

Dexon grinned and engulfed Lord Duirsar in a bear hug.

While the elf lord endeavored to extract himself, Vala turned to Takari and said, "And you're free to do as you please, too."

Takari frowned. "Free?" she asked. "Of course I'm free. I'm Sy'Tel'Quess."

"Let me put this another way," Vala said. "As the bearer of Kuhl's child and his darksword, you have a home with us in Vaasa."

"With you?" Takari said, She smiled broadly and came over to stand with Vala and Galaeron. "We're all going to Vaasa to live in the Granite Tower . . . together?"

"If you like, yes."

Vala glanced at Galaeron as though looking for rescue, but of course he only smiled and used fingertalk to thank her. She went pale, but quickly collected herself and took Takari by the arm.

"We have some very interesting customs in Vaasa," Vala said, narrowing her eyes at Galaeron. "Our men sleep in the snow."

EPILOGUE

3 Eleasias, the Year of Wild Magic

No sooner had Shade Enclave stopped wobbling than the summons came to Malygris, the Blue Suzerain of Anauroch. Though it took a mighty act of will to resist the call of the Most High, the dracolich lingered atop his perch, watching to see if the thread of shadow that ran between the enclave and the dark lake beneath would dissolve, or if the capsized mountain would rise to its former place high in the sky. When neither happened, Malygris deigned to answer. Lifting his boneless magnificence off the peak where he'd been resting, he flew into the city.

Before entering the cave where the Most High always met him, Malygris took a turn over the enclave and found that the magnificent metropolis had degenerated overnight into a drab city of hovels and tenements. The Palace Most High, whose grandeur had awed even him, was in the light of Anauroch's sun little more than a barren field, with a freestanding arch to mark the entrance and a handful of stairwells leading down into the ground.

When Malygris finally entered the Cave Gate, he found Telamont Tanthul waiting with a pile of freshly decapitated heads large enough to hold a dragon. The stench was awful, but that would change with a decade of curing. Though he tried not to show it, Malygris was impressed. The next time the accursed Cult of the Dragon priests came to his lair with some errand, he would enjoy watching their faces when they looked upon his new nest.

Malygris was so grateful that instead of forcing the Most High to come to him as usual, the dracolich landed in front of the shade. The platinum glow of Telamont's eyes seemed less bright, but there was another sign of his weariness.

"You were occupied, Mighty One?" Telamont asked.

"That is none of your concern." Malygris raised his horny snout bone toward the pile of heads and asked, "You have gifts?"

The Most High nodded and waved an empty sleeve toward the heap. If he realized his confidence was being tested, he showed no sign.

"The Cult of the Dragon," said he shade.

Malygris's jaw dropped.

"The *whole* cult?"

"Only the fools who knew of your bondage," Telamont clarified.

"All? You're sure?" Malygris asked. He could hardly believe what he was hearing. "I am free?"

Telamont inclined his head.

"Did you not tell me it was impossible to free me of the Cult?"

"It was *then*," Telamont answered. "We acted when we could be certain."

"And when your need was greatest," Malygris said, turning toward the cave mouth. "You may deliver the heads to my lair."

He spread his wings, but found himself unable to launch. The weight of Telamont's will pressed down on him so hard he thought it might crush one of his minor wing bones, and he found himself speaking thoughts he had intended to keep private.

"I have seen the true face of Shade, and I am no longer awed."

Malygris tried to stop there, but Telamont's will forced him to continue, "The Chosen mammals are peeling your blankets from the High Ice, and the strength of the other warmblood realms will soon return. It will not be long, I think, before your city crashes into the lake or flees back into the shadow."

"You are mistaken, my friend, but I will not hold it against you."

Telamont pointed at the floor by his feet, and Malygris found himself clattering over to lay his magnificent chin on the cold stone. He thought instantly of the amulet the cult priests used to control him, but it was not hanging from the Most High's neck. Telamont Tanthul had his own magic.

"Shade is here to stay."

"Shade is here to stay," Malygris found himself repeating.

"We have many enemies, but we are accustomed to enemies."

"We have many enemies—" Malygris tried to resist saying "we," but the will of the Most High was as heavy as all of his coin piles together—"but we are accustomed to enemies."

"Shade will prevail as it always prevails, by hiding in the darkness and striking from the shadows."

Malygris's resistance crumbled, and he found himself repeating the words of his own will.

"Shade will prevail as it always prevails, by hiding in the darkness and striking from the shadows."

"Good," Telamont said. He raised his sleeve and wrapped five tendrils of cold shadow around Malygris's nose horn. "Together, we will triumph."

When he spoke this time, Malygris believed what he was saying.

R.A. Salvatore's
War of the Spider Queen

New York Times best-selling author R.A.
Salvatore, creator of the legendary dark elf
Drizzt Do'Urden, lends his creative genius to
a new FORGOTTEN REALMS® series that delves
deep into the mythic Underdark and even
deeper into the black hearts of the drow.

DISSOLUTION
Book I
Richard Lee Byers sets the stage as the delicate power structure
of Menzoberranzan tilts and threatens to smash apart. When
drow faces drow, only the strongest and most evil can survive.

INSURRECTION
Book II
Thomas M. Reid turns up the heat on the drow civil war and
sends the Underdark reeling into chaos. When a god goes silent,
what could possibly set things right?
December 2002